AN EVIL MIND

About the author

Born in Brazil of Italian origin, Chris Carter studied psychology and criminal behavior at the University of Michigan. As a member of the Michigan State District Attorney's Criminal Psychology team, he interviewed and studied many criminals, including serial and multiple homicide offenders with life-imprisonment convictions.

Having departed for Los Angeles in the early 1990s, Chris spent ten years as a guitarist for numerous rock bands before leaving the music business to write full-time. He now lives in London and is a Top Ten *Sunday Times* bestselling author.

Visit www.chriscarterbooks.com or find him on Facebook.

Also by Chris Carter

The Crucifix Killer
The Executioner
The Night Stalker
The Death Sculptor
One by One

Chris Carter

AN EVIL MIND

**SIMON &
SCHUSTER**

London · New York · Sydney · Toronto · New Delhi

A CBS COMPANY

First published in Great Britain by Simon & Schuster UK Ltd, 2014
A CBS COMPANY
Copyright © Chris Carter 2014

3 5 7 9 10 8 6 4 2

Simon & Schuster UK Ltd
1st Floor
222 Gray's Inn Road
London WC1X 8HB

www.simonandschuster.co.uk

Simon & Schuster Australia, Sydney
Simon & Schuster India, New Delhi

A CIP catalogue record for this book is available from the British Library

HB ISBN: 978-1-47113-219-3
TPB ISBN: 978-1-47113-220-9
EBOOK ISBN: 978-1-47113-222-3

Typeset by Hewer Text UK Ltd, Edinburgh
Printed and bound in Great Britain by CPI Group (UK) Ltd, Croydon CR0 4YY

This novel differs immensely from all my previous books, mainly because this is the first thriller I've written in which most of the plot and characters are based on real facts and people I met during my criminal-behavior-psychology days. The names have been changed for obvious reasons.

I would like to dedicate this novel to all the readers who have entered the competition that was run in the UK to become one of the victims in this thriller, and especially to the winner, Karen Simpson, who lives in South Wales and who has been a great sport. I hope you all enjoy it.

Part One

The Wrong Man

One

'Morning, Sheriff. Morning, Bobby,' the plump, brunette waitress with a small heart tattoo on her left wrist called from behind the counter. She didn't have to check the clock hanging from the wall to her right. She knew it would be just past 6:00 a.m.

Every Wednesday, without fail, Sheriff Walton and his deputy, Bobby Dale, came into Nora's truck-stop diner, just outside Wheatland in southeastern Wyoming, to get their sweet-pie fix. Rumor had it that Nora's Diner baked the best pies in the whole of Wyoming. A different recipe every day of the week. Wednesday was apple-and-cinnamon-pie day, Sheriff Walton's favorite. He was well aware that the first batch of pies always came out of the oven at 6:00 a.m. sharp, and you just couldn't beat the taste of a freshly baked pie.

'Morning, Beth,' Bobby replied, dusting rainwater off his coat and trousers. 'I'll tell you, the floodgates from hell have opened out there,' he added, shaking his leg as if he'd peed himself.

Summer downpours in southeastern Wyoming were a common occurrence, but this morning's storm was the heaviest they'd seen all season.

'Morning, Beth,' Sheriff Walton followed, taking off his hat, drying his face and forehead with a handkerchief, and quickly looking around the diner. At that time in the morning, and with such torrential rain outside, the place was a lot less busy than usual. Only three out of its fifteen tables were taken.

A man and a woman in their mid-twenties were sitting at the table nearest to the door, having a pancake breakfast. The sheriff figured that the beat-up, silver WV Golf parked outside belonged to them.

The next table along was occupied by a large, sweaty, shaved-headed man, who must've weighed at least 350 pounds. The amount of food sitting on the table in front of him would've easily been enough to feed two very hungry people, maybe three.

The last table by the window was taken by a tall, gray-haired man, with a bushy horseshoe mustache and a crooked nose. His forearms were covered in faded tattoos. He'd already finished his breakfast and was now sitting back on his chair, toying with a packet of cigarettes and looking pensive, as if he had a very difficult decision to make.

There was no doubt in Sheriff Walton's mind that the two large trucks outside belonged to those two.

Sitting at the end of the counter, drinking a cup of black coffee and eating a chocolate-coated donut, was a pleasantly dressed man who looked to be in his forties. His hair was short and well kept, and his beard stylish and neatly trimmed. He was flipping through a copy of the morning's newspaper. His had to be the dark-blue Ford Taurus parked by the side of the diner, Sheriff Walton concluded.

'Just in time,' Beth said, winking at the sheriff. 'They're just out of the oven.' She gave him a tiny shrug. 'As if you didn't know.'

The sweet smell of freshly baked apple pie with a hint of cinnamon had already engulfed the entire place.

Sheriff Walton smiled. 'We'll have our usual, Beth,' he said, taking a seat at the counter.

'Coming right up,' Beth replied before disappearing into the kitchen. Seconds later she returned with two steamy, extra-large slices of pie, drizzled with honey cream. They looked like perfection on a plate.

'Umm . . .' the man sitting at the far end of the counter said, tentatively raising a finger like a kid asking his teacher's permission to speak. 'Is there any more of that pie left?'

'There sure is,' Beth replied, smiling back at him.

'In that case, can I also have a slice, please?'

'Yeah, me too,' the large truck driver called out from his table, lifting his hand. He was already licking his lips.

'And me,' the horseshoe-mustache man said, returning the cigarette pack to his jacket pocket. 'That pie smells darn good.'

'Tastes good too,' Beth added.

'Good doesn't even come close,' Sheriff Walton said, turning to face the tables. 'Y'all just about to be taken to pie heaven.' Suddenly his eyes widened in surprise. 'Holy shit,' he breathed out, jumping off his seat.

The sheriff's reaction made Bobby Dale swing his body around fast and follow the sheriff's stare. Through the large window just behind where the mid-twenties couple was sitting, he saw the headlights of a pick-up truck coming straight at them. The car seemed completely out of control.

'What the hell?' Bobby said, getting to his feet.

Everyone in the diner turned to face the window, and the shocked look on everyone's face was uniform. The vehicle was coming toward them like a guided missile, and it was showing no signs of diverting or slowing down. They had two, maybe three seconds before impact.

'EVERYBODY TAKE COVER!' Sheriff Walton yelled, but he didn't have to. Reflexively, everybody in the restaurant was already scrambling on their feet to get out of the way. At that speed, the pick-up truck would crash through the front of the diner and probably not stop until it reached the kitchen at the back, destroying everything in its path, and killing everyone in its way.

A chaotic mess of desperate screams and movement took over the restaurant floor. They all knew they just didn't have enough time to get out of the way.

CRUUUUNCH-BOOM!

The deafening crashing noise sounded like an explosion, making the ground shake under everyone's feet.

Sheriff Walton was the first to look up. It took him a few seconds to realize that somehow the car hadn't crashed through the front of the building.

Frowning was followed by confusion.

'Is everyone all right?' the sheriff finally called out, frantically looking around.

Mumbled confirmation was returned from all corners of the room.

The sheriff and his deputy immediately got to their feet and rushed outside. Everyone else followed just a heartbeat later. The rain had gotten heavier in the past few minutes, now coming down in thick sheets, severely reducing visibility.

Out of sheer luck, the pick-up truck had hit a deep pothole on the ground just a few yards from the front of the diner, and had drastically veered left, missing the restaurant by just a couple of feet. As it detoured, it had clipped the back of the dark-blue Ford Taurus parked outside, before smashing head-first into a side building that housed two bathrooms and a storage room, completely destroying it. Thankfully, there was no one inside either of the bathrooms, or the storage room.

'Holy shit!' Sheriff Walton breathed out, feeling his heart race inside his chest. The collision had turned the pick-up truck into a totally mangled wreck, and the outside building into a demolition site.

Skipping over the debris, the sheriff was the first to get to the truck. The driver was its only occupant – a gray-haired man who looked to be somewhere in his late fifties, but it was hard to be sure. Sheriff Walton wasn't able to recognize him, but he was certain he'd never seen that pick-up truck around Wheatland before. It was an old and rusty, early 1990s Chevy 1500, no airbags, and though the driver had been wearing his seatbelt, the impact had been way too violent. The front of the truck, together with its engine, had caved backward and into the driver's cabin. The dashboard and steering wheel had crushed the driver's chest against his seat. His face was covered in blood, torn apart by shards of glass from the windscreen. One had sliced through the man's throat.

'Goddammit!' Sheriff Walton said through clenched teeth, standing by the driver's door. He didn't have to feel for a pulse to know that the man hadn't survived.

'Oh, my God!' he heard Beth exclaim in a trembling voice from just a few feet behind him. He immediately turned to face her, lifting his hands in a "stop" motion.

'Beth, do not come here,' he commanded in a firm voice. 'Go back inside and stay there.' His stare moved to the rest of the diner patrons who were moving toward the truck fast. 'All of you go back into the diner. That's an order. This whole area is now out of bounds, y'all hear?'

Everybody stopped moving, but no one turned back.

The sheriff's eyes searched for his deputy, and found Bobby standing all the way at the back, by the Ford Taurus. The look on his face was a mixture of shock and fear.

'Bobby,' Sheriff Walton called. 'Call for an ambulance and the fire brigade *now*.'

Bobby didn't move.

'Bobby, snap out of it, goddammit. Did you hear what I said? I need you to get on the radio and call for an ambulance and the fire brigade right now.'

Bobby stood still. He looked like he was about to be sick. Only then did the sheriff realize that Bobby wasn't even looking at him or at the mangled pick-up truck. His eyes were locked onto the Ford Taurus. Before crashing into the bathroom building, the truck had clipped the left side of the Taurus' rear-end hard enough to release its trunk door.

All of a sudden Bobby broke out of his trance and reached for his gun.

'No one move,' he yelled out. His shaky aim kept jumping from person to person. 'Sheriff,' he called in an unsteady voice. 'You better come have a look at this.'

Two

Five days later.
Huntington Park, Los Angeles, California.

The petite, dark-haired checkout girl rang the last item through and looked up at the young man standing at her register.

'That'll be $34.62, please,' she said, matter-of-factly.

The man finished packing his groceries into plastic bags before handing her his credit card. He couldn't have been any older than twenty-one.

The checkout girl swiped the card through the machine, waited a few seconds, bit her bottom lip, and with doubtful eyes looked up at the man.

'I'm sorry, sir, this card's been declined,' she said, offering the card back.

The man stared back at her as if she'd spoken to him in a different language.

'What?' His eyes moved to the card, paused, and then returned to the checkout girl. 'There's gotta be some sort of mistake. I'm sure I still have some credit left on that card. Could you try it again, please?'

The checkout girl gave him a tiny shrug and swiped the card through one more time.

A tense couple of seconds went by.

'I'm sorry, sir, it's been declined again,' she said, handing the card back to him. 'Would you like to try another one?'

Embarrassed, he took the card from her and faintly shook his head. 'I don't have another one,' he said shyly.

'Food coupons?' she asked.

Another sad shake of the head.

The girl waited as the man started searching through his pockets for whatever money he could find. He managed to come up with a few dollar bills, and a bunch of quarters and dimes. After quickly adding up all his change, he paused and looked back at the checkout girl, apologetically.

'I'm sorry. I'm about twenty-six dollars short. I'll have to leave a few things behind.'

Most of his shopping consisted of baby stuff – diapers, a couple of pots of baby food, a can of powdered milk, a bag of baby wipes, and a small tube of diaper rash ointment. The rest was just everyday essentials – bread, milk, eggs, some vegetables, a few pieces of fruit, and a can of soup – all of it from the budget range. The man didn't touch any of the baby stuff, but returned everything else.

'Could you see how much that comes to now, please?' he asked the girl.

'It's OK,' the man standing behind him in the checkout line said. He was tall and athletically built, with sharp, chiseled, attractive features and kind eyes. He handed the checkout girl two twenty-dollar bills.

She looked up at him and frowned.

'I'll get this,' he said, nodding at her before addressing the young man. 'You can put your groceries back in the bags. It's my treat.'

The young man stared back at him, confused, and unable to find any words.

'It's OK,' the tall man said again, giving him a reassuring smile. 'Don't worry about it.'

Still stunned, the young man's gaze moved to the check-out girl, and then back to the tall man.

'Thank you so much, sir,' he finally said, extending his hand, his voice catching in his throat, his eyes becoming just a little glassy.

The man shook his hand and gave him a reassuring head nod.

'That was the kindest thing I've ever seen happen in here,' the checkout girl said once the young man had collected his groceries and left. Tears had also welled up in her eyes.

The tall man simply smiled back at her.

'I'm serious,' she reiterated. 'I've been working at the checkout in this supermarket for almost three years. I've seen plenty of people come up short when it comes to paying, plenty of people having to return items, but I've never seen anybody do what you just did.'

'Everybody needs a little help every now and then,' the man replied. 'There's no shame in that. Today, I helped him, maybe someday he'll help someone else.'

The girl smiled as her eyes filled with tears again. 'It's true that we all need a little help every once in a while, but the problem is, very few are ever willing to help. Especially when they need to reach into their pockets to do so.'

The man silently agreed with her.

'I've seen you in here before,' the checkout girl said, ring-ing through the few items the man had with him. It came to $9.49.

'I live in the neighborhood,' he said, handing her a ten-dollar bill.

She paused for a moment and locked eyes with him. 'I'm Linda,' she said, nodding at her nametag, and extending her hand.

'Robert,' the man replied, shaking it. 'Pleasure to meet you.'

'Listen,' she said, returning his change. 'I was wondering. My shift ends at six this evening. Since you live in the neighborhood, maybe we could go for a coffee somewhere?'

The man hesitated for a brief moment. 'That would be really nice,' he finally said. 'But unfortunately, I'm flying out tonight. My first vacation in . . .' He paused and narrowed his eyes at nothing for an instant. 'I don't even remember when I last had a vacation.'

'I know the feeling,' she said, sounding a little disappointed.

The man collected his groceries and looked back at the checkout girl.

'How about if I call you when I get back, in about ten days? Maybe we can have a coffee then.'

She looked up at him and her lips stretched into a thin smile. 'I'd like that,' she replied, quickly jotting down her number.

As the man stepped outside the supermarket, his cellphone rang in his jacket pocket.

'Detective Robert Hunter, Homicide Special,' he answered it.

'Robert, are you still in LA?'

It was the LAPD's Robbery Homicide Division's captain, Barbara Blake. She was the one who, just a couple of days ago, had ordered Hunter and his partner, Detective Carlos

Garcia, to take a two-week break after a very demanding and exhausting serial killer investigation.

'Right now, yes,' Hunter replied, skeptically. 'I'm flying out tonight, Captain. Why?'

'I really hate to do this to you, Robert,' the captain replied, sounding sincerely sorry. 'But I need to see you in my office.'

'When?'

'Right now.'

Three

In lunchtime traffic, the 7.5-mile drive from Huntington Park to the LAPD headquarters in downtown Los Angeles took Hunter a little over forty-five minutes.

The Robbery Homicide Division (RHD), located on the fifth floor of the famous Police Administration Building on West 1st Street, was a simple, large, open-plan area crammed with detectives' desks – no flimsy partitions to separate them or silly floor lines to delimit workspace. The place sounded and looked like a street market on a Sunday morning, alive with movement, murmurs and shouts that came from every corner.

Captain Blake's office was at the far end of the main detectives' floor. The door was shut – not that unusual due to the noise – but so were the blinds on the oversized internal window that faced the floor, and that was undoubtedly a bad sign.

Hunter slowly started zigzagging his way around people and desks.

'Hey, what the hell are you doing here, Robert?' Detective Perez asked, looking up from his computer screen as Hunter squeezed past Perez and Henderson's desks. 'I thought you were supposed to be on vacation?'

Hunter nodded. 'I am. I'm flying out tonight. Just having a quick chat with the captain first.'

'*Flying?*' Perez looked surprised. 'That sounds rich. Where are you going?'

'Hawaii. My first time.'

Perez smiled. 'Nice. I could do with going to Hawaii right about now too.'

'Want me to bring you back a lei necklace or a Hawaiian shirt?'

Perez pulled a face. 'No, but if you can manage to slip one or two of those Hawaiian dancers into your suitcase, I'll take them. They can do the hula up on my bed every goddamn night. You know what I'm saying?' He nodded like he meant every word.

'A man can dream,' Hunter replied, amused by how vigorously Perez was nodding.

'Enjoy yourself over there, man.'

'I'm sure I will,' Hunter said before moving on. He paused before the captain's door, and instinct and curiosity made him tilt his head to one side and check the window – nothing. He couldn't see past the blinds. He knocked twice.

'Come in.' He heard Captain Blake call from the other side in her usual firm voice.

Hunter pushed the door open and stepped inside.

Barbara Blake's office was spacious, brightly lit and impeccably tidy. The south wall was taken by bookshelves packed by perfectly arranged, and color-coordinated hardcovers. The north one was covered by framed photographs, commendations and achievement awards, all symmetrically positioned in relation to each other. The east wall was a floor-to-ceiling panoramic window, looking out over South Main Street. Directly in front of the captain's twin-pedestal desk were two leather armchairs.

Captain Blake was standing by the panoramic window. Her long jet-black hair was gracefully styled into a bun, pinned in place by a pair of wooden chopsticks. She was wearing a silky white blouse, tucked into an elegant navy-blue pencil skirt. Standing next to her, holding a steaming cup of coffee, and wearing a conservative black suit, was a slim and very attractive woman, who Hunter had never seen before. She looked to be somewhere in her early thirties, with long, straight blonde hair, and deep blue eyes. She looked like someone who would normally be entirely at ease in whatever situation she found herself in, but there was something a little apprehensive about the way she held her head.

As Hunter entered the office and closed the door behind him, the tall and slim man who was sitting in one of the armchairs, also in a soberly dark suit, turned to face him. He was in his mid-fifties, but the heavy bags under his eyes and his fleshy, saggy cheeks, which also gave him a somewhat hound-like look, made him look at least ten years older. The thin flock of gray hair he still had left on his head was neatly combed back over his ears.

Taken by surprise, Hunter paused, narrowing his eyes.

'Hello, Robert,' the man said, standing up. His naturally hoarse voice, made worse by years of smoking, sounded surprisingly strong for a man who looked like he hadn't slept in days.

Hunter's gaze stayed on him for a couple of seconds before moving to the blonde woman, and finally to Captain Blake.

'Sorry about this, Robert,' she said with a slight tilt of the head, before allowing her stare to go rock hard as it honed in on the man facing Hunter. 'They simply turned up unannounced about an hour ago. Not even a goddam courtesy call,' she explained.

'I apologize again,' the man said in a calm but authoritative tone. He was definitely someone who was used to giving orders, and having them followed. 'You look well.' He addressed Hunter. 'But then again, you always do, Robert.'

'So do you, Adrian,' Hunter replied unconvincingly, stepping toward the man and shaking his hand.

Adrian Kennedy was the head of the FBI's National Center for the Analysis of Violent Crime (NCAVC) and its Behavioral Analysis Unit – a specialist FBI department that provided support to national and international law enforcement agencies involved in the investigation of unusual or serial violent crimes.

Hunter was well aware that unless it was absolutely mandatory, Adrian Kennedy never traveled anywhere. He now coordinated most of NCAVC operations from his large office in Washington, DC, but he was no career bureaucrat. Kennedy had begun his life with the FBI at a young age, and quickly demonstrated that he had tremendous aptitude for leadership. He also had a natural ability to motivate people. That didn't go unnoticed, and very early in his career he was assigned to the prestigious US President protection detail. Two years later, after foiling an attempt on the president's life by throwing himself in front of the bullet that was destined to kill the most powerful man on earth, he received a high commendation award, and a "thank you" letter from the president himself. A few years after that, the National Center for the Analysis of Violent Crime was officially established in June 1984. They needed a director, someone who was a natural leader. Adrian Kennedy was the name at the top of the list.

'This is Special Agent Courtney Taylor,' Kennedy said, nodding at the blonde woman.

She moved closer and shook Hunter's hand. 'Very nice to meet you, Detective Hunter. I've heard a lot about you.'

Taylor's voice sounded incredibly seductive, combining a sort of soft, girlish tone with a level of self-assurance that was almost disarming. Despite her delicate hands, her hand-shake was firm and meaningful, like that of a business-woman who had just closed a major deal.

'It's a pleasure to meet you too,' Hunter replied, politely. 'And I hope that some of what you've heard wasn't so bad.'

She gave him a shy, but truthful smile. 'None of it was bad.'

Hunter turned and faced Kennedy again.

'I'm glad we managed to catch you before you'd left for your break, Robert,' Kennedy said.

Nothing from Hunter.

'Going anywhere nice?

Hunter held Kennedy's stare.

'This has got to be bad,' he finally said. 'Because I know you're not the sort to sugar-talk anyone. I also know you couldn't care less about where I am going on my break. So how about we drop the bullshit? What's this about, Adrian?'

Kennedy took a moment, as if he had to carefully consider his answer before finally replying.

'You, Robert. This is about you.'

Four

Hunter's attention wandered over to Captain Blake for a brief moment; as their eyes met, she shrugged apologetically.

'They didn't tell me much, Robert, but the little I know sounds like something you would want to hear.' She went back to her desk. 'It's better if they explain.'

Hunter looked at Kennedy and waited.

'Why don't you have a seat, Robert?' Kennedy said, offering one of the armchairs.

Hunter didn't move.

'I'm fine standing, thank you.'

'Coffee?' Kennedy asked, indicating Captain Blake's espresso machine in the corner.

Hunter's gaze hardened.

'All right, fine.' Kennedy lifted both hands in a surrender gesture, while at the same time giving Special Agent Taylor an almost imperceptible nod. 'We'll get on with it.' He returned to his seat.

Taylor put down her cup of coffee and stepped forward, pausing just beside Kennedy's chair.

'OK,' she began. 'Five days ago, at around six in the morning, while driving south down US Route 87, a Mr John Garner suffered a heart attack just outside a small town called Wheatland, in southeastern Wyoming. Needless to say, he lost control of his pick-up truck.'

'It was raining heavily that morning, and Mr Garner was the sole occupant of the truck,' Kennedy added before signaling Taylor to carry on.

'Maybe you already know this,' Taylor continued. 'But Route 87 runs all the way from Montana to southern Texas, and like most US highways, unless the stretch in question is going through what's considered a minimum populated area or an high accident-risk one, there are no guardrails, walls, high curbstones, raised center island divisions ... *nothing* that would keep a vehicle from leaving the highway and venturing off in a multitude of directions.'

'The stretch that we're talking about here doesn't fall under the minimum populated area, or high accident-risk category,' Kennedy commented.

'By pure luck.' Taylor moved on. 'Or lack of it, depending what point of view you take, Mr Garner suffered the heart attack just as he was driving past a small truck-stop diner called Nora's Diner. With him unconscious at the wheel, his truck veered off the road and drove across a patch of low grass, heading straight for the diner. According to witnesses, Mr Garner's truck was in a direct line of collision with the front of the restaurant.

'At that time in the morning, and because of the torrential rain that was falling, there were only ten people inside the diner – seven customers plus three employees. The local sheriff and one of his deputies were two of the customers.' She paused to clear her throat. 'Something must've happened right at the last second, because Mr Garner's truck drastically changed course and missed the restaurant by just a few feet. Road accident forensics figured that the truck hit a large and deep pothole just a few yards before getting to the diner, and that caused the steering wheel to swing hard left.'

'The truck crashed into the adjacent lavatory building,' Kennedy said. 'Even if his heart attack hadn't killed Mr Garner, the collision would have.'

'Now,' Taylor said, lifting her right index finger. 'This is the first twist. As Mr Garner's truck missed the diner and headed toward the lavatory building, it clipped the back of a blue Ford Taurus that was parked just outside. The car belonged to one of the diner's customers.'

Taylor paused and reached for her briefcase that was by Captain Blake's desk.

'Mr Garner's truck hit the Taurus rear hard enough to cause the trunk door to pop open,' Kennedy said.

'The sheriff missed it.' Taylor again. 'Because as he ran outside, his main concern was to attend to the truck driver and passengers, if there had been any.'

She reached into her briefcase and retrieved an 11x8-inch colored photograph.

'But his deputy didn't,' she announced. 'As he ran outside, something inside the Taurus' trunk caught his eye.'

Hunter waited.

Taylor stepped forward and handed him the photograph.

'This is what he saw inside the trunk.'

Five

For the past ten minutes Special Agent Edwin Newman had been standing inside the holding cells control room in the basement of one of the several buildings that made up the nerve center of the FBI Academy. Despite the many CCTV monitors mounted on the east wall, all of his attention was set on a single and very specific one.

Newman wasn't one of the academy's trainees. In fact, he was a very experienced and accomplished agent with the Behavioral Analysis Unit, who had completed his training over twenty years ago. Newman was based in Washington DC, and had specially made the journey to Virginia four days ago just to interview the new prisoner.

'Has he moved at all in the past hour?' Newman asked the room operator, who was sitting at the large controls console that faced the monitors' wall.

The operator shook his head.

'Nope, and he won't move until lights off. Like I told you before, this guy is like a machine. I've never seen anything like it. Since they brought him in four nights ago, he hasn't broken his routine. He sleeps on his back, facing the ceiling, hands locked together and resting on his stomach – like a cadaver in a coffin. Once he closes his eyes, he doesn't move – no twitching, no turning, no restlessness, no scratching, no snoring, no waking up in the middle of the night to go pee, no nothing. Sure, at times he looks scared, as if he has no fucking idea why he's here, but most of the time he sleeps like a man with absolutely no worries in life, crashed out in the most comfortable bed money can buy. And I can tell you this –' he pointed at the screen – 'that bed ain't it. That is one goddamn uncomfortable piece of wood with a paper-thin mattress on top.'

Newman scratched his crooked nose but said nothing.

The operator continued.

'That guy's internal clock is tuned to Swiss precision. I shit you not. You can set your watch by it.'

'What do you mean?' Newman asked.

The operator let out a nasal chuckle. 'Every morning, at exactly 5:45 a.m., he opens his eyes. No alarm, no noise, no lights on, no call from us, and no agent bursting into his cell to wake him up. He just does it by himself. 5:45, on the dot – *bing* – he's awake.'

Newman knew that the prisoner had been stripped of all personal possessions. He had no watch or any other kind of timekeeper with him.

'As he opens his eyes,' the operator continued, 'he stares at the ceiling for exactly ninety-five seconds. Not a second more, not a second less. You can watch the recording from the past three days and time it if you like.'

No reaction from Newman.

'After ninety-five seconds,' the operator said, 'he gets out of bed, does his business at the latrine, and then hits the floor and starts doing push-ups, followed by sit-ups – ten reps of each in each set. If he isn't interrupted, he'll do fifty sets with the minimum of rest in between sets – no grunting, no puffing, and no face-pulling either, just pure determination. Breakfast is brought to him sometime between 6:30 and 7:00 a.m. If he hasn't yet finished his sets, he'll carry on until he's done, only then will he sit down and calmly eat his food. And he eats all of it without complaining. No matter what tasteless shit we put on that tray. After that, he's taken in for interrogation.' He turned to look at Newman. 'I'm assuming *you* are the interrogator.'

Newman didn't reply, didn't nod, and didn't shake his head either. He simply carried on staring at the monitor.

The operator shrugged and carried on with his account.

'When he's brought back to his cell, whatever time that might be, he goes back to a second battery of his exercise routine – another fifty sets of push-ups and sit-ups.' He chuckled. 'If you lost count, that's one thousand of each every day. When he's done, if he isn't taken away for further interrogation, he does exactly what you can see on the screen right now – he sits on his bed, crosses his legs, stares at the blank wall in front of him, and I guess he meditates, or prays, or whatever. But he never closes his eyes. And let me tell you, it's fucking freaky the way he just stares at that wall.'

'For how long?' Newman asked.

'Depends,' the operator replied. 'He's allowed one visit to the shower every day, but prisoners' shower times change from day to day. You know the drill. If we come get him while he's wall-staring, he'll simply snap out of his trance, step off the bed, get shackled and go to the shower – no moaning, no resisting, no fighting. When he comes back, he goes straight back to the bed-sitting, wall-staring thing again. If he isn't interrupted at all, he'll carry on staring at that wall until lights off at 9:30.'

Newman nodded.

'But yesterday,' the operator added. 'Just out of curiosity, they kept the lights on for an extra five minutes.'

'Let me guess,' Newman said. 'It made no difference. At exactly 9:30, he lay down, went back to his "body in a coffin" position, and went to sleep, lights off or not.'

'You got it,' the operator agreed. 'Like I said, he's like a machine, with a Swiss precision internal clock.' He paused and turned to face Newman. 'I'm no expert here, but from what I've seen in the past four nights and four days, mentally, this guy is a fucking fortress.'

Newman said nothing.

'I don't want to overstep my mark here, but . . . has he talked at all during any of the interrogation sessions?'

Newman considered the question for a long moment.

'The reason I ask is because I know the drill. If a special prisoner like this one hasn't talked after three days of interrogation, then the VIP treatment starts, and we all know how tough that gets.' Instinctively the operator checked his watch. 'Well, it's been three days, and if the VIP treatment was about to start, I would've gotten word of it by now. So I'm guessing – he talked.'

Newman observed the screen for a few more seconds before nodding once. 'He spoke for the first time last night.' He finally looked away from the wall monitor and stared back at the room operator. 'He said seven words.'

Six

As Hunter studied the photograph Special Agent Courtney Taylor had handed him, he felt his heartbeat pick up speed inside his chest, and a rush of adrenaline surge through his body. Several silent seconds went by before he allowed his stare to finally leave the picture and wander over to Captain Blake.

'Have you seen this?' he asked.

She nodded.

Hunter's eyes returned to the photograph.

'Clearly,' Kennedy said, standing up again. 'Mr Garner's pick-up truck clipped the back of the Ford Taurus hard enough not only to release the trunk door, but also to knock that ice container over.'

The photograph showed a family-size, picnic-style ice container that had been tipped on its side inside the Taurus' trunk. Large cubes of ice had spilled out of it, rolling off in all directions. Most of the ice cubes were crimson with what could only have been blood. But that was only secondary. Hunter's full attention was on something else – the two severed heads that undoubtedly were being preserved inside the container until it was disturbed by the accident. Both heads were female: one blonde – longish hair; one brunette – short, pixie-styled hair. Both heads had been severed from their bodies at the base of the neck. From what Hunter could tell, the cut looked clean – experienced.

The blonde woman's head was lying on its left cheek, her long hair covering most of her face. The brunette woman's head, on the other hand, had rolled away from the container and, with the help of several ice cubes, had wedged itself in such a way that the back of her head was flat against the trunk's floor, her features clearly exposed. And that was what made Hunter pause for breath. Her facial wounds were more shocking than the decapitation itself.

Three small, locked, metal padlocks crudely and savagely pierced the flesh on both of her lips at uneven intervals, keeping her mouth shut, but not completely sealed. Her delicate lips, crusty with blood, still looked swollen, which indicated that the padlocks had ripped through her flesh while she was still alive. Her eyes had been removed. Her eye sockets were empty. Just two black holes caked with dried blood, which had also run down her cheeks, creating a crazy, dark red, lightning bolt effect.

She didn't have the skin of an old woman, but guessing her age from the picture alone was practically impossible.

'That photograph was taken by Sheriff Walton just minutes after the accident,' Kennedy offered, walking over and pausing next to Hunter. 'As Agent Taylor mentioned earlier, he was having breakfast in the diner that morning. Nothing was touched. He acted fast because he knew the rain would start destroying evidence pretty quickly.'

Taylor reached inside her briefcase and retrieved a new photograph, handing it to Hunter.

'This one was taken by the forensics team,' she explained. 'They had to travel all the way from Cheyenne, which is only about an hour away, but when you add delay time, assembling the team together and getting on the road, they only got there about four hours after the accident had happened.'

In this new photograph, both heads had been placed side by side, facing up, still inside the Taurus' trunk. The blonde woman's face showed exactly the same wounds as the brunette's. Again, guessing the second woman's age was nearly impossible.

'Were their eyes inside the container?' Hunter asked, his attention never leaving the picture.

'No,' Taylor replied. 'There was nothing else inside the ice container.' She looked at Kennedy, and then back at Hunter. 'And we have no idea where their bodies might be.'

'And that's not all,' Kennedy said.

Hunter's eyes left the picture and settled on the man from the FBI.

'Once those padlocks were removed from their lips,' Kennedy explained, nodding at the photograph. 'It was revealed that they'd both had all of their teeth extracted.' He paused for effect. 'And their tongues cut off.'

Hunter stayed silent.

'Since we have no bodies,' Taylor said, taking over again. 'And consequently no fingerprints, one could argue that the perpetrator removed their teeth, and possibly their eyes, to avoid identification, but the sheer brutality of the wounds inflicted on both victims . . .' She paused and lifted her right index finger to emphasize her point. '. . . *prior to death*, tells us otherwise. Whoever killed them, enjoyed doing it.' She phrased her last few words as if she'd just revealed a big secret. It sounded a little patronizing.

Kennedy pulled a face while at the same time giving Taylor a sharp look because he knew that she hadn't told anyone in that room anything they hadn't already figured out. Despite not being part of the FBI National Center for the Analysis of Violent Crime, or the Behavioral Analysis Unit, Robert Hunter was the best criminal profiler Kennedy had ever met. He had tried to recruit Hunter into the FBI for the first time many years ago, when he first read Hunter's Ph.D. thesis paper titled *An Advanced Psychological Study in Criminal Conduct*. Hunter was only twenty-three years old at the time.

The paper had impressed Kennedy and the then FBI Director so much, that it became mandatory reading at the NCAVC, and still remained so. Since then and over the years, Kennedy had tried several times to recruit Hunter into his team. In his mind, it made no sense that Hunter would rather be a detective with the LAPD's Special Homicide Division than join the most advanced serial-killer-tracking task force in the USA, arguably in the world. True, he knew Hunter was the lead detective for the Ultra Violent Crimes Unit, a special unit created by the LAPD to investigate homicides and serial homicides where over-whelming brutality and/or sadism had been used by the perpetrator, and Hunter was the best at what he did. His arrest record proved that, but still, the FBI could offer him a lot more than the LAPD could. But Hunter had never shown even an ounce of interest in becoming a federal agent, and had declined every offer made to him by Kennedy and his superiors.

'Interesting case,' Hunter said, handing the pictures back to Taylor. 'But the FBI and the NCAVC have investigated a ton of similar cases ... some even more disturbing. This isn't exactly something new.'

Neither Kennedy nor Taylor disputed that.

'I take it that you don't have an identity on either of the two victims,' Hunter said.

'That's correct,' Kennedy replied.

'And you said that their heads were found in Wyoming?'

'That's also correct.'

'You can probably guess what my next question is going to be, right?' Hunter asked.

A second of hesitation.

'If we don't know who the victims are,' Taylor said, nodding at him. 'And their heads were found in Wyoming, what are we doing in Los Angeles?'

'And why am I here?' Hunter added, quickly checking his watch. 'I have a plane to catch in a few hours, and I still need to pack.'

'We're here, and you're here, because the federal government of the United States needs your help,' Taylor replied.

'Oh please,' Captain Blake said, with a smirk on her lips. 'Are you going to give us the patriotic bullshit speech now? Are you for real?' She stood up. 'My detectives put their lives on the line for the city of Los Angeles, and consequently for this country, day in, day out. So do yourself a favor and don't even go there, sweetheart.' She pinned Taylor down with a stare that could melt metal. 'Does that bullshit actually work on people?'

Taylor looked like she was about to reply, but Hunter cut in just a second before.

'Need me? Why?' He addressed Kennedy. 'I'm not an FBI agent, and you guys have more investigators than you can count, not to mention a squad of criminal profilers.'

'None of them as good as you,' Kennedy said.

'Flattery will get you nowhere in here,' Captain Blake said.

'I'm not a profiler, Adrian,' Hunter said. 'You know that.'

'That's not really why we need you, Robert,' Kennedy replied; he paused a moment, and nodded at Taylor. 'Tell him.'

Seven

The tone Kennedy used caused Hunter's right eyebrow to twitch up just a fraction. He turned, faced Agent Taylor, and waited.

Taylor used the tip of her fingers to tuck her loose hair behind her ears before beginning.

'The Ford Taurus belonged to one of the customers who was having breakfast in the diner that morning. According to his driver's license, his name is Liam Shaw, born February 13, 1968, in Madison, Tennessee.' Taylor paused and observed Hunter for a second, trying to pick up any signs that he'd recognized the name. There were none.

'According to his driver's license?' Hunter questioned, his gaze ping-ponging between Taylor and Kennedy. 'So you have doubts.' He stated rather than asked.

'The name checks out,' Kennedy said. 'Everything looks above board.'

'But you still have doubts.' Hunter pushed.

'The problem is . . .' Taylor this time. 'Everything looks above board if we go back a maximum of fourteen years. Beyond that . . .' She faintly shook her head. 'We could find absolutely nothing on a Liam Shaw, born February 13, 1968, in Madison, Tennessee. It's like he never existed before then.'

'And judging by the way you were observing me when you mentioned his name,' Hunter said, 'you were looking for signs of recognition. Why?'

Taylor looked impressed. She'd always been very proud of her poker face, the way she could study people without them noticing it, but Hunter had read her like a book.

Kennedy smiled. 'I told you he's good.'

Taylor seemed to take no notice of the comment.

'Mr Shaw was arrested on the spot by Sheriff Walton and his deputy,' she said. 'But Sheriff Walton also quickly realized that he had stumbled upon something that he and his small department simply wouldn't be able to handle. The Taurus' license plates were from Montana, which created a cross-state reference. With that, the Wyoming sheriff department had no option but to bring us in.'

She paused and shuffled through the contents of her briefcase for a new document.

'Now, here is the second twist to this story,' she said, moving on. 'The Taurus isn't registered under Mr Shaw's name. It's registered under a Mr John Williams of New York City.'

She handed the document to Hunter.

Hunter barely glanced at the sheet of paper he'd been given.

'Surprise, surprise,' Kennedy said. 'There was no John Williams at the address the car was registered to.'

'John Williams is quite a common name,' Hunter said.

'Too common,' Taylor agreed. 'About fifteen hundred in New York City alone.'

'But you have Mr Shaw in custody, right?' Hunter asked.

'That's correct,' Taylor confirmed.

Hunter looked at Captain Blake, still a little confused. 'So, you've got Mr Shaw, who is apparently from Tennessee, two unidentified female heads, a vehicle with Montana license plates, which is registered to a Mr Williams from New York City.' He shrugged at the room. 'My original question still stands – why are you in LA? And why am I here and not at home packing?' He checked his watch one more time.

'Because Mr Shaw isn't talking,' Taylor replied, her voice still calm.

Hunter stared hard at her for a couple of seconds.

'And how does that answer my question?'

'Agent Taylor's statement isn't one hundred percent accurate,' Kennedy cut in. 'We've had Mr Shaw in our custody for four days. He was transferred to us a day after he was arrested. He's being held in Quantico. I assigned Agent Taylor and Agent Newman to the case.'

Hunter's eyes moved to Taylor for just a second.

'But as Agent Taylor said . . .' Kennedy moved on. '. . . Mr Shaw has been refusing to speak.'

'So?' Captain Blake interrupted, a little amused. 'Since when has that stopped the FBI from still extracting information from anyone?'

Kennedy was unfazed by the spiked remark.

'During last night's interrogation session,' he continued, 'Mr Shaw finally spoke for the first time.' He paused and walked over to the large window on the east wall. 'He said only seven words.'

Hunter waited.

'He said, "*I will only speak to Robert Hunter.*"'

Eight

Hunter didn't move. He didn't even flinch. His facial expression remained unchanged. If Kennedy's words had affected him in any way, he showed no signs of it.

'I'm sure I'm not the only Robert Hunter in America,' he finally said.

'I'm sure you aren't,' Kennedy agreed. 'But we're also sure that Mr Shaw was talking about you, not someone else.'

'How come you're so sure?'

'Because of his tone of voice,' Kennedy replied. 'And his posture, his confidence, his attitude ... everything about him, really. We've analyzed the footage countless times. You know what we do, Robert. You know that I have people who are trained to read the faintest of telltale signs, to recognize the slightest change of voice intonation, to identify body-language signals. This guy was confident. No hesitation. No trepidation. Nothing. He was certain that we would know who he was referring to.'

'You can watch the recording if you like,' Taylor offered. 'I've got a copy right here.' She gestured toward her briefcase.

Hunter remained silent.

'That's why we thought that maybe you might recognize the name,' Kennedy said. 'But then again, we had our suspicions that Liam Shaw was just a bogus name anyway.'

'Have you tried Tennessee, where this Mr Liam Shaw is supposedly from?' Captain Blake asked. 'There might be a Robert Hunter somewhere over there.'

'No, we haven't,' Taylor replied. 'No need. As Director Kennedy said, Mr Shaw was too confident. He knew that it would take us no time to find out exactly whom he was referring to.'

Kennedy took over. 'As soon as I heard the name, I knew that he could only be talking about one person. You, Robert.'

'Do you have that footage?' Hunter asked.

'I do,' Taylor replied. 'I also have a photograph of Mr Shaw.' She retrieved one last picture from her briefcase and handed it to Hunter.

Hunter stared at the photograph for a very long, silent moment. Again, neither his facial expression nor his body language gave anything away. Until he took a deep breath, and his eyes moved up to meet Kennedy's.

'You have got to be shitting me.'

Nine

The man who called himself Liam Shaw sat on the bed inside the small cell located deep underground – sublevel five of a nondescript building inside the FBI Academy complex in Quantico, Virginia. His legs were crossed under his body, his hands loosely clasped together, resting on his lap. His eyes were open, but there was no movement in them, just a dead, half-scared, half-uncertain look, staring straight ahead at the blank wall in front of him. In fact, there was no movement from him at all. No slight head-shake, no twitching of the thumbs or fingers, no tiny adjust-ment of the legs under him, no shifting or rocking of the body, nothing, except for the unavoidable physical motor-reaction of blinking.

He'd been in that position for the past hour, simply star-ing at that wall, as though if he stared at it for long enough he'd be magically transported somewhere else. His legs should've cramped by now. His feet should've been tingly with thousands of pins and needles. His neck should've been stiff from the lack of movement, but he looked as comfortable and as stress-free as a man sitting in his own luxurious living room.

He'd taught himself that technique a long time ago. It had taken him many years to master it, but he could now practically empty his mind from most thoughts. He could easily block out sounds and blind himself to what was happening around him, despite having his eyes wide open. It was a sort of meditation trance that elevated his mind onto an almost unearthly level; but most of all, it kept him mentally strong. And he knew that that was exactly what he needed right now.

Since last night, the agents had stopped bothering him. But he knew they would. They wanted him to talk, but he just didn't know what to say. He knew enough about police procedure to know that whatever explanation he gave them wouldn't suffice, even if it were the truth. In their eyes, he was already guilty, no matter what he said or didn't say. He also understood that the fact that he wasn't being held by a regular police or sheriff's department, but had been turned over to the FBI, complicated matters immensely.

He knew he had to give them something soon, because the interrogation methods were about to change. He could feel it. He could sense it in the tone of voice of both of his interrogators.

The attractive blonde woman who called herself Agent Taylor was softly spoken, charming and polite, while the big man with the crooked nose who called himself Agent Newman was much more aggressive and short-tempered. Typical good-cop-bad-cop team play. But their frustration due to his total commitment to staying silent was starting to show. The charm and politeness were about to end. That had become obvious in the last interrogation session.

And then the thought came to him, and with it came a name:

Robert Hunter.

Ten

Hunter eventually made it back to his apartment to pack his bags, but the flight he took just a couple of hours later wasn't the one he had booked to Hawaii.

After taxiing its way up the runway, the private Hawker jet finally received the takeoff 'go ahead' from the Van Nuys airport control tower.

Hunter was seated toward the back of the plane, nursing a large cup of black coffee. His job didn't really allow him to travel much, and when he did, if at all possible, he usually drove. He'd been on a few commercial planes before, but this was his first time inside a private jet, and he had to admit that he was impressed. The plane's interior was both luxurious and practical in equal measures.

The cabin was about twenty-two feet long by seven feet wide. There were eight very comfortable, cream leather seats, set out in a double-club configuration – four individual seats on each side of the aisle, each with their own power outlet and media system. All eight seats could swivel 360 degrees. Low-heat LED overhead lights gave the cabin a nice, bright feel.

Agent Taylor was sitting on the seat directly in front of Hunter, typing away on her laptop, which was sitting on the fold-out table in front of her. Adrian Kennedy was sitting to Hunter's right, across the aisle from him. Since they left Captain Blake's office, he seemed to have been on his cellphone the whole time.

The plane took off smoothly and quickly climbed up to a cruising altitude of 30,000 feet. Hunter kept his eyes on the blue, cloudless sky outside his window, wrestling with a multitude of thoughts.

'So,' Kennedy said, finally coming off his phone and placing it back inside his jacket pocket. He had swiveled his seat around to face Hunter. 'Tell me about this guy again, Robert. Who is he?'

Taylor stopped typing into her laptop and slowly rotated her seat around to face both men.

Hunter kept his eyes on the blue sky for a moment longer.

'He's one of the most intelligent people I've ever met,' he said at last. 'Someone with tremendous self-discipline and control.'

Kennedy and Taylor waited.

'His name is Lucien, Lucien Folter,' Hunter carried on. 'Or at least that's the name that I knew him by. I met him on my first day at Stanford University. I was sixteen.'

Hunter grew up as an only child to working-class parents in Compton, an underprivileged neighborhood of South Los Angeles. His mother lost her battle with cancer when he was only seven. His father never remarried and had to take on two jobs to cope with the demands of raising a child on his own.

Hunter had always been different. Even as a child his brain seemed to work through problems faster than anyone else's. School bored and frustrated him. He finished all of his sixth-grade work in less than two months and, just for something to do, he read through all the modules for the rest of his lower-school years. After doing so, he asked his school principal if he was allowed to take the final exams for grades seven and eight. Out of sheer curiosity and intrigue, the principal allowed him to. Hunter aced them all.

It was then that his principal decided to get in contact with the Los Angeles Board of Education; after a new battery of exams and tests, at the age of twelve, he was accepted into the Mirman School for the Gifted.

But even a special school's curriculum wasn't enough to slow his progress down.

By the age of fourteen he'd glided through Mirman's high school English, History, Math, Biology and Chemistry curriculums. Four years of high school were condensed into two and at fifteen he'd graduated with honors. With recommendations from all of his teachers, Hunter was accepted as a 'special circumstances' student at Stanford University.

By the age of nineteen, Hunter had already graduated in Psychology – *summa cum laude* – and at twenty-three he received his PhD in Criminal Behavior Analysis and Biopsychology.

'You said he was your roommate?' Taylor asked.

Hunter nodded. 'From day one. I was assigned to a dorm room on my first day in college.' He shrugged. 'Lucien was assigned to the same room.'

'How many sharing the room?'

'The two of us, that's all. Small rooms.'

'Was he also a psychology major?'

'That's right.' Hunter's gaze returned to the sky outside his window as his memory started to take him back to a long time ago. 'He was a nice guy. I never expected him to be so friendly to me.'

Taylor frowned. 'What do you mean?'

Hunter shrugged again. 'I was a lot younger than anyone around. I had never been too much into sports, going to the gym, or any sort of physical activity, really. I was very skinny and awkward, long hair, and I didn't dress like most people did at the time. In truth, I was a bully magnet. Lucien was almost nineteen then, loved sports and worked out regularly. The kind of guy who'd usually have a field day with someone who looked like me.'

From Hunter's look and physique, no one would ever have guessed that he'd been a skinny and awkward kid when young. He looked like he'd been a typical high school jock. Maybe even captain of the football or the wrestling team.

'But he didn't,' Hunter continued. 'In fact, it was because of him that I didn't get picked on as much as I would have. We became best friends. When I started going to the gym, he helped me with workouts and diet and all.'

'And how was he on a day-to-day basis?'

Hunter knew that Taylor was referring to Folter's inner-character traits.

'He wasn't the violent kind, if that's what you're asking. He was always calm. Always in control. Which was a good thing, because he sure knew how to fight.'

'But you just said that he wasn't the violent kind,' Taylor said.

'That's right.'

'But you've also just implied that you've seen him in a fight.'

Half a nod. 'I have.'

Taylor's eyes and lip-twist asked a silent question.

'There are certain situations that, no matter how calm or easy-going you are, you just can't get out of,' Hunter replied.

'Such as?' Taylor insisted.

'I only remember seeing Lucien in a fight once,' Hunter explained. 'And he really tried to get out of it without using his fists, but it didn't work out that way.'

'How so?'

Hunter shrugged. 'Lucien had met this girl in a bar at the weekend and spent the night chatting to her. As far as I am aware, that was it. There was no sex, no kissing, nothing bad, really, just a few drinks, a little flirting and loads of laughs. On the Monday after that weekend, we were coming back from a late study session at the library, when we got cornered off by four guys, all of them pretty big. One of them was the girl's "very pissed off" ex-boyfriend. Apparently, they'd split not that long ago. Now the thing about Lucien was that he'd always been a great talker. As the saying goes: He could sell ice to an Eskimo. He tried to reason his way out of that situation. He said that he was sorry, that he didn't know that she had a boyfriend, or that they had just split. He said that if he'd known, he would've never approached her and so on. But the guys didn't want to know. They said that they weren't there for an apology. They were there to fuck him up, full stop.'

'So what happened then?' Taylor asked.

'Not much. Until then I had never seen anything quite like it. They just went for him. Me? As skinny as I was, I wasn't about to sit and watch my best friend get beat up by four Neanderthals, but I barely got a chance to move. The whole thing was over in ten . . . fifteen seconds, tops. I couldn't really tell you what happened in detail, but Lucien moved fast . . . too fast, actually. In absolutely no time, all four of them were on the floor. Two had a broken nose, one had about three or four broken fingers, and the fourth one had his genitals kicked to the back of his throat. After we got out of there, I asked him where he learned to do that.'

'And what did he say?'

'He gave me a bullshit answer. He said he watched a lot of martial arts movies. One thing I had learned about Lucien was that there was no point in trying to push him for an answer when he didn't want to give you one. So I just left it at that.'

'You said that he's a great talker,' Taylor said with a slight lilt in her voice. 'Well, he hasn't made that much conversation in the past few days.'

'When did you last see him?' Kennedy asked.

'The day I got my PhD diploma,' Hunter explained. 'In college I graduated a year before him.'

Taylor knew from Hunter's résumé that he had sped through his college years as well, condensing four years into three.

'But I stayed in Stanford,' Hunter said. 'I was offered a second scholarship to carry on studying for a PhD So I took it. Lucien and I continued to share the dorm room for one more year, until he graduated. After that, he left Stanford.'

'Did you keep in touch?'

'We did, but not for very long,' Hunter confirmed. 'He took a few months off after he graduated. Went traveling for a little while, and then decided that he wanted to go back to university. He also wanted to get a PhD.'

'Did he go back to Stanford?'

'No. He went to Yale.'

'Connecticut?' Taylor was surprised. 'That's all the way on the east coast. Why so far away when you have Stanford, Berkley, Caltech, and UCLA right there in California? Four of the best universities in the whole of the country.'

'Yale is also a great university,' Hunter countered.

'I know that. But you know what I mean. Connecticut is a hell of a hike from California. I'm guessing that, after living there for so many years, he probably had lots of friends and some sort of life back in LA. Why the sudden change? Is that where his family is from, Connecticut?'

Hunter paused for a second, trying to remember.

'I don't know where his family is from,' he said. 'He never talked about them.'

Taylor's gaze slowly moved to Kennedy and then back to Hunter.

'Don't you think that's a little odd?' she asked. 'You two spent years together sharing a dorm room. As you've put it, you became best friends. He never said anything about his family at all?'

Hunter shrugged matter-of-factly.

'No, and I don't think that's odd at all. I never talked about my family, to him, or anyone else for that matter. Some people are more private than others.'

'So you last saw him when you received your PhD diploma,' Kennedy said.

Hunter nodded. 'He flew over for the graduation ceremony, stayed for a day, and flew back the next morning. I never heard from him again since.'

'He just flew back to Connecticut and disappeared?' Taylor spoke again. 'I thought you were best friends.'

'Maybe I was the one who disappeared,' Hunter said.

Taylor hesitated for an instant.

'Why? Did he try to get in contact with you?'

'Not that I am aware of,' Hunter replied. 'But I didn't try to keep in touch with him either.' He paused and looked away. 'After my graduation I didn't keep in touch with anyone.'

Eleven

The private Hawker jet touched down on Turner Field landing strip in Quantico, Virginia, almost exactly five hours after taking off from Van Nuys airport in Los Angeles.

After Hunter's conversation with Kennedy and Taylor about what he could remember of his old best friend, they all sat in silence for the rest of the long flight. Kennedy fell asleep for a couple of hours, but Hunter and Taylor stayed awake for the duration, each one lost in their own thoughts. For some reason Taylor's memory took her back to when she was still a child, and how she was forced to learn how to take care of herself at a very young age.

Her seemingly healthy father died of an unexpected heart attack, triggered by a coronary aneurysm, when she was fourteen years old. Taylor took his death very badly, and so did her young mother. The next couple of years became a tremendous battle, emotionally and financially, as her mother – who had been a housewife for the past fifteen years – struggled with a series of odd jobs and the pressures of being a recent widow, and consequently a single parent.

Taylor's mother was a tender woman with a kind soul, but she was also one of those people who just couldn't handle being by herself. What followed was a string of deadbeat boyfriends, some of them abusive. Taylor was just about to graduate from high school when her mother became pregnant again. Her mother's boyfriend at the time told her that he just didn't want that kind of responsibility, that he wasn't ready to become a father and have a family, and that he had no intention of becoming a father to someone else's daughter – a girl that he couldn't care less for. When Taylor's mother refused to follow through with the abortion clinic appointment he'd set up for her, he simply dumped her and left town the next day. They never heard from him again.

With her mother heavily pregnant and unable to work, Taylor gave up on the idea of going to college and started working full time at the local mall. A month later, her mother gave birth to a baby boy, Adam – but unfortunately Adam was born with an abnormality on chromosome eighteen, resulting in moderate mental retardation, muscle atrophy, craniofacial malformation, and huge difficulty in coordinating movement. Instead of bringing her joy, Adam's birth threw Taylor's mother into an out-of-control depression spiral. She didn't know how to cope with it and found solace in sleeping tablets, antidepressants and alcohol. At the age of seventeen, Taylor had to become 'big daughter', 'big sister', and 'man of the house'.

Government subsidy wasn't nearly enough so, for the next three years, Taylor worked whatever jobs she could get and took care of her little brother and mother, but despite all the medical support, Adam's health kept on deteriorating, and he died two months after his third birthday. Her mother's depression worsened considerably, but without medical insurance, professional help was nearly impossible to find.

One rainy night, when Taylor came back from working a late waitress shift in a restaurant downtown, she found a note from her mother on the kitchen table:

Sorry for not being a good mother to you or Adam, honey. Sorry for all the mistakes. You're the best daughter a mother could ever hope for. I love you with all my heart. I just hope that you can one day forgive me for being so weak, so stupid, and for all the burden I've put you through. Please be happy, honey. You deserve to.

Reading the note filled Taylor with a heart-stopping dread, and she rushed to her mother's room . . . but it was way too late. On her mother's bedside table there were three empty bottles – one of sleeping pills, one of antidepressants, and one of vodka. Taylor still has nightmares about that night.

A black GMC SUV with tinted windows, FBI-style, was already waiting for them on the runway when they landed.

Hunter stepped off the plane and stretched his six-foot frame against the early morning breeze. It felt good to be breathing clean air again, and to finally get out of such confined space. No matter how luxurious the jet's passenger cabin was, after five hours locked inside it, it felt like a sky prison.

Hunter checked his watch – the sun wouldn't be up for another two hours, but surprisingly, the night air in Virginia at that time of year felt just as warm as it did back in Los Angeles.

'We all need to try to get some sleep,' Kennedy said, coming off his cellphone again. All three of them boarded the SUV. 'And a decent breakfast later on. Your quarters are ready,' he addressed Hunter. 'I hope you don't mind staying at one of the recruit dorms at the academy.'

Hunter gave him a subtle headshake.

'Agent Taylor will come get you at ten a.m.' Kennedy consulted his timepiece. 'That'll give everyone around six hours' break. Get some sleep.'

'Can't we make it any earlier than that?' Hunter asked. 'Like now? I'm here already. I don't see the point of delaying this any longer.'

Kennedy looked straight into Hunter's eyes. 'We all need some rest, Robert. It's been a long day and a long flight. I know that you can work on very little sleep, but that doesn't mean that your brain doesn't get tired like everyone else's. I need you sharp when you walk in there to talk to your old friend.'

Hunter said nothing. He simply watched the lampposts fly by as the SUV drove off.

Twelve

Special Agent Courtney Taylor knocked on Hunter's dorm room door at exactly 10:00 a.m. She had managed five hours' sleep, had showered, and was now wearing a businesslike but elegant black pinstripe suit. Her blonde hair had been pulled back into a very slick ponytail.

Hunter opened the door, checked his watch, and smiled.

'Wow, I guess you timed your arrival to absolute perfection.'

Hunter's hair was still wet from his shower. He was wearing black jeans, a dark blue T-shirt under his usual thin black leather jacket, and black boots.

Dozing on and off, he had only managed to sleep a total of two and a half hours.

'Are you ready, Detective Hunter?' Taylor asked.

'Indeed,' Hunter replied, closing the door behind him.

'I trust that you got breakfast OK?' she said, as they started walking down the corridor toward the staircase.

At precisely 9:00 a.m., an FBI cadet carrying a healthy breakfast tray of fruit, cereal, yogurt, scrambled eggs, coffee, milk and toast had knocked on Hunter's door.

'I did,' Hunter said with a questioning smile. 'But I didn't know the FBI did room service.'

'We don't, this was a one-off. You can thank Director Kennedy for that.'

Hunter nodded once. 'I'll make sure I do.'

Downstairs, another black SUV was waiting to drive them across the compound to the other side. Hunter sat in silence in the back seat, while Taylor sat in front with the driver.

The FBI Academy was located on 547 acres of a Marine Corps base forty miles south of Washington, DC. Its nerve center was an interconnected conglomerate of buildings that looked a lot more like an overgrown corporation than a government training facility. Recruits in dark blue sweat suits, with the bureau's insignia emblazoned on their chests and FBI in large golden letters across their backs, were just about everywhere. Marines with high-powered rifles stood at every intersection and at the entrance to every building. The sound of helicopter blades cutting the air seemed to be constant. There was no way of escaping the palpable sense of mission and secrecy that soaked the entire place.

After a drive that seemed to have lasted forever, the SUV finally reached the other side of the complex, and stopped at the heavily guarded gates of what could only be described as a compound within a compound, completely detached from the main network of buildings. After clearing security, the SUV moved inside and parked in front of a three-story brick building fronted by dark-tinted, bulletproof-glass windows.

Hunter and Taylor exited the car, and she escorted him past the armed Marines at the entrance and into the building. Inside they went through two sets of security doors, down a long hallway, through two more sets of security doors and into an elevator, which descended three floors down to the Behavioral Science Unit, or BSU. The elevator opened onto a long, shiny and well-lit hardwood corridor, with several portraits in gilded frames lining the walls.

A big man with a round face and a crooked nose stepped in front of the open elevator doors.

'Detective Robert Hunter,' he said in a harsh voice that came across as a little unfriendly. 'I'm Agent Edwin Newman. Welcome to the FBI BSU.'

Hunter stepped out of the lift and shook Newman's hand.

Newman was in his early fifties, with combed-back peppery hair and bright green eyes. He was wearing a black suit with a pristine white shirt and a silky red tie. He smiled, flashing gleaming white teeth.

'I thought that we could have a quick chat in the conference room before we take you to see ...' Newman paused and looked at Taylor. '... your old friend, as I understand.'

Hunter simply nodded and followed Newman and Taylor to the opposite end of the hallway.

The conference room was large and air-conditioned to a very pleasant temperature. The center of the room was taken by a long, polished mahogany table. A very large monitor showing a detailed map of the United States glowed at the far wall.

Newman took a seat at the head of the table and nodded for Hunter to take the seat next to him.

'I know you've been made completely aware of the delicate situation we have here,' Newman began, once Hunter took his seat.

Hunter agreed with a head gesture.

Newman flipped open the folder on the table in front of him. 'According to what you told Director Kennedy and Agent Taylor, the real name of the man we have in our custody is Lucien Folter, and not Liam Shaw, as it was stated in his driver's license.'

'That's the name I knew him by,' Hunter confirmed.

Newman nodded his understanding. 'So you think that Lucien Folter could also be a made-up name?'

'That's not what I said,' Hunter replied calmly.

Newman waited.

'I see no reason why he would use a false name back in college,' Hunter said, trying to clear things up. 'You also have to remember that we're talking about Stanford University here, and someone who was just nineteen at the time.'

Newman gave Hunter a very subtle frown, not quite following the detective's line of thought.

Hunter read it and explained. 'That means that this nineteen-year-old kid would've had to have expertly falsified several records to be accepted into a very prestigious university, in an era when personal computers did not exist.' He shook his head. 'Not an easy task.'

'Not easy,' Newman agreed. 'But it was doable.'

Hunter said nothing.

'The only reason I ask is because of the hidden meaning in his name,' Newman said.

'Hidden meaning?' Hunter looked at the agent curiously.

Newman nodded. 'Did you know that the word Folter means *torture* in German?'

Hunter agreed with a head gesture. 'Yes, Lucien told me.'

Newman carried on staring at him.

Hunter didn't look too impressed. 'Is that what you mean by hidden meaning?' He glanced at Taylor, then back at Newman. 'Did you also know that the name Lucien comes from the French language and it means "light, illumination"? It's also a village in Poland, and the name of a Christian saint. Most names have a history behind them, Special Agent Newman. My family name means "he who hunts"; nevertheless, my father was never a hunter in any shape or form. A great number of American family names will, by coincidence, mean something in a different language. That doesn't actually constitute a hidden meaning.'

Newman said nothing back.

Hunter took a moment, and then allowed his gaze to move to the folder on the table.

Newman got the hint and began reading. 'OK. Lucien Folter, born October 25, 1966, in Monte Vista, Colorado. His parents – Charles Folter and Mary-Ann Folter, are both deceased. He graduated from Monte Vista High School in 1985, with very good grades. No youth record whatsoever. Never got into any trouble with the police. After graduating from high school, he was quickly accepted into Stanford University.' Newman paused and looked up at Hunter. 'I guess you know everything that happened during the next few years.'

Hunter remained silent.

'After obtaining his psychology degree from Stanford,' Newman continued, 'Lucien Folter applied to Yale University in Connecticut for a PhD in Criminal Psychology. He was accepted, did three years of his degree, and then simply disappeared. He never completed his PhD.'

Hunter kept his eyes on Newman. He didn't know that his old friend hadn't completed his doctorate.

'And when I say disappeared,' Newman said. 'I mean *disappeared*. There's nothing else out there on a Lucien Folter after his third year at Yale. No job records, no pass-port, no credit cards, no listed address, no bills ... no anything. It's like Lucien Folter ceased to exist.' Newman closed the folder. 'That's all we have on him.'

'Maybe that was when he decided to take up a new iden-tity,' Taylor offered. She was sitting across the table from

Hunter. 'Maybe that was when he got tired of being Lucien Folter and became someone else. Maybe Liam Shaw, or maybe even someone completely different that we don't know about.'

Silence took over the room for the next few seconds, before Newman broke it again.

'The truth is that whoever this guy really is, he's a living, breathing, walking mystery. Somebody who might've lied to everyone throughout his whole life.'

Hunter chewed on that thought for a moment.

'I wanted you to understand this before you go talk to him,' Newman added, 'because I know that things can get a little emotional when we're dealing with people from our past. I'm not trying to tell you what to do. I've read your file, and I've read your thesis on "An Advanced Psychological Study in Criminal Conduct". Everybody in BSU has, it's mandatory reading, and so I know that you know what you're doing better than most. But you're still human, and as such you have emotions. No matter how clued-up a person is, emotions can and will cloud best judgments and opinions. Keep that in mind when you walk in there.'

Hunter stayed quiet.

Newman then proceeded to explain to Hunter how unconventional and mysterious Lucien Folter had appeared to be since he had arrived in Quantico – the extreme silence, the up-to-the-second biological internal timekeeping, the long exercise sessions, the wall staring, the extraordinary mental strength, everything.

From what he knew of his old friend, Hunter wasn't too surprised Lucien could be that mentally focused.

'He's waiting,' Newman said at last. 'I guess we better get going.'

Thirteen

Newman and Taylor guided Hunter out of the conference room, back down the hallway, and into the elevator, which descended another two floors to sublevel five. This level was nothing like the Behavioral Science Unit's floor. There was no shiny hallway, no fancy fixtures on the walls, no pleasant feel to the place whatsoever.

The elevator opened onto a small concrete-floored anteroom. On the right, behind a large safety-glass window, Hunter could see what had to be a control room, with wall-mounted monitors and a guard sitting at a large console desk.

'Welcome to the BSU holding cells floor,' Taylor said.

'Why is he being held here?' Hunter asked.

'A couple of reasons, really,' Taylor replied. 'First, as was mentioned before, the sheriff's department in Wheatland had no idea how to deal with a case of this magnitude, and second, because everything indicates that this is probably a cross-state double-homicide case. So until we're able to establish where your old friend should be rightly held, we'll keep him here.'

'Also because your friend's potential psychopathy has triggered several bells within the behavioral unit,' Newman added. 'Especially his incredible mental strength, and the way he's able to hold firm under pressure. No one in the unit has ever come across anyone quite like him. If he really is a killer, judging by the level of brutality that was used on the two victims' heads found, then we might have stumbled upon a Pandora's box.'

Taylor signaled the guard inside the control room and he buzzed open the door directly across the room from them. The US Marine standing by the door took a step to the side to allow them through.

The door led them into a long corridor where the walls were made of cinder block. There was a distinct sanitized smell in the air, something that tickled the inside of the nose, similar to what one would find in a hospital, but not as strong. The corridor led them to a second heavy metal door – breach and assault proof. As they got to it, Taylor and Newman looked up at the security camera high on the ceiling above the door. A second later, the door buzzed open. They zigzagged through another two smaller hallways and two more breach/assault proof doors, before arriving at the interrogation room, halfway down another nondescript hallway.

This new room was nothing more than a square box, 16 feet by 16 feet, light gray cinder-block walls, and white linoleum floor. The center of the room was taken by a square metal table with two metal chairs at opposite ends. The table was securely bolted to the floor. Also bolted to the floor, just by where the chairs were, were two sets of very thick metal loops. On the ceiling, directly above the table, two fluorescent tube lights encased in metal cages bathed the room in crisp brightness. Hunter also noticed the four CCTV cameras, one at each corner of the ceiling. A water cooler was pushed up against one of the walls, and the north wall was taken by a very large two-way mirror.

'Have a seat,' Taylor said to Hunter. 'Get comfortable. Your friend is being brought here.' She gestured with her head. 'We'll be next door, but we'll have eyes and ears in this room.'

Without saying anything else, Taylor and Newman exited the interrogation room, allowing the heavy metal door to shut behind them, and leaving Hunter alone inside the claustrophobic square box. There was no handle on the inside of the door.

Hunter took a deep breath and leaned against the metal table, facing the wall. He'd been inside interrogation rooms countless times. Many of them face to face with people who turned out to be very violent, brutal and sadistic killers. Some of them serial. But not since his first few interrogations had he felt the choking tingle of anticipation that was now starting to strangle at his throat. And he didn't like that feeling. Not even a little bit.

Then the door buzzed open again.

Fourteen

To Hunter's own surprise, he found himself holding his breath while the door was being dragged open.

The first person to step through it was a tall and well-built US Marine, carrying a close-quarters combat shotgun. He took two steps into the room, paused, and then took one step to his left, clearing a pathway from the door into the room.

Hunter tensed and stood up straight.

The second person to step into the room was about one inch taller than Hunter. His hair was brown and cropped short. His beard was just starting to become bushy. He was wearing a standard, orange prisoner jumpsuit. His hands were cuffed and linked together by a metal bar that was no longer than a foot. The chain that was attached to that metal bar looped around his waist and then moved down to his feet, hooking on to thick and heavy ankle cuffs, restricting his movements, and forcing him to shuffle his way along as he walked – like a Japanese Geisha girl.

His head was low, with his chin almost touching his chest. His eyes were focused on the floor. Hunter couldn't clearly see his face, but he could still recognize his old friend.

Directly behind the prisoner followed a second Marine, armed identically to the first.

Hunter took a step to his right, but remained silent.

Both guards guided the prisoner to the metal table and to one of the chairs. As they sat him down, the second Marine quickly shackled the prisoner's ankle chain to the metal loop on the floor. The prisoner never lifted his head up, keeping his eyes low throughout the entire procedure. Once all was done, both guards exited the room without uttering a word, or even looking at Hunter. The door closed behind them with a heavy clang.

The tense silent seconds that followed seemed to stretch for an eternity, until the prisoner finally lifted his head up.

Hunter was standing across the metal table from him, immobile . . . transfixed. Their eyes met, and for a moment they both simply stared at each other. Then, the prisoner's lips stretched into a thin, nervous smile.

'Hello, Robert,' he finally said, in a voice that sounded full of emotion.

Lucien had gained a little more weight since Hunter had last seen him, but it looked to be all muscle. His face looked older, but leaner. He still had the same unmistakably healthy hue to his skin as he had all those years ago, but the look in his dark brown eyes had changed. They now seemed to possess a penetrating quality often associated with greatness, looking at everything with tremendous focus and purpose. With his high cheekbones, full, strong lips and a squared jaw, Hunter had no doubt that women would still refer to him as handsome. The one-inch-long diagonal scar on his left cheek, just under his eye, gave him a rough, 'bad boy' look that Hunter was sure would come across as charming to many people.

'Lucien,' Hunter said, as if he couldn't believe his eyes.

The staring continued for several seconds.

'It's been a very long time,' Lucien said, looking down at his shackled hands. 'If I could, I'd hug you. I've missed you, Robert.'

Hunter stayed quiet simply because he didn't really know what to say. He'd always hoped that one day he would see his old college friend again, but he'd never imagined that it would be in the situation they found themselves in at that moment.

'You look well, my friend,' Lucien said with a renewed smile, his eyes analyzing Hunter. 'I can tell you've never stopped working out. You look like . . .' He paused, searching for the right words. '. . . a lean boxer ready for his championship fight, and you barely look like you've aged. Looks like life has been good to you.'

Hunter finally shook his head, just a subtle movement, as if awaking from a trance.

'Lucien, what the hell is going on?' His voice was calm and composed, but his eyes were still showing surprise.

Lucien took a deep breath and Hunter saw his body tense uncomfortably.

'I'm not sure, Robert,' he said. His voice was a little weaker.

'You're not sure?'

Lucien's eyes returned to his cuffed hands and he shuffled himself on his seat, looking for a more comfortable position, a clear sign that he was struggling with his own thoughts.

'Tell me,' he said, avoiding eye contact. 'Have you ever heard from Susan?' For an instant he seemed surprised by his own question.

Hunter frowned. 'What?'

'Susan. You remember her, don't you? Susan Richards?'

Flashes of memory exploded inside Hunter's head. He remembered Susan very well. How could he not? The three of them were almost inseparable during their years at university. Susan was also a psychology major, and a very bright student. She had moved from Nevada to California after being accepted into Stanford. Susan Richards was one of those happy-go-lucky kind of girls, always smiling, always positive about everything, and very little ever fazed her. She was also very attractive – tall and slim, with chestnut hair, beautiful almond-shaped hazel eyes, a petite nose, and plump lips. Susan had inherited most of her Native American mother's delicate features. Everyone used to say that she looked more like a Hollywood star than a psychology student.

'Yes, of course I remember Susan,' Hunter said.

'Have you ever heard from her in all these years?' Lucien asked.

Hunter's psychological training took over, and he finally realized what was happening. Lucien's defense and fear mechanisms were kicking in. Sometimes, when a person is afraid, or too nervous, to talk about a delicate subject, he/she might, almost unconsciously, try to steer the conversation away from that fragile topic, and avoid talking about it, at least for a little while, until their nerves settle. That was exactly what Lucien was doing.

As a psychologist, Hunter knew that the best way to deal with that was to just play along. Nerves would settle in time.

'No,' he replied. 'After her graduation, I never heard from her again. Did you?'

Lucien shook his head. 'Same here. Not even a little note.'

'I remember she'd said that she wanted to go traveling. Europe or something. Maybe she did and decided to stay over there for some reason. Maybe she met somebody and got married, or found a career opportunity.'

'Yes, I remember she talked about traveling, and maybe she did,' Lucien agreed. 'But even so, Robert. We were together pretty much all the time. We were friends . . . good friends.'

'Things like that do happen, Lucien,' Hunter said. 'You and I were best friends, and we didn't keep in touch after college.'

Lucien looked up at Hunter. 'That's not entirely true, Robert. We did keep in touch for a while. A few years, actually. Until you finished your PhD. I went to the ceremony, remember?'

Hunter nodded once.

'I thought that maybe she had kept in touch with you.' Lucien shrugged. 'Everyone knew that Susan was into you.'

Hunter said nothing.

Lucien gave Hunter a friendly smile. 'I know that you never got together with her because you knew that I really liked her.

'That was very cool of you. Very . . . considerate, but I don't think I would've minded. The two of you probably would've made a very nice couple.'

Lucien's eyes avoided Hunter's for a second.

'Do you remember when we went with her to that tattoo parlor because she wanted to get that horrible thing on her arm?' he asked.

Hunter did remember it. Susan had decided to get a tattoo of a red rose, where its stem, full of thorns, was wrapped around a bleeding heart, giving the impression that it was strangling it.

'I do remember it,' Hunter said with a melancholic smile.

'What the hell was that? A rose strangling a heart?'

'I liked that tattoo,' Hunter said. 'It was different, and I'm sure it meant something to her. I thought it looked very good on her arm. The tattoo artist did a great job.'

Lucien pulled a face. 'I don't really like tattoos. Never did.' He paused and his eyes moved to a random spot on the cinder-block wall. 'I miss her. She could always make us laugh, even in the worst of situations.'

'Yes, I miss her too,' Hunter said.

Silence took over the room for several seconds. Hunter filled a paper cup with water from the cooler and placed it on the table in front of Lucien.

'Thank you,' he said, taking a quick sip.

Hunter poured himself one as well.

'They've got the wrong man, Robert,' Lucien finally said.

Hunter paused and looked back at his old friend. It sounded like Lucien's nerves were finally starting to settle, and he was now ready to talk. Hunter questioned with his eyes.

'I didn't do it,' Lucien said, his voice full of emotion again. 'I didn't do what they're saying I did. You have to believe me, Robert. I'm not a monster. I didn't do those things.'

Hunter stayed quiet.

'But I know who did.'

Fifteen

Behind the large two-way mirror, inside the observation room next door, Special Agents Taylor and Newman were attentively watching every movement made and listening to every word spoken by Lucien Folter. Doctor Patrick Lambert, a forensic psychiatrist with the FBI Behavioral Science Unit was also present.

On a table by the east wall, two CCTV monitors were showing highly detailed images of Lucien taken from different angles. Doctor Lambert was patiently examining every facial movement, and scrutinizing every different voice inflection the prisoner produced, but that wasn't all. Both monitors were also hooked up to a computer equipped with state-of-the-art facial analysis software, which was capable of reading and evaluating the most minuscule of facial or eye movements. Movements that could not be controlled by the interviewee, triggered subconsciously as his state of mind altered from calm to nervous, to anxious, to irritated, to angry, or to any other state. Inside that observation room, they were all sure that if Lucien Folter lied about anything at all, they would know.

Neither Doctor Lambert, nor Special Agents Taylor and Newman, needed the facial analysis program to pick up all the anxiety and nervousness in Lucien's tone of voice, eye movement and facial expressions. That was something they were already expecting. After all, he was talking for the first time since he'd been arrested for a very brutal double homicide. Add to that the fact that he was now face to face with an old friend he hadn't seen since his college days, and Lucien was bound to be nervous and anxious. It was a common psychological human reaction. As was the initial avoidance of the subject. Talking about something common to him and his old friend was an easy and secure way to calm his nerves, to steady his uneasiness. They all waited, knowing that Detective Hunter would soon start slowly steering Lucien toward talking, but Hunter didn't even need to. Lucien went back to the subject of his own accord. But his last few words caught everyone by surprise.

'*They've got the wrong man, Robert.*'

The tension inside the observation room went up a notch, and instinctively everyone craned their heads forward in the direction of the monitors, as if that would make them see or hear better.

'*I didn't do it. I didn't do what they're saying I did. You have to believe me . . .*'

'Of course he didn't,' Newman said with a half-chuckle, looking over at Taylor. 'They never do. Our prison system is full of innocent people, isn't that right?'

Taylor said nothing. She was still carefully watching the screens, and so was Doctor Lambert.

'*But I know who did.*'

Those last five words were something no one was expecting, because in truth, those words equated to an admission of complicity. Even if Lucien Folter hadn't been the one who'd murdered and decapitated both of those women, by admitting that he knew who'd done it, not alerting the police, and being picked up transporting the women's heads cross-state, made him an accessory to murder with at least a couple of aggravating circumstances. And in Wyoming, where he was arrested and the death penalty was still enforced, the District Attorney's office would no doubt push for it.

Sixteen

Despite his surprise, Hunter did his best to appear calm and relaxed. He was certain that Lucien's last five words had been enough to bring the tension inside the observation room next door up a few degrees, but now that Lucien's nerves seemed to have settled down enough for him to start talking, Hunter knew he had to keep the conversation between them going as smoothly as possible. Simply steer it in the right direction and allow his old friend to talk.

Hunter pulled a chair and sat across the table from Lucien. 'You know who did it?' he asked, his tone as tranquil as someone asking for the time.

Interrogators usually hold a standing, more authoritative position, while the person being interrogated is kept in an inferior, sitting-down one. The theory behind it is that it works as an intimidation technique – the person asking the questions is at a higher level, talking down at the person who is answering them. It plays on, and appeals to, a childhood memory that most people will probably have of a parent reprimanding them when they'd been bad. But the last thing Hunter wanted right now was for Lucien to feel any more intimidated than he already was. Having a seat directly in front of him did away with the authoritative position, bringing Hunter level with Lucien. Psychologically,

Hunter's move would hopefully have an unthreatening effect, keeping the tension in the room down to a minimum.

'Well,' Lucien said, leaning forward and placing his elbows on the table, 'I don't really know "exactly" who did it, but it's a logical conclusion. It has to be either the person who I was supposed to be delivering the car to, or the one who delivered the car to me. If they didn't directly do it, they'll know who did. They are the ones you have to go after.' Lucien paused and let go of a deep, heartfelt breath. 'You have to help me, Robert. I'm not the one the FBI wants. I didn't do this. I'm just a delivery boy.'

For the first time, Hunter noticed a slight emotional trepidation in Lucien's voice. He knew the car wasn't registered in Lucien's name. The FBI had told him that, but this was the first he'd heard of Lucien delivering the car to someone else.

'You were taking that blue Ford Taurus to someone?' Hunter asked.

Lucien's eyes averted Hunter's once again. When he finally spoke, his tone was back to being calm and controlled, but it carried a hint of anger this time.

'The reality is, life doesn't treat everyone equally, my friend. I'm sure you know that.'

Hunter was uncertain of what Lucien was really talking about, so he waited.

Lucien's gaze quickly moved to the cameras on the ceiling, and then to the large two-way mirror just behind Hunter. He knew he was being recorded. He knew that nothing he said would be private to only Hunter and himself, and for the briefest of moments he looked embarrassed.

Hunter picked up on his friend's sudden discomfiture, followed his stare, but there was nothing he could do about others listening in. This was the FBI's show, not his. He gave Lucien a moment.

'After I left Stanford, I made a few mistakes,' Lucien said. Paused. Rethought his words. 'Actually I made *quite* a few mistakes. Some of them very bad.' He finally looked back at Hunter. 'I guess I should start from the beginning.'

Seventeen

For some reason, Lucien's words had an atmospheric chilling effect, as if all of a sudden someone had switched on an air-conditioner unit inside the interrogation room.

Hunter felt the awkward chill trickle down his neck and travel down his spine, but held steady.

Lucien had another sip of his water, and as he did so, the look in his eyes became melancholic.

'I met a woman during my second year at Yale,' he began. 'Her name was Karen. She was British, from a place called Gravesend, in southeast England. Have you heard of it?'

Hunter nodded.

'I hadn't,' Lucien said. 'I had to look it up. Anyway, Karen was …' He considered what to really say. '… different from what most people would expect a Yale PhD student to be like … or look like.'

'Different?' Hunter asked.

'In every aspect. She was a free spirit, if you believe people can be such things. You remember the kind of girls I used to go for, right?'

Hunter nodded again, but said nothing, allowing his old friend to carry on uninterrupted.

'Karen was nothing like any of them.' A timid smile

parted his lips. 'When we met, she was forty-two. I was twenty-five.'

Hunter had started taking mental notes.

'She was five-foot-one. A whole twelve inches shorter than me . . . and curvy.'

Hunter remembered that Lucien used to be attracted only to tall, slim women – five-foot-ten or over, with a lithe, dancer's body.

'She also had quite a few tattoos,' Lucien continued. 'A lip piercing, a nose piercing, her left ear was stretched to a full centimeter, and she had this Bettie Page-style fringe.'

This time it was hard for Hunter not to show surprise.

'I thought you didn't like tattoos.'

'I don't. And I don't much care for facial piercings either. But there was just something about Karen. Something I can't really explain. Something that grabbed hold of me and didn't let go.' Another sip of his water. 'We started dating just a few months after we met. It's funny how life is always full of surprises, isn't it? Karen looked nothing like any of the girls I used to go for, she didn't act like them either, but nevertheless, she was the one I fell head over heels for.' Lucien paused and looked away. 'I guess I can say that I was truly in love.'

Hunter saw a muscle flex on his friend's jaw.

'She was a very sweet woman,' Lucien said. 'And we got along fantastically well. We did everything together. Went everywhere together. Spent every second together. She became my haven, my heaven, my heart. I was living a dream, but there was one problem.'

Hunter waited.

'Karen had gotten involved with some very bad people.'

'What kind of bad?' Hunter asked.

'Drugs bad,' Lucien said. 'The kind of bad you don't mess with, unless you've grown tired of this life and feel like exiting it in a very violent way.' He finished the rest of his water in three large gulps before crushing the paper cup in his right hand.

Hunter took note of his friend's silent angry outburst, stood up, poured him a new cup of water, and placed it back on the table.

'Thank you.' He stared at the cup. 'I'm sorry to say that I wasn't strong enough, Robert,' Lucien continued. 'I'm not sure if it was because I was too much in love, or if I was just swallowed up by the moment, but instead of talking her out of it, I ended up joining her, and trying some of the stuff she was using.'

There was a pain-stricken, embarrassed pause.

Hunter carried on observing his friend.

'The problem is,' Lucien moved on, 'and I'm sure you know this, some of this shit is hard to only *try*.' He looked down at his hands. 'So I got hooked.'

'What kind of drugs are we talking about here?'

Lucien shrugged. 'The heavy kind. Instant hook stuff . . . and alcohol. I started drinking a lot.'

Hunter had seen so many strong people fall victim to those kind of drugs, he'd lost count.

'From then on everything went downhill, and in a hurry. All the money I had went into supplying Karen's habit and mine. It ate away at my finances faster than you could imagine. My entire life started suffering. I dropped out of Yale in my third year, and would do anything to get my daily fix. I ran up debts everywhere, and with the wrong kind of people. The people Karen had introduced me to. The really bad kind.'

'You didn't have anyone you could turn to for help?' Hunter asked. 'I'm not talking about financial help. Someone who could help you kick the habit, bring you back.'

Lucien's gaze met Hunter's and he chuckled derisively. 'You know me, Robert. I never had that many close friends. The few I had, I had broken contact with.'

Hunter read the hint. 'You could've still looked me up, Lucien. You knew where I was. We were best friends. I would've helped you.' Hunter paused and his stare went hard as he realized his mistake. 'Shit, you were already hooked when you flew down for my PhD graduation, weren't you? That's why you only stayed in LA less than twenty-four hours. But I was so consumed by the moment that I didn't even notice. That was you asking for my help.'

Lucien looked away.

Hunter felt a stab of guilt cut through his flesh. 'You should've said something. I would've helped you. You know I would've. I'm sorry I didn't notice it.'

'Maybe I should have. Maybe that's just another one of my bad mistakes. But I'm not going to cry about things long gone, Robert. Things that can't be changed. Everything that happened to me was my own doing, my own fault, nobody else's. I know it, and I accept that. And yes, I know that everyone needs a little help every once in a while. I just didn't know how to ask for it.'

It was Hunter's turn to have a sip of his water. 'Were you still with Karen when you went to LA?' he asked.

Lucien nodded. 'She also quit Yale, and did some very . . . very stupid things to get hold of cash.' He hesitated, took a deep breath, and his eyes saddened. 'We stayed together for three years. All the way until she overdosed.' A long pause. 'She died in my arms.'

Lucien looked away as his toughness began showing cracks. Tears came into his eyes, but he held steady.

Silence took over the room for a long moment.

'I'm so sorry,' Hunter finally said.

Lucien nodded and rubbed his face with his shackled hands.

'What happened then?' Hunter asked.

'Then I really went to hell, and I did it a step at a time. I lost my way, big time. I hit depression hard and at full speed. Instead of learning from what happened to Karen and kicking the habit, I got deeper into it.' Lucien stole a peek at the two-way mirror once again. 'I should've been dead by now, and in many ways I really wish I were. The fight-back was very long, very slow, and very painful. It took me many years to manage to get my addiction under control. A few more to finally kick it. All the while I just got myself into more and more debt, and involved with the worst kind of characters society has to offer.'

Blood tests run by the FBI had shown that Lucien Folter was clean. Hunter knew that.

'So when did you finally kick it?' he asked.

'Several years ago,' Lucien said, being deliberately vague. 'By then, I had lost all hope of a career in psychology or in anything decent, really. I went through a series of odd jobs, most of them awful, some of them not quite legit. In the end, I hated what I had become. Even though I was clean, I just wasn't the person I once was anymore. I wasn't Lucien Folter. I had become someone completely different. A lost soul. Someone I didn't recognize. Someone *no one* recognized. Someone I really didn't like.'

Hunter could guess what was coming next.

'So you decided to change identities,' he said.

Lucien looked straight at Hunter and nodded.

'That's right,' he agreed. 'You know, being a junkie, living life as "scum" for as long as I did, puts you in contact with some very colorful folks. People who are able to get you anything you want . . . for a price, obviously. Getting hold of a new identity was as easy as buying a newspaper.'

Hunter knew Lucien wasn't lying because he understood the reality of the world they lived in. All one needs to obtain whatever documents one likes in a different name is to know the right people, or wrong people, depending which way you look at it. And these people aren't even that hard to find.

'Once I became Liam Shaw,' Lucien said, 'I then concentrated on getting healthy again. It took me quite a while to manage to put weight back on . . . to regain focus. With all the drugs, I had the body of an anorexic. My stomach had shrunk. My mouth was full of ulcers. My health had deteriorated to a hair away from death. I had to keep on forcing myself to eat.' He paused and looked at his arms and torso. 'I look OK on the outside now, but my insides are royally fucked up, Robert. I've caused a lot of damage to my body. Much of it irreversible. Most of my internal organs are so damaged, I'm not even sure how they're still working.'

Despite his words, Hunter picked up no self-pity in Lucien's tone of voice or in the look in his eyes. He had simply accepted what he had done to himself. He had acknowledged his mistakes, and he seemed OK with paying the price.

'Tell me about this car delivery thing,' Hunter said.

Eighteen

Lucien's eyebrows bobbed up and down once, as he looked back at his old friend.

'The problem with getting involved with the kind of people I got involved with, is that they get their claws very deep into you right at the beginning. And once they do that, they never really let go. They own you for life. I'm sure you understand that these people can be very persuasive when they want to be.'

Hunter said nothing.

'It started about a year and a half ago.' Lucien moved on. 'The way it happens is, I get a call on my cellphone telling me where to pick up the car from. They give me a delivery address and a time-frame. No names. When I get there, there's always someone waiting to collect the car. I hand the car over, he gives me enough money for a ticket back ... maybe a little extra, and that's all. Until the next phone call.'

'I'm guessing you don't always deliver the cars to the same place,' Hunter said.

'Not so far,' Lucien agreed. 'A different pick-up and delivery address every time.' He paused and looked at Hunter. 'But I've always delivered to the same person.'

That came as a surprise.

'Can you describe him?' Hunter asked.

Lucien pulled a face. 'About six-foot tall, well built, but deliveries were always made at night, in some dark field. The person receiving the car was always wearing a long coat with its collar up, a baseball cap, and dark glasses.' He shrugged. 'That's as good a description as I can give.'

'So how do you know it was the same person?'

'Same voice, same posture, same mannerisms.' Lucien sat back on his chair. 'It wasn't hard to tell, Robert. I'm telling you, it was the same person every time.'

Hunter saw no reason to doubt Lucien. 'How about the person who delivered the car to you?' he asked.

'As I've said, the instructions came over the phone. Car was left in a car park. Keys, car park ticket and delivery address were left inside an envelope in a safe place for me to collect. No human contact.'

'And you had no idea what you were delivering?' Hunter asked. 'I mean – you didn't know what was in the trunk?'

Lucien shook his head. 'It was always part of the instructions – *don't ever look in the trunk.*'

Hunter pondered over that for a second or two, but Lucien anticipated his next question, and offered an answer before Hunter could even ask it.

'Yes, I was curious about it. Yes, I thought about taking a quick peek many times, but like I said, these are the kind of people you simply don't fuck with. If I'd opened that trunk, I'm sure they would've had a way of knowing it. Curious or not, that was one stupid mistake that I wasn't prepared to make.'

Hunter had a quick sip of his water.

'You said that this all started about a year and a half ago?'

Lucien nodded.

'How many deliveries were there?'

'This was supposed to be my fifth car delivery.'

Hunter held steady, but alarm bells started ringing every-where inside his head. *Five* deliveries. If Lucien was telling the truth, and he was delivering the same or very similar cargo every time, then this whole thing had just escalated into a serial-murderer investigation. And judging by what he'd seen, a very brutal and sadistic one.

Lucien paused and looked at Hunter differently, like a rookie poker player who'd just gotten a great hand and was unable to disguise it. 'My trump is – I know who the person over the phone was.'

Hunter's eyebrows arched.

Lucien took a moment before speaking again. 'For now, I'll keep that information to myself, together with all the previous pick-up and delivery locations.'

That answer caught Hunter completely by surprise and he frowned.

'I know you're not running this show, Robert,' Lucien explained. 'The FBI is pulling all the strings here. The only reason you're here is because I asked for you. I know they've probably told you that you're only here as a guest ... a listener. You have no authority over anything. You can't guarantee me anything because here you have no bargain-ing powers. My only bargaining power, on the other hand, is information.'

'I understand that,' Hunter agreed. 'But I don't see how withholding it can help you, Lucien. If you are innocent, you have to help the FBI prove that, not play games with them.'

'And I will do that, Robert, but I'm scared. Even a child

can see that the evidence against me is overwhelming. I know that I'm facing death row here, and I'm petrified. Yes, I'll admit that paranoia has set in in here.' Lucien lifted his shackled fists and hit them three times against his forehead before looking straight into Hunter's eyes. 'I didn't tell them anything so far because I didn't think they'd believe me.'

It was easy to see how paranoia and fear could've easily distorted Lucien's vision of reality. Hunter had to reassure him. 'It doesn't quite work like that, Lucien. Why wouldn't the FBI believe you? They're not out to send you, or just anyone to prison. They want to find the person who's responsible for those murders, and if you can help them, of course they'll listen to you. Of course they'll follow up on what you tell them.'

'OK, maybe they would, but I panicked.' He took a deep breath. 'Then I thought of you. I have no family left, Robert, everyone's gone. There's no one on this earth who even cares if I live or die. I met a lot of people in my life, but you're the only real friend I've ever had. The only one who knew the real me, and you were also a cop. So I just thought that maybe . . .' Lucien's voice was filled with emotion one more time. His toughness cracked again. 'I didn't do this, Robert. You have to believe me.'

Back in college, Hunter could usually tell when Lucien was lying because he had a very subtle tell. Hunter had identified it in their second semester at Stanford. As he was telling a lie, Lucien's stare would harden, become more determined, as if somehow the tough look in his eyes could hypnotized you into believing him. Consequently, for just a fraction of a second, his lower left eyelid would tighten, producing not exactly a twitch, but a very delicate movement. He couldn't help it because he didn't even know he was doing it. It's been over twenty years, but Hunter hoped he could still identify it because he knew what to look for. But there had been no hardening of the stare. No movement of the lower left eyelid whatsoever, no matter how subtle.

'Remember when I told you that I didn't know how to ask for help, your help?' Lucien paused for breath. 'Well, I'm doing it now. Please help me, Robert.'

Hunter felt the stab of guilt slash through him for the second time.

'How can I help you, Lucien?' he asked. 'You said so yourself just a moment ago. I'm here as a listener. I have no authority over anything. I'm not even an FBI agent. I'm a detective with the LAPD.'

Lucien locked eyes with Hunter for a long moment, and then, all of a sudden, his gaze softened.

'If I'm brutally honest, Robert, I don't think I really care if I live or die anymore. I messed up a long time ago. I made way too many mistakes, and since then, I've done nothing but live a sub-life. I lost everything, including my dignity and the only person I truly loved. I guess I can say that I'm ashamed of most of my life, but I'm not a murderer. I know that this might sound silly, but I don't care what anyone thinks of me, except you, Robert. Regardless of what happens to me, I want *you* to know that I'm not a monster.'

Hunter was about to say something, but Lucien interrupted him.

'Please don't say that you already know that, or that you don't believe I am one, because I don't want your pity, Robert. I want you to know. *Really know*. That's why I'm going to tell you what I'm going to tell you, because I know that you will check on everything I say, with or without the FBI.'

Still no telltale signs from Lucien.

Hunter knew Lucien was right. There was no way he would walk away from that interrogation room and forget about everything Lucien was about to tell him, no matter what sort of pressure the FBI tried to put him under.

'So what is it that you want to tell me?' he asked. 'What is it that you want me to go check out?'

Lucien looked down at his hands before meeting Hunter's stare . . . and then he started speaking again.

Nineteen

Special Agents Taylor and Newman, together with Doctor Lambert, stepped into the interrogation room thirty seconds after Lucien was taken back to his cell. Hunter was leaning against the metal table, facing a blank wall, a pensive look on his face.

'Detective Hunter,' Taylor said, grabbing his attention. 'This is Doctor Patrick Lambert. He's a forensic psychiatrist with the BSU. He also watched the entire interview from the observations room.'

'It's a pleasure to meet you, Detective Hunter,' Doctor Lambert said, shaking Hunter's hand. 'Impressive work.'

Hunter gave him a subtle frown.

'Your paper. Impressive work. And to think that you wrote that when you were so young.'

Hunter accepted the compliment with a simple head gesture.

'For someone who had said only seven words in five days, you sure got him talking,' Taylor said.

Hunter looked at her, but said nothing back.

'We didn't pick up anything relevant,' Newman announced, pouring himself a cup of water from the cooler.

'What do you mean?' Hunter asked.

Newman told Hunter about the facial analysis software

they were using inside the observation room.

'There were a few nervy eye, head and hand movements,' Doctor Lambert said. 'A few emotional qualities here and there in his tone of voice, but nothing that would flag as too anxious or too nervous. Bottom line is – we have no clear indication that he was lying about anything.' He paused for effect. 'But we also have no clear indication that he was telling the truth about anything.'

So much for your expensive facial analysis software, Hunter thought.

'And that includes everything he told you in the last few minutes of your interview,' Doctor Lambert added.

Lucien had tried keeping his voice quiet; quieter than throughout the entire session, but the powerful multi-directional microphone on the ceiling directly above the metal table had picked up every word he had said to Hunter.

'*I'm sending a riddle your way, Robert. A riddle that only you will know the answer to.*' Lucien had placed both elbows on the table, leaned forward, and looked over Hunter's shoulder at the two-way mirror behind him. '*I don't trust those fuckers.*'

His voice had become almost a whisper.

'*For the past several years, I've been living – or hiding, if you prefer – in North Carolina. The house is rented, and I pay cash in advance directly to this old couple, so the place can't be traced back to me.*' A pause, followed by a sip of water. '*In our dorm room back in Stanford, I used to have several posters on the wall by my bed. But there was a particular one. The largest of them all. The one that you also liked . . . with the sunset. If you think about it, you will remember it. The county in North Carolina carries the same name as the figure in that poster.*'

Hunter's expression had turned thoughtful.

'*I'm sure you'll also remember Professor "Hot Sauce".*' The right edge of Lucien's mouth had lifted in a semi-devious smile. '*Susan's dare? Halloween night?*' He'd waited just a second before seeing recognition dance across Hunter's face. '*By sheer coincidence, the city I've been living in shares his name.*'

Hunter had said nothing.

'*After I got the first phone call asking me to make the first car delivery, something inside my head told me that this would probably end very badly. So, out of precaution, I started keeping a diary, so to speak. Actually, it was more like a notebook, and I noted down everything I could – date, time and duration of calls, conversation details, pickup times and locations, car type and license plate numbers, stops I did on the way, the name of the person at the other end of the line ... everything. I keep the notebook in the house, down in the basement.*'

Hunter had caught a new glint in his old friend's eyes. Something that wasn't there before.

'*The house is right at the end of the wood's edge. The keys are in my jacket pocket, which I believe was seized by the FBI. You have my authorization to use it and get into the house, Robert. You'll find a lot in there. Things that can help you clear this mess up.*'

That was all Lucien had said.

'So,' Newman said to Hunter. 'Do you know the answers to all that crap he threw at you at the end?'

Hunter said nothing, but Newman seemed to read his demeanor as a positive answer.

'Great. So if you give us the name of the county and the town in North Carolina where his house is at, your job here is all done.' He finished drinking his water. 'I understand that you were on your way to Hawaii for a long-overdue vacation.' For no reason at all, Newman checked his watch. 'You've only missed a day. You could be there by tomorrow morning.'

Hunter's gaze lingered on Newman for a few seconds, before moving to Taylor, and then back to Newman.

'That's exactly why Lucien made the location of his house into a riddle that only I could figure out,' he said, standing up straight and adjusting the collar on his leather jacket. 'Because the only way any of you are getting there, is if I take you there.'

Twenty

Neither Newman nor Taylor had the authority to make that sort of decision. All they knew was that the man in their custody had refused to talk, saying he would only speak to Detective Robert Hunter of the LAPD. Hunter had been brought in, but as far as everyone was concerned, he was there simply as a listener. His job was to get Lucien Folter to talk. He wasn't supposed to be involved in the investigation, and he certainly wasn't part of the team. This was not a joint venture between the LAPD and the FBI.

'I thought that you couldn't wait to go on vacation, Robert,' Adrian Kennedy said, staring straight into the web camera.

Hunter, Taylor and Newman had gone back up to the BSU floor and were now sitting inside an ample office, facing a very large flat-screen monitor mounted onto the west wall. The dot-sized green light at the top of the monitor indicated that the in-built camera was on.

Despite being less than an hour away, Director Adrian Kennedy's overbooked schedule prevented him from making the trip back to Quantico. He was speaking to everyone via a video link from his office in Washington, DC.

'Well, that plan got screwed up yesterday when you showed up in LA, Adrian,' Hunter said, matter-of-factly.

'I'm sure we can fix it, Robert,' Kennedy replied. 'If you just give Agents Taylor and Newman the information they need to proceed, I can arrange to have a jet fly you over to Hawaii tonight.'

Hunter looked impressed. 'Wow. Is the FBI budget that loose that you can actually justify getting a jet just to take me all the way to Hawaii from Virginia? Damn, and at the LAPD we don't even get a big enough budget to supply us with enough bulletproof vests.'

'Robert, I'm serious. We need this information.'

'So am I, Adrian.' Hunter's voice went grave all of a sudden and his stare hardened. 'I didn't ask for this. You came to me, remember? You threw me into this mix. Now I'm part of it, whether you like it or not. If you think I'm just going to hand over the information and walk away like an obedient little boy, then you don't know me at all.'

'Nobody really knows you, Robert,' Kennedy hit back, his voice still calm. 'You've always been this cryptic enigma for as long as I've known you. But you're now playing a very risky game . You do understand that what you're doing is withholding information that's pertinent to a federal homicide investigation. I can have your ass for that.'

Hunter looked unfazed.

'If that's how you want to play it,' he replied evenly. 'I've never explicitly told anyone that I understood what Lucien's little riddle meant. I can't be withholding information if I have none, Adrian, because I don't think I remember seeing any posters in my old dorm room, and Professor "Hot Sauce" is no professor I can recall.' Hunter paused and, from the corner of his eye, saw frustration start to color Agent Newman's face. 'You're not the only one who knows how to play hardball, Adrian, and I'm not one of your puppets.'

Kennedy didn't look angered or offended. In fact, he wasn't really expecting Hunter to react in any other way, not after watching the footage recorded from the interrogation room. Hunter was being asked for help, on one side by the FBI, on the other by his old best friend.

'Sorry to interrupt, Director Kennedy,' Newman said, leaning forward on his seat. 'But we still have the subject in our custody. If Detective Hunter is refusing to cooperate, sorry, but fuck him. Let him go back to LA.' He looked at Hunter. 'No offense, pal.'

He got absolutely zero reaction from Hunter.

'We can still extract the information directly out of the subject,' Newman continued. 'Just give me a few more sessions with him.'

'Of course we can,' Kennedy said. 'Because that has worked brilliantly so far, hasn't it, Special Agent Newman?'

Newman was about to say something else but Kennedy lifted a finger, indicating that he'd heard enough. The look in his eyes was a clear indication that he was running through a few possibilities in his head.

'OK, Robert,' Kennedy said, after several silent seconds. 'I'll play nice if you play nice. You and Agent Taylor go check out this property in North Carolina. Agent Newman, I need you back in Washington ... today. I've got something else I want you on.'

Newman looked like he'd been slapped across the face. His mouth half opened to say something but Kennedy cut him short again.

'*Today*, Agent Newman. Is that understood?'

Newman took a deep breath. 'Yes, sir.'

Kennedy addressed Hunter again. 'Robert, no more games. You do know what this Lucien character was talking about in his riddle, right? You know the answers to those questions?'

Hunter nodded once.

'OK.' Kennedy consulted his watch. 'We're lucky. North Carolina is close enough that we can move fast. Agent Taylor, get everything organized. I want you and Robert there by tonight, at the latest. Let's go seize this diary, or notebook, or whatever it is, and let's start figuring this whole mess out. Call me with any news as soon as you get it, no matter the time. Is that understood?'

'Yes, sir,' Taylor replied as she peeked at Hunter.

Kennedy cut the connection.

Twenty-One

'OK,' Agent Taylor said, using a wireless keyboard to type a new command into a desktop computer.

Taylor and Hunter had gone back to the same conference room they were in earlier, the one with the large monitor showing a detailed map of the United States on the far wall. As she hit the 'Enter' key, the map changed to a county-detailed version of the entire state of North Carolina.

'So what was this poster that Lucien Folter had on his wall?' Taylor asked. 'The one you liked. The one with the sunset.'

Hunter gave her a subtle shrug, stepped closer to the map, and allowed his eyes to carefully study it.

'It was a poster of the mountains,' he said. 'The sun was just about to set over them. The sky had taken this striking reddish-purple color. And that was what I really liked about that poster – the sky color. And there was also a camp fire.'

'A camp fire?'

'That's right,' Hunter agreed.

'Was that it?' Taylor asked.

'No, there was a lone figure sitting by the fire, watching the sunset.'

'What figure?'

Hunter's eyes had stopped searching the map.

'An old man.'

Taylor frowned. 'An old man?' she said, joining Hunter by the map. 'So what are we looking for here? Oldman County? Granddad County? Or did this old man have a name? Lucien Folter said that the county carried the same name as the figure in that poster.'

'No name,' Hunter clarified. 'But that old man was a Native American. More precisely, a . . .' He pointed to a county on the far left-hand side of the map. The county of Cherokee.

The state of North Carolina is divided into three regions – Eastern, Piedmont and Western. Cherokee County is the westernmost county in the Western Region. It borders both Georgia and Tennessee.

'A Cherokee Indian,' Taylor said with a different rhythm to her voice. 'I'll be damned.'

Hunter paused and looked at her. The expression on his face asked the question.

Taylor tilted her head to one side. 'My ex-husband was half-Cherokee. We just got through a tough divorce. Strange coincidence, that's all.'

Hunter nodded.

Taylor's attention returned to the map as she considered the county's position in relation to their location. 'Damn,' she said, returning to the computer. 'That will be a hell of a long drive.'

'At least eight hours there, and eight hours back,' Hunter agreed.

Taylor typed a new command in, and on the map a route was immediately traced between the FBI Academy in Quantico and the eastern border of Cherokee county. On the left-hand side, a detailed, step-by-step breakdown of the entire itinerary was displayed. According to it, and with zero stops, the 535-mile journey would take them approximately eight hours and twenty-five minutes.

Hunter checked his watch – 12:52 p.m. He sure as hell wasn't in the mood for a seventeen-hour drive there and back.

'Can we fly there?' he asked.

Taylor pulled a face. 'I don't have the kind of clearance necessary to authorize a plane,' she said.

'But Adrian does,' Hunter added.

Taylor nodded. 'Director Kennedy can authorize anything he likes.'

'So let's get him to authorize one,' Hunter said. 'Just minutes ago he was ready to authorize a jet to take me on vacation to Hawaii, and I'm not even with the FBI.'

Taylor had no argument against that.

'OK, I'll call him. So where are we going?'

Hunter looked at her.

'The second part of the riddle,' she clarified. 'The name of the city? Who was this Professor "Hot Sauce"? Susan's dare? Halloween night?'

Hunter wasn't ready to show all his cards yet, at least not while they were still at the FBI academy. He checked his watch. 'One step at a time, Agent Taylor. Let's get going first. I'll tell you when we're airborne.'

Taylor studied him for an instant. 'What difference does it make?'

'My point exactly. If it makes no difference, then I can either tell you now or later. I'll do it later. We need to get going.'

Taylor lifted both hands, giving up. 'Fine, we'll play it your way. I'll call Director Kennedy.'

Twenty-Two

Taylor's telephone conversation with Director Adrian Kennedy lasted less than three minutes. He didn't need much convincing.

Lucien Folter had been arrested six days ago. The FBI had two decapitated and mutilated female heads in their hands – no bodies – no identities. The questions were piling up like dirty dishes, and so far they had nothing. Kennedy wanted answers, and he wanted them pronto, whatever it took.

Within ninety minutes, everything was arranged and a Phenom 100 light jet was waiting for Hunter and Taylor at the Turner Field landing strip. This plane was about half the size of the one they took from Los Angeles to Quantico, but just as luxurious inside.

The cabin lights dimmed momentarily, and the plane took off swiftly. Hunter sat nursing a large cup of strong black coffee, while his brain tried to carefully revisit every word that was said that morning inside the interrogation room.

Taylor was sitting in the black-leather swivel chair directly in front of Hunter. Her laptop computer was resting on her lap; its screen displayed a detailed map of Cherokee County with all its cities and towns. 'OK, we're airborne, so where exactly are we heading? Who's Professor "Hot Sauce"?'

Hunter smiled as he remembered it.

'Lucien, Susan and I went to a Halloween party in an Irish bar in Los Altos. There we bumped into our neuropsychology professor. Nice guy, great professor, and he loved to drink. That night we'd all had a few, but then, out of the blue, he decided to challenge us to a shot-drinking competition. Lucien and I declined, but to our surprise, Susan took him up on the offer.'

'Why were you surprised?'

'Susan wasn't that good a drinker,' Hunter said, with a slight shake of the head. 'Four, five shots, and Susan was gone. What we didn't know was that she had a trick up her sleeve.'

Interest bathed Taylor's face. 'What trick?'

'Susan's grandparents were Latvian, and because of that, she knew a few Latvian words, including the word for water – "ūdens". The deal was, each one took turns downing a shot of their favorite drink. Susan knew the barman, who was actually Latvian. The professor was drinking Tequila, and Susan kept on ordering a shot of "ūdens" from the barman. Fourteen shots later, the professor threw in the towel. His forfeit penalty was to drink an entire two-ounce bottle of Hot Sauce, which he did. He didn't turn up for class for the next three days. From that day on, the three of us only referred to him as Professor Hot Sauce.'

Hunter quickly studied the map on Taylor's screen. It took him just a second to find what he was looking for.

'So who was your neuropsychology professor?' Taylor asked.

Hunter pointed at the screen. 'His name was Steward Murphy.'

The city of Murphy was the largest city in Cherokee county, situated at the confluence of the Hiwassee and Valley Rivers.

'It doesn't look like there's an airport in Murphy,' Taylor said, analyzing the map, before typing in a new command. A second later she had an answer. 'OK, the closest airport to Murphy is Western Carolina Regional Airport. About thirteen and a half miles away.'

'That will do,' Hunter said. 'You can tell the pilot that that's where we're heading.'

Taylor used the intercom phone on the wall to her right to give the pilot his instructions.

'We should be there in about an hour and ten minutes, give or take a few,' she told Hunter.

'Much better than eight and a half of driving,' he commented.

'Do you mind if I ask you something, Detective Hunter?' Taylor said after they'd been airborne for a few minutes.

Hunter peeled his eyes from the blue sky outside his window and looked at her.

'I do if you're going to carry on calling me Detective Hunter. Please call me Robert.'

Taylor seemed to hesitate for a moment. 'OK, Robert, as long as you call me Courtney.'

'Deal. So what would you like to ask me, Courtney?'

'You felt guilty, didn't you?' She waited a couple of seconds and decided to clarify. 'When Lucien told you about his drug problem and how he got involved with it all.'

Hunter stayed quiet.

'While everyone in the observation room had all their attention focused on Lucien, I was observing you. You felt guilty. You felt like it'd been your fault.'

'Not like it'd been my fault,' Hunter finally said. 'But I know I could've helped him. I should've noticed he was hooked when he came to see me in LA for the last time. I don't even know how I missed that.'

Taylor bit her bottom lip and looked away, clearly debating if she should say what she was thinking. She decided that there was no point in being coy. 'I know he was your friend, and I'm sorry to say this, but junkies don't get a lot of sympathy from me. I've worked on too many cases where someone, high on some cheap fix, or trying to get some cash to buy some cheap fix, committed the most atrocious murder, or murders.' She paused for breath. 'He could be lying, you know? He could still be hooked on something, and he could've killed those two women while under the influence.'

Hunter picked up on something different underlying Taylor's tone. Hidden anger, maybe.

'Your lab tests showed that he was clean,' he said.

'Certain drugs exit your system in a matter of hours, you know that,' Taylor came back. 'Plus, those heads had been preserved in ice containers for who knows how long. Those two women could've been murdered months ago.'

'That's true.' Hunter couldn't counter-argue her point. 'And certain drugs do exit your system in a matter of hours, but you've seen junkies before, right? They just can't stay away from drugs for too long, and they all show typical psychological and physical signs of dependency – skin, eyes, hair, lips . . . paranoia, anxiety . . . you know what to look for. Lucien showed none of it.' Hunter shook his head. 'He isn't hooked anymore.'

This time it was Taylor who couldn't debate Hunter's argument. Lucien really showed no physical or psychological signs of dependency anymore. But she wasn't ready to let it rest quite yet.

'OK, I agree, he does appear to be clean, but he still gets no sympathy. According to what he told you, nobody forced him to take any drugs. He decided to do so of his own free will. He could've just as easily walked away from it. People all over, and of all ages, are offered drugs every day. You know this better than most, Robert. Some go for it, some don't. It's a *choice*. In his case, it was *his* choice, no one else's. No one but Lucien should feel guilty about him becoming a junkie.'

Hunter said nothing for a long instant. The plane hit a spot of turbulence and he waited until it was all clear before speaking again.

'It's not quite that simple, Courtney.'

'Isn't it?'

'No.' Hunter sat back in his seat.

'I was offered drugs many times,' Taylor said. 'In school, in college, on the streets, around the neighborhood, at parties, on vacation, everywhere really, and I still managed to stay away from them.'

'And that's great, but I bet that you also know people who weren't as strong as you, right? People who didn't manage to stay away from them. People who got hooked?'

Something seemed to change inside Taylor's eyes. 'I do, yes.' Hunter could tell that she was struggling to keep her voice calm. 'But I don't feel guilty because of it.'

For some reason that sounded like a lie.

'We're all different, Courtney, and that's why we all react differently to any given event,' Hunter said. 'Our reactions directly depend on the circumstances surrounding that event, and on our psychological mood at that particular time.'

Taylor *did* know that. She'd seen it before – someone who's feeling happy – things are going great at home and at the workplace – gets offered a highly addictive drug at a party or somewhere else. That person says 'no' because he/she sees no need for it. At that particular time, that person's feeling naturally happy, naturally high. That same person, just a day later, gets laid off, or has a bad argument at home, or something that bumps his/her mood down a notch – gets offered the same highly addictive drug. This time the person says 'yes' because his/her mood has changed, the circumstances have changed, and right at that particular moment that person is psychologically, and maybe even physically, very vulnerable. Drug pushers have some sort of sixth sense when it comes to picking those people out of a crowd, and they really know how to sweet-talk a person into believing that if he/she takes whatever drug they are being offered, all their problems will be gone in a flash. Paradise awaits.

Taylor began chewing on her bottom lip.

'You know that there are many drugs out there that all it takes is a single hit, don't you?' Hunter continued. 'Like Lucien said: "instant hook stuff". Even very strong people can't be very strong all the time, Courtney. It's a fact of life. All you need is to be approached when, for one reason or another, you're not so mentally strong, you're feeling lonely, or depressed, or neglected or something, and they've got you. We don't know all the facts. And we also don't know how many times Lucien walked away from it before he finally failed.'

'I'll admit,' Taylor said. 'You fight a good argument on behalf of junkies.'

'I'm not trying to defend junkies, Courtney,' Hunter said calmly. 'I'm just saying that a very large number of addicts out there know that they've made a mistake, and all they want is to find the strength to kick the habit. Most of them can't seem to find that strength on their own, they need help ... help that most of the time isn't very forthcoming. Probably because so many out there share the same thoughts as you do.'

Taylor's blue eyes honed in on Hunter intensely before darting away.

'So how do you think you could've helped him?' she asked. 'What would you have done?'

'Everything I could,' Hunter replied without missing a beat. 'I would've done *everything* I could. He was my friend.'

Twenty-Three

An hour and eight minutes after taking off, the Phenom 100 jet touched down at Western Carolina Regional Airport. The weather outside had started to change. Several large clouds were now lurking around in the sky, keeping the sun from properly shining through, and bringing the temperature down a few degrees. In spite of the lack of sunshine, Taylor put on her sunglasses as soon as they stepped out of the plane. It was basic FBI training – once in public, always hide your eyes.

Outside the airport, Hunter and Taylor met a representative from a local car-rental company she had spoken to on the phone. He delivered them a top-of-the-range, black Lincoln MKZ sedan.

'OK,' Taylor said, flipping open her laptop as she and Hunter got into the car. She took the driver's seat. The car looked and smelled brand new, as if it had been purchased that morning just to accommodate them. 'Let's figure out where we need to go from here.'

Taylor used the laptop's touchpad and quickly called up a satellite-view application. In a fraction of a second, she had a photographic bird's-eye-view map of the city of Murphy on her screen.

'Lucien said that the house was at the end of a wood's edge,' she continued, angling the laptop Hunter's way.

They both studied the screen for a long moment and, as Taylor used the touch pad to drag the map from left to right and top to bottom, her demeanor changed.

'Was he kidding?' she finally said. Her voice was still calm, but it now had a sliver of annoyance to it. She lifted her sunglasses and placed them on her head before pinning Hunter down with a concerned stare. 'This place is surrounded by woodland. It's everywhere, inside and outside the city. Just look at this.'

Her gaze returned to her screen as she used the touchpad again to zoom out on the map. She wasn't joking. The city of Murphy looked like it had been built slap-bang in the middle of a large, hilly forest. There seemed to be more woodland around than buildings.

'What are we supposed to do? Find a house at the edge of every woodland we come across and go see if any of his keys fit?'

Hunter said nothing. He was still staring at the screen, trying to figure it all out.

'He was fucking with us, wasn't he?' Taylor chuckled those words. 'Even if this house does exist, which I now doubt, it could take us a couple of days to find it, maybe more. He sent us on a wild goose chase, Robert. He's play-ing games.' She took a moment to think about it. 'I'm sure he's been here before. Maybe even lived here for a while. He knows Murphy is surrounded by woodland. That's why he sent us here with that crazy riddle. We could spend days here, and never come across this . . . fantasy house.'

Hunter spent a few more seconds analyzing the map before shaking his head. 'No, this is wrong. This isn't what he meant.'

Taylor's eyebrows arched. 'What do you mean? That's

exactly what he said: "*The house is at the end of a wood's edge.*" Unless you've got this riddle wrong, and we came to the wrong place.'

'I didn't,' Hunter assured her. 'We came to the right place.'

'OK then, so Lucien *is* playing games. Just look at that map, Robert.' She nodded at her laptop. '"*The house is at the end of a wood's edge,*"' she repeated. 'Those were his words. I've got the recording here with me if you want to listen to it again.'

'I don't have to,' Hunter replied, turning the laptop to face him. 'Because that's not exactly what he said.'

'I'm sorry?'

'He said that the house was at the end of *the* wood's edge, not *a* wood's edge. And there's a big difference. Can you get us a searchable map of Murphy? Locations, street names, things like that?'

'Yeah, sure.'

A few keystrokes later and the bird's-eye-view map on the screen was substituted by an up-to-date satellite street map of the city of Murphy.

'Here we go,' she said, passing the laptop over to Hunter, who quickly typed something into the search feature. The map panned out, rotated left, and then zoomed in on a narrow dirt road located between two woodland hills on the south side of the city. The road's name was – Woods Edge.

Even Hunter was a little surprised. He was expecting that perhaps one of the woodlands, or maybe even a park, carried the name "Woods Edge", but not a road.

'Oh, ye of little faith,' he said.

'I'll be damned,' Taylor breathed out.

The road seemed to carry on for about half a mile. There was nothing on either side of it, except woodland, until the very end, where a single house stood – the house at the end of the Woods Edge.

Twenty-Four

Taylor took the wheel, and the drive from the airport to the south side of Murphy took her just under twenty-five minutes. The entire journey was punctuated by hills, fields and woodlands. As they approached the city of Murphy, a few small ranches sprang up by the side of the road, with horses and cattle moving lazily around the yard. The typical smell of farm manure coated the air, but neither Hunter nor Taylor complained. Hunter, for one, couldn't remember ever being in a place where everywhere he looked was painted by trees and green fields. It was striking scenery, they both had to admit.

As Taylor exited Creek Road and veered right into Woods Edge, the road got bumpier by the yard, forcing Taylor to slow down to almost a snail's crawl.

'Jesus, there's absolutely nothing here,' she said, looking around. 'Did you notice that we haven't seen a lamppost for way over a mile?'

Hunter nodded.

'I'm glad we still have daylight to guide us,' Taylor commented. 'There's no doubt Lucien was hiding from something, or someone. Who in their sane mind would want to live down here?'

She tried her best to avoid the larger potholes and bumps,

but no matter how carefully she swerved, or how slowly she drove, it still felt as if they were driving through a warzone.

'This is like a minefield,' she said. 'Car companies should bring their vehicles down here for a suspension test.'

A couple of slow and very bouncy minutes later, they finally reached the house at the end of the Woods Edge.

The place looked like a single-story ranch house, but on a much smaller scale. A low wooden fence, in desperate need of repair and a new paint job, surrounded the front of the property. The grass beyond the fence looked like it hadn't been cropped in months. Most of the cement slabs that made up the crooked pathway that led from the gates to the house were cracked, with weed growing through the cracks and all around the slabs. An old and full-of-holes Stars and Stripes fluttered from a rusty flagpole on the right. The house was once white fronted, with pale blue windows and doors, but the colors had faded drastically, and the paint was peeling off from just about everywhere. The hipped roof also looked like it could do with a few new tiles.

Hunter and Taylor stepped out of the car. A cool breeze started blowing from the west, bringing with it the smell of damp soil. Hunter looked up and saw a couple of darker clouds starting to close in.

'He certainly didn't take very good care of this place,' Taylor said, closing the car door behind her. 'Not really the best of tenants.'

Hunter checked the dirt road around him and all the way up to the wooden fence. Except for their own, there were no other tire tracks. The house had no car garage, so Hunter looked for a place where a car could park by the house. In places like this, people tend to always park in the same spot.

That would've undoubtedly left some sort of lasting impression on the ground, maybe even some oil marks or residues. He saw none. If Lucien Folter really lived here, it didn't look like he owned a car.

Hunter also checked the postbox by the fence. Empty.

As they both moved toward the house, Hunter paused a second, allowing Taylor to take the lead. As it had been pointed out to him more than once, this wasn't his investigation.

The single wooden step that led up to the porch creaked liked a warning signal under Taylor's weight. Hunter, who was right behind her, decided to skip it, stepping straight up onto the porch instead.

They checked the windows on both sides of the front door. They were all locked, with their curtains drawn shut. The heavy door on the right of the house that led to its backyard was also locked. The wall above it was high enough to dissuade anyone who might've been thinking about climbing over.

'OK, let's try these,' Taylor said.

Lucien's keychain could've belonged to a building supervisor – a single, thick metal loop, packed with similar-looking keys. There were seventeen in total.

Taylor pulled open the mesh-screen door and tried the first key. It didn't even go into the lock. The second, third, fourth and fifth keys all slid in easily, but none of them turned. Taylor just kept on calmly going through them.

The smell of damp soil became stronger and the air cooler as the first drops of rain came down. Taylor paused a second and looked up, wondering how many holes would reveal themselves on the porch's roof once the rain got stronger.

Keys number six and seven were a repeat of the first one
– wrong fit. Key number eight, on the other hand, slid into
the lock with tremendous ease, and as Taylor turned it, the
lock came undone with a muffled clunk.

'Bingo,' she said. 'I wonder what all these other keys are
for.'

Hunter said nothing.

Taylor turned the handle and pushed the door open.
Surprisingly, there was no creaking or squeaking noise, as if
the hinges had been well oiled recently.

Even before stepping into the house, they were both hit
by a disinfectant, mothball sort of smell that came from
inside. Instinctively, Taylor brought a hand to her nose.

The smell didn't bother Hunter.

Taylor found a light switch on the inside wall to the right
of the door and flicked it on.

The front door led into a very small and completely bare,
white-walled anteroom. They quickly moved past it and to
the next room along – the living room.

Once again, Taylor found the light switch by the door
and flicked it on, activating a single light bulb that hung
from the center of the ceiling. The thick red and black shade
around it dimmed its already weak strength considerably,
throwing the room into a penumbra.

It wasn't the most spacious of living rooms, but with
almost no furniture to speak of, it also didn't feel cramped.
The disinfectant, mothball smell was much stronger in this
room, making Taylor cringe and look like she was about to
heave.

'You OK?' Hunter asked.

Taylor nodded unconvincingly. 'I hate the smell of moth-
balls. It messes my stomach up.'

Hunter gave her a few seconds, and allowed his eyes to slowly scan the room. There was nothing to indicate that the house was home to anyone, no pictures, no paintings on the walls, no decorative items anywhere, no personal touches, nothing. It was like Lucien was hiding even from himself.

The open door on the west wall led into a dark kitchen. Across from where they'd entered the living room, a corridor led deeper into the house.

'Do you want to check the kitchen?' Hunter asked with a head gesture.

'Not particularly,' Taylor said. 'I just want to find this diary, and go get some fresh air.'

Hunter nodded his agreement.

They crossed the living room and entered the corridor on the other side. The light here was just as weak as the one in the living room.

'I guess he liked moody lighting,' Taylor commented.

There were four doors down the hallway – two on the left, one on the right, and one down the far end. The two on the left and the one at the far end were wide open. Even with the lights off, Hunter and Taylor could tell that they led into two bedrooms and a bathroom. The thick and heavy door on the right side of the corridor, on the other hand, was securely locked with a large padlock.

'This has got to be the door to the basement,' Taylor said.

Hunter agreed, checking the padlock, which surprised him. It was a military-grade padlock, made by Sargent and Greenleaf – supposedly resistant to every form of attack, including liquid nitrogen. Lucien certainly didn't want anyone going down into that basement uninvited.

'And we're back to the key roulette,' Taylor said, retrieving Lucien's keychain once again.

As she started going through the keys, Hunter quickly checked the first room on the left – the bathroom. It was small, tiled all in white, with a heavy musty and wet smell. There was nothing interesting in there.

Click.

Hunter heard the metal noise coming from the corridor and stepped out of the bathroom.

'Got it,' Taylor said, letting the padlock drop to the floor. 'Took me twelve tries this time.' She twisted the door handle and pushed the door open.

There was a light cord hanging from the ceiling on the inside of the door. Taylor clicked it on. A yellowish fluorescent tube flickered on and off a couple of times before finally engaging, revealing a narrow cement staircase that bent right at the bottom.

'Do you want to go first?' Taylor asked, taking a step back.

Hunter shrugged. 'Sure.'

They both took the steps down slowly and carefully. At the bottom, another two yellowish fluorescent light bulbs lit a space about the same size as the living room upstairs, with a crude cement floor and tired white walls. Furniture wise, it could also be compared to the sparsely decorated living room upstairs. A tall wooden bookcase overflowing with books hugged the north wall. A large rug, together with a flowery sofa, centered the room. Directly in front of it, there was a beech-wood module with an old tube TV on it. To the left of the module was a chest of drawers and a small beer fridge. A few framed drawings adorned the walls. Everything was covered in a thin layer of dust.

'The diary must be there,' Taylor said, nodding at the bookcase.

Hunter was still looking around the room, taking everything in.

Taylor stepped forward toward the bookcase; she paused before it, and let her eyes quickly browse through all the titles. Several of them looked to be on psychology, a few on engineering, a few on cooking, a few on mechanics, several paperback thrillers, and a few on self-motivation and how to overcome adversity. In one corner, a small collection of books looked a little different from all the others. The main difference was – they had no title. They weren't printed books. They were hardcover notebooks, the kind easily found in any stationery store.

'It looks like we've got more than one diary here,' Taylor announced, reaching for the first book.

She got no reply from Hunter.

Without looking at him she flipped the book open, and as she started flicking through it, she frowned. There was nothing written on any of the pages. They were all covered by hand drawings and sketches.

'Robert, come have a look at this.'

Still no reply from Hunter.

'Robert, can you hear me?' Taylor finally turned to face him.

Hunter was standing in the middle of the room, immobile, staring at the wall straight in front of him. The look on his face had changed to something Taylor couldn't quite recognize.

'Robert, what's going on?'

Silence.

She followed his stare toward one of the framed drawings.

'Wait a second,' she said, squinting at it and moving a little closer. It took her several seconds to understand what she was looking at, and as she did, her whole body was suddenly covered in gooseflesh.

'Oh, my God,' she whispered. 'Is that . . . human skin?'

Hunter finally nodded slowly.

Taylor breathed out, took a step back, and looked around the room again.

'Jesus Christ . . .' Her throat went completely dry and she felt as if she was being choked by a pair of invisible hands.

There were five different frames adorning the walls.

Hunter still hadn't moved. His stare was still locked onto the frame directly in front of him. But the fact that what seemed to be framed drawings, were actually framed human skin, wasn't what had shocked him the most. What had frozen Hunter to the spot was what was drawn onto the human skin in the frame he was staring at. A very unique tattoo. One that Hunter remembered well, because he had been there when it was done. And so was Lucien. A tattoo of a red rose, where its thorny stem wrapped itself around a bleeding heart, giving the impression that it was strangling it.

Susan's tattoo.

Part Two

The Right Man

Twenty-Five

This time, Lucien Folter was already sitting at the metal table inside the interrogation room when the door buzzed open and Hunter and Taylor walked in. Just like before, his hands were cuffed, linked together by a metal chain. His feet were also shackled, with the ankle chain already securely fastened to the thick metal loop on the floor by his chair. Standing right behind him were two armed US Marines. They both nodded at Hunter and Taylor before exiting the room without saying a word.

Lucien was leaning forward on his chair. His hands were resting on the table with his fingers interlaced together. He was very slowly and calmly tapping his thumbs against each other in a steady rhythm, as if he was doing it to the beat of some song that only he could hear. His head and his eyes were low. His stare was fixed on his hands.

Taylor deliberately allowed the door to slam shut behind her, but the loud bang didn't seem to reach Lucien's ears. He didn't flinch, didn't look up, didn't stop with the thumbs tapping. It was like he was in a world of his own.

Hunter stepped forward and stopped across the table from him, his arms loose and relaxed by the side of his body. He didn't take a seat. He didn't say a thing. He simply waited.

Taylor stood by the door, anger burning inside her eyes. On their trip back to Quantico, she had promised herself that she wouldn't let that anger show, that she would be pragmatic ... professional ... detached. But seeing Lucien again, sitting in that room seemingly unperturbed, made her blood boil inside her veins.

'You sick sonofabitch,' she finally blurted out. 'How many have you actually killed?'

Lucien just kept staring at his thumbs, following the beat that no one else could hear.

'Did you skin them all?' Taylor carried on.

No reply.

'Did you make one of those sick trophies out of every victim?'

Still no reply, but this time Lucien stopped with the thumbs tapping, slowly lifted his head, and locked eyes with Hunter. Neither of them said anything for a very long moment. They simply studied each other like two complete strangers who were about to go into battle. The first thing Hunter noticed was that Lucien's demeanor had totally changed from their previous interview. The emotional Lucien, the one who seemed scared that a huge injustice was being done to him, the one who needed help, that Lucien was all but gone. The new Lucien sitting before Hunter now looked stronger ... more confident ... fearless. Even his face looked tougher, like a fighter who wouldn't walk away from any sort of confrontation – someone who was ready for come what may. There was also something very different about the look in his dark brown eyes. Something very cold and disconnected, void of any emotion. It was an empty look that Hunter had seen several times before, but never in Lucien's eyes. It was a psychopathic look.

Lucien breathed out.

'By the look on your face, Robert, I'm sure you've recognized the tattoo on one of the frames on my wall.'

Hunter realized now that that had been the real reason why Lucien had mentioned Susan and her tattoo earlier. Not because he was trying to steer the conversation away from a fragile topic until his nerves settled, but because he wanted to make absolutely sure Hunter would remember it before sending him to the house.

Hunter wasn't exactly sure of what to say, so he remained silent.

'That piece is by far my favorite,' Lucien continued. 'Do you know why, Robert?'

No reply from Hunter.

Lucien gave him a pleased smile, as if the memories filled his heart with joy.

'Susan was my first.'

'You sick sonofabitch,' Taylor said again, stepping forward as if she was about to launch onto Lucien, but sense seemed to take over right at the last second and she paused by the metal table.

Lucien's icy gaze slowly moved to her. 'Please stop repeating yourself, Agent Taylor. You've already called me a sick sonofabitch.' His voice was flat. No emotion. No warmth. 'Maybe I *am* one, but swearing doesn't really suit you.' He ran his tongue over his lips to wet them. 'Name-calling is for the weak. For people who lack the intellect to argue intelligently. Do you think you lack the intellect, Agent Taylor? Because if you do, you have no business being an FBI agent.'

Taylor took a deep breath to steady herself. Though her eyes still burned with anger, she knew Lucien was just trying to push her.

'I understand that right now you're still a little in shock from your discovery back in the house,' Lucien continued, 'so your emotions are running a little high.' He shrugged, unconcerned. 'Understandable. But I bet that little outburst of yours isn't really what's expected from a senior FBI agent, is it? I bet it surprised even you, because I bet you promised yourself that you wouldn't lose it. You promised yourself that you would remain calm and professional, didn't you, Agent Taylor?' Lucien gave her no time to reply. 'But being able to control one's emotions is a very tricky thing. Even with the best of intentions, your emotions can still easily boil up inside you. It takes a lot of training to be able to properly control them.' Another shrug. 'But I'm sure you'll get there someday.'

Taylor strained to hold her tongue. It was obvious to her that Lucien was counting on another emotional reaction, but she didn't comply.

'How many were there, Lucien?' Hunter asked in a steady voice, finally breaking his silence. 'You said Susan was your first. How many victims were there?'

Lucien sat back and smiled a smile that looked rehearsed.

'That's a very good question, Robert.' He looked deep in thought for a long instant. 'I'm not really sure. I lost count after a while.'

Taylor felt her skin starting to goose-bump again.

'But I have it all written down,' Lucien said, as he began nodding. 'Yes. There really is a diary, Robert. Actually, there is more than one, where I documented everything – places I've been, people I've taken, methods I've used . . .'

'And where are they?' Taylor asked.

Lucien chuckled and moved his hands, making the chain rattle against the metal table. 'Patience, Agent Taylor,

An Evil Mind   119

patience. Haven't you ever heard the saying: "*Good things will come to those who wait*"?'

Though Lucien's words were intended for Taylor, all of his attention was on Hunter.

'I know that right now you have a thousand questions tumbling over each other inside that brain of yours, Robert. I know that all you want is to understand the why's and how's . . . and obviously, since you're a cop, to identify all the victims.' Lucien rotated his neck from side to side, as if trying to release some tension. 'That could take a while. But believe me, Robert, I really do want you to understand the why's and how's. That's the real reason why I called you here.'

Lucien looked past Hunter at the two-way mirror behind him. He wasn't speaking to Hunter or Taylor anymore. He knew that after what they had uncovered in North Carolina, a more senior FBI figure would be on the other side of that glass. Someone with the authority to call all the shots.

'I know that *you* also want to know the why's and how's,' he said in a chilling tone, staring at his own reflection. 'After all, this is the famous FBI Behavioral Science Unit. You live to study the minds of people like me. And believe me, you have never encountered anyone quite like me.'

Lucien could practically feel the tension growing behind the glass.

'More than that,' he continued. 'You need to identify the victims. It's your duty. But I'm telling you now, you'll never be able to do that without my cooperation.'

Hunter saw Taylor uneasily shift her weight from foot to foot.

'The good news is that I'm willing to do that,' Lucien said. 'But I'll do it on my terms, so listen up.' His voice seemed to have gone even more serious. 'I will only speak to Robert, no one else. I know he isn't with the FBI, but I also know that that can easily be remedied.' He paused and looked around the room. 'The interviews will not be conducted in this room anymore. I don't feel comfortable here, and . . .' He lifted his hands and moved them about, allowing the chain between his wrists to rattle against the metal table once again. 'I really don't like being shackled. It puts me in a very bad state of mind, and that's not good, for me, or for you. I also like to move around when I talk. It helps me think. So from now on, Robert can come down to my cell. We can talk there.' He stole a quick peek at Taylor. 'Agent Taylor can sit in on the interviews if she wants. I like her. But she'll have to learn how to control that temper of hers.'

'You don't get to negotiate,' Taylor said, keeping her voice as calm as she could muster.

'Oh, I think I do, Agent Taylor. Because I take it that by now you'll have a team of agents going over every inch of my house in Murphy. And if they're competent in the least, they should find out that what you and Robert saw in that house earlier . . .' Lucien paused and he and Hunter locked eyes once again. 'Well . . . that's only the beginning.'

Twenty-Six

Lucien was right in his assumption – a specialized FBI team had already been deployed to scrutinize every inch of his house back in Murphy.

Special Agent Stefano Lopez was the agent in charge of the very experienced, eight-strong search team. That particular crew had been put together eight years ago by Director Adrian Kennedy himself, who had little trust in forensic specialists. A few years back, most forensic work around the country had started to be outsourced to private companies. Their overpaid forensic agents, if one could call them that, no doubt fueled by the increasing number of forensic-investigation TV shows that had hit the airwaves in the past decade, truly believed they were stars, and acted accordingly.

Kennedy's team had been highly trained in the collection and analysis of forensic evidence, and all eight of them had a degree either in chemistry, or biology, or both. Three of the agents, including Lopez, the team leader, had also been pre-med students before joining the FBI. They were all qualified, and had brought with them enough lab equipment and gadgets to perform a variety of 'on the spot' basic tests.

To expedite the search, Agent Lopez had compartmentalized the house and split the crew into four teams of two:

Team A – Agents Suarez and Farley – was in charge of going through everything in the living room and kitchen; Team B – Agents Reyna and Goldstein – was searching both bedrooms down the corridor, and the small bathroom; Team C – Agents Lopez and Fuller – was downstairs in the basement; Team D – Agents Villegas and Carver – was outside searching the property grounds.

Team C had already photographed the entire basement in its original state, and was now in the process of sieving through everything as it was collected, tagged, and placed inside plastic evidence bags for further analysis. The first items to be taken down were the framed human skin pieces.

As Agents Lopez and Fuller carefully unhooked the first frame from the east wall, they both realized that the frames had been simply, but cleverly homemade. First, the human skin piece had been either soaked or sprayed with a preserving substance like formaldehyde or formalin, which is a solution of gas formaldehyde in water. Then, the piece had been stretched out and placed flat against a sheet of Plexiglas that was about 2 millimeters thick – equivalent to two regular microscope slides stacked together. A second sheet of Plexiglas, of identical thickness, was then placed over the human skin piece, sandwiching it between both Plexiglas sheets. To keep skin deterioration down to a minimum, the Plexiglas/human skin sandwich was finally airtight locked using a special sealant, before being framed just like any regular painting or picture.

'This is one hundred percent fucked up,' Lopez said, after dusting the last of the frames for fingerprints. There were none.

Lopez was tall and slim, with short curly hair, piercing dark brown eyes, and a hooked nose that had earned him the nickname Hawk.

'No shit, Hawk,' Agent Fuller said as he started tagging and bagging the frames. 'You know we've seen enough killers' trophies over the years, among them quite a few body parts, but this is pushing the boundaries.' He made a head gesture toward the frames. 'This guy didn't just cut a finger or an ear off his victims. He *skinned* them, at least partially, maybe even while they were still alive, and to me that puts him in a new category I haven't seen before.'

'And what category is that?'

'Psychopath freak show – level: grandmaster. One with a lot of skill and patience too.'

Hawk agreed with a nod. 'Yeah, that *is* messed up, but what really gets me is this room.' He looked around him.

Fuller's gaze circled the room, following Hawk's. 'What do you mean?'

'How many serial killers' trophy rooms would you say that we've seen over the years?'

Fuller pulled a face and shrugged. 'I don't know, Hawk. More than enough, for sure.'

'Since this unit was put together, thirty-nine,' Hawk confirmed. 'But we've all seen hundreds of photographs of other trophy rooms, and you know they all look similar – small, smelly, grimy, dark, you know what I'm talking about. It's usually just a cupboard-sized space or a shed somewhere where the perpetrators keep whatever parts they chopped off their victims. Somewhere they can go to jerk off, or fantasize, or whatever it is they do when they're reliving the time they spent with their victims. You've seen them. They all look like some sort of sick shrine out of a Hollywood horror movie.' Hawk paused, turned both of his gloved hands upward, and looked around the room again. 'But look at this place. It looks like an average family's sitting room. It's just a little dusty.' He ran two fingers over the top of the chest of drawers, showing the result to Fuller just to emphasize his argument.

'OK, and your point is?'

'My point is that I don't think this guy came down here to be reminded of his murders, or of the time he spent with his victims. I think this guy came down here to watch TV, drink beer and read, just like regular folk. The difference is that he did all that surrounded by the framed skin of his victims.'

Hawk had walked the entire house before assigning the agents to their teams. He knew that the only TV set in the house was the old tube one down in the basement. He also knew that the small fridge in the corner had nothing but a few bottles of beer inside.

Something in Hawk's voice concerned Fuller.

'So what are you really saying, Hawk?'

Hawk paused by the bookcase and scanned through some of the titles.

'What I'm saying is that I don't think those were trophies.' He pointed to the evidence bags on the floor now holding the five frames. 'Those were just simple decorating items. If this guy really has a trophy room somewhere, this isn't it.' He paused and breathed in a worried breath. 'I'm saying brace yourself, Fuller, because if this guy has a trophy room, we haven't found it yet.'

Twenty-Seven

Upstairs in the house, Team B – Agents Miguel Reyna and Eric Goldstein, had just finished their swipe of the small bathroom and the first bedroom. They'd managed to collect several fingerprints from both rooms, but even without a more in-depth analysis, Goldstein, who was the team's expert when it came to fingerprints, could tell that their patterns seemed identical, which hinted that they'd all come from the same person. The size of all the thumbprints found also indicated that the prints had probably come from a male subject.

The shower's plughole had given them several hair strands, all of them short and dark brown in color. The high-intensity UV-light test they'd conducted in the first bedroom and in the bathroom had revealed no traces of semen or blood anywhere, not even in the bathroom's washbasin from what could've been an old shaving cut. Several spots, some small, some large, did light up on the floor all around the toilet seat, and on the seat itself, but that was to be expected. Urine is extremely fluorescent when illuminated with ultraviolet light.

Just to be sure, they also ran a UV-light test on the walls. It's not uncommon for perpetrators to try to cover bloodstained walls by giving them a new coat of paint.

Though that would make them completely invisible to the naked eye, paint-covered bloodstains will still quite clearly reveal themselves under high-intensity UV-light scrutiny.

A few scattered speckles did light up on the corridor walls. Reyna and Goldstein collected samples of them all, but none of them were hidden behind the topcoat of paint. Both agents had their doubts that the samples they collected in the hallway would turn out to be blood.

They approached the last room at the end of the corridor, the master bedroom, and paused by the door, allowing their eyes to take everything in before proceeding.

The décor inside was sparse, cheap and messy, like a college dorm room furnished on a very low budget. The double bed pushed up against one of the walls looked like it had come from a Salvation Army shop, and so did the mattress and the black and gray bed cover and pillow cases. A wooden, drawerless bedside table, with a reading lamp on it, was also pushed up against the same wall, on the right side of the bed. An old-looking double-door wardrobe was centered against the west wall. The only other piece of furniture in that room was a small bookcase, crammed with books.

'At least this shouldn't take very long,' Reyna said, slipping on a brand-new pair of latex gloves.

'Good,' Goldstein agreed. Even with the nose mask the strong mothball smell was starting to burn the inside of his nostrils.

They started like they had in the two previous rooms, with a high-intensity UV-light test, and as soon as they switched the UV light on, the bed covers lit up like a Christmas tree.

'Well, no surprise there,' Goldstein said. 'Those sheets look like they've never been washed.'

While a variety of body fluids are fluorescent under high-intensity UV light – semen, blood, vaginal secretion, urine, saliva and sweat – using the light alone will not confirm exactly what sort of stain one is looking at. More tests are certainly needed. Also, several other non-body-fluid substances, like citric fruit juices or toothpaste, will certainly light up bright under a UV-light test.

'Let's bag all the bed covers and sheets,' Goldstein said. 'The lab will have to deal with this.'

Reyna quickly pulled everything off the bed and placed each item into individual evidence bags. The white mattress under the sheets showed no visible signs of any blood splatter, but they ran a UV test on it anyway. Once again, several speckles lit up here and there, but nothing that could get any alarm bells ringing. Nevertheless, Reyna and Goldstein marked and collected samples of them all.

When they were all done, Goldstein crossed over to where the small bookcase was, and carefully began retrieving each and every book. Reyna stayed by the bed, dusting its frame for fingerprints. As he moved over to the other side, he noticed something different on the side of the mattress – a long, horizontal makeshift flap, made from a thick white fabric that blended easily with the mattress, hiding it extremely well. He frowned at it and slowly ripped it from the mattress. Concealed underneath the flap, he found a long slit in the mattress.

'Eric, come have a look at this,' he called with a hand gesture.

Goldstein put down the book he was looking through, and walked back over to where Reyna was.

'What do you think this is?' Reyna asked, pointing to the long opening in the mattress.

Goldstein's eyes widened a touch. 'A hiding place.'

'You bet,' Reyna replied, slipping his fingers into the slot, and horizontally, pulling both sides apart, as wide as he could.

Goldstein bent down and shone his flashlight into the aperture. Neither of them could see anything past Reyna's hands.

'I'll check,' Goldstein said, putting his flashlight down, and slowly slipping his right hand into the gap. Very carefully he started touch-feeling his way around the inside of the mattress. First left, then right – nothing. He slid his arm in a little deeper, all the way up to his elbow. Left, right. Still nothing.

'Maybe whatever was hidden here is already gone,' Reyna offered.

Goldstein wasn't about to give up just yet. He bent forward and shoved his whole arm into the mattress – all the way up to his shoulder. This time he didn't have to feel around. His fingers immediately collided with something solid.

Goldstein paused and looked at Reyna in a particular way.

'You've got something?' Reyna asked, instinctively bending his head to one side to look into the gap again. He saw nothing.

'Give me a sec,' Goldstein said, spreading his fingers to grab whatever object was hidden inside the mattress. Whatever it was, it was about five inches thick.

'Hold on,' he said. 'I've got it.' He tried to pull it out, but the object slipped from his grip. 'Hold on, hold on,' he said again, now sliding his other arm into the mattress. With his arms shoulder-length apart, he grabbed hold of the object with both hands. 'It feels like some sort of box,' he announced, and slowly started dragging it out.

Reyna waited.

'OK, here we go,' Goldstein said as he got the object to the opening.

Reyna moved his hands out of the way, and felt an odd excitement run up and down his spine.

Goldstein dragged the whole object out of the mattress and placed it on the floor between them. It was a box. A wooden box of about twenty-nine inches long by twenty-one wide.

'Gun box,' Reyna said, but without much conviction.

Goldstein's thick eyebrows arched up inquisitively. The box was actually large enough to hold a submachine gun like an MP5 or an Uzi, or even two or three handguns.

'Only one way to find out,' Goldstein said.

Surprisingly the box had no locks, just two old-style flip latches. Goldstein undid them both, and flipped the lid open.

There were no guns inside, but still its contents made both agents pause, their eyes opening wide.

The box had a division down the center of it, splitting it into two separate compartments.

After several seconds of complete silence and absolute stillness, Goldstein finally used a pen to cautiously rifle through the contents inside both compartments.

'Holy shit,' he whispered before looking over at Reyna. 'You better go get Hawk.'

Twenty-Eight

At 01:30 a.m., Hunter and Agent Taylor were called into a special NCAVC meeting, which was held inside a sound-proof conference room on the third floor of the BSU building. Four men and three women sat around a long, polished red oak table. A large, white projection screen had been lowered from the ceiling toward the far wall. As soon as Hunter was ushered into the room, he could sense the heavy, worried atmosphere, which was further emphasized by the tense look on everyone's faces. Director Adrian Kennedy was sitting at the head of the table.

'Please come in and have a seat,' he said without standing up, indicating the two empty seats by his side, one to his right, one to his left.

Hunter took the seat to Kennedy's right.

'OK, let's start with introductions,' Kennedy continued. 'I know everyone here is familiar with Detective Robert Hunter's paper,' he said to the group, 'but I believe this is the first time most of you have met the man behind that work.' He glanced at Hunter then in turn nodded at each person around the table. 'Jennifer Holden oversees our PROFILER computer system; Deon Douglas and Leo Hurst are with our Criminal Investigative Analysis Program – CIAP; Victoria Davenport is with the FBI's Violent Crime

Apprehension Program – VICAP; Doctor Patrick Lambert, who you met earlier, is our chief of forensic psychiatry, and Doctor Adriana Montoya is one of our chief pathologists.'

They all nodded a silent 'Hello' at Hunter, who returned each and every one a nod of his own.

'To my left, is FBI Special Agent Courtney Taylor,' Kennedy said. 'She'll be heading this investigation.'

More silent nods.

'I already took the liberty of contacting your captain with the LAPD once again, Robert,' he said to Hunter. 'We now need you in this case, and I know you want in, but we've got to do this by the book. A request has already been expedited and sanctioned by both sides.' He drew quotations in the air with his fingers. 'You're now officially "on loan" to the FBI.' He placed an FBI ID card with Hunter's name and photograph on the table in front of him. 'So, until we've got this all figured out, you are Special Agent Robert Hunter.'

Hunter seemed to cringe at the title. He left the ID card where it was.

'OK,' Kennedy said to the whole room. 'Sorry to have dragged you all out here for such a late, unscheduled meeting, but there's no doubt that today's turn of events constitutes a major game changer.' He sat back on his seat, locked his fingers together, and rested his hands on his lap before addressing Hunter and Taylor directly.

'Doctor Lambert and I were in the observation room earlier today, during your second interview with Lucien Folter.'

Hunter didn't look surprised. He knew that Taylor had called Kennedy from the house in Murphy right after their discovery. She had also used her smartphone to email him pictures of the framed human skin pieces, and a short video of Lucien's basement room. Hunter had expected that Kennedy would've postponed whatever he had on for the rest of the day, and made the trip back from Washington, DC to Quantico, ASAP.

'Everyone in this room has also watched the recorded footage of both interviews at length,' Kennedy added before nodding at Doctor Lambert, who took over.

'The transformation Mr Folter went through in the space of just a few hours, from interview one to interview two, was nothing less than astounding.' He looked a little embarrassed. 'I must admit that after the first interview, after the drug addiction story he told you, some part of me had started to believe him. I felt sorry for him.'

Victoria Davenport with VICAP nodded her agreement before Doctor Lambert carried on.

'I had really started to entertain the possibility that Mr Folter had in fact been just another victim of an elaborate plan by a very sadistic killer, or killers. That he'd been just a pawn, a delivery boy in something much bigger.' The doctor ran a hand through the little hair he had left on his head, just a handful of white strands that never seemed to want to stay in place. 'In all my years as a forensic psychiatrist, I've seen very few people who were able to lie so convincingly, and most of those suffered from dissociative identity disorder.' He looked straight at Hunter. 'And you know that's not the case we have here.'

Hunter said nothing, but he knew Doctor Lambert was right. Lucien had shown absolutely no indications of split personality. He never claimed to be, or hinted at being, two or more different people.

With someone suffering from dissociative identity disorder, once an identity takes over, it's like a whole new person, with his/her own feelings, emotions, history and memories. Feelings, emotions, history and memories that aren't shared between identities. So if Lucien suffered from DID, causing him to display a different identity in the second interview from the identity he'd displayed during the first one, the second identity wouldn't have remembered the first interview, or anything that was said during it. The crimes committed by one of his identities also would not be remembered, and possibly not even known, by any other identity his brain had developed. But that hadn't been the case. Lucien knew exactly how he'd acted, and what he'd said in both interviews.

'After what I saw,' Doctor Lambert said, 'I have very little doubt that Mr Folter had simply acted a very well-thought part during the first interview to perfection. The real Lucien Folter is the one we all saw and heard in the second interview – cold, emotionless, psychopathic and in total control of his actions.'

He paused, allowing his words to hang in the air for a moment before proceeding.

'He might have been caught by chance after that freak accident in Wyoming, but he willingly guided Detective Hunter and Agent Taylor to his house in North Carolina, knowing very well that they would find the framed human skin pieces. Knowing that Detective Hunter would personally recognize one of them. That shows a very high level of cruelty, arrogance, and pride, together with a tremendous sense of achievement and pleasure in what he's done.' The doctor paused for breath. 'This guy really likes hurting people . . . physically and emotionally.'

Twenty-Nine

Doctor Lambert's last few words caused almost everyone sitting inside the conference room to shift uneasily in their seats.

Kennedy took the opportunity to glance over at the pathologist in the room, Doctor Adriana Montoya. She had short black hair, striking hazel eyes, full lips, and a tiny tattoo of a broken heart on her neck, just behind her left ear.

'DNA analysis might still take a couple of days,' she said, leaning forward and placing her elbows on the table. 'We might have the results of the skin pigmentation test and epidermis analysis sometime later today. There's a chance that they will show that the pieces came from five different people.' A short pause. 'If that's the case, that'll gives us seven victims so far, which already makes Lucien Folter a very prolific serial killer. One the FBI had no knowledge of until about a week ago. And I have to agree with Doctor Lambert. His level of brutality and cruelty is astonishing. The two victims in his trunk were decapitated. The five in his basement were skinned.' She softly shook her head as she considered the possibilities. 'And, according to him – *this is only the beginning.*'

Hunter noticed that for some reason Doctor Montoya's last words made Kennedy tense a fraction further.

Leo Hurst from CIAP – early forties, heavily built, somber – flipped a page on the document sitting on the table in front of him. It was a transcript of both interviews.

'This guy knows his game,' he said. 'He knows that the FBI doesn't give in to a psychopath's demands. Whatever the situation is, we dictate the rules ... always. The problem is that in this case he has managed to tip the scales in his favor, and there isn't much we can do about it. He knows that we'll have to play ball because the investigation's priority has just shifted from arresting a subject to identifying the victims.'

Everyone's attention moved to him.

'OK, let's suppose for a moment that he's lying about this being only the beginning,' he continued. 'Let's suppose that all we get are these seven "possible" victims. Yes, there's a likelihood that we could positively identify all seven of them without his help, depending on DNA analysis, and if they had all been added to the national missing-persons database.' He scratched the skin between his two very thin eyebrows. 'But even if we manage to identify them all without his help, then we're faced with problem number two.'

'Finding the bodies,' Kennedy said, and for a brief moment he locked eyes with Hunter.

'Precisely,' Deon Douglas, Hurst's partner at CIAP, agreed. He was African-American and also looked to be in his early forties, with a shaved head and a stylish goatee that no doubt took some maintenance. 'Their families will want closure. They'll want to give the bodies, or whatever remains are found, a proper burial, and this Folter character knows that without his cooperation, we probably won't have a prayer finding the location where he disposed of them.'

Again, Hunter noticed that Kennedy seemed to tense up more than anyone else in the room, which seemed very uncommon. Adrian Kennedy had been with the FBI NCAVC and the Behavioral Science Unit for as long as Hunter could remember. He wasn't easily rattled by any sort of crime or perpetrator, no matter how brutal or unusual. Hunter sensed that there was something else. Something that Kennedy wasn't telling them, at least not yet.

'He could be lying about this being only the beginning,' Jennifer Holden said. 'As you've said –' she nodded at Leo Hurst '– he seems to know his game. He knows that by saying that, the scales would tip in his favor. Maybe we should put him through a polygraph test.'

Hunter shook his head. 'Even if he's lying, he'd easily beat it.'

'He would beat a lie-detector test?' Jennifer Holden asked, a little surprised.

'Yes,' Hunter replied with absolute conviction. 'I've seen him do it before just for fun, twenty-five years ago, and my guess is that he's gotten better at it.'

A few odd looks circled the room.

'You all saw the recording of the first interview,' Hunter offered. 'Even the facial analysis software that was being used failed to pick up any significant changes in his expressions. It looks to me that Lucien has almost no psychological response to lying. His pupil dilation and breathing remained exactly the same throughout. I'm sure that he's trained himself, and we'll find that even his pore size and skin flush will remain unchanged. He's probably counting on a polygraph test. Whether we put him through one or not, it will make no difference to him.'

Doctor Lambert nodded his agreement. 'Long, elaborate lies take a certain type of individual and a great amount of talent to do it convincingly. It requires creativity, intelligence, control, great memory and, most of the time, very high improvisational skills. And I'm only talking about regular circumstances here. When a person has to do all that before an authoritative figure, like a cop, or a federal agent, knowing that his freedom is on the line, those qualities will multiply themselves by a factor of X. Judging by how convincing he was in that first interview, I really wouldn't be surprised if Lucien Folter waltzed his way through a polygraph test.'

'Do you think he's lying about this being only the beginning?' Taylor asked Hunter.

'No, I don't, but what I, or any of us think, is irrelevant. Like Leo said, Lucien knows his game. He knows that after what we've seen, we don't have the luxury to doubt. Right now, he's calling the shots.'

No one said anything, because no one really knew what to say.

Hunter took the silent break opportunity and turned to face the man sitting at the head of the table.

'How's the house searching going, Adrian?' he asked. 'Any news?'

Kennedy looked at him as if Hunter had read his thoughts.

There was a stretched, worried pause.

'Well,' Kennedy said at last, 'that's the real reason we're here tonight. The search team found something inside Lucien Folter's bedroom. It was hidden inside his mattress.'

The tension in the room climbed up a few degrees.

Everyone waited.

'And this is what they found.'

Kennedy clicked a button on the small remote-control unit on the table in front of him, and the image of the closed wooden box Goldstein and Reyna had found was immediately projected onto the white screen on the far wall.

'Looks like a gun case,' Deon Douglas commented. 'Big enough for a machine gun, or a disassembled long-range rifle. Has it been opened yet?'

Kennedy nodded. 'Unfortunately, a weapon wasn't what was found inside it,' he replied.

'So what did we get?' Taylor asked.

Kennedy's eyes circled the table and paused on Hunter before he pressed the remote-control button one more time.

'We got this.'

Thirty

Despite lights off and the total darkness that surrounded him, Lucien Folter lay awake in his cell down in sublevel five of the BSU building. His eyes were open, and he was staring at the ceiling as if some fascinating movie that only he could see were being projected against it. But this time he wasn't lost in one of his meditation trances. The time for meditation was well and truly over. He was simply reorganizing his thoughts, putting them in an appropriate order of execution.

A step at a time, he thought. *Take it a step at a time, Lucien.*

And step one seemed to have gone perfectly so far.

Lucien would've given anything to have seen Hunter's face when he entered the basement down in the house in Murphy and finally realized that the wall frames weren't drawings. He would've given anything to have seen Hunter's face when he finally recognized Susan's tattoo.

Yes, that would've been worth a small fortune.

He felt his blood warming as memories of his last night with Susan came rushing back to him. He could still remember the sweet smell of her perfume, how soft her hair felt, how smooth her skin was. He reminisced on those memories for just a while longer before pushing them aside.

Lucien wondered how long it would take the FBI search team to find the box he had hidden inside the mattress in the master bedroom.

Probably not that long, if they're any good.

Instinctively, he started going over the contents of the box in his head, and that filled him with excitement, bringing a proud but curbed smile to his lips. He could remember every item. But that box and its contents were nothing compared to what was still to come. They were all in for a big surprise.

Lucien swallowed his smile down and finally closed his eyes.

One step at a time, Lucien. One step at a time.

Thirty-One

The next image to appear on the projection screen was a snapshot of the same wooden box they'd all seen seconds earlier, but this time the lid was open. They could all clearly see that the box had a division down its center, creating two distinct compartments. As if on cue, everyone in the room, with the exception of Adrian Kennedy, craned their necks forward and squinted at the screen at the same time.

The compartment on the right was packed full of what at first seemed like just a bunch of colorful fabrics. The compartment on the left was filled with a variety of different jewelry items.

Silence.

More squinting.

A few chairs shuffled.

'Are those women's underwear?' Agent Taylor finally asked, indicating the compartment on the right.

'Let me clear that up for you,' Kennedy said, clicking the remote control button yet again.

The image on the screen changed one more time. It now showed all the contents from the box neatly arranged over a white surface. Taylor was right. The fabrics that were in the right compartment were all women's underwear, panties to be more precise, in a multitude of colors, sizes and styles, but now that they were all unbundled and plainly displayed in rows, an unseen detail became clear to everyone. Many of the garments were covered with dried blood.

The jewelry items that had occupied the left box compartment were also clearly arranged in rows, divided by type – rings, earrings, necklaces, bracelets, watches, chains, and even a couple of belly button bars.

The air inside the conference room seemed to have become stale and intoxicating all of a sudden.

'Inside the right compartment, we found fourteen pairs of women's underwear,' Kennedy said, standing up. 'Out of those, eleven were covered with blood.' He allowed the gravity of what he'd just said to sink in before continuing. 'All the items have already been expedited to our forensics lab. The garments vary in size, from extra small, or size zero, to large – size thirty-four – which would indicate that they belonged to different people.'

'They would have,' Hunter said, more as an instinctive comment to himself than to the room, but Kennedy heard it.

'Sorry, what was that, Robert?'

Hunter paused for an instant.

'Those are tokens, Adrian, and I'm sure that everyone in this room knows that, in general, token collectors only take one token from each victim.'

Like a Mexican wave, agreement nods started with the person to Hunter's right, and moved around the table all the way to Taylor.

Token collectors do *in general* take only one token from each victim. Usually a very intimate item. Something that will easily trigger very strong memories of the victim and the murder act, and remind them of how powerful they are.

A lot of the time they go for intimate items of clothing because they're in close contact with the victim's skin, more precisely sexual parts, and they'll frequently hold the victim's smell. Some perpetrators even believe they'll be able to smell the victim's fear on the item for months afterward, maybe years if properly stored, heightening their exhilaration, because many of them become aroused, sexually or otherwise, by the fear they command over their prey. With that in mind, taking two or more intimate items that belonged to the same victim would become pointless because they would not increase the satisfaction perpetrators get from reliving the murder act. One is usually more than enough.

'Detective Hunter is right,' Doctor Lambert said. 'There'd be very little point in taking more than one token from each victim.'

'Jesus Christ!' Jennifer Holden from PROFILER exclaimed. 'So you're saying that we now might have another fourteen "possible" victims to add to the "possible" seven we've already got?'

'Twenty-six "possible" new victims,' Hunter corrected her, pointing to the jewelry pieces on the screen.

Six pairs of wide-open eyes honed in on him. Kennedy and Doctor Lambert were the only ones who showed no surprise.

'Right again,' Doctor Lambert confirmed, nodding at the group. 'Following the double-token theory, if Mr Folter had already taken an underwear item from a victim, also taking a piece of jewelry from the same victim makes the second token pointless.' He nodded at the screen. 'We've got twelve pieces of jewelry. It would be safe to assume that the jewelry came from different victims, increasing the total to a possible twenty-six. Add that to what was found in his trunk and in his basement, and we might be looking at thirty-three victims so far.'

A few headshakes were followed by a couple of deflated sighs and whispers.

'There's something else,' Hunter said.

The room's attention returned to him.

'Two of those rings, all three watches, and one of those necklaces aren't feminine pieces of jewelry.'

All eyes moved back to the screen.

'If these really belonged to his victims,' Hunter moved on, 'it doesn't look like Lucien killed only women.'

Thirty-Two

At 7:30 a.m. sharp, the heavy metal door to the cell corridor in sublevel five of the BSU building buzzed open. The hallway beyond it was wide, well lit and about seventy-five yards long. The cinder-block wall on the right was painted a dull shade of gray. The shining resin floor carried almost the same color, just a touch darker, with two guiding yellow lines running along the edge of it. The left wall was a series of high-security cells. Ten in total. Each cell was separated by a wall as wide as the cell itself, which was about eleven feet. There were no metal bars. The cells were all fronted by very thick, shatterproof Plexiglas. On the Plexiglas, positioned in a cluster at the center of it and about five and a half feet from the floor, there were eight small conversation holes, about half an inch in diameter each. The cells were all empty, their lights turned off, with the exception of the one at the far end of the corridor.

Hunter and Taylor stepped through the door and into the echoey hallway. Despite being with the FBI for several years now, and having visited the BSU building on many occasions, this was the first time Taylor had been down in sublevel five. Hunter had never seen it either.

There was definitely something quite ominous and sinister about that long stretch of corridor, as if they had just stepped over the threshold between good and evil. The air inside it felt a touch too cold, a touch too dense, a touch less breathable.

Taylor did her best to fight the awkward shiver that sped up and down her spine as she took the first steps toward the last cell, but failed miserably. Something about that place reminded her of the Halloween haunted houses she used to be so scared of when she was a kid.

'I don't know about you,' she said, steadying her body. 'But I'd much rather do this up in the interrogation room.'

'Unfortunately we don't have that choice,' Hunter replied as their shoes click-clacked against the shiny floor with every step. He suddenly stopped and faced Taylor. 'Courtney, let me tell you something about Lucien.' His voice was barely louder than a whisper. He didn't want it to echo all the way to the last cell. 'He always liked to play games – mind games – and he was very good at it. He's probably even better now. I'm sure he'll target you more than he will me. He'll try to get under your skin with comments, innuendos, direct digs, whatever. Some will probably be very nasty. Just be prepared for it, OK? Don't let it affect you. If he manages to get into your mind, he'll rip you apart.'

Taylor made a face as if she already knew all this.

'I'm a big girl, Robert. I know how to take care of myself.'

Hunter nodded. He hoped she was right.

Thirty-Three

Two metal fold-up chairs had already been placed side by side at the end of the corridor, directly in front of the last cell.

Lucien Folter was lying on his bed, motionless, eyes open, staring at the ceiling. He could hear the steps coming down the hallway toward him. He stood up, faced the Plexiglas and waited. He looked and felt completely relaxed. Not an ounce of any sort of emotion showing on his face. A couple of seconds later Hunter and Taylor came into his line of sight, and the blank mask vanished, like an experienced actor who'd just been given his cue for the big scene.

He gave them a warm smile.

'Welcome to my new home,' he said in a calm voice, looking around himself. 'As temporary as it may be.'

The cell was a rectangular box, eleven feet wide by thirteen feet deep. Just like the corridor outside, its walls were made up of cinder blocks painted a dull shade of gray. Other than the bed, which was mounted against the left wall, there was only a latrine and a washbasin against the far wall, and a small metal table with a metal bench, both bolted to the right wall and floor.

As if about to conduct a business meeting, Lucien pointed to the two chairs in the corridor.

'Please have a seat.'

He waited for Hunter and Taylor to be seated before taking a seat himself at the edge of the bed.

'Seven-thirty in the morning,' Lucien said. 'I love an early start. And as far as I can remember, so do you, Robert. Still can't sleep?'

Hunter said nothing, but his insomnia wasn't a big secret, or something he kept hidden from anyone, anyway. He had started experiencing sleepless nights at the early age of seven, just after cancer robbed him of his mother.

With no family other than his father, coping with his mother's death proved to be a very painful and lonely task. He would lie awake at night, too sad to fall asleep, too scared to close his eyes, too proud to cry.

It was just after his mother's funeral when he started fearing his dreams. Every time he closed his eyes he saw her face, crying, contorted with pain, begging for help, praying for death. He saw her once fit-and-healthy body so drained of life, so fragile and weak, she couldn't even sit up on her own strength. He saw a face that had once been beautiful, that had once carried the brightest smile and the kindest eyes he'd ever seen, transformed during those last few months into something unrecognizable. But it was still a face he'd never stopped loving.

Sleep and his dreams became the prison he'd do anything to escape from. Insomnia was the logical answer his body and brain found to deal with his fear and the ghastly nightmares that came at night. A simple but effective defense mechanism.

Lucien studied Hunter and Taylor's faces for several seconds. 'You're still very good at not giving anything away, Robert,' he said, shaking his finger in Hunter's direction.

'Actually, I'd say you got better at it, but you, Agent Taylor.' His finger moved to her. 'Are close, but not quite there yet. I assume you've found the box.

'See, Agent Taylor.' A new smile found its way onto Lucien's lips. 'That quick glance you gave Robert just confirmed my suspicion. You still have a bit to learn.'

Taylor looked unfazed.

Lucien's smile widened.

'You see Agent Taylor,' he said. 'Keeping a steady poker face takes a lot of practice. Creating a deceptive façade takes a lot more energy though, isn't that right, Robert?' Lucien knew Hunter wouldn't reply, so he moved on. 'Even you have to admit that I've now got mine down to perfection, haven't I? You thought you could always tell when I was lying, didn't you?' He breathed in. 'And you could, all those years ago, but not anymore.' Lucien paused and scratched his chin. 'Let me see now. What was it again? Oh yes . . . this.'

Lucien looked straight into Hunter's eyes, and suddenly his stare became a touch more focused, more determined. Then, for fraction of a second, his lower left eyelid tightened in an almost imperceptible movement. If you weren't looking for it, you wouldn't have seen it.

'Did you catch that, Agent Taylor?' Lucien followed his question with a smile. 'Of course you didn't, but don't beat yourself up just yet. It's not your fault. You had no idea what you were looking for or where to look.' His gaze moved to Hunter. 'Robert noticed it because he knew he had to look at my eyes, especially my left one. I'll do it again, a little slower this time. Don't blink or you'll miss it, Agent Taylor.'

He repeated his eye movement, this time with so much control it was almost frightening.

'You told me about it in college once, Robert, after a party, remember? We were both a little drunk and you thought I'd taken no notice of it, didn't you?'

Hunter cast his mind back, and a hazy memory surfaced.

'But it *stayed* with me,' Lucien continued. 'You said that it was something very subtle, not everyone would notice, but I know that you could always pick it up. You always had a great eye for that kind of stuff, Robert. I know I didn't do it often. At least not if I was telling just a simple white lie, but if it were anything more serious ... BANG, my eye movement always gave me away.' Lucien used his thumb and forefinger to rub his eyes a couple of times. 'So I practiced, and practiced, and practiced in front of a mirror until it was all gone. No more telltale signs. No more being betrayed by psychological motor reactions. It took me a while, a long while actually, but I learned to control them. In fact, I got so good at it that I can flash-create new ones any time I like, just to throw people off course. That is a terrifying thought, isn't it?'

Hunter and Taylor stayed quiet.

'I knew that you'd be looking for the eye movement giveaway, Robert. I could sense your concentration in order to read me.' A new smile. 'I was fucking great, wasn't I? A performance worthy of an Oscar.' Without losing a beat, Lucien changed the subject and moved on. 'I'd offer you a drink,' he said. 'But all I've got is tap water, and I only have one cup.' Again, he studied his two interviewers for an awkward moment. 'Coffee would be nice, but I don't have any.' His stare lingered on Taylor.

She got the hint, looked up at the CCTV camera on the ceiling high above the cell, and gave it a single nod.

'Black with two sugars, if you please,' Lucien said, looking up at the same camera before addressing Hunter and

Taylor again. 'OK, let me tell you how this is going to work. I'll allow you to ask me a few questions. I'll answer them truthfully, and I mean that. I won't lie. Then it's my turn to ask you a question. If I sense that you haven't answered me honestly, the interview is over for twenty-four hours, and we can start again the next day. I tell you the truth, you tell me the truth. Does that sound fair to you?'

Taylor frowned. 'You want to ask us questions? About what?'

Her reaction amused Lucien.

'Information is power, Agent Taylor. I like feeling powerful, don't you?'

They all heard the door at the end of the corridor buzz open again. A Marine carrying a steaming cup of coffee made his way toward them. Taylor took the cup, placed it in the Plexiglas slide tray, and slid it into the cell toward Lucien.

'Thank you, Agent Taylor,' he said, retrieving the cup. He brought it to his nose and drew in a deep breath before sipping it. If the coffee was too hot, he showed no reaction. 'Very nice.' He nodded his approval. 'OK,' he said, sitting back down, 'let's start the great reveal. What's your first question?'

Thirty-Four

Hunter had been silently studying his old friend since he and Taylor got to his cell. Lucien had an even more victorious, self-glorifying air about him that morning than he had the day before, but that wasn't all that surprising. Lucien knew he was holding the upper hand. He knew that, at least for now, they all had to dance to his tune, and that seemed to please him immensely. But there was something else. Something new about Lucien's persona – conviction, confidence, deep pride even, as if he really wanted everyone to know the truth about what he'd done.

Taylor glanced at Hunter, who made no move to ask the first question.

'So far we've found indications that you might've committed thirty-three murders,' she began, her voice flat, calm, calculated, her eyes not shying away from Lucien's. 'Is that correct, or have there been any more victims we don't yet know about?'

Lucien sipped his coffee again before shrugging matter-of-factly.

'That's a good first question, Agent Taylor, straight away trying to figure out just how big a monster I am.' He tilted his head back ever so slightly and started running his index finger from his Adam's apple to the tip of his chin, in a shaving motion. 'But tell me this, if I'd murdered only one person, savagely or not, would that make me less of a monster than if I'd murdered thirty-three, or fifty-three, or one hundred and three?'

Taylor kept her cool. 'Is that one of your questions for us?'

Lucien smiled, unconcerned. 'No, it isn't. I was just curious, but never mind, 'cos like I said, Agent Taylor, it was a good first question. It just wasn't the right one. And that's very disappointing coming from a senior FBI agent like yourself. I was really expecting more from you.' He looked at her in a derogatory way. 'But I don't mind schooling you this once. After all, life is nothing but a big learning experience, isn't that right, Agent Taylor?'

Taylor said nothing, but a tiny hint of anger trickled into her eyes.

'Your first question should've had more purpose. It should've addressed the main topic of why you're here. The question should've prompted an answer that would've indicated if you're wasting time or not.' Lucien sipped his coffee again before addressing Hunter. 'But let's see if we can fix that for her, shall we? I still remember how good you used to be in college, Robert, always a step ahead of everyone, including all the professors. Now, with so many years of experience as an LAPD detective, I'm guessing you've got better, sharper, wittier even. So, for the grand prize, let's hear it, Robert. In this situation, what would your first question have been? And please don't disappoint Agent Taylor here. She wants to learn.'

Hunter didn't have to look. He could feel Taylor's eyes on him.

Hunter was sitting back against the chair's backrest. His position was relaxed and calm. His left leg was crossed over his right one. His hands were resting on his thighs. There was no tension in his shoulders or neck, and his facial expression didn't seem worried.

'Don't keep us waiting, Robert,' Lucien urged him. 'Patience is a virtue, but a pain in the ass to master.'

Hunter knew he had no alternative but to play Lucien's game.

'Location,' he said at last. 'Do you really know the exact location of every body you disposed of?'

Clap, clap, clap.

Lucien had put his cup of coffee down on the floor, and had begun clapping slowly.

'He's good, isn't he?' Lucien asked Taylor in a sarcastic tone. 'If I were you, I'd pay attention, Agent Taylor. You might learn a thing or two here today.'

Taylor did her best not to glare at him.

'You know why that's the right question, Agent Taylor?' he asked rhetorically, like a lecturing teacher. 'Because if I answer "no" to it, this whole thing is over. You can pack me up and send me off to the electric chair. I'm no use to you, or the FBI anymore.' Without taking his eyes off Taylor, he picked up his coffee cup from the floor. 'You're not here to get a confession from me, Agent Taylor. That part is done and dusted. I am a killer. I murdered *all* those people . . . brutally.' There was a chilling pride in Lucien's last few words. 'The only reason I'm still here is because you desperately need something from me.' He glanced at Hunter. 'The location of all the bodies. Not really because you need proof of what I've done, but because families need closure. They need to give their loved ones a proper burial, isn't that right, Agent, Taylor?'

Again Taylor didn't reply.

'If I answer "no" to Robert's question, there's no point in having any more interviews. There's no point in asking any more questions. There's no point in keeping me here, because I can't give you what you need.' A ghost of a smile graced Lucien's lips. This was certainly amusing him. 'Tell me, Agent Taylor, does it make you mad that an outsider can do your job better than you?'

Don't let it get to you, the voice inside Hunter's head said to Taylor. *Don't get upset. Don't let him under your skin.* From the corner of his eye he could see Taylor struggling with her anger, and if he could see it, so could Lucien.

Taylor didn't take the bait. She did struggle with her anger, but she kept it under wraps.

Lucien chuckled proudly and his attention returned to Hunter.

'The answer to your question, Robert, is – *yes*. I can tell you the location of all the bodies that *can* be found.' He calmly sipped his coffee. 'As you might understand, some can never be found. It's a physical impossibility. Oh,' he said casually, 'and I also know all of their identities by heart.'

Once again, Lucien tried to read Hunter's expression. Once again he failed, but he detected a hint of doubt in Taylor's eyes.

'I'm willing to sit through a polygraph test if you think I'm deceiving you, Agent Taylor.'

He'll easily beat it. Hunter's words from the early-morning meeting came back to her. *He's probably counting on a polygraph test.*

'That won't be necessary,' she finally said.

Lucien laughed animatedly. 'I see. Did Robert tell you that we both beat the polygraph when we were in college, just for fun?'

Taylor didn't confirm it, but she didn't know that Hunter had beaten it as well.

'He was much better than I was, though,' Lucien said. 'It took me months to master the technique, but he got it down in just a few weeks.' He looked at Hunter. 'Robert always had tremendous self-discipline and concentration control.'

Something different coated Lucien's last few words. Taylor thought it was jealousy, but she was wrong.

Lucien lifted a hand in a 'wait' gesture.

'But why should you believe a word I'm saying? I haven't done much other than lie to you up to now.' There was a lengthy pause. 'As I've suggested, you could try a lie-detector test.' Lucien threw his head back and laughed a full-fat laugh. 'I wish you had. That would've been fun.'

Neither Hunter nor Taylor looked amused.

'You don't have to say it, Robert,' Lucien commented, anticipating what Hunter was about to say. 'I'm pretty sure I know the procedure. To establish a thread of trust between us, you'll need some sort of token of good faith, isn't that right? If I were a terrorist holding hostages, this is the point where you would ask me for a hostage, just to prove that I'm willing to play fair.'

'You've got to give us something, Lucien,' Hunter agreed. He hadn't shifted from his relaxed sitting position yet. 'Like you've said, you've given us nothing but lies so far.'

Lucien nodded and finished his coffee.

'I understand that, Robert.' He closed his eyes and drew in a deep, tranquil breath, as if he were just sitting in a flowery garden outside somewhere, appreciating the delicate perfume that traveled the air. 'Megan Lowe,' Lucien said without opening his eyes. 'Twenty-eight years old. Born December 16 in Lewistown, Montana.' He slowly ran the tip of his tongue across his upper lip, as if his mouth had started to salivate at the memory. 'Kate Barker, twenty-six years old. Born eleventh of May in Seattle, Washington. Megan was abducted on July second, Kate on July fourth. Both were independent street-working girls, working in Seattle, Washington. Megan was the brunette whose head was found inside the trunk of the car I was driving. Kate was the blonde one.'

Lucien finally opened his eyes and looked at Hunter.

'The remains of their bodies are still in Seattle. Would you like to write down the address?'

Thirty-Five

Director Adrian Kennedy, who was watching and listening to the interview from the holding cells' control room, immediately got the bureaucratic machine running to obtain a federal search warrant. Being an FBI director has its advantages, and despite the early hour and the fact that Washington State is three hours behind Virginia, Kennedy managed to get a warrant signed by a Seattle federal judge in record time.

Even though Lucien had told Hunter and Taylor that the key to the location where the two victims' remains were stored was on the same keychain they had used for the house in Murphy, Kennedy wasn't willing to wait. He wasn't about to send Hunter, Taylor or any other agent all the way from Quantico to Seattle, just to check if Lucien was lying again or not.

With a federal search warrant secured, Kennedy placed a call to the FBI field office on 1110 3rd Avenue in Seattle, Washington. At 8:30 a.m. Pacific Time, a team of two agents was dispatched to the address Lucien had given Hunter and Taylor – a commercial storage unit.

'So where are we going, Ed?' Special Agent Sergio Decker asked, as he took the driver's seat and switched on the engine of the midnight-black Ford SUV.

Special Agent in charge, Edgar Figueroa, had just climbed

into the passenger seat. He was in his mid-thirties, tall and broad-shouldered, with a bodybuilder's physique. His dark hair was cropped to a centimeter of his skull, and one just needed to look at his nose to know that it had been broken at least a couple of times.

'To check a self-storage unit on North 130th Street,' he replied, buckling up.

Decker nodded, backed the car up, took a right on 3rd Avenue and headed northwest toward Seneca Street.

'What case is this?' he asked.

'Not ours,' Figueroa replied. 'I think a call came in from high above in Washington, DC or Quantico. We're just going to verify the veracity of the address.'

'Narcs?' Decker questioned.

Figueroa shrugged and shook his head at the same time. 'Not sure, but I don't think so. DEA isn't involved as far as I know. I wasn't told much, but I think this is supposed to be victim's remains.'

Decker's eyebrows arched. 'Stashed in a commercial storage unit?'

'That's the address we have,' Figueroa confirmed.

Decker took another right and merged onto the I-5 North, heading toward Vancouver, British Columbia. Traffic was slow, as expected at that time in the morning, but not excessively so.

'Do they have somebody in custody?' Decker asked.

'As far as I understand, yes. And again, I think they're holding him either in DC or Quantico.' Another shrug from Figueroa. 'Like I said, I wasn't told very much, but I did get the impression that this is something big.'

'Do we have a warrant, or are we just going to talk our way through this, using our FBI charm?' Decker joked.

'We do have a warrant,' Figueroa said, consulting his watch. 'A court marshal is meeting us at the address.'

The trip from the FBI office on 3rd Avenue to the independent self-storage building, located on the north side of the city, took them about twenty-five minutes. Just like most self-storage buildings, from the outside this one also looked like a regular warehouse. It was painted all in white, with the self-storage trade name in huge green letters across the front of the building. The large customers' car park at the front of the unit was practically empty, with only a handful of cars scattered around the lot. A young couple was unloading the contents of a rented white van onto an industrial-size wheeled cart. The van was parked by loading dock number two.

Decker parked the SUV by the side of a small decorative green garden directly in front of the unit's main office. The ground was still wet from the rain that had stopped about forty minutes earlier, but judging from how dark the sky looked, rain was on its way back.

As both agents stepped out of the car, a woman, probably in her early forties, exited a white Jeep Compass that was parked just a few yards away, four spaces to their right.

'I'm US Court Marshal Joanna Hughes,' she said, offering her hand. She didn't have to ask. She could easily tell that Figueroa and Decker were the two FBI agents she was supposed to meet.

Hughes' chestnut hair was pulled back into a tight ponytail, which made her forehead seem too large for her round face. She wasn't exactly an attractive woman. Her nose looked a little too pointy, her lips too thin, and her eyes seemed to be constantly squinting, as if trying to read something that was just a touch too far away. She was elegantly dressed in a cream business suit and beige, pointed high-heel shoes. The agents formally introduced themselves and shook hands.

'Shall we?' Hughes gestured toward the reception.

An electronic 'ding-ding' bell rang as Figueroa pushed the office door open and he, Decker and Hughes stepped into the excessively brightly lit rectangular room. Both FBI agents kept their dark shades on. Hughes just wished she had hers with her.

There was a small seating area to the left of the door. A light brown four-seater sofa and two matching armchairs had been positioned around a round chrome and glass low table. A few magazines and several brochures of the storage facility were neatly arranged on the tabletop. There was also a water cooler in the corner. Sitting behind the wood and acrylic reception counter was a young man who looked to be no older than twenty-five. His eyes were glued to his smartphone. He seemed to be either texting ferociously, or really absorbed in some ridiculously entertaining videogame. It took him at least five seconds to finally look up from the tiny screen.

'Can I help you?' he asked, putting the phone down next to the computer monitor in front of him and standing up. He gave the visitors an overenthusiastic smile.

'Are you the person in charge here?' Marshal Hughes asked.

'That would be correct, ma'am.' The kid nodded once. 'How can I help you today?'

Hughes stepped closer and displayed her credentials. 'I'm US Federal Marshal Joanna Hughes,' she said. 'These two gentlemen are federal agents with the FBI.'

Figueroa and Decker reached into their suit jacket pockets, producing their IDs.

The kid checked them before taking a step back. He looked a little confused. 'Is there some sort of a problem?' His enthusiastic smile had completely vanished.

Hughes handed him a piece of paper with the US government stamp on it.

'This is a federal search warrant giving us legal permission and right to search storage unit number 325 in this establishment,' she said calmly but in a very authoritative voice. 'Would you be so kind as to open it for us?'

The kid looked at the warrant, read a few lines, pulled a face as if it were written in Latin, and hesitated for a second. 'I . . . I think I need to call my boss for this.'

'What's your name, kid?' Decker asked.

'Billy.'

Billy was about five-foot-eight with short blond hair, which was spiked at places with styling gel. He had a three-day-old stubble and a couple of earrings in each ear.

'OK, Billy, you can call whoever you like, but we don't really have time to wait.' He nodded at the warrant. 'As Federal Marshal Hughes has explained, that piece of paper, which has been signed by a US federal judge, gives us the legal right to look inside unit 325, with or without your cooperation. Neither you nor we need your boss's permission to do so. That's all the permission we need right there. If you don't open the door for us, unfortunately for you, we're just going to have to bust it open, using any means necessary.'

'And we won't be legally responsible for any damage caused,' Figueroa added. 'Do you understand what I'm saying?'

Billy had started to look very uncomfortable. His cellphone beeped on the counter, announcing a new incoming text message, but he didn't even glance at it.

'That copy of the warrant stays with you,' Decker added. 'So you can show it to your boss, your lawyer, or whoever you please. That guarantees that you're not breaking the law, or company rules, or doing anything you shouldn't be doing.' He paused and checked his watch. 'We're on a pretty tight schedule here, Billy. So what's it going to be? Are we going to let us into the unit, or are we busting it open? You've got to make a choice.'

'You guys aren't punking me, are you?' Billy asked, his stare moving to the glass window behind both agents, as if he was trying to spot a candid camera somewhere.

'This is official, Billy,' Hughes replied, her tone telling Billy that that was no joke.

'You guys really FBI?' Billy now sounded a little thrilled.

'We really are,' Decker replied.

'Look, I'd like to help,' Billy said. 'I can let you into the building. No problem. But I can't open the door to unit 325 because it's padlocked. None of our doors has an actual key locking mechanism, just a very thick sliding bolt. Our customers can buy a padlock from us.' He quickly indicated a display just behind him with several padlocks in all different sizes. 'Or bring their own, but they're not required to supply us with an extra key, so none do. Once a unit is rented out, we don't have access to it anymore. It's a completely private affair.'

Figueroa nodded, and thought about it for a moment. 'OK. Can you give us the details of that account?'

'Sure.' Billy started typing something into the computer behind the reception desk. 'Here we go,' he said after just a few seconds. 'The unit is one of our medium, special ones – ten feet by ten feet.'

'Special?' Decker asked.

'Yeah,' Billy said. 'It's one of our units that's fitted with a power socket.'

'OK.'

'It was rented out eight months ago, on the fourth of January, to a Mr Liam Shaw,' Billy continued reading from his screen. 'He paid for it a whole year in advance . . . cash.'

'No surprise there,' Decker said.

'The unit is located on Corridor F,' Billy added. 'I can take you there now if you like.'

'Let's go,' Figueroa and Decker said at the same time.

Thirty-Six

Until they had some sort of confirmation that Lucien was telling the truth about the self-storage unit in Seattle, no one saw any point in moving forward with the interviews. Director Adrian Kennedy told Hunter and Taylor that Washington FBI agents, armed with a federal search warrant, had already been sent to verify the veracity of Lucien's statements, and they should have an answer in the next sixty minutes or less.

Taylor was sitting alone inside one of the conference rooms on sublevel three of the BSU building, staring at the untouched cup of coffee on the table in front of her, when Hunter opened the door and stepped inside.

'Are you OK?' he asked.

For a moment it seemed like Hunter's question hadn't reached her, then she slowly turned and looked up at him.

'Yeah, I'm fine.'

An awkward few silent seconds followed.

'You did well down there,' Hunter said in a non-patronizing or condescending tone.

'Oh, yeah,' Taylor replied with a sarcastic nod. 'Except for starting out with the wrong first question, you mean.'

'No,' Hunter told her, taking a seat across the table from her. 'That's where you're wrong, you see. No matter what first question you came up with, Courtney, Lucien would've thrown it back at you and tried to discredit you, tried to make you feel inferior, tried to shake your confidence and make you believe you're not good enough, because he wants to get under your skin. And he knows he's good at it. In college he used to bully professors that way.'

Taylor kept her eyes on Hunter.

'He wants to get under my skin too, but he knows me a little better than he does you, or at least he did, so right now he'll want to test the water with you to see how you respond, and he's going to keep on pushing harder and harder, you know that, don't you?'

'Let him push,' Taylor replied firmly.

'Just remember that to Lucien this is like a game, Courtney . . . his game, because he knows he has the upper hand. Right now, there's only one thing we can do.'

Taylor looked back at Hunter. 'We play the game,' she said.

Hunter shook his head. 'Not the game, we play *his* game. We give him what he wants. Make him believe he's winning.'

Adrian Kennedy pushed the conference-room door open and peeked inside. 'Ah, here you are.' He was carrying a blue dossier with him.

'Anything from Seattle yet?' Hunter asked.

'Not yet,' Kennedy responded. 'We're still waiting, but it doesn't look like Lucien was lying about the identities of the women found in his trunk.' He flipped open the dossier. 'Megan Lowe, twenty-eight years old. Born December 16 in Lewistown, Montana. She left Lewistown when she was sixteen, six months after her mother allowed her then boyfriend to move into their house.' Kennedy instinctively nodded at Hunter. 'She first moved to Los Angeles, where she spent the next six years. All indicates that she was indeed a street-working girl. After LA, Megan moved to Seattle. Line of work seemed to have stayed the same.' He turned a page on the report he was reading. 'Kate Barker, twenty-six years old. Born May 11 in Seattle, Washington. She left home when she was seventeen and moved in with a boyfriend, who at the time was an "aspiring musician". Not confirmed, but it seems like the boyfriend was the one who first got Kate to prostitute herself.'

'Money for drugs?' Taylor asked.

Kennedy shrugged. 'Probably. The abduction dates Lucien gave us, July second for Megan and July fourth for Kate, will be hard to confirm, as neither of them were ever reported missing.'

That wasn't surprising. Prostitutes account for the third-largest number of unsolved murders in the USA, just behind gang and drug-related killings. Every day thousands of street-working girls in America are raped, beaten up, robbed or abducted. They aren't targeted because of how attractive they look, or because they carry cash with them. They are targeted because they are easily accessible and extremely vulnerable, but most of all because they are anonymous. The vast majority of street-working girls live alone, or share with other working girls. They don't normally have a part-ner for obvious reasons. Many of them are runaways with little or no links to their families anymore. They live lonely lives, with very few friends. Statistically, only two in every ten street workers that go missing are ever reported to miss-ing persons.

Kennedy handed a copy of the report to Hunter and one to Taylor. The reports each carried a mugshot of their subjects. Both women, Megan Lowe and Kate Barker, had been arrested a couple of times for prostitution. Despite the mugshots, it was impossible for anyone to match the photographs to the two heads found inside Lucien's trunk, such was the brutality of the wounds inflicted on them.

'If Lucien wasn't lying about their identities,' Kennedy said, as he was leaving the room, 'chances are, he isn't lying about Seattle either.'

Thirty-Seven

The inside of the storage facility was just as brightly lit as the reception office, with extra-wide corridors and rounded corners for ease of movement with wheeled carts and pallet trucks. The resin floor had been painted in light green. The storage unit doors were all white with their respective numbers painted in black at the center of it, and again on the wall to the right of the door. It took Billy about two minutes to guide them through all the turns and hallways until they reached corridor F. Unit 325 was the third door on the left.

'Here we are,' Billy said, indicating the unit.

Just as he'd explained earlier, centered on the right-hand edge of the rolling door was a metal bolt, locked in place by a thick, brass-colored padlock.

Figueroa and Decker moved forward to have a better look at it.

Unlike the military-grade padlock that Lucien had used to secure the door to the basement in the house in Murphy, this one was a Master ProSeries, shrouded padlock, not as impenetrable, but still formidable.

'This is a pretty heavy duty padlock,' Figueroa said, looking at Decker and then at Billy. 'Do you think you can breach it with that bolt cutter?'

Billy had already assumed that he'd have to breach the padlock to the unit, and had brought with him a red and yellow forty-two-inch bolt cutter.

'No problem,' Billy said, stepping forward. 'We had to cut through a similar one a few weeks ago. I'm pretty sure this one will be no different.'

'So go right ahead and do your thing, Billy,' Figueroa said, stepping out of the way.

Billy moved closer, opened the jaws of the cutter as wide as it would go and carefully positioned them around one of the shrouded ends of the padlock's shackle. He put most of his weight behind the cutter, and gave it a firm squeeze.

Clank.

The cutter slid off the padlock as if nothing had happened, but they all saw something bounce onto the floor and slide away a couple of yards down the corridor. Billy had managed to cut off part of the protective shroud. Now the shackle was exposed on one side.

'I told you,' Billy said, nodding at the cutter. 'This bad boy is the shit. Now comes the easy part.' He placed the cutter jaws around the exposed shackle and gave it one more firm squeeze.

Click.

This time the cutter didn't slide off the padlock. Its jaws simply cut through the shackle as if slicing through wet clay.

Everyone looked impressed.

'I need to cut it again,' Billy explained. 'The shackle is too thick and too sturdy for us to be able to twist it out of place and free the lock. I need to cut a chunk off the shackle.'

'Knock yourself out, Billy,' Decker said.

Billy repeated the same steps as seconds earlier, this time placing the cutter's jaws about three centimeters up the shackle from where he'd cut through the first time.

Click.

As the cutters sliced through the metal again, a small piece fell to the ground, leaving a sizable gap on the padlock's shackle.

'And Bob's your uncle,' Billy announced triumphantly, removing the padlock from the door bolt.

'Great work, Billy,' Figueroa said.

Billy stepped away and Figueroa slid the door bolt back and rolled the metal door up. All four of them stood still for a moment, staring into the almost empty, ten feet by ten feet, storage unit. There was nothing there, except a large industrial chest freezer pushed up against the back wall.

'Thanks, Billy,' Decker said, slipping on a pair of latex gloves. Figueroa did the same. 'You can go back now. We'll call you if we need anything else.'

Billy looked disappointed. 'Can't I stay and have a look?'

'Not this time, Billy.'

They all waited until Billy had rounded the corner before entering the storage unit. Hughes stayed a couple of paces behind both agents.

A low hum that came from the freezer's motor provided a very unnerving and creepy background soundtrack. There was no padlock or lock on the freezer's lid.

Figueroa moved closer and studied the freezer for several seconds, checking underneath and behind it as well.

'Looks OK,' he said at last.

'So let's check inside,' Decker replied.

Figueroa nodded and lifted the lid open.

They all frowned in almost perfect synchronization as Figueroa, Decker and Hughes looked inside.

'What exactly are we looking for here, guys?' Hughes asked in a semi-sarcastic tone. 'Supplies for an ice-cream parlor?'

All they could see inside the large freezer were stacks of two-liter plastic tubs of ice cream. In fact, they were about three layers high. From the labels they could see on the top layer, they had a rainbow of flavors: chocolate, vanilla, strawberry, pistachio, cookies and cream, apple cinnamon, and banana choc-chip.

Decker was still frowning at all the tubs, but Figueroa had a much more concerned look on his face.

'Jesus Christ,' he finally said in a deflated breath, reaching for one of the tubs. He picked up a strawberry one.

Hughes and Decker were now frowning at him.

Holding the opaque white ice-cream tub with his left hand, Figueroa slowly pulled the lid undone.

Hughes' eyes went wide as she saw what was inside it. A second later, she vomited.

Thirty-Eight

Hunter and Taylor were called into Director Adrian Kennedy's office fifty-five minutes after Kennedy had left them with the report on Megan Lowe and Kate Barker.

The office, which was located on the third floor of the BSU building, was spacious and nicely decorated, without being too imposing. There was an old-fashioned mahogany desk, two dark brown Chesterfield leather armchairs, a furry rug that looked comfortable enough to sleep on, and a huge bookcase with at least one hundred leather-bound volumes. The walls were mostly adorned with framed diplomas, awards and photographs of Kennedy posing next to political and government notables.

Kennedy was sitting behind his desk, his reading glasses high up on his nose, staring at his 27-inch computer screen. 'Come in,' he called in response to the door knock.

Taylor pushed the door open and stepped inside. Hunter was just a couple of paces behind her.

'Don't sit down,' Kennedy said, motioning them to come closer and nodding at his screen. 'We got word from Seattle. Come have a look at this.'

Hunter and Taylor moved past the armchairs and positioned themselves behind Kennedy's desk. Hunter was to his left, Taylor to his right. The screen showed only Kennedy's desktop. He had minimized the application he was looking at.

'About forty minutes ago,' Kennedy began, 'two of our agents and a US federal marshal breached the padlock on the storage unit's door in Seattle. This is what they found inside.'

Kennedy clicked his mouse and brought back the application he had minimized seconds earlier. It was a regular image-viewing program.

'I received these photographs about five minutes ago,' he explained.

The first picture on the screen was taken from just outside storage unit 325's open door. It was a standard, wide-angle 'crime-scene' photograph, depicting the whole room. It gave everyone a good idea of the size of the unit. It also indicated how unsuspicious the space looked. Pushed up against the back wall, they could all see the large chest freezer.

Kennedy clicked the mouse again.

The second picture showed the freezer by itself, with its lid closed. Again, nothing suspicious there either.

Another click.

The third photograph was taken from an up/down view angle, showing what the agents saw as they lifted the freezer's lid.

For a moment, Taylor frowned at all the ice-cream tubs.

'From now on it gets sick,' Kennedy said, clicking his mouse again.

The image on the screen was substituted by a close-up snapshot of an agent holding one of the ice-cream tubs in his left hand. Its lid had been pulled open.

Taylor hesitated for a split second while squinting, trying hard to understand what exactly she was looking at . . . and then she finally saw it.

'Oh, Christ,' she whispered, bringing a hand to her mouth.

Hunter's stare stayed on the screen.

Frozen inside the ice-cream tub were two pairs of human eyeballs and a pair of human tongues.

It was easy to see why Taylor had struggled to understand the image at first. Due to dehydration and lack of blood, everything had shrunk in size. The eyeballs were on the left of the picture, stuck together like a bunch of grapes. The tongues sat to their right, also stuck together, one on top of the other, creating an odd X shape.

Kennedy gave Hunter and Taylor a few more seconds to study the picture before clicking his mouse again. The next image showed a second ice-cream tub. Inside it was a frozen human hand, severed at the wrist. No fingers. They had all been cut off.

Another click.

A second frozen hand inside an ice-cream tub.

One more click.

A different severed and frozen body part.

Kennedy stopped clicking.

'It carries on,' he said. 'There were sixty-eight ice-cream tubs inside that freezer. Every single one of them holding a frozen body part. Some of them held internal organs too, or parts of it . . . heart, liver, stomach . . . you get the picture, right?'

Hunter nodded.

'That section of the self-storage facility in Seattle has been locked down for the time being,' Kennedy explained.

'They guaranteed me two, three hours max, just so our forensics team can go over the entire unit and collect the freezer with all the ice-cream tubs. The lab will do a DNA analysis and compare it to the one we've got from the severed heads in Lucien's trunk. Not that I have too much doubt they'll match.'

Neither Hunter nor Taylor seemed to have any doubt either.

'The clerk working at the storage facility helped the agents breach the unit's door earlier, but he had no idea what was kept inside,' Kennedy moved on. 'We're keeping this as under wraps as we can. The press has got no word of it yet, and we'll try to keep it that way for as long as possible but, as we all know, Lucien Folter will have to be tried by a US court of law, so this story will eventually break. And when it does, it'll break big, because now I have no doubt that what we have locked up downstairs is a fucking monster, and this really is only the beginning.'

Thirty-Nine

Lucien Folter had just finished the last set of his exercise routine when he heard the heavy metal door at the end of the corridor unlock, followed shortly by the sound of footsteps. He got up from the floor, used the sleeve of his orange jumpsuit to wipe the sweat from his forehead, took a seat at the edge of his bed, and calmly waited. When Hunter and Taylor appeared before him and took the seats in front of his cell, Lucien had a proud smirk on his lips.

'I'm guessing you had confirmation from Seattle,' he said, his eyes slowly moving from Hunter to Taylor. Both of their faces carried nothing more than a blank expression. 'Too bad you didn't go there to see it for yourself. I think that I can safely say that my dismembering and chopping skills have become very polished over the years.'

'Have you disposed of all the bodies in the exact same way?' Taylor asked. She didn't seem affected by Lucien's bragging. 'By dismembering them?'

Lucien and Taylor held each other's stare for several seconds.

'No, not all of them,' he replied matter-of-factly. 'You see, Agent Taylor, at first, like all the scientists in your BSU, I was curious. I really wanted to understand what drives a person to kill without emotion or remorse. The big question in my head was – are all psychopaths born that way, or can one be created out of sheer will? I read everything on the subject I could get my hands on, and I found that none of it had any of the answers I was looking for. There's nothing out there, Agent Taylor, no book, no thesis paper, no detailed work of any kind that will tell you what really goes on in here.' He tapped his index finger against his right temple a couple of times. 'Inside the mind of someone who became a senseless killer, someone who taught himself to be a psychopath.' Lucien smiled cryptically. 'But you never know. Maybe one day that will change. But allow me to give you a little preview.'

Calmly Taylor crossed her right leg over her left one and waited.

Lucien began.

'What so many seem to fail to understand, Agent Taylor, is that there's a huge learning curve when it comes to becoming a man like me. I've had to evolve, adapt, improvise and become more resourceful throughout the years.' He gave them a quick shrug. 'But I always knew I would have to. Right from the start I wanted to try different things ... different methods ... different approaches, and though death is universal, essentially every victim has to be handled differently.' Lucien made it sound as if killing was nothing more than a simple lab experiment. 'But someone like me will always face one huge problem.'

'And that is?' Taylor asked, her interest measured.

Lucien smiled at her humorlessly.

'Well, while you have countless resources and teams of agents and officers working around the clock to catch criminals, Agent Taylor, people like me are lone souls. My resources were very limited. Everything I had to rely on was in my head.' He stared Taylor down coldly, still ignoring Hunter's gaze. 'I'm sure you are aware that not so long ago, the FBI published a study showing that at any one time there are at least five hundred serial killers loose in the USA.' He chuckled. 'Astonishing, isn't it? People like me are a lot less rare than what many might believe. I've encountered several other murderers throughout the years. People who *want* to torture and kill for no reason other than pure pleasure. People who hear voices, or think they do, telling them to go out and kill. People who believe they are doing some divine work on earth, ridding God's creation from sinners, or whatever. Or people who simply want to give their darkest desires wings. Some of them want to learn. They want to find someone who'd teach them. Someone like me.'

Lucien gave Hunter and Taylor a few seconds to fully savor the implications of what he'd said.

'If I wanted to take on an apprentice, do you really think it would take me long to find one? All I would have to do is search the streets of any major city in this great country of ours.' He spread his arms wide as if wanting to embrace the world. 'The streets of America are overflowing with the next Ted Bundy, the next John Wayne Gacy, the next Lucien Folter.'

As outrageous as the boastful claim sounded, Hunter knew Lucien was right.

'We could even have a talent show to search for America's next Superstar Serial Killer.' Lucien pulled a face as if he were seriously considering it. 'I should actually suggest that to some cable TV channels. And it wouldn't surprise me if one did consider such a show, because one thing is for sure – they would have a bigger audience than most of their other shit.'

Memories of Hunter's latest investigation with the LAPD exploded in his mind like fireworks – a serial killer who had created his own reality Internet murder show. And just like Lucien had suggested, the audience logged in to watch it in droves.

Lucien stood up, grabbed the plastic cup from the small metal table, walked over to the washing basin in the corner, and poured himself some water before returning to the edge of the bed.

'But returning to your question, Agent Taylor,' Lucien continued. 'I didn't always disposed of my bodies in the same way.' He had a sip of his water.

'Susan,' Hunter said, breaking his silence. 'You said she was your first victim.'

Lucien's attention turned to Hunter.

'I knew you'd want to start with her, Robert. Not only because she was a friend, but also because you're right. I *did* tell you that she was my first one. And that really is the perfect place to start, isn't it?' He took a deep breath and the look in his eyes changed, as if he weren't bound by the walls around him anymore. As if the memory and the images were so vivid he could touch them. 'So let me tell you how it all began.'

Forty

Palo Alto, California.
Twenty-five years earlier.

'So, are you really going to go traveling?' Lucien asked, placing a new round of drinks on the table.

Susan Richards nodded. 'I sure am.'

Lucien and Susan had both graduated in psychology from Stanford University just a week ago, and were still flying high on their achievement. They'd been celebrating every night since.

'Before I have to start job-hunting,' Susan said, reaching for her drink – a double Jack Daniel's and Coke. 'I want to take a little time for myself, you know? Visit some different places. Maybe even take a trip to Europe. I always wanted to go there.'

Lucien laughed. 'Job hunting? Have you gone mad? We just graduated from *Stanford*, Susan, which is the top psychology university in the country. If you decide not to start your own, practices from all over will be hunting you.'

'Is that what you're going to do?' Susan asked. 'Start your own practice?'

'Nah, I don't think so. I've been giving it a little thought lately, and I think that I might do the same as Robert.'

'PhD?'

'I've been thinking about it, yeah. What do you think?'

'Yeah, if that's what you really want, go for it, Lucien.'

Lucien tilted his head to one side and shrugged at the same time. 'I just might.'

'Talking about Robert,' Susan said, adjusting herself in her seat, 'it's a pity that he had to go back to LA today.'

Young Robert Hunter had been there for their graduation ceremony and for the first three nights of their week-long party spree, but he had taken the bus back to Los Angeles that morning to spend a week with his father, before he had to go back to Palo Alto to start his summer job.

'Yeah, I know,' Lucien replied, sipping his new cocktail.

They were sitting at The Rocker Club in Crescent Park, on the north side of Palo Alto. It was their favorite lounge – the staff were friendly, the booze was cheap, the crowd was usually young and up for a good time, and the music was rocking and upbeat.

'He does miss his father quite a bit,' Lucien added. 'It's the only family he's got left.'

'Yes, I know,' Susan said. 'His mother passed away when he was very young, didn't she?'

Lucien nodded. 'I think he was about seven or eight, but he never really talks about it. Even when he's a little drunk, Robert still manages to avoid the subject. I think that there's more to it than just standard trauma of losing a parent when young, you know?'

Susan paused halfway through sipping her drink. 'Oh, please don't.'

'What?'

'Please tell me that you're not going to be one of those dopey psychology graduates who can barely have a conversation with someone without psychoanalyzing them, Lucien. Especially your friends.'

'I . . .' Lucien shook his head with a half-embarrassed smile on his lips. 'I wasn't psychoanalyzing Robert.'

'Yes, you were.'

'No, I wasn't. I was just saying that we've shared the same tiny dorm room for four years. He's an odd person. Brightest guy I've ever met, but odd nonetheless, and I think that his mother's death might go a little deeper than he lets on.'

'Oh, really?' Susan said, putting her drink down on the table and pulling a face. 'Like what, for example, Doctor Lucien? Let's hear your theory.'

'I'm not a doctor, and I don't have a theory,' Lucien replied, pulling a face of his own. 'I was just saying . . .' He waved his hand in a dismissive gesture. 'Look, never mind. I'm not even sure why we're talking about this. We're here to party and celebrate.' He reached for his drink. 'So let's party and celebrate.'

Susan raised her glass. 'Yeah, I'll drink to that.'

Guns N' Roses' 'Sweet Child of Mine' started playing through the speakers. Lucien finished his cocktail in two big gulps.

'C'mon, let's go dance,' he said, getting to his feet.

'But . . .' Susan pointed at her drink.

'Drink it down, girl . . . rock and roll style,' Lucien replied, urging her with a series of hand movements. 'C'mon, c'mon, c'mon.'

Susan gulped her drink down, took Lucien's hand and allowed him to drag her to the dance floor.

A couple of hours and several drinks later they were both ready to leave. Susan looked to be really drunk, while Lucien looked in much better shape.

'I think we should leave your car here and take a cab,' Susan said. Her words were starting to skid into each other. 'You can pick it up tomorrow sometime.'

'Nah,' Lucien came back. 'I'm still good. I can drive.'

'No, you can't. You drank just as much as me, and I . . . am . . . wasted.'

'Yeah, but I was drinking cocktails, not double shots of JD and Coke. You know the cocktails here are mainly juice with a splash of booze. I could drink them all night and still be OK to drive home.'

Susan paused and regarded Lucien for a long instant. He did look quite steady on his feet, and he was right, the cocktails at the Rocker Bar weren't very strong.

'Are you sure you're OK to drive?'

'Positive.'

Susan shrugged. 'OK then, but you're driving slowly, you hear? I'm going to keep my eye on you.' She made a V with her index and middle fingers, pointed at her eyes, and then slowly moved her hand in the direction of Lucien's.

'Ten-four, ma'am,' Lucien said, giving her a military salute.

Lucien had parked down the road, just around the corner. At that time in the morning, the street looked deserted.

'Buckle up,' he said, taking the driver's seat. 'It's the law.' He smiled.

'Says the man who had a truckload of cocktails before taking the wheel,' Susan joked, struggling with the seatbelt.

Lucien waited, giving her the look.

'I'm trying, all right?' she said, a little flustered. 'I can't find the goddamn hole.'

'Here, let me help you.' Lucien leaned over, grabbed her seatbelt buckle, and quickly slid it into its lock. Then, with no warning, he moved a little closer and kissed her full on the lips.

Susan pulled back, surprised. 'Lucien, what are you doing?' It looked like she had gone sober all of a sudden.

'What do you think I was doing?'

A very awkward few seconds flew by.

'Lucien . . . I'm . . . very sorry if I've given you the wrong impression tonight, or any other night. You're a fantastic person, a really good friend, and I get along with you great, but . . .'

'But you don't have those kind of feelings for me.' Lucien finished Susan's sentence for her. 'Is that what you were about to say?'

Susan just stared at him.

'What if instead of me being the one sitting here, it were Robert?'

Susan was taken aback by the question.

'I bet you wouldn't pull back like you did. I bet you'd be all over him like a two-dollar whore. Your clothes would probably be gone, and you'd be sitting on his lap, undoing his belt with the utmost urgency.'

'Lucien, what the hell is going on? It's like I don't even know you right now.'

Lucien's eyes went stone cold, as if all the life and emotion had been sucked out of them.

'And what makes you think you knew me at all?'

The arctic tone of Lucien's words made Susan shiver. She was still struggling to understand what was happening when Lucien exploded into action, violently launching his body forward, and using his left hand to pin Susan's head against the passenger window.

Lucien hadn't fastened his seatbelt, which gave him a lot more freedom of movement.

Susan tried to scream, but Lucien rapidly slid his hand over her mouth, muffling whatever sounds came out of it. With his right hand, he opened the small compartment that sat between the two front seats and reached inside.

Susan grabbed at Lucien's left hand and tried to push it away ... tried to free her mouth ... her head, but even if she'd been sober, he'd still be way too strong for her.

'It's OK, Susan,' he whispered in her ear. 'It'll all be over soon.'

With incredible speed, Lucien's right hand shot toward Susan's face. She felt something prick the side of her neck, and in that instant their eyes met.

Hers full of fear.

His full of evil.

Forty-One

Lucien recounted the events that took place that night with the same enthusiasm as someone recollecting what he'd had for breakfast. All the while his eyes were locked on Hunter.

Hunter tried his best to remain impassive, but hearing Lucien's account of how he had subdued Susan had started to slowly tighten a knot in his throat. He shifted his weight in his chair, but never once broke eye contact with Lucien.

Lucien paused, had another sip of his water, and said nothing else.

Everyone waited.

Silence.

'So you drugged her,' Taylor said.

Lucien gave her an unenthusiastic smile. 'I injected her with Propofol.'

Taylor glanced at Hunter.

'It's a fast-acting general anesthetic,' Lucien clarified. 'It's incredible what you can get your hands on when you manage to get access to the medical school building at Stanford.'

'So what happened next?' Taylor asked. 'Where did you take her? What did you do?'

'No, no, no,' Lucien said with a slight shake of the head. 'It's my turn to ask a question. That was the agreement, was it not? So far, this "question game" has been very one-sided.'

'Fair enough,' Taylor agreed. 'Tell us what happened next and then ask your question.'

'No deal. It's my turn now. Time to finally feed my curiosity.' Lucien massaged the back of his neck for a moment before looking back at Hunter. 'Tell me about when you were a kid, Robert. Tell me about your mother.'

Hunter's jaw tightened.

Taylor looked a little confused.

'*Quid pro quo*,' Lucien said. 'You as cops, or profilers, or federal agents, or whatever, are always looking to try to understand what makes people like me tick, isn't that right? You're always trying to figure out how the mind of a ruthless killer works. How can a human being have such disregard for another human life? How can someone become a monster like me?' Lucien delivered every word in a steady, mono-sounding rhythm. 'Well, on the other hand, a monster like me would also like to know what makes people like you tick. The heroes of society ... the best of the best ... the ones who'd risk their lives for people they don't even know.' He paused for effect. 'You want to understand me. I want to understand you. It's as simple as that. And as Freud would tell you, Agent Taylor, if you want to delve deep into someone's psyche, if you want to understand the person they became, the best place to start is with their childhood and their relationship with their mother and father. Isn't that right, Robert?'

Hunter said nothing.

Lucien slowly cracked every knuckle on both of his hands. The creepy, bone-creaking sound reverberated against the walls in his cell.

'So, Robert, please indulge me in a twenty-five-year-old curiosity of mine, will you?'

'I don't think so, Lucien,' Hunter said, his voice as serene as a priest's in a confessional.

'Oh, but I do, Robert,' Lucien replied in the same peaceful tone. 'I really do. Because if you want to know any more about what happened to Susan, including where you could find her remains, you will indulge me.'

The knot in Hunter's throat got a little tighter.

'Tell me what happened, Robert? How did your mother die?'

Silence.

'And please don't lie to me, Robert, because I can assure you that I'll know if you do.'

Forty-Two

For a moment Hunter's memory flashed back to Susan
Richards' parents. He and Lucien had met them a couple of
times when they'd made the trip from Nevada to Stanford
to visit their daughter. They were a very sweet couple.
Hunter couldn't remember their names, but he remembered
how thrilled and proud they were of Susan for being
accepted into such a prestigious university. She was the first
person in either of their families to have ever gone to college.

Just like Hunter's parents, Susan's mother and father had
come from very poor backgrounds, and neither of them had
been able to finish high school, having to drop out before
their freshmen year and find jobs of their own to help their
families. When Susan was born, they'd promised themselves
that they would do whatever it took to offer their daughter
a better chance at life than the ones they had. When they
started saving for her college fund, Susan was only three
months old.

According to the law in the USA, death *in absentia*, or
presumption of death, occurs when a person has been missing from home and has not been heard from for seven years
or more, though the amount of years may vary slightly from
state to state. Despite what the law says, in the absence of
remains or any concrete proof, Hunter was sure that if

Susan Richards' parents were still alive, they'd still be holding on to a sliver of hope. The least he could do was give them some closure, and the chance to bury their daughter with dignity.

'My mother died of cancer when I was seven years old,' Hunter said. He still looked pretty relaxed in his seat.

Lucien smiled triumphantly. 'Yes, that much I already know, Robert. What type of cancer?'

'Glioblastoma multiforme.'

'The most aggressive type of primary brain cancer,' Lucien said, his voice emotionless. 'That must've been a tough blow. How fast did it develop?'

'Fast enough,' Hunter said. 'Doctors found it too late. Within three months of the diagnosis she passed away.'

It was Taylor's turn to shift her weight in her chair.

'Did she suffer?' Lucien asked.

Hunter's jaw tightened again.

Lucien leaned forward, placed his elbows on his knees, and very subtly started rubbing his hands against each other.

'Tell me, Robert.' The next four words were delivered slowly, with a pause between each of them. 'Did your mother suffer? Did she scream in pain at night? Did she go from being the strong, smiling, full-of-life person to an unrecognizable sack of skin and bones? Did she beg for death?'

Hunter could see that Lucien had switched his game, at least for the time being. He wasn't interested in getting under Taylor's skin anymore. Today, Hunter was his target. And Lucien was doing a damn good job.

'Yes,' Hunter replied.

'Yes?' Lucien said. 'Yes to what?'

'To everything.'

'So say it.'

Hunter breathed in.

Lucien waited.

'Yes, my mother suffered. Yes, she did scream in pain at night. Yes, she did go from being a strong, smiling, full-of-life person to an unrecognizable sack of skin and bones, and yes, she did beg for death.'

Taylor stole a peek at Hunter and felt goose bumps creep up all over her body.

'What was her name?' Lucien asked.

'Helen.'

'Was she in a hospital or at home when she died?'

'At home,' Hunter said. 'She didn't want to be in a hospital.'

'I see.' Lucien nodded. 'She wanted to be with her family . . . with her loved ones. Very noble, though strange and a little sadistic that she'd want her seven-year-old son to witness first-hand all of her suffering, all of her pain . . . and I'm guessing it must've been something quite excruciating.'

Through the avalanche of memories, keeping a steady face had become impossible. Hunter looked away and pressed his lips together, taking a moment. When he spoke again, his voice was as steady as he could muster, but there was no hiding the sadness in it.

'My mother worked as a cleaner for minimum wage. My father worked nights as a security guard, and to comple-ment the little money he earned, during the day he would take any odd job he could get. The end of each and every month was always a struggle in our house, even when they were both healthy. We had no savings because there was never anything left to save. My father's small health insurance wouldn't cover the costs. We couldn't afford the hospital bills. Back home was the only place she could be.'

A long, dragged silence.

'Wow, that's *one* sad story, Robert,' Lucien finally said coldly. 'I can practically hear the violins. Tell me, were you at home when your mother died?'

Hunter shook his head. 'No.'

Lucien returned to a regular seating position and nodded calmly before standing up. 'I told you that if you lied to me, Robert, I'd know. And that was a lie. This interview is over.'

Taylor's surprised gaze waltzed between Hunter and Lucien.

'Fuck Susan's remains,' Lucien said. 'You will never find those. Good luck explaining that to her family.'

Forty-Three

Lucien turned and slowly walked over to the washbasin.

Taylor tensed on her seat, but the awkward moment lasted just a few seconds before Hunter lifted both of his hands in a surrender gesture. 'OK, Lucien, I'm sorry.'

Lucien ran a hand through his hair, but kept his back to Hunter and Taylor. He took his time, as if he was considering Hunter's apology.

'Well, I guess I can't really blame you, can I, Robert?' he said at last. 'You needed to give it a shot to see if I could really tell if you were lying or not. It's only logical. Why would you trust me now? I could never tell with you before, could I? You never really had any telltale signs. You were always the one who could keep a straight face through any situation.' He finally turned to face his interrogators again. 'Well, old friend, I guess you're getting old, or perhaps it's because I've gotten much, much better at reading people.'

Hunter didn't doubt that for a second. Many serial killers become experts in observing people and reading their body language and hidden signs. It helps them choose the right victim and pick the precise moment to strike.

'So,' Lucien continued. 'For old times' sake, I'm going to let this one slide, but don't lie to me again, Robert.' He sat back down. 'Maybe you would like to rephrase your answer?'

A short pause.

'Yes, I was home when my mother died,' Hunter began again. 'As I'd said, my father worked nights as a security guard, and my mother passed away during the night.'

'So you were alone with your mother?'

Hunter nodded.

Lucien waited, but Hunter offered nothing more. 'Don't stop now, Robert. Did her screams scare you at night?'

'Yes.'

'But you didn't go hide in your room, did you?'

'No.'

'And why not?'

'Because I was more scared of not being there for her if my mother needed me.'

'And did she? On that last night? Did she need you?'

Hunter held his breath.

'Did she need you, Robert?'

Hunter saw something in Lucien's eyes that he hadn't noticed before – total certainty, as if he already knew all the answers, and if Hunter deviated from the truth even a little bit, Lucien would know.

'Yes,' Hunter finally replied.

'How did she need you?' Lucien asked. 'And remember, don't lie to me.'

'Pills,' Hunter said.

'What about them?'

'My mother used to take them. They made the pain go away, at least for a little while. But as the cancer grew stronger inside her, the effect of the pills grew weaker.'

'So she needed more,' Lucien said.

Hunter nodded.

A pensive look came over Lucien's face; a moment later, his lips stretched into a wicked smile.

'But they were prescription painkillers, right?' he said. 'Probably very strong, probably schedule two, probably opioids, which means that exceeding the dosage was a big no-no. Those pills weren't by her bedside, were they, Robert? They couldn't have been. The risk of accidental overdose would've been too great. So where were they? In the bathroom? In the kitchen? Where?'

Silence.

'The pills, Robert, where were they kept?' Lucien insisted. Hunter could hear the threat in his voice.

'My father kept them in the cupboard, in the kitchen.'

'But your mother asked you for them that night.'

'Yes.'

Lucien scratched the scar on his left cheek.

'She couldn't handle the pain anymore, could she?' he pushed. 'She'd rather be dead. In fact, she begged for death, and you were the messenger, because you brought them to her, didn't you? How many pills did you bring her, Robert?' Then it dawned on him and he lifted a hand at the same time as his eyes widened a touch. 'No, wait. You brought her the whole bottle, didn't you?'

Hunter said nothing, but his memory took him back to that night.

Nights were always worse. Her screams sounded louder, her groans deeper and heavier with pain. They always made him shiver. Not like when he felt cold, but an intense shiver that came from deep within. Her illness had brought her so much pain, and he wished there was something he could do to help.

Seven-year-old Robert Hunter had heard his mother's painful screams and had cautiously opened the door to her room. He felt like crying. Since she'd gotten ill, he felt a lot like crying, but his father had told him he mustn't.

Her illness had made her look so different. She was so thin he could see her bones poking at her sagging skin. Her striking long blonde hair was now fine and frizzled. Her once-sparkling eyes had lost all the life in them and had sunk deep into their sockets.

Shaking, he paused by the door. His mother was curled up into a ball on the bed. Her knees pushed up against her chest. Her arms wrapped tightly around her legs. Her face contorted in pain. She screwed up her eyes and tried to focus on the tiny figure standing at the door.

'Please, baby,' she whispered as she recognized her son. 'Can you help me? I can't take the pain anymore.'

It took all his strength to keep his tears locked in his throat. 'What can I do, Mom?' His voice was as weak as hers. 'Do you want me to call Dad?'

She managed only a delicate shake of the head. 'Dad can't help, honey, but you can. Could you come here . . . please. Can you help me?'

His mother looked like a different person now. Her eyes had the darkest bags under them. Her lips were cracked and crusted.

'I can heat up some milk for you, Mom. You like hot milk.'

He would do anything he could to see his mother smile again. As he stepped closer, she winced as a new surge of pain took over her body.

'Please, baby. Help me.' Her breath was coming in short gasps.

Despite what his father had told him, he simply couldn't hold his tears anymore. They started rolling down his face.

His mother could now see he was scared and shaking. 'It's OK, honey. Everything will be fine,' she said in a trembling voice.

He stepped closer still and placed his hand in hers.

'I love you, Mom.'

His words brought tears to her eyes. 'I love you too, honey.' She gave his hand a subtle squeeze. It was all she could muster with the little strength she had left in her. 'I need your help, honey . . . please.'

'What can I do, Mom?'

'Can you get my pills for me, honey. You know where they are, don't you?'

He ran the back of his right hand against his running nose. He looked scared. 'They're very high up,' he said, hiding his eyes from her.

'Can't you reach them for me, baby? Please, the pain has been going on for so long. You don't know how much it hurts.'

His eyes were so full of tears everything appeared distorted. His heart felt empty, and he felt as if all his strength had left him. Without saying a word, he slowly turned around and opened the door.

His mother tried calling after him, but her voice was so weak, it didn't travel more than just a few yards.

He came back a few minutes later carrying a tray with a glass of water, two cream biscuits and the bottle of medicine. She stared at it, hardly believing her eyes. Very slowly, and through unimaginable pain, she pushed herself up into a sitting position. He stepped closer, placed the tray on the bedside table and handed her the glass of water.

She wanted to hug him so much, but she barely had the strength to move; instead, she gave him the most honest smile he'd ever seen. She tried, but her fingers were way too weak to twist the bottle cap open. She looked at him, and her eyes begged for help.

He took it from her trembling hands, pressed down on the cap and twisted it counterclockwise, before pouring two of the pills onto her hand. She placed them in her mouth and swallowed them down without even sipping the water. Her eyes pleaded for more.

'I read the label, Mom. It says you shouldn't have more than eight a day. The two you just had make it ten today.'

'You're so intelligent, my darling.' She smiled again. 'You're very special. I love you so much and I'm so sorry I won't see you grow up.'

His eyes filled with tears once again as she wrapped her bony fingers around the medicine bottle.

He held on to it tightly.

'It's OK,' she whispered. 'It'll all be OK now.'

Hesitantly, he let go. 'Dad will be angry with me.'

'No, he won't be, baby. I promise you.' She placed two more pills in her mouth.

'I brought you these biscuits.' He pointed to the tray. 'They're your favorite, Mom. Please have one. You didn't eat much today.'

'I will, honey, in a while.' She had a few more pills. 'When Daddy comes home in the morning, tell him I love him, and that I always will. Can you do that for me?'

The boy nodded. His eyes locked on the now almost empty medicine bottle.

'Why don't you go read one of your books, darling? I know you love reading.'

'I can read in here, Mom, so you're not alone. I can sit in the corner if you like. I won't make a noise, I promise.'

She extended her hand and touched his hair. 'I'll be OK now, honey. The pain's starting to go away.' Her eyelids looked heavy.

'I'll guard the room then. I'll sit just outside the door.'

She smiled a pain-stricken smile. 'Why do you wanna guard the room, honey?'

'You told me that sometimes God comes and takes ill people to heaven. I don't want him to take you, Mom. I'll sit by the door and if he comes I'll tell him to go away. I'll tell him that you're getting better and not to take you.'

'You'll tell God to go away?'

He nodded vigorously.

She started crying again. 'I'm going to miss you so much, Robert.'

Taylor looked at Hunter and felt her heart shrivel inside her chest.

A cold smile began to crack on Lucien's lips, like ice over a dark, frozen lake. 'So you left the room,' he said.

Hunter nodded.

'And that was when the nightmares started,' Lucien said in conclusion, like a psychologist who had finally broken through a patient's barrier.

A disconcerting silence took over the entire basement corridor, but not for long. With his gaze fixed on Lucien, Hunter finally let go of the memory.

'Susan, Lucien,' he said. The sadness had vanished from his voice. 'You have what you wanted, now tell us what happened after you drugged her in the car?'

Forty-Four

La Honda, 18 miles from Palo Alto, California.
Twenty-five years earlier.

Susan Richards was jolted awake by the loud sound of a heavy door slamming shut. Despite the sudden noise, her eyes opened slowly, blinking constantly, as if grains of sand had been blown into them and were now scratching at her cornea. Her eyelids felt heavy and tired, and no matter how hard she tried, she couldn't get her eyes to focus on anything. Everything around her came as nothing but a big blur.

The first thing she realized was how dizzy she felt, as if she were stuck in a hazy dream with no way of waking up. Her mouth was bone dry and her tongue felt like sandpaper. Then she noticed the smell – dirty, damp, moldy, old and sickening. She had no idea where she was, but it smelt as if the place had been neglected for years. In spite of the horrible stench, Susan's lungs demanded that she took in a full breath of air, and as she did, she could almost taste the rancid quality of the room. One deep breath and it made her gag.

All of a sudden, between desperate coughs, sharp and excruciating pain came to her. It took her exhausted body a few seconds to finally home in on it. It was coming from her right arm.

Susan realized then that she was sitting down on some sort of hard and terribly uncomfortable chair. Her wrists were tied together behind the chair's backrest, her ankles to the chair's legs. She was soaking wet, drenched with sweat. She tried lifting her head, which was awkwardly slumped forward, and the movement sent waves of nausea rippling through her stomach.

She couldn't identify the light source inside the room, maybe a corner lamp or an old light bulb hanging overhead, but whatever it was, it bathed the room in a weak yellowish glow. Her eyes finally moved right and tried to focus on her arm and the source of the pain. She still felt groggy, so it took a moment for her vision to steady itself and for the blurriness to dissipate. When it did, her heart was filled with terror.

'Oh, my God.' The words dribbled out of her lips.

An enormous chunk of skin was missing from her arm – from her shoulder all the way down to her elbow. In its place she saw raw, blood-soaked flesh. For an instant, it looked as if the wound were alive. Blood was cascading down her arm, over her hands, through her fingers, and onto the concrete floor, forming a large crimson pool at the feet of the chair.

Instantly, Susan jerked her head away and vomited all over her lap. The effort made her feel even weaker, even dizzier.

'Sorry about that, Susan,' she heard a familiar voice say. 'You could never really stand the sight of blood, could you?'

Susan coughed a few more times and tried to spit the awful vomit taste from her mouth. Her eyes moved forward, finally focusing on the figure standing in front of her.

'Lucien . . .' she said in a feeble whisper.

Flash images of last night at the Rocker Club came back to her. Then she remembered sitting in Lucien's car . . . the angry way he had looked at her. And then nothing.

'What . . .' She was unable to finish the sentence, her throat way too frail to produce the sounds. Instinctively, her eyes shot toward the raw flesh in her right arm once again and her whole body shivered.

'Oh,' Lucien said, unconcerned, reaching behind him. 'Don't worry about that. I don't think you'll miss this horrible thing, will you?'

He showed her a large glass jar filled with some pale pink liquid. Something was floating in it. Susan squinted, forcing her tired eyes, but still couldn't tell what it was.

'Oh, sorry,' Lucien said, picking up on her confusion and reaching inside the jar with his gloved hand to collect the floating object. 'Allow me to show you. The edges have curled in a little bit now.' He uncurled them and stretched the wet piece of skin he had carved off her arm less than an hour ago. 'This is a hideous tattoo, Susan. I have no idea why you'd think that this is cool in any way.'

Acid-tasting bile found its way back into Susan's mouth, resulting in a new desperate gagging/coughing frenzy.

Amused, Lucien waited until it was over.

'But I think that it will make a great token,' he said, nodding a couple of times. 'And do you know what? I do think that I will give the "token collector" thing a shot. See how it makes me feel. Test the theory behind it. What do you think?'

Susan's head throbbed with the rhythm of her thudding heart. The rope that had been used to tie her wrists and ankles felt as if it had cut through to her bones. She wanted to speak, but fear seemed to have erased every word from her terrified mind. Her eyes, on the other hand, mirrored her fear and desperation.

Lucien returned the tattooed piece of skin to the jar.

'You know,' he said, 'I've had that syringe hidden in my car for almost a year now. I thought about using it many times.'

Susan breathed in and the air seemed to travel into her nose in lumps.

'But never on you,' Lucien moved on. 'I thought about picking up a prostitute many times. As I know you'll remember from our criminology classes, they are easy targets – approachable, accessible and, most of the time, anonymous.' He shrugged indifferently. 'But unfortunately it didn't quite work out that way. I never really felt ready for it before, but tonight I felt different. I guess I can say that tonight I felt my first *real* "killer's" impulse.'

Tears welled up in Susan's eyes. To her, the air inside the room became denser, even more polluted ... almost unbreathable.

'I felt this amazing drive to simply do it and not think of the consequences,' Lucien said.

His eyes shone with a new purpose. Susan saw it, and that sent a new current of panic traveling through her body.

'So I decided not to fight it,' he proceeded, moving a step closer. 'I decided to act on it. So I did. And here we are.'

Susan tried to calm her breathing, tried to think, but everything still felt like a horrible dream. But if it were, why wasn't she waking up?

'Lucien ...' she said, her voice rasping, catching on her swollen throat, '... I don't kno—'

'No, no, no,' Lucien interrupted, shaking his left index finger at her. 'There's nothing you can say. Don't you see,

Susan? There's no turning back now.' He stretched his arms out to his sides, calling attention to the room. 'We're here now. The process has started. The floodgates are open, or any cliché sentence you'd care to come up with. But no matter what, this is happening.'

That was when Susan noticed the look in Lucien's eyes – distant and ice cold, like a man without a soul. And it paralyzed her.

Her fear filled Lucien with excitement. He was expecting that excitement to conflict with something inside of him – maybe morals, or emotions . . . he wasn't quite sure what, but something. That conflict never came. He felt nothing but exhilaration to be finally doing something he'd fantasized about for so long.

Susan wanted to speak, to scream, but her panic-frozen lips wouldn't move. Instead, her eyes begged him for mercy . . . mercy that never came.

Without any warning, Lucien exploded forward, and in a flash his hands were on Susan's neck.

Her eyes went wide with terror, her neck muscles tightened as her body tried to defend itself from the attack, her jaw dropped open, gasping for air, but her brain knew that the battle was already lost. Lucien's thumbs were already compressing Susan's airway, while his large palms were applying enough pressure to the carotid arteries and jugular veins to cause significant occlusion, and interfere with the flow of blood in her neck.

When Susan's body started kicking and wriggling on the chair, Lucien placed most of his body weight on her lap to keep her steady. That was when he felt something collapse under his thumbs. He knew then he had just crushed her larynx and trachea. Susan would be dead in seconds, but

Lucien never stopped squeezing, at least not then. He carried on until he had fractured the hyoid bone in her neck, all the while his mad and frantic-looking eyes locked on to Susan's dying ones.

Forty-Five

Hunter sat in silence. Not once did he interrupt Lucien's account of events, which was conveyed coldly and without sentiment, but all throughout it Hunter fought to keep his emotions in check.

Taylor had also listened to everything in silence, no interruptions, but she found herself shifting in her chair at least a couple of times. Every tiny nervy movement she made seemed to please and amuse Lucien more and more.

'Before you ask,' Lucien said, looking at Hunter, 'there was no sexual gratification. I did not touch Susan in that way.' He shrugged. 'Truth be told, she was never supposed to be my first. She was never supposed to be a victim at all. She was never part of the thousands of fantasies I had before that day. It was just very unfortunate that it happened that way.'

'Thousands?' Taylor asked.

Lucien smiled. 'Please don't be so naive, Agent Taylor. Do you think that people like me just suddenly decide to start killing and that's that? We're ready to go out the next day and pick our first victim?' He shook his head sarcastically. 'People like me fantasize about hurting others for a long time, Agent Taylor. Some might start fantasizing when kids, some a lot later in life, but we all do, and we do it all the time. Me, I guess I can say that my fascination with death started very early. You see, my father was a great hunter. He used to take me hunting up on the mountains in Colorado, and there was something about waiting, stalking, and looking straight into the animal's eyes just before pulling the trigger that captivated me.'

Lucien scratched his chin while regarding Hunter. Then he smiled.

'Look at you, Robert. I can practically hear your brain working. The psychologist in you already starting to make theoretical connections between my early hunting days and the killer I became.' He laughed. 'Before you ask, I didn't wet the bed when I was a kid, and I never liked setting fire to anything.'

Lucien was referring to the Macdonald triad: a psychology-based theory that suggests that a set of three behavioral individualities – animal cruelty, obsession with fire setting, and persistent bedwetting past the age of five – if all are present together while young, can be associated with violent tendencies later in life, particularly homicidal behavior. Though studies have shown that statistically no significant links between the triad and violent offenders have been found, if the triad is split, animal cruelty is by far the individuality that had been proven to manifest itself in the early lives of a great number of apprehended serial killers. Hunter was well aware of that.

Lucien used his index finger to pick at something that was stuck between his two front teeth. 'Well, knock yourself out, old buddy. Analyze what you like, but I'm sure I will surprise you.'

'You already have.'

The edges of Lucien's lips curved up smugly.

'Despite my hunting days,' he continued, 'it was during my first year in high school that I started having dreams.'

Interest grew across Taylor's face.

'In these dreams I wasn't hunting. I was hurting people. Sometimes people I knew, sometimes people I had never seen before ... just random creations of my imagination. They were very violent, and supposedly scary dreams, but they filled me with excitement, they made me feel good, so good that I didn't want to wake up. I didn't want them to stop ... and that was when I started fantasizing during the day, while wide-awake. The star role in these ...' Lucien searched the air around him for the right words: '... let's say, "intense fantasies" of mine, usually belonged to people I disliked ... teachers, school bullies, some family members ... but not always.' He paused and made a 'whatever' face. 'Anyway, Susan was never one of them. She was never part of any of my violent fantasies or dreams. She just happened to fit the *perfect* profile that night.'

Lucien stood up, crossed over to the washbasin and refilled his cup with water.

'That was the real reason I wanted to study psychology and criminal behavior,' he continued, returning to the edge of the bed. 'To try to understand what was going on in my head. Why I had these violent fantasies swimming around in here.' He tapped his right temple with the tip of his index finger. 'Why I enjoyed them so much, and if there was anything I could do to get rid of them.' He chuckled. 'But wouldn't you know it? College had the adverse effect. The more I studied and the more theories I read about how psychologists believed the mind of a killer worked, the more intrigued I became.' Lucien paused and had a sip of water. 'I wanted to test them.'

'Test them?' Taylor asked. 'Test who, or what?'

'The theories,' Hunter said, reading between the lines.

Taylor looked at him.

Lucien pointed at him and made a face as if saying, *You got it in one, Robert.* 'I wanted to test the theories.' He leaned forward a little. 'Weren't you intrigued, Robert? As a student with such an eager mind, didn't you want to understand what *really* goes on inside a killer's head? What *really* makes them tick? Didn't you want to know if the theories we were taught were true, or just a pile of shit guesses put together by a bunch of nerd psychologists?'

Hunter continued studying Lucien in silence.

'Well, I did,' Lucien said. 'The more theories I studied, the more I compared them to how my fantasies made me feel. And then, one of those theories finally proved true for me.'

Lucien looked at Taylor in a way that made her feel naked, vulnerable.

'Care to take a guess at what theory that was, Agent Taylor?'

Taylor refused to be intimidated. 'The theory that says you need to be a sick scumbag and fucked in the head to do what you did?' Taylor replied, no anger or excitement in her voice.

It only made Lucien smile. 'Robert?' His gaze moved toward Hunter and his eyebrows arched.

Hunter wasn't in the mood for games, but Lucien was still holding all the cards.

'Fantasies may one day not be enough,' he said.

Lucien's smile widened before he addressed Taylor again. 'He really *is* good, isn't he? That's right, Robert. I carried on fantasizing until one day I realized that the fantasies just weren't enough. They weren't making me feel as good as they used to. I realized that to get the same high, I needed to move it to the next level.' His stare settled back on Hunter as if he owed him a debt of gratitude. 'Then you said something that triggered everything, Robert.'

Forty-Six

If Lucien was expecting any sort of reaction from Hunter, he was disappointed. Hunter stayed perfectly still, matching Lucien's stare. It was Taylor who showed surprise.

'How do you mean?' she asked, wiggling her body on her chair.

Lucien kept his eyes on Hunter a little longer, still looking for a reaction.

Nothing.

'Robert and I used to have very long discussions about many of those theories,' Lucien began. 'It was only natural. Two young and hungry minds trying to make sense of the crazy world we lived in, trying to be the best students we could be. But it was during a debate in our second year at Stanford that Robert said something that really got my brain going.'

Taylor peeked at Hunter.

Hunter kept his attention on Lucien.

'I'll clarify it for you, Agent Taylor,' Lucien offered with a smirk. 'We were studying brain physiology. The debate was whether science would one day find a way to identify a sector of our brain, no matter how small, that controlled our urges to doing something, anything, including becoming a killer.'

Lucien looked at Hunter. Even without any acknowledgment, he knew Hunter remembered that debate.

'I hope you don't mind if I use the same example as you did then, Robert,' Lucien said. 'I still remember it well.' He didn't wait for a reply from Hunter. 'Two brothers,' Lucien began, addressing Taylor, 'identical twins. Grew up under identical circumstances and environment. Both were shown the same amount of love and affection by their parents. They went to the same schools, attended the same classes, and were taught the same moral values. Both very popular students. Both very good students.' Lucien shrugged. 'Attractive too. The point I'm trying to put across here, Agent Taylor, is that there was absolutely no difference in their upbringing.'

Taylor's frown was minimal, but Lucien noticed it.

'Stay with me,' he said, 'things will get clearer. Now, let's say that these two brothers became avid music fans.' Lucien winked at Hunter. 'And they both liked the same style of music and the same music groups. They changed their looks and hairstyles to match the ones of their idols. They bought the albums.' Lucien paused and smiled. 'Well, that was back then, now they would just download the music, isn't that right? Anyway, they had the T-shirts, the baseball hats, the posters, the badges ... everything. They went to every concert that came to their town. But there was one difference. Brother "A" was content in just being a music fan. He was happy with just going to the gigs, listening to the songs back in his room, and dressing up like his idols. Brother "B", on the other hand, wanted something more. Just being a fan, going to gigs, and listening to the music wasn't enough for him. Something inside him told him that he needed to be part of the music circus. He needed to experience the real deal for himself. So brother "B" learns how to play an instrument, and he joins a band. And there we have it.'

Lucien allowed his words to float in the air, giving Taylor a moment to digest them before moving on.

'It's that little difference that makes *all* the difference, Agent Taylor. Why does brother "B", after growing up in identical circumstances, wants something that little bit more than brother "A"? Why is one content with just being a fan, and the other isn't?'

If Taylor was trying to think of an answer, Lucien didn't wait.

'That same theory can be easily transposed across to the desire to murder.' This time his smirk was even more confident. 'Some people with violent tendencies may be content with just fantasizing, with watching violent films, or reading violent books, or looking at violent pictures on the Internet, or punching a punch bag, or whatnot, but some . . .' He shook his head slowly. 'Some will feel the need to go that little bit further. To become brother "B". And it's this drive, the drive that makes us want something more than others, that Robert argued he didn't think science will ever be able to pinpoint, at least not physically, because that drive is what makes us individuals. It's what makes us all different from each other.'

Hunter kept on observing Lucien. He was getting excited with his own discourse, like a preacher in a church. Even more so because he could see that he'd made Taylor wonder.

'Are you saying that Robert's debate argument all those years ago is what tipped you into starting killing?' Taylor said with a sarcastic lilt to her voice. 'Are you looking for someone else to blame for everything you've done? Well, that's typical.'

Lucien threw his head back and laughed animatedly. 'Not at all, Agent Taylor. I've done what I've done because I wanted to.' He pointed a finger at Hunter. 'But physiology aside, that argument got me thinking, old friend, because that was when I realized that that was exactly what I needed to do. I needed to stop fantasizing. I needed to stop fighting the urge. I needed to move it to the next level . . . brother "B". So I started planning. You see, one of the great things about studying criminology, Agent Taylor, is that we learn about some of the most infamous killers that have walked this earth. And believe me, I studied them in depth. I read and subscribed to specialized newspapers and magazines. I studied the writings of numerous prominent forensic psychiatrists. I learned about sex murderers, serial murderers, military murderers, mass murderers, and professional murderers. I studied massacres and murder conspiracies. I learned just about everything I could on the subject, but the one thing I paid particular attention to was . . . perpetrators' mistakes. Especially the mistakes that led to their capture.'

Taylor decided to bite back. 'Well, it looks like you didn't pay that much attention after all, given your current predicament.' She allowed her eyes to circle around his cell.

Lucien didn't seem bothered by Taylor's sharp comment.

'Oh, I paid more than enough attention, Agent Taylor. Unfortunately no one can foresee accidents. The only reason I'm sitting here right now is not because I made a mistake, or due to any merit of your own or the organization you work for, but because an unfortunate chain of chance events took place seven days ago. Events that were out of my control. Admit it, Agent Taylor, the FBI had no idea I existed. You weren't investigating me, any of my aliases, or any of the acts I committed.'

'We would have eventually got to you,' Taylor said.

'But of course you would.' Lucien grinned confidently. 'Anyway, as I was saying, I started planning. And the first thing on my list was to find an isolated and anonymous place. Somewhere where I wouldn't be disturbed. A place where I could take my time.'

'And you found such a place in La Honda,' Hunter said.

'I sure did,' Lucien confirmed. 'Just an old, abandoned little house in the middle of the woods. It was close enough to Stanford that it wouldn't take me long to get there. And the best thing about it was that I could use remote back roads to reach it. No one would spot me.'

Lucien stood up and stretched his powerful frame.

'The place is still there,' he said. 'I visited it not that long ago.' He didn't sit back down. 'You know what? I've got a little bit of a headache and I'm getting hungry. So what do you say we all take a break?' He pulled his sleeve up and looked at his wrist as if he had a watch. 'Let's start again in two hours, how does that sound?'

'Not good, Lucien,' Hunter said. 'Susan's remains, where are they?'

'Another two hours before you find out won't make a difference, Robert. It's not like you have to rush to save her, is it now?'

Forty-Seven

Outside, the sun was shining bright in yet another cloudless sky. It was the kind of warm and joyful day that made most people smile for no apparent reason, but the magic of the day didn't seem to reach as far as the BSU building.

Hunter had found an empty meeting room somewhere on the second floor. He was standing by the window, staring out at nothing at all, when Taylor stepped inside and softly closed the door behind her.

'So there you are.'

Without turning, Hunter checked his watch. It had only been ten minutes since they'd left Lucien in his cell, but to him it felt like hours.

'Are you all right?' Taylor asked, stepping closer.

'Yeah, I'm fine,' Hunter replied, his voice firm and confident.

Taylor hesitated an instant. 'Listen, I need to get out of here for a while.'

Hunter turned and looked at her.

'I need to go outdoors for an hour or so, breathe some fresh air or something before I go back down into that basement.'

Hunter could easily sympathize with her argument.

'I know a place not very far from here where on a day like this, they'll have tables outside,' Taylor added. 'Their food is great, but if you're not hungry, their coffee is even better. What do you say we get the hell out of here for a bit?'

She didn't have to ask twice.

Forty-Eight

Despite them having had their last meal over four and a half hours earlier, neither Hunter nor Taylor felt like eating. Hunter ordered a simple black coffee, while Taylor went for a double espresso. They were sitting at one of the outside tables at a small Italian cantina-style restaurant in Garrisonville Road, less than fifteen minutes' drive from the FBI Academy.

Taylor stirred her coffee and watched the thin layer of dark brown foam slowly disappear from the surface. She thought about telling Hunter how sorry she was for what had happened to his mother. She thought about maybe telling him about her own mother, but as she thought better of it she decided that neither subject would benefit anyone. She finished stirring her coffee and placed the spoon down on the saucer.

'What did Lucien mean when he said that your friend Susan just happened to fit the perfect profile that night?' she asked.

Hunter was waiting for his coffee to cool down a little. He'd never been one of those people like Carlos Garcia, his partner back at the LAPD, who could pretty much pour boiling hot coffee into a cup, give it five seconds, and then drink it down as if it were just lukewarm.

Hunter raised his eyes at Taylor.

'Lucien and Susan, had both just graduated from Stanford,' he said. 'For Susan, her college days were over. She didn't need to be in class anymore. She had no job, no boss, no boyfriend, no husband, no "punching the clock" anywhere, so to speak. Her family lived in Nevada. No one was expecting to hear from Susan again soon, especially because she had already let everyone know that after graduation, she had her mind set on traveling.'

'So, if she disappeared,' Taylor said, picking up on Hunter's line of thought, 'people would've just assumed that she'd really acted on her promise of traveling. No reason for anyone to get worried, at least not for a while.'

'Exactly,' Hunter agreed. 'The circumstances of that particular moment in time made her the best possible kind of victim. The anonymous kind. The unmissed. And Lucien knew that very well.'

A tall and young-looking waitress, with her long dark hair pulled back into a fishtail braid, stepped up to their table.

'Are you sure you wouldn't like to have a look at the menu?' she asked with a hint of an Italian accent. 'I can recommend the gnocchi with the chef's special cheese, tomato and basil sauce.' She gave them a charming smile. 'It's so good you'll want to lick the plate.'

Gnocchi was Hunter's favorite Italian dish, but he still had no appetite.

'Wow, that does sound very tempting,' he said, matching her smile. 'But I'm not very hungry today. Maybe another time.' He nodded at Taylor.

'Yeah, I'm not hungry either. Just the coffee for me today, thanks.'

'No problem,' the waitress said. She paused. Looked back at them. 'I hope you guys work things out,' she added kindly. 'You look good together.' She gave them one last sympathetic smile before moving over to take the order of a small group sitting just a few tables away.

'Is that the vibe we're giving out?' Taylor asked once the waitress was out of earshot. 'That we're a couple trying to work things out?'

Hunter had an amused smile on his lips. He shrugged. 'I guess.'

For an instant, Taylor almost looked embarrassed, but in a flash her game face was back on. 'Do you really believe that Susan was never part of any of Lucien's violent fantasies?' she asked. 'Do you believe she really was his first ever victim? And that he didn't rape her?'

Hunter leaned back on his chair. 'Why do you think he would lie about any of that?'

'I'm not sure. I guess that what I'm trying to understand is – if Susan really was Lucien's first ever victim, and he'd never had any "violent fantasies" about her, how come he went for her and not someone else . . . a stranger?'

Hunter frowned. 'I thought we just covered that a minute ago.'

'No, I'm not talking about that particular night, or even that week, Robert. What I'm talking about is that despite the circumstances back then, giving Susan the quality of "perfect victim", unless it was all an act, she and Lucien were supposed to be "friends". From what he said, he even had some romantic interest in her, which suggests some sort of emotional attachment.'

Hunter's coffee had cooled down enough for him to have a healthy sip. 'And you're thinking, it's got to be a lot harder for a perpetrator to kidnap, partially skin, and then kill someone he knew, someone who was supposedly a friend, someone who he had a crush on.'

'Exactly.' Taylor nodded. 'Especially if that person is his first ever victim. If Lucien hadn't fantasized about killing Susan in particular, then why torture and kill a "friend"? He could've easily found another anonymous victim – a total stranger – someone he could've picked up in a bar or a club, a hooker, I don't know, but someone who he had zero feelings for, someone he couldn't care less about.'

'And to Lucien, that was exactly who Susan was.'

Taylor frowned.

'You're trying to look at it with your own eyes, Courtney,' Hunter said, putting his coffee cup back down on the table. 'You're trying to understand it with your own mind. And when you do that, your emotions get in the way. You have to try to look at it through Lucien's eyes. His psychopathy isn't victim-centered.'

Taylor held Hunter's gaze for a long while. Every agent with the FBI's Behavioral Science Unit is aware that there are two major types of aggressive psychopaths. The first kind – victim-centered – are the ones to whom the victim is the most important part of the equation. The perpetrator fantasizes about a *specific* type of victim, so everyone he chooses has to match that type, fit the profile. And it usually boils down to physical type. With victim-centered psychopaths, the whole fantasy revolves around the way the victim looks. It's the victim's physical attributes that excites and 'turns them on'. Most of the time because it reminds them of someone else. In those cases, there's always some sort of strong emotional connection, and nine out of ten times their fantasies will involve some sort of sexual act. The victim being sexually assaulted either before or after being murdered is almost a certainty.

The second major type of aggressive psychopaths – violence-centered – are the ones to whom the victim is secondary. The most important part of the equation is the violence, not the victim. It's the killing act that pleasures them. They don't fantasize about a certain type of victim. They don't fantasize about having sex with the victim, because sex will bring them little, or no pleasure at all. On the contrary, it's a distraction from the violence. What they fantasize about is torture, about how to inflict pain, about the God-like power that it gives them. To those psychopaths, anyone can become a victim, even friends and family. There is no distinction. Because of that, they achieve a much higher level of emotional detachment than the victim-centered ones. They can easily kidnap, torture and kill a friend, a relative, a lover, a spouse ... To them it doesn't matter. Emotions simply have no relevance.

'How do you know Lucien's psychopathy isn't victim-centered?' Taylor finally asked.

Hunter finished his coffee and used a paper napkin to dab his mouth.

'Because of what we have so far.'

Taylor leaned in slightly and cocked her head.

'The tokens that were found inside that box in Lucien's house, remember?' Hunter elaborated. 'Not all of them came from women, and the ones that did drastically varied in size. That tells us that the victim's physical type and even the gender aren't that important to him. But Lucien also told us so himself ... twice.'

Taylor paused, and Hunter could tell that she was searching her mental record of that morning's interview.

'He told us that when he was in high school he dreamed of hurting people.' Hunter reminded her. 'Sometimes people he knew, sometimes people he had never seen before . . . just random creations of his imagination – not a specific type.

Taylor remembered Lucien saying that, but she hadn't fully made the connection.

'Then he told us that when he started fantasizing while wide-awake, the star roles in his violent fantasies usually belonged to people he disliked. Sometimes teachers, some-times school bullies, sometimes family members . . . but not always. No physical attributes, or gender came into play. In Lucien's dreams and fantasies, who he was hurting made no difference to him. What excited him was the act of murder, itself.'

Hunter consulted his watch. It was time to get going.

'Trust me, Courtney, whatever feelings Lucien felt for Susan wouldn't have stopped him. Not even love.'

Forty-Nine

For lunch Lucien had been given an aluminum tray containing one portion of bread, lumpy mashed potatoes, a small amount of vegetables, and two pieces of chicken, which were swimming in some sort of yellowish sauce. Everything lacked salt and seemed to have been seasoned with an extra pinch of absolutely nothing at all. Lucien was convinced that the FBI had redefined tasteless food, but he didn't really mind. He wasn't eating for taste or pleasure. He ate to keep his body and mind fed, to give his muscles at least some of the nutrients they needed. And he ate every last scrap.

Just ten minutes after he'd finished his lunch, Lucien heard the familiar buzzing and unlocking sound that came from the door at the end of the corridor.

'Two hours almost to the second,' he said, as Hunter and Taylor came into his line of sight. 'I had a feeling you two would be punctual.' Lucien waited for them to sit down. 'Do you mind if I stand up and walk about a little while we talk? It gets the blood flowing to my brain better, and it helps me digest that crap you guys call food around here.' He jabbed his head toward the empty tray.

No one had any objections.

'So,' Lucien said. 'Where were we?'

Hunter and Taylor both knew that Lucien hadn't forgotten where they'd left off. The question was just part of his game.

'Susan Richards,' Taylor said, calmly crossing her legs, interlacing her fingers together, and resting her right elbow on one of the chair's arms.

'Oh, yeah,' Lucien replied as he slowly started pacing from left to right at the front of the cell. 'What about her again?'

'Her remains, Lucien,' Hunter said in a firm but unthreatening tone. 'Where are they?'

'Oh, that's right. I was about to tell you, wasn't I?' There was a perverse quality to Lucien's new smile. 'Have you contacted her parents yet, Robert? Are they still alive?'

'What?'

'Susan's parents. We met them a couple of times, remember? Are they still alive?'

'Yes. They're still alive,' Hunter confirmed.

Lucien nodded his understanding. 'They seemed to be nice people. Will you be the one in charge of giving them the news?'

Hunter suspected he would be, but he was getting tired of Lucien's games. The way he saw it, right then, any answer was an answer, as long as it got Lucien talking.

'Yes.'

'Will you be doing it over the phone, or do you intend to do it face to face?'

Any answer.

'Face to face.'

Lucien chewed on that for a beat before returning to Hunter's original question. 'You know, Robert, that night I experienced things ... feelings, actually, that until then I had only read about in criminology books, interview transcripts, and accounts from apprehended offenders. Personal and intimate feelings that the more I read about them, the more I wanted to experience them for myself, because that'd be the only real way to find out if they'd be true for me or not.'

He paused and stared at the wall in front of him, as if fascinated by some invisible work of art hanging from it.

'That night, Robert, I could actually feel Susan's life-light fading away right at my fingertips.' Lucien's gaze moved down toward his hands before continuing. 'I could feel her heart pulsating in my palms, and the more I squeezed, the weaker it got.' He turned and faced Hunter and Taylor one more time. 'And that was when I was elevated, like an out-of-body experience. That was when I realized that what so many had testified to, the feeling we read about so many times, was indeed true.'

Taylor's eyes darted toward Hunter and then back to Lucien. 'What feeling are you talking about?'

Lucien didn't answer, but his eyes passed the question over to Hunter.

'The "God-like feeling",' Hunter said.

Lucien nodded once. 'Right again, Robert. The "God-like feeling". A feeling of such supreme power that until then I believed it was reserved only for God. The power to extinguish life. And let me tell you, it's true what they say. That feeling changes your life forever. It's intoxicating, Robert, addictive, hypnotizing even. Especially if you're looking straight into their eyes as you squeeze the life out of their bodies. That's the moment when you *become* God.'

No, Hunter thought. *That's the moment when you delude yourself that you had, for the quickest of instants, equated yourself to God. Only a deluded person would believe that he or she could become God, however briefly.* He said nothing, but noticed Lucien's fingers slowly closing into fists before he turned and faced Taylor.

'Tell me, Agent Taylor, have you ever killed someone?'

The question caught Taylor completely by surprise, and in a whirlwind of memory, her heartbeat took off like a fighter jet.

Fifty

It'd happened three years after Taylor had graduated from the FBI Academy. She'd been assigned to the New York field office, but the events that took place that night had nothing to do with any of the investigations she'd been working on at that time.

That night, Taylor had spent hours poring over NYPD's and New Jersey PD's combined investigation files into a serial killer that they had named 'The Ad Killer', or TAK for short.

In the past ten months, TAK had sodomized and killed six women – four in New York and two in New Jersey. All six of them had been private sex workers. All six of them fitted a specific physical profile – dark, shoulder-length hair, brown eyes, aged between nineteen and thirty-five, average weight, average height. The pseudonym 'The Ad Killer' was used because the only solid fact that the police had been able to gather over nine months of investigations was that all six women had placed private advertisements, offering their 'tantric massage' services, in the back pages of free local newspapers.

After nine months and not much to show for it, the Mayor of New York had demanded that the chief of police requested the assistance of the FBI. Courtney Taylor was one of the two agents assigned to assist with the case.

It was past midnight by the time Taylor left the FBI office on the twenty-third floor of the Federal Plaza building that late October night. She drove slowly through Manhattan before crossing the Midtown Tunnel in the direction of her small one-bedroom apartment in Astoria, in the northwest corner of Queens. Her mind had been so busy, sifting through an earthquake of thoughts and trying to piece together a few aspects of the investigation, that it was only after spotting a 24-hour grocery store on 21st Avenue, that she remembered she had completely run out of several supplies back home.

'Oh, damn!' she breathed out, quickly swinging her car right and taking a parking spot just past the store. As she turned off the engine, her stomach also decided to remind her of how hungry she was by demonstrating its own version of a whale's mating call.

At that time in the morning the store wasn't busy at all – two, maybe three customers browsing the aisles. The young clerk at the counter nodded a robotic 'good morning' at Taylor, before returning his attention to whatever paperback he was reading.

Taylor grabbed a basket by the entrance and, without putting too much thought into what she needed, started throwing items into it. She'd just picked up a half-gallon of milk from one of the fridges at the back of the store when she heard some sort of loud commotion up front. She frowned and took a glance around the corner but saw nothing out of the ordinary. Still, her instincts told her that something wasn't right, and Taylor had learned a long time ago to always trust her instincts. She put the basket on the floor and walked around to the next aisle along.

'Hurry the fuck up, man, or I'll blow your fucking brains all over this dirty floor. I ain't got all fucking night,' she heard somebody say in a very anxious voice, even before she had a chance to peek around the corner again.

Instantly, Taylor reached for her Glock 22, thumbed the safety off, and very quietly chambered a round. Her stomach's mating whales had gone quiet all of a sudden, giving way to a heavy-metal drum solo from her heart. This was no well-prepared and thought-out FBI operation. This was no drill. This was sheer bad luck. This was real, and this was happening right there and then.

Crouching down to keep herself hidden from view from the front counter, Taylor moved stealthily up the aisle. She paused before reaching the end of it, and through a gap between some items on one of the shelves, was able to check the round surveillance mirror in one of the ceiling corners.

'Motherfucker, you think I'm playing wit' you?' she heard the anxious voice say again. 'You think this is a fucking game? You better speed the fuck up or I'll pop a cap in your ugly ass. You dig what I'm saying, holmes?'

The drum solo in Taylor's heart gathered momentum. Through the mirror she could see a single perpetrator. He looked young. He was tall and skinny, wearing blue jeans, a dark, loose, New York Yankees sweatshirt, and had a red and black bandana covering most of his face. He was pointing a Beretta 92 semi-automatic pistol directly at the terrified store clerk's head.

Like a frantic chicken, the perpetrator kept on quickly turning his head every few seconds to check the store's entrance and aisles. Even from a distance, Taylor could tell that he was completely wasted, wired up on some kind of drug. And that made everything a lot worse.

Despite his incessant checking, the kid with the Beretta was so out of it that he didn't even notice the police car that had parked just outside the shop.

Officer Turkowski wasn't responding to a distress call. That small grocery store, stashed away in a dark corner of Queens, had no silent alarm or panic button hidden behind the counter. No, Officer Turkowski simply got hungry and decided to grab a couple of donuts and maybe a few Twinkies to keep him going for the next hour or so. He thought about grabbing a burrito from the Taco Bell on Jackson Avenue, but he was just around the corner from the 24-hour grocery store, and he decided that he fancied something sweet.

Turkowski was a young officer who had been with the NYPD for two and a half years. He'd only started doing solo patrols – twice a week – in the past two months. Tonight, as luck would have it, was a solo-patrol night.

He stepped out of his Crown Vic and, for once, closed the driver's door without slamming it shut – no noise.

Inside the shop, the terrified store clerk had finished placing all the cash from the register into a paper bag, and was about to hand it over to his assailant when he saw the young police officer appear at the shop's door.

Turkowski saw the kid with the Beretta a second before the kid saw him. No time to call for backup. Hardcore police training kicked in, and in a flash he had unholstered his gun and, in a two-hand grip, had it aimed at the kid.

'Drop it,' he called out in a steady voice.

The kid had already forgotten everything about the money and the store clerk. His only concern now was the cop with the gun. He swung his body around, and in a split second he had his Beretta aimed at Turkowski's chest.

'Fuck that, cop. You drop it,' the kid said, holding his gun sideways in a one-hand grip – street gangster-style.

It was obvious the kid was nervous, but he was no first-timer. In a very agile move, as he pivoted his body to face the police officer, he had taken a step back and strategically positioned himself with his back to the front of the shop. He now had the store clerk slightly to his left, the police officer slightly to his right, and the shop aisles directly in front of him, giving him, out of the three of them, the best overall viewpoint of the entire scene.

Hiding in the aisle, Taylor had the kid's inverse viewpoint.

'I said drop it,' Turkowski repeated, easing himself one step to his right. 'Put your weapon on the ground, take a step forward, and kneel down with your hands behind your head.'

Still crouching down, Taylor had silently moved up the aisle and was now almost at the front of the shop. No one had noticed her yet. From her hidden position, she got a better look at the entire scene, especially the perpetrator. The kid's eyes were wild with a mixture of adrenaline, anxiety and drugs. His posture was rigid, but fearless, as if he'd been in that position before. As if he had everything under total control. Turkowski, on the other hand, seemed edgier.

'Fuck you, cop,' the kid said, using his left hand to pull the red and black bandana down from his nose and mouth, allowing it to hang loosely around his neck, and revealing his face.

Taylor instantly knew that that was a bad sign. She instantly knew it was time to act before the whole situation got out of control.

Too late.

Like a film on the big screen, as Taylor started getting up from her crouching position, the entire scene switched into slow motion. The kid hadn't yet noticed her, and no one will ever know if he sensed her presence before she revealed herself, but he gave Officer Turkowski no chance ... no warning. He squeezed the trigger on his Beretta 92 three times in quick succession.

The first bullet hit Turkowski on his right shoulder, rupturing tendons, shattering bone, and blowing up a red mist of blood. The second and third hit him square on the chest, directly over his heart, destroying the organ's left and right atria, and the pulmonary artery and veins. Turkowski was dead before he hit the ground.

Despite the mess and the blood, the kid didn't panic. He quickly swung on the balls of his feet to face the store clerk again, grabbed the bag with the cash, and raised his gun. The way he saw it, since he'd already killed a cop, why leave a living witness?

Taylor had read that resolve in the kid's crazed eyes and movement. She could foresee what was coming, and before he could turn the nightmare into a reality, Taylor was up on her feet. She had stepped away from her aisle cover and into clear view, her Glock 22 firmly aimed at the kid with the Beretta.

Through the corner of his eye, the kid caught a glimpse of movement coming from his right. Instinctively he began spinning his body around, his finger already starting to apply pressure to the trigger.

Taylor had no time to shout out a command or a warning, but she also knew that it would make no difference. The kid wouldn't have responded. He would've shot her with the same determination with which he had shot the police officer.

Taylor squeezed her trigger only once.

The .40 Smith & Wesson bullet was intended to just wound. To hit the kid on the upper arm or shoulder. To force him to drop his weapon, but the shot had been hurried and the kid was in mid-movement. The bullet hit him higher than intended and a few inches to the right. The kid fell back. A chunk of his throat splattered onto the wall behind him. It took him three and a half minutes to bleed out. It took the ambulance ten minutes to get to the store.

He was only eighteen years old.

Fifty-One

Doing her best to keep her face and movements as steady as she could manage, Taylor blinked away the memory.

'Excuse me?' She angled her head in a way that suggested she hadn't heard Lucien's question properly.

'I'm sure you've been involved in hundreds of FBI investigations, Agent Taylor,' Lucien said. 'What I want to know is: have you, in any of them, had to pull out your gun and kill someone, even if in "self-defense"?'

Taylor wasn't prepared to go through any of what had happened that night all those years ago with Lucien, but she knew that if she answered truthfully he would pick at that wound until it bled again. Trying to concentrate on her breathing, her eyes, and everything else that could give her away, she gave him her answer.

'No.'

Lucien was observing Taylor, but this time her poker face worked. If anything had betrayed her answer, he didn't seem to notice it.

'Robert?' Lucien moved the question over. His head skewed sideways. 'Don't lie to me now.'

Once again, Hunter had the feeling that somehow Lucien already knew the answer.

'Yes,' he said. 'Unfortunately, I've killed people in the line of duty.'

'How many?'

Hunter didn't have to think about it. 'I've shot and killed six people.'

Lucien savored those words for an instant. 'And you weren't overcome by a feeling of tremendous power? You didn't get the "God-like feeling"? Not even once?'

'No, I didn't.' Hunter didn't hesitate. 'If I could have avoided it, I would've.'

For several seconds, they exchanged a fierce stare, as if their eyes were fighting their own private tug-of-war.

'Susan's remains, Lucien,' Hunter finally said. 'Where are they?'

'Very well,' Lucien agreed, breaking eye contact. He breathed in deeply. 'Like I said before, Robert, the place I used in La Honda is still there. Once the magic of the moment had worn off that night, once I stopped shaking from the adrenaline rush, I knew I had to dispose of the body in a way that no one would find it. But I had already given that a lot of thought. That was just another reason why I chose that place – it was surrounded by wild woods.' A careless shrug. 'I didn't know it would happen that night though,' he added. 'It wasn't my intention when I left the dorm to go meet Susan. As I said, it just turned out that way.'

He started pacing his cell again, his hands behind his back.

'So I dug for the rest of the night, all the way until morning. Ended up with a four, maybe five-foot-deep grave. I had already bought bags and bags of coffee powder and a few bottles of mountain lion urine.'

Both Hunter and Taylor knew that coffee powder is a very strong animal scent distractor. It confuses them, and usually makes them lose a scent trail, if they were on to one. Mountain lion urine can be easily bought in several shops around America, and it's used for its predator scent quality. Its smell scares away a multitude of other animals, like foxes, wolves and coyotes. It's a simple law of nature – the stronger and deadlier the predator, the more animals its scent will scare off.

'I buried her body in the woods behind the house,' Lucien said, 'under layers of dirt, coffee powder and mountain lion urine. Covered it all with some leaves and sticks. And I can tell you, it's never been disturbed by man or animal.'

'So where is this house?' Hunter asked.

Lucien spent the next two minutes giving Hunter and Taylor specific instructions of how to get to it from Sears Ranch Road.

Lucien paused directly in front of Hunter. 'Will you tell them everything? Will you tell them the truth?'

Hunter knew Lucien was talking about Susan's parents again.

'Yes.'

'Um ... I wonder how they'll feel. What their reaction will be?'

'What do you care?' Taylor spat the words. 'At least they'll have closure at last. They'll be able to bury their daughter's remains with dignity. And they'll also have the certainty that the monster who took her away from them will be locked up for the rest of his natural life.'

Lucien was still pacing his cell, but instead of moving from left to right, he'd started walking back and forth between the back wall and the Plexiglas at the front.

'Oh, no, I wasn't talking about that, Agent Taylor.' Lucien's lips broke into something that looked like half a smirk, half an amused smile. 'I meant ... I wonder how they'll feel when they find out that they *ate* their own daughter.'

Fifty-Two

Adrian Kennedy had decided to cancel all of his appoint-
ments back in Washington, DC and stay at the FBI Academy
in Quantico, at least for another day or so. In all his years
with the Bureau, no single investigation or suspect had
intrigued him as much as Lucien Folter had.

He'd ordered a check on Susan Richards' parents late last
night. That was how Hunter knew they were still alive. Her
father was now seventy-one and her mother sixty-nine,
both retired. Kennedy had also told Hunter that they were
still living in the same old house in Boulder City, Nevada,
and they were still calling the police departments in Palo
Alto and Santa Clara County at least once a month asking
for any news.

Kennedy and Doctor Lambert had been following all the
interviews through the monitors in the holding cells' control
room. Every once in a while one of them would make a
brief comment on something that was said, but mostly they
watched in silence. As soon as Kennedy heard Lucien's
instruction of how to get to Susan Richards' grave behind
the house in La Honda, he reached for the phone on the
desk in front of him.

'Get me the Special Agent in charge of our field office in
San Francisco . . . ASAP!'

Within seconds Kennedy was speaking to Special Agent Bradley Simmons, a softly spoken man who had been with the FBI for twenty years, nine of those with the San Francisco office. He still had a strong southern Texas accent.

Kennedy had paid intense attention to Lucien's instructions. He didn't even need to listen back to the recording or check his notes. He could easily recount word for word.

'Get in touch with the La Honda Police Department and County Sheriff's office *only* if you need to, you understand?' Kennedy said, once Agent Simmons had taken everything down. 'This is *exclusively* an FBI operation. From what we understand the location is isolated by woods, no neighbors, no one around, that was the main reason why it was chosen, so if there's no need for you to let anyone else know ... *don't let anyone else know*. Get on to it now, and get back to me the second you find anything.'

Kennedy put the phone down and returned his attention to the monitors and the interview just in time to hear Lucien's last comment. His body tensed and he looked at Doctor Lambert.

'Did he just say that they *ate* their own daughter?'

Doctor Lambert was sitting before one of the monitors with a disbelieving look on his face. He wanted to play back the recording just to be sure, but he knew he didn't need to. He knew he'd heard right. Without diverting his attention from the monitor, he nodded slowly.

At that precise moment there was a knock on the door to the control room. The person didn't wait for a reply, pushing the door open.

'Director Kennedy,' the man said, stepping into the room.

Chris Welch was in his early forties with short blond hair that was brushed back off his forehead. He was carrying what looked to be a notebook of some sort.

'Sorry to disturb you, sir.' Welch was with the FBI's Behavioral Analysis Unit. 'You asked me to notify you immediately if we came across anything that seemed relevant in any of these books.' He nodded at the notebook he was holding. It was a regular 8x10.5-inch notebook, with a marbled brown and black hardcover.

All the books and notebooks that were retrieved from Lucien's house in Murphy had been handed in to the FBI's BAU. Their task was to scrutinize their content.

'I thought you'd like to have a look at this.' Welch flipped the notebook open and handed it to Kennedy.

Kennedy's eyes scanned through several pages before he let out a heavy breath.

'Jesus!'

Fifty-Three

Even with the ventilation system on full blast, the heat down in sublevel five of the Behavioral Science Unit building seemed oppressive. Hunter felt beads of sweat form on the nape of his neck and slowly start to trickle down his back, only to be frozen in place by Lucien's words. They seemed to have chilled the air like an arctic blast.

'They what?' he asked, his voice puncturing the silence that had clouded the air since Lucien last spoke.

Lucien had reached the back wall again and had stopped pacing. His back was toward Hunter and Taylor.

'Yes, you heard right, Robert,' he said. 'Susan's parents ate her . . .' He bobbed his head to one side. 'I mean . . . not all of her, of course, just a few diced-up organs.'

Taylor felt something start to spin circles inside her stomach.

'How?' Hunter asked. 'By then they'd already traveled back to Nevada after her graduation.'

'Yes, I know,' Lucien said. 'I visited them.'

'You what?' Taylor this time.

Lucien faced them. 'I visited them two days after that night . . . took a gift with me . . . a pie I baked myself.'

The circles inside Taylor's stomach became scary roller coasters.

'A trip from Stanford to Boulder City in Nevada doesn't take that long,' Lucien said to Taylor. 'Susan had introduced them to us – Robert and I, that is – a year or two before. We met them again after the graduation ceremony. Susan and I had both graduated *cum laude*, and they were very proud of her. Any parent would be.'

It was barely noticeable, but Hunter picked up a sting of pain in Lucien's last few words.

'They were a sweet couple,' Lucien proceeded. 'Susan was a sweet girl. I decided it was the right thing to do.'

'The right thing to do?' Taylor had been knocked off balance so hard that she couldn't contain herself. She had to ask. 'How could that be the right thing to do?'

'You're the investigator in this case, Agent Taylor. You tell me.' Lucien sounded condescending. 'Let me throw you a pop quiz. Let's say this was a completely different investigation. Let's say that you didn't have me in custody. Let's say that you had a case where you found out that the UNSUB had fed some of his victim's organs to her family, what would your conclusion be, Agent Taylor? I'm interested to know.'

'*Play his game. Let him believe he's winning.*' Hunter's words came back to Taylor. She knew that what Lucien wanted was to get under her skin, to shake her confidence. She now understood that every time she lost her temper, Lucien felt like he'd won another battle. '*Give him what he wants.*'

'Because you're a deranged psychopath?' she said. 'Because to you it sounded like something fun to do? Because it fed your "God" delusion?'

Lucien crossed his arms over his chest and looked at Taylor, intrigued. A challenging smile threatened to stretch his lips.

'That's a very interesting conclusion, Agent Taylor,' he replied, sarcasm dripping off his words. 'Spoken like a true professional. You know, I always found that there's nothing as entertaining as seeing people feed off their emotions. The problem with it is that it takes away objectivity. It clouds judgment. It opens the door to a world of mistakes. I learned that a long time ago.'

As if he didn't have a care in the world, Lucien pulled his sleeve up and again looked at his wrist as if he had a watch.

'Anyway, I'm quite bored of all these questions, and I guess you two have got a lot of work to do now, don't you? You know . . . bones to dig up, explanations to make, stories to tell.'

Leisurely, Lucien lay down on the bed and interlaced his fingers behind his head.

'Give Susan's parents my best for me, will you, Robert? Oh, and by the way, if you're wondering . . . yes, I did sit down and have dinner with them that night.'

Fifty-Four

Hunter's fist connected with the punch bag with so much force, it sent it swinging backward almost a whole meter. He'd been hitting one of the 45-kilo leather bags that hung from the ceiling in the BSU building's boxing gym for a little under an hour. His shirt and shorts were drenched in sweat, which was pouring down from his forehead like rain. His whole body was sore from the grueling workout and he felt mentally exhausted. But he needed some time to think, to try to organize the mess of thoughts inside his head, to disconnect, even if only for a few minutes, and for Hunter, more times than not, heavy exercise did the trick.

Today was *not* one of those times. Frustration ran through his body like bad blood, and no matter how hard Hunter punched that bag or how much weight he lifted, he just couldn't seem to get rid of it.

'If I were thirty years younger, I'd spot you with that punch bag,' Kennedy said, standing at the door to the gym. The place was deserted, except for Hunter. 'But even so, the way you're punching that thing, you'd probably put me through the wall. I'm surprised your hand isn't broken yet.'

The long day and a full pack of cigarettes made Kennedy's hoarse voice sound even weaker, even more guttural.

Hunter delivered one quick final series of heavy punches to the bag – jab, jab, cross, left hook, cross. The bag swung back and sideways awkwardly, as if it'd had enough and had been finally defeated, before Hunter embraced it into a stop. His breath was tortured, his face a dark shade of pink, the veins on his arms and shoulders swollen from the whole effort and the extra blood flow. Panting, he rested his head against the bag for a moment, taking his time, waiting for his breathing to slowly return to normal. Sweat dripped from his chin onto his shoes and the floor.

Kennedy stepped closer.

'Any news from La Honda?' Hunter asked at last, his arms still hugging the punch bag.

Kennedy nodded with very little enthusiasm.

Hunter used his teeth to pull free the Velcro straps on both of his gloves and turned to face the director.

'I had four agents check the site.'

Hunter used the inside of his left arm and the left side of his torso to grab his right glove and pulled his hand free, before undoing his left glove.

'They found the house Lucien mentioned.' Kennedy threw Hunter a towel. 'The agents followed Lucien's instructions to the specific location and began digging. They dug for an hour.' He handed Hunter an A4-size envelope. 'And this is what they found.'

Hunter quickly dried his face and hands before reaching inside the envelope and retrieving a couple of printed-out photographs. As his eyes devoured the images, his heartbeat picked up speed once again.

The first photograph showed a full human skeleton, its bones old and time-discolored, lying inside what looked to be a five-foot-deep grave.

The second one was a close-up snapshot of the skull.

In silence, Hunter stared at both pictures for a long time, dwelling on the second one for a lot longer than the first, as if he were mentally reconstructing Susan's face over her skull.

Kennedy took a step back, giving Hunter a moment before he spoke again. 'Since we already know that Lucien is a serial offender, protocol dictates that we now dig up the entire site,' Kennedy said, 'looking for possible remains of other bodies. It's a huge operation, and there's no way of doing that without getting the local authorities involved and bringing a Hollywood-size spotlight to this case.'

'I'd wait a while, Adrian,' Hunter said. He'd never been a big fan of protocol. 'At least until we're finished interviewing him. So far Lucien has been straight with us. If there are other bodies buried around that same area, I have a feeling he will tell us. Bringing a spotlight to this investigation right now won't benefit anyone.'

Kennedy usually played by the book, but right then he was inclined to agree with Hunter.

'It will take at least a couple of days and a few tests to confirm if what we've got really is Susan Richards' skeleton,' Kennedy said.

'It will be,' Hunter replied, returning the printouts to the envelope.

Kennedy looked a question at Hunter.

'Lucien had no reason to lie,' Hunter said.

The question remained in Kennedy's eyes.

'We already know he killed Susan,' Hunter clarified. 'He told us that, and the framed tattooed piece of skin in his basement confirmed it. If he had disposed of Susan's body in a way where no remains could be found, he would've just told us so.' He jabbed a finger at the envelope. 'If those were the remains of someone else's body, who he'd also have killed, because he knew the exact location where it was buried, there was no point in telling us it was Susan's, because he knows we will be testing it anyway.'

Kennedy's head bobbed down once. 'I understand, but just to be on the safe side, I think you'd better wait for official confirmation before contacting her parents.'

Hunter nodded slowly before using the towel on his face and arms again. Bringing the news to Susan's parents was one job he wasn't looking forward to. 'I've got to take a shower.'

'Come up to my office when you're done,' Kennedy said. 'There's something else I need to show you.'

Fifty-Five

Twenty minutes later, Hunter, his hair still wet from his shower, was back inside Director Kennedy's office. Special Agent Taylor was also there. She had lost the ponytail. Her blonde hair was loose and wavy, falling naturally over her shoulders. She was wearing a dark pencil skirt with a tucked-in blue blouse, black nylon stockings, and black strappy court shoes. She was sitting in one of the armchairs in front of Kennedy's desk. In her hands, the same photographs Hunter had looked at down in the gym, the ones of Susan Richards' remains.

Kennedy got up from behind his desk.

'You still drink Scotch?' he asked Hunter.

Single-malt Scotch whisky was Hunter's biggest passion. Unlike so many, he knew how to appreciate its palate instead of just getting drunk on it. Though sometimes getting drunk worked just fine.

Hunter nodded. 'Do you?'

'When at all possible.' Kennedy walked over to the cabinet to his left, opened it and retrieved three tumblers and a bottle of Tomatin 25-year-old.

'Not for me, sir, thank you,' Taylor said, placing the photographs back inside the envelope.

'Relax, Agent Taylor,' Kennedy said in a reassuring tone. 'This is an informal meeting, and after what we've all been through today, I'd say a drink is more than appropriate.' A hesitant pause. 'Unless you don't drink Scotch. In that case I can get you something else.'

'Scotch is fine, sir,' Taylor replied confidently.

'Ice?'

Hunter shook his head. 'Just a drop of water, please.'

'Same here,' Taylor said.

Kennedy smiled. 'Looks like I've got a couple of true Scotch drinkers in my office.'

He poured the three of them a healthy dose, added a splash of water, and handed a glass to Hunter and one to Taylor.

'I need to ask you something, Robert,' Kennedy said in a more serious tone.

Hunter sipped his Scotch. It was pleasantly rich without being overpowering, with notes of citrus and fruit. A complex but very smooth palate. He enjoyed the taste for a moment.

Taylor did the same.

'Do you think Lucien was lying about the cannibalism?' Kennedy asked. 'That's something that we have no way of proving.'

'I can't see what he would achieve by lying about that,' Hunter replied.

'Maybe he was going for the "shock" effect, Robert,' Kennedy said. 'People with a "God" complex thrive on the attention. You both know that.'

Hunter shook his head. 'Not Lucien. He doesn't want notoriety. At least not yet. As sickening as it sounds, I don't think he's lying about what he's done . . . about eating some of Susan's flesh or organs . . . or about feeding it to her parents.'

Kennedy paused, doubt bubbling in his eyes. 'You know I don't come from a psychology background, Robert, so let me ask you the same question Lucien asked Agent Taylor.' His head jerked in her direction. 'Why would he do that? Lucien drove across state lines with parts of her cooked into a dish just to offer it to her parents, for chrissakes. That's beyond deranged, beyond evil, beyond immoral, beyond anything I've ever seen or heard. And I've seen and heard a lot in my life. What kind of evil mind drives anyone to do such a thing?' He had another mouthful of Scotch.

Taylor looked at Hunter curiously.

He shrugged and looked away.

'I've read studies, books, papers, theses ... you name it, about cannibal killers, serial or not,' Kennedy added. 'God knows, we've had many of them down in those same cells over the years. And I understand that a good number of them believe that they do it because to them their victims are special, and the act of eating them solidifies their bond with their victims. They feel that if they eat even a small part of them, the victims will stay with them forever and all that crap.' He gave Hunter and Taylor a subtle headshake. 'I guess everyone deludes in their own way. But feeding it to others ...? That's just pure sadism and psychosis. What else can explain it?'

Hunter said nothing.

Kennedy pushed it.

'So if you have anything that could throw any sort of light on the "whys" of this madness, Robert, please humor me, because I can't figure it out. Why did he feed her to her parents? Was it pure sadism?'

Hunter sipped his drink again and leaned against the bookcase. 'No, I don't think it was sadism. I think he did it because he felt guilty.'

Fifty-Six

Kennedy's doubtful look bounced between Hunter and Taylor. The FBI Agent didn't look at all surprised.

'Could you please elaborate, Robert,' he said in his whispering voice. 'Because to me, feeding someone to her own parents doesn't quite sound like the actions of a person stricken by guilt.'

Hunter looked around him, as if searching for an answer that might've been floating around in the air.

'We could theorize as much as we like here, Adrian, but the only one who really knows what was going on inside his head is Lucien himself.'

'I understand that,' Kennedy agreed. 'But I still would like to know your thoughts on why you think guilt had anything to do with it.'

'If Lucien is being truthful about Susan being his first ever victim,' Hunter said, 'and right now we have no reason to doubt that, then, as you know, guilt and remorse are the first two common psychological emotions that usually torment a first-time killer.'

Kennedy and Taylor both *did* know that. According to the FBI's Behavioral Science Unit, 'serial murder' is defined as: *a series of three or more killings, committed on three or more separate occasions, with a 'cooling-off' period between*

murders. These murders must also have common character-
istics such as to suggest the reasonable possibility that the
crimes had been committed by the same person or persons.

That cooling-off period, Kennedy knew, especially
between the initial killings of a series, was almost always
due to the perpetrator or perpetrators experiencing intense
feelings of guilt and/or remorse directly after committing
the crime.

That was easily understandable. Most aggressors who
eventually become serial murderers struggle with fantasies,
urges, destructive impulses and even rage attacks for a long
time, sometimes years, finding them harder and harder to
resist until the urges finally win the battle. The simple fact
that they *struggle* with these impulses for such a long time
clearly indicates that they know that killing another human
being is wrong. It then becomes a simple psychological
human response.

Most people usually experience some level of guilt if they
do something they know to be wrong – cheat in an exam,
steal the paper from the neighbor's door, cheat on a partner,
tell a lie, or whatever. That sense of guilt is directly propor-
tional to how wrong they believe their actions were – the
worse the actions, the bigger the guilt trip. And bad actions
don't come much worse than murder. For that reason, many
first-time murderers will be thrown into the depths of dark
depression and experience a tremendous feeling of guilt
directly after killing someone. With that in mind, it stood to
reason that Lucien had also experienced enormous lows,
and was overwhelmed by incredible feelings of guilt after
his first ever murder.

'OK, I agree that Lucien must've struggled with different
stages of guilt in the aftermath of murdering Susan,'

Kennedy admitted. 'But I still can see no reason why, over-whelmed by guilt or not, he would've fed parts of her body to her own parents, Robert.'

'I can see two *possible* reasons,' Hunter said, with a hand gesture. 'The first one you mentioned just a moment ago.'

Kennedy's eyes squinted a fraction. 'And what was that?'

'The belief that by consuming the flesh of their victims, the victims will then stay with them forever. They will become part of them,' Taylor said in a half whisper. 'Or whoever eats them.' She allowed Kennedy a few seconds to reanalyze that statement.

Kennedy caught on quickly. 'Jesus! Third-party transfer-ence.' He looked at Hunter for confirmation but proceeded anyway. 'So Lucien believed that if her parents consumed some of her flesh, then Susan would stay with *them* forever?'

'As Lucien said,' Taylor commented, 'she was never meant to be a victim, and he also thought that her parents were nice people. So Robert could be right. He might've done it because he felt guilty at taking their daughter away from them.'

Kennedy considered that for a long, silent moment.

'And the second possible reason?' he finally asked.

'The second reason links to the first,' Hunter said. 'Lucien told us that he used to hunt with his father, right?'

'Yes, I remember that.' Kennedy said.

'He also said that his father was a great hunter.'

'Yes, I remember that too.'

'OK, many hunters inherit a belief that's been passed down through generations and generations of Native Americans,' Hunter explained.

Kennedy's eyebrows arched curiously.

'Native Americans never hunted for fun or sport. They hunted exclusively for food, and they believed that they must eat whatever they killed, always, because to eat their prey was to honor them. They believed that it kept their spirit alive in this world. It showed respect. To let their flesh go to waste, that would be a dishonor.'

Kennedy didn't know that, but his memory and his eyes instantly flashed back to Susan Richards' file sitting on his desk. Her mother was second-generation Shoshone, a Native American tribe, mostly from the area that became the state of Nevada. Her family name was Tuari, which meant 'young eagle'. Kennedy was well aware that Lucien knew that too.

Taylor looked at Hunter intriguingly.

'I read a lot,' Hunter offered before she was able to ask the question.

'So you think that, in his mind at least, Lucien was redeeming himself, even if only a little bit,' Kennedy stated rather than asked. 'He was being compassionate, by feeding her flesh to her own parents, he was trying to keep Susan's spirit alive *for them*, even without their knowledge.

'*Everyone deludes in their own way*.' Hunter repeated Kennedy's words from a little earlier. 'But like I said, we can theorize as much as we like here, but the only one who really knows what was going on inside his head is Lucien himself.'

'So in that case, let me ask you this,' Kennedy said. 'Why do you think he took part? Lucien said that he *did* sit down to have dinner with them that night.'

'Because Lucien was experimenting.'

Kennedy pinched the bridge of his nose as if he could feel an oncoming headache.

'In college, Lucien didn't exactly doubt any of the theories behind these sadistic acts,' he said. 'He knew they were based on true accounts from apprehended offenders, but he was on the verge of almost obsessing with the *feelings and emotions* described by such offenders.'

Kennedy remembered something Lucien had said during one of the interviews. 'He wanted to experience them for himself.'

'Back then, he never said so in so many words,' Hunter agreed. 'But now we know that that was exactly what he wanted, to experiment. And that's what makes Lucien so different from most psychopaths I've ever come up against.'

Kennedy's eyebrows moved up inquisitively.

'We know that he killed Susan, his first victim, by strangulation,' Hunter elaborated. 'But if we compare her murder to his latest one, the two victims in his trunk . . . the MO, the level of violence, everything has skyrocketed. I'm willing to bet that the violence in every murder he'd committed in between moved up a step at a time. But Lucien escalates not because he's being guided by uncontrollable urges inside of him.'

'He does it consciously,' Taylor said, picking up Hunter's thread of thought. 'He does it because he wants to know how he would feel as he becomes more and more violent.'

'That's a frightening thought,' Kennedy said. 'The level of determination and self-discipline one needs to carry on escalating murder after murder for twenty-five years is mindboggling. And you think he did it just so he could experience the feeling?'

Hunter had paused, his memory digging out something long forgotten. 'I'll be damned!' He finally exclaimed.

'What?' Kennedy asked.

'I can't believe he's really doing it,' Hunter murmured.

'Doing what?'

'I think Lucien might've been writing an encyclopedia.'

Fifty-Seven

Kennedy's shoulder's stiffened as he felt an awkward shiver grab hold of his whole body, something that didn't happen very often when it came to BSU investigations. He waited for Hunter to continue.

'I remember this discussion we had once.' Hunter's memory searched the past. 'I think it was during our second year in college. We were discussing emotional triggers and drives in extreme violent murders – what psychological factors could drive an individual to sadistically and brutally offend and reoffend.'

'OK,' Kennedy said, still intrigued.

'Back then, all we had were a bunch of theories put together by several psychologists and psychiatrists, and a handful of accounts by apprehended killers. Now bear in mind that notorious cannibal killers like Jeffrey Dahmer, Armin Meiwes, or Andrej Chikatilo hadn't been caught yet. Their interviews, accounts and thoughts weren't on file.'

Kennedy and Taylor both nodded together.

'As I've said,' Hunter moved on, 'Lucien didn't doubt the veracity of the accounts we had then, but he wasn't quite convinced by many of the psychological theories. What I remember he used to say a lot was: *"How can they know for sure?"*'

'They couldn't,' Taylor said. 'That's why it was a theory, not a fact.'

'Precisely,' Hunter agreed. 'And Lucien understood that.'

'But he wasn't satisfied,' Kennedy concluded.

'No, he wasn't. And that day he suggested something so far-fetched, I had completely forgotten about it.'

'And that was?'

Hunter took a deep breath while trying to remember the details.

'The surreal possibility of someone becoming a killer solely to experiment,' he finally said. 'Lucien argued how ground-breaking it would be for criminal behavior psychology if a fully mentally capable individual went on a killing rampage, escalating his or her way through different levels of violence, and experimenting with different methods and fantasies, while at the same time taking comprehensive notes of everything, including feelings and psychological state of mind at the time, and in the aftermath of each murder. Some sort of in-depth psychological study of the mind of a killer, written by the killer himself.'

Kennedy's body tensed just a little, fighting the same awkward shiver that had run deep inside him just moments ago.

'He believed that a notebook, or even a series of note-books, filled with such true accounts would become an encyclopedia of knowledge, a bible of sorts to criminal behavioral scientists.'

Kennedy scratched his left cheek. He couldn't help thinking that, as absurd as it sounded, Lucien was right. If such a book, or books, existed, they'd prove invaluable and probably become one of the most referred-to works by criminologists, psychologists and law enforcement officials and agents all around the world. Such a book, especially if written by someone with a criminal psychology degree, someone who understood the importance of such information and knew exactly what to add, would no doubt become some sort of holy book in the never-ending fight against violent predators.

'I think that might be what he was doing,' Hunter said, his thoughts beginning to turn his stomach. 'Jumping from murder to murder, escalating the violence with each one, trying different things, different methods . . . and keeping a diary of how he felt, especially emotionally.' In his mind, that would give him the excuse he wanted.'

Kennedy's forehead creased as he looked at Hunter. 'Excuse?'

'Lucien is a sociopath, no doubt about that, we know it and he knows it. The difference is: he's known it for a long time. He told us that, remember?'

Taylor nodded. 'He started fantasizing while still in school.'

'That's right, and I think that that knowledge hurt him. A regular kid shouldn't be fantasizing about killing people. Maybe it all made him feel like something inside his brain was broken, that he didn't belong. He even told us that the reason why he decided to study criminal behavior psychology was to understand himself.'

'But that backfired,' Kennedy said.

'No, it didn't,' Hunter replied. 'If anything, it pushed his imagination further. It made him come up with what to him sounded like a plausible motive.'

'What better excuse to commit atrocious acts of violence than to fool yourself into believing that you're doing it for a noble cause,' Taylor said, following Hunter's line of thought. 'All in the name of research.'

'That false belief would've eased his internal pain,' Hunter added. 'Lucien could then start feeding his hunger because in his mind, he wasn't a sociopath anymore . . . he was a scientist, a researcher. Everyone deludes in their own way, remember?'

Kennedy broke eye contact.

'Is there something else?' Hunter asked. 'Something you're not telling us?'

Kennedy shrugged and pursed his lips in reply. He walked over to his desk, opened the top right-hand drawer and pulled out a notebook. It was the same notebook Special Agent Chris Welch had handed him in the holding cells' observation room earlier.

Hunter immediately recognized the notebook as one of those he and Special Agent Taylor had seen in Lucien's basement.

'Unfortunately, you might be right, Robert,' Kennedy said. 'Because we found this.'

Fifty-Eight

As if it were something he'd been dreading for years, Hunter took the notebook from Kennedy's hands and flipped open its cover.

Taylor moved to Hunter's side.

On the first page all they saw was a crude, black-and-white pencil sketch of a female face, screaming, contorted in agony.

Hunter's eyes left the page and moved to Kennedy.

The BSU Director gestured for Hunter to carry on.

Hunter turned to the second page. No more drawings, just plain handwritten text. Hunter immediately recognized Lucien's handwriting.

He began reading:

I guess my head is starting to change. At first, after every kill, I was overwhelmed by intense feelings of guilt, as I expected I would be. Sometimes for months. I came close to turning myself in many times. Many times I promised myself I'd never do it again. But as time went by and the guilty feeling began to lessen, slowly and very steadily, the desire to do it all again would come back. I wanted it to come back. With every victim, my guilt phase grew shorter and shorter, to the point that they are now almost non-existent – a couple of days long, if that.

There's no doubt that my mind has adapted. Murder has become something that feels natural to me now. When I'm out, I often look around, and as my eyes settle on someone in a bar, on a train, on the streets . . . wherever I am, I find myself thinking of how easily I could kill anyone. How much I could make them scream. How much pain I could inflict before I actually kill them. And those thoughts excite me more than ever.

Getting rid of these thoughts has become harder and harder, but the truth is, I don't want to get rid of them. I now understand that killing can indeed become a very powerful drug. More powerful than any drug I've ever tried. And I am completely hooked. But despite my addiction, one thing I've learnt is that I need some sort of trigger to finally push me over the edge.

That trigger can be anything – a certain physical type that matches a specific look, the way someone talks or looks at me, the way someone dresses, the scent they're wearing, an action they take, a mannerism they have . . . anything. I don't know it until I see it.

I saw it again last night.

Hunter flipped the page but stopped reading to look at Kennedy again. He had his hands tucked deep inside his trouser pockets. His saggy cheeks seemed to have gained more weight in the past few days, and the dark circles under his eyes had taken an even more morbid appearance. His gaze was locked on the notebook in Hunter's hands.

Hunter went back to the words on the pages:

It was late. I had just ordered my third double Scotch. I wasn't looking for anything or anyone. I just felt like getting drunk, that's all. Actually, I felt like getting obliterated. It was by chance that I found myself in Forest City, Mississippi. I hadn't booked into a motel or anything. I figured I'd just get hammered, pass out in my car outside in the parking lot, wake up sometime the next day and be on my way.

But things didn't happen that way.

I was sitting at the far end of the bar, keeping to myself. It was a slow night with not many customers. The barman tried to be friendly and start a conversation, but I was curt enough that he quickly got the hint.

As the bartender poured me my next drink, a new face walked into the bar. He was big, a lot bigger than me – a mixture of muscle and greasy fat. He was taller too, by at least three to four inches. The bartender called him Jed.

Jed's hair was cut so short I wondered why he didn't just shave it all off. He had a jagged half-moon scar on the underside of his chin, clearly the result of someone taking the rear end of a broken bottle to his face. His nose had also been broken more than once, and his right ear looked a little out of shape, as if it'd been smashed against his skull. It didn't take someone with a lot of brainpower to know that Jed liked to get himself into fights.

He took a seat at the bar, four stools to my left, and as he did, two other customers who were at the tables behind us got up and left.

It didn't look like Jed was a very popular guy either.

He stank of cheap booze and stale sweat.

'Gi'me a fucking beer, Tom,' he called, his voice dragging a little. His pupils were the size of dinner plates, so he was definitely loaded on something heavier than just alcohol.

'C'mon, Jed.' The barman hesitated, keeping his voice even. 'It's late, and you've certainly had enough for one night.'

Jed's Bulldog brow creased even further.

'Don't fucking tell me I've had enough, Tom.'

His voice grew louder by a few decibels, and another customer sneaked out the door.

'I'll tell you when I've had enough. Now gi'me a fucking beer before I shove one up your pussy little ass.'

Tom grabbed a bottle of beer from the fridge, unscrewed its top and placed it on the bar in front of Jed.

Jed took it and swallowed half of it down in three large gulps.

I didn't realize I was staring until Jed turned to me.

'What the fuck are you looking at?' he said, pushing his beer bottle to one side.

'Are you some kind of fag?'

I didn't answer him, and still didn't look away.

'I asked you a question, fag.'

Jed took another swig of his beer.

'You like what you see, fag?' He lifted his right arm and flexed his bicep like a bodybuilder before blowing me a kiss.

I was hypnotized by that sack of shit that called himself Jed.

'C'mon, Jed,' the bartender tried to intervene, clearly foreseeing what was to come. 'Let it go, man. The guy is just trying to have a quiet drink.'

He looked at me with a face that said – 'Dude, please just go. You don't want this trouble, trust me.'

I didn't move. I probably wasn't even blinking.

'Shut the fuck up, Tom,' Jed said, pointing a finger at him, but looking at me. 'I want to know why this fag likes looking at me so much. Do you want to fuck a real man tonight? Is that it, fag? Would you like a piece of this?' Jed used both hands to point to his massive gut.

My eyes slowly ran the length of his body, and that seemed to piss him off way past his limit. His jaw locked in anger. His face became even redder, and he stood up from his stool threateningly.

And that was it.

That was the trigger.

It wasn't his obnoxious way, or his smell, or the name calling, or the fact that he was so damn ugly he probably had to sneak up on his mirror. It wasn't even that he didn't allow me to get drunk in peace. It was the fact that he thought he could assert his superiority over me that did it. That pushed me over the edge.

Right there and then, I knew Jed would die that night.

Fifty-Nine

Hunter stopped reading and looked at Kennedy.

Even though he was looking at the words upside down, Kennedy had been following Hunter's eyes and he knew exactly where he'd paused.

'Read on,' he said. 'There's a twist.'

I didn't face up to Jed. Not there. I wasn't about to get into a fistfight with him in a public place. That would've been way too reckless.

I placed thirty dollars on the bar to cover my drinks, got up and took a couple of steps back.

'What's the problem, fag?' Jed said, sounding and moving his hands like a ghetto rapper. 'Too scared?'

Tom, who had moved from behind the bar, quickly jumped in, putting himself between Jed and myself.

'C'mon, Jed, there's no problem here. The guy didn't say anything, and he was just leaving, right?'

Tom twisted his neck to look at me, his eyes begging me not to engage, and leave.

I finally snapped out of my staring trance, looked down at the floor, and began walking away.

'That's right, fag, get your pussy ass out of here before I fuck you up.'

I opened the door and stepped outside into the warm and damp night.

I didn't go anywhere. I just got into my car, drove it over to the other side of the road, and parked it in a dark spot, next to a rusty dumpster. From there, I had a clear view of the bar's entrance.

I waited.

Jed walked out the door forty-six minutes later and staggered over to a battered Ford pick-up truck. It took him almost a minute to manage to slot his keys into the keyhole and open the door. He didn't drive off straight away either, and for a moment I thought that he would fall asleep in the truck, but he didn't. He lit up a spliff and smoked the whole damn thing before he turned on his engine.

I followed him as he pulled onto the road. I kept my distance, but I didn't really have to. Jed's senses were mushed. He wouldn't have noticed a pink elephant in a golden tutu following him.

Jed's driving was all over the place, and what scared me the most was the possibility of him being stopped by a cop. If that had happened, Jed would've spent the night in a cell for driving under the influence, and I would've probably walked away from the whole situation. Unfortunately for Jed, Forest City in Scott County, Mississippi, seemed deserted of cops that night.

Jed lived just outside town, in a single-story, dirty, old and faded-blue wooden house by the side of the road. There was no garage, and the driveway was nothing but dirt and gravel, flanked by shrubs and overgrown grass. He parked his truck by the rusty metal fence that circled the property, and smoked another spliff before finally wobbling his way into the house.

I found a hidden place to park, waited twenty minutes, and very quietly crossed over to the house. The front door was locked, but it didn't take me long to find an open window. I knew there'd be one. With no air conditioning, the night was too hot and stuffy for Jed to have kept all the windows and doors shut.

The inside of the house smelled of grease, fried onions, stale cigarettes and dry rot. The place was filthy and looked an absolute mess but, after meeting Jed, I expected nothing less.

I tiptoed my way deeper into the house. Finding the bedroom was easy. All I had to do was follow the snoring sound. And Jed snored like a dinosaur in heat. But I decided that I didn't want to kill him in his bed. That would've been too easy.

I felt my blood bubbling inside my veins with excitement as my heart changed rhythm. My adrenal glands caught up to the new beat and began pumping full throttle, while my mouth salivated like a hungry dog in a butcher's shop. I wanted to prolong that feeling for as long as I could. Nothing is more exciting than hiding inside the victim's house and waiting for the right moment.

I chose a sharp knife from his kitchen. Thankfully, there was a good selection to choose from. I knew that a fat greaseball like Jed would no doubt get up in the middle of the night and either hit the kitchen for some more food, or the bathroom to go piss a gallon. With that much booze inside of him, the bathroom was a safer option. I hid behind the shower curtain where he wouldn't see me until it was too late.

I covered my shoes with plastic bags that I'd also found in the kitchen, carefully pulled the shower curtain back, climbed into his soiled bathtub, leaned back against the tiled wall, and waited. I can stay still for hours if I have to.

The waiting made my whole body tingle as if I were soaked in an Alka-Seltzer bath, high on my power.

Jed finally came into the bathroom ninety-four minutes later, dragging his feet.

I took a deep breath to keep myself from going for him too early. I had carved a small slit in the plastic curtain so I could see out. Looking lost, Jed paused once he entered the bathroom.

And then the right moment came.

Sixty

As if hypnotized by the words, Hunter and Taylor's eyes just couldn't tear themselves away from the pages in Lucien's notebook. It was like reading a blockbuster paperback book, with the added difference that every single word was true.

Still drunk, high, and half-asleep, Jed faced the shower curtain and stretched his huge arms high above his head. His mouth opened into a black hole as he started yawning, and even from behind the curtain I could smell his putrid breath. His eyes were bloodshot from a combination of the weed he'd smoked earlier, alcohol, and the heavy sleep he'd just woken up from. He was wearing nothing but a pair of filthy boxer shorts. It almost made me laugh.

For an instant, it looked to me as if his eyes tried to focus on the shower curtain. Maybe he'd noticed the tear I'd created, I'm not sure, but I knew that that was my cue.

I was so wired up from adrenaline and excitement that I must've moved twice as fast as normal. Jed's brain and reflexes were so screwed up from the alcohol, the drugs and the sleep that he would've reacted twice as slow as normal. Put those two factors together, and Jed never saw me coming.

With my left hand I pulled the shower curtain to one side, while already throwing my body forward. My right hand and the knife were also moving fast, creating a high arc from right to left.

The blade hit Jed exactly where I wanted it to – across his neck and throat. The combination of how sharp the blade was and the strength of the movement would've proven lethal to anyone. The knife cut through skin and muscle as if they were made of rice paper. From the amount of arterial spray that flew high into the air, hitting first my face, then the curtain and wall behind me, I knew I had sliced through both of Jed's internal jugular veins. I also ruptured his upper airway. His eyes settled on me for a brief moment, but I'm not sure he recognized me, or even understood what was happening.

I didn't care if he knew or not. My body was already floating on air with the ecstasy of it all. I grabbed the back of Jed's head with my left hand and pulled it back hard, exposing the fatal wound further. I enjoyed watching the blood squirt out of his neck, cascade down his body, and froth in his mouth. A muffled, gurgling sound was all his vocal cords could produce. I held him in that position until his crazed eyes went still. Until the gurgling sound was gone. Until his body became nothing but a dead weight.

After Jed fell to the ground, I stayed in the bathroom for another seven minutes, still high on all the natural chemicals that my brain had thrown at me. I felt no guilt. No remorse.

I washed my face and hands, but wasn't very concerned with my clothes. I would just burn them as soon as I left the house.

It was time to move on.

But fate is a funny thing, and as I walked down the short corridor and past Jed's room, something grabbed my eyes and I stopped. The door was wide open, and that was the first time I saw her.

It was hard to believe that a large bag of human excrement like Jed would have a girlfriend. I know she wasn't his wife because neither of them had a wedding ring. But still, he did, and there she was, passed out on the bed. Surprisingly, she wasn't nearly as big or as ugly as Jed was: short dark hair, high cheekbones, delicate lips, and smooth honey-colored skin. She was attractive, very much so. How she ended up with Jed will always be a mystery to me.

I stood by the door, staring at her asleep in bed for a little while. I was still buzzing from cutting Jed's throat. How can anyone, high on his favorite drug, walk away when some more is so freely offered to him?

I felt my body start to tingle again, and I felt the trigger being pulled inside my head for the second time in the same night. I decided that I wouldn't fight the urges anymore, so I carefully and quietly walked into the room and lay in bed beside her. I could still feel the warmth from where Jed had lay.

I didn't move for twenty-two minutes. I just lay there, watching Jed's girlfriend asleep, waiting, inhaling the scent from her hair, feeling the warmth of her body so close to mine.

Then she moved.

She rolled over and threw her arm over my chest in a sleepy hug, like couples do. Her eyes remained closed. Her hand fell on my shoulder, and I couldn't contain myself. As softly as I could, I took her hand, brought it over to my lips, and began kissing and licking her fingers. They smelled and tasted of hand cream.

I guess she enjoyed the kissing and nibbling, because she moaned quietly and slowly threw her leg over me. As it settled over my body, subconsciously and understandably, she missed Jed's body volume. That's what she was used to. The nerves in her leg registered it, but it took a few seconds for the signals to be decoded by her drowsy brain. As they did, she frowned even before her eyes blinked open.

The light in the room wasn't great. All she had to go by was the full moon, now low in the sky outside the open window on the east wall. My face was half obscured by shadows.

I guess I hadn't washed myself as well as I thought I had, because at that exact moment, a drop of Jed's blood dripped from my hair onto my forehead, ran down over my eyebrow, and onto the white pillowcase.

The woman blinked again. This time a nervous, full-of-fear kind of blink. Her brain, registering that something wasn't right and sensing danger, became awake fast. She jerked her head back a couple of inches so her eyes could better focus, and as they did, fear froze them in place.

All she saw was a stranger with his clothes soaked in blood, lying where her boyfriend was supposed to be, staring straight into her eyes, with two of her fingers stuck into his mouth.

Sixty-One

Hunter stopped reading and closed the notebook.

An uncomfortable Special Agent Taylor took a step back and finished her Scotch in one gulp.

'Where are the others?' Hunter asked, nodding at the notebook.

'That's the only one,' Kennedy answered. 'All the other notebooks found in the house in Murphy contained nothing. A few drawings and sketches but nothing else. Nothing like this.'

'But there must be others.' Hunter sounded a little confused. 'Are you sure they've checked through all the books and notebooks they found?'

'Yes, I'm sure,' Kennedy confirmed. 'Lucien must've kept them somewhere else, or even scattered around several different locations. That wouldn't surprise me, and that's something else you must find out during the course of your interviews.'

Hunter's stare hardened.

Kennedy read it. Tiredness began really showing in his hoarse voice, which was now starting to croak.

'Look, Robert, there's no way on earth I approve of what Lucien has done, but if you're right about him writing down everything he's done and experienced into notebooks, then it's already done, and it cannot be *undone*. If these note-books do indeed exist, then we might as well have them. For one, they'll constitute evidence in a serial murder case that I have no doubt will go down in history. Two, the psychological and behavioral knowledge, the understanding that we'll gain from those notes and texts, may prove to be a game changer in our fight against extreme violent repeat offenders. As a law-enforcement officer and as a psychologist, you know that full well, Robert.'

Hunter had no argument to come back with.

'Nothing inside the storage facility in Seattle?' Taylor asked.

'Nothing but the chest freezer and the severed body parts,' Kennedy confirmed.

Everyone appeared to have gone into thinking mode for a beat.

'I checked with the Scott County Sheriff's Department in Mississippi,' Kennedy moved on. 'Jed Davis and his girl-friend, Melanie Rose, were butchered inside the house they shared just outside Forest City twenty-one years ago. They were found by her mother who had dropped by with a homemade apple pie about two days after the incident. No one was ever arrested.' He paused for effect and to catch his breath. 'According to the medical examiner, Melanie Rose's head was hacked off with a kitchen knife. The head was left on the dining table in the living room. That was the first thing her mother saw when she looked in through the window.' Kennedy looked at Hunter, the expression on his face as serious as a heart attack. 'He killed her just because she was home, Robert. He killed her for pure pleasure.'

Hunter closed his eyes and pressed his lips against each other.

'You read the accounts,' Kennedy added. 'They were written the day after he butchered them. The narrative and the words are clear and concise, not hysterical or even nervous. We all know that that spells total emotional detachment. As you've said, his accounts are like a study into what goes on inside the mind of a vicious killer – how he thinks, how he feels, what drives him – prior, during, and after each attack. Call me selfish, Robert, but I want that knowledge. We *need* that knowledge. If those books exist, I want them.'

Hunter walked over to the window and had a look outside. Night and rainy clouds had darkened the sky, but it somehow made him see things clearer, understand something that until now he hadn't. And he cursed himself for not having seen it earlier.

'I guess you will have them, Adrian,' he said. 'Because Lucien wants you to have them.'

Taylor frowned and Kennedy threw Hunter a skewed look.

'What do you mean?'

'This was all planned,' Hunter said.

Taylor and Kennedy's confused looks intensified.

'What was all planned, Robert?' Taylor asked.

'Being caught.' Hunter turned to face them. 'Well, maybe the timing wasn't one hundred percent there. Maybe Lucien would've liked to carry on doing what he's been doing for a while longer. He could never have predicted the accident in Wyoming that led us to him, but I think that he was always counting on being caught one day.'

Kennedy took just a few seconds to board Hunter's thought ship. 'Because what's the point in writing an encyclopedia on killing and behavioral motivation if no one will read it . . . or study it, right?'

Hunter agreed in silence.

Taylor thought about it for a second but wasn't as convinced. 'Yeah, but then why would he want to be caught? He could've arranged for the books to be delivered to the FBI, or he could've sent them in anonymously, or something.'

'It wouldn't have had the same effect,' Hunter disagreed.

'Robert is right.' Kennedy backed him up. 'The notebooks on their own wouldn't have had the same "weight" as if we'd caught the perpetrator. It would've taken us a lot longer to follow it up because there would always be doubts as to whether the books were a hoax or not. Having Lucien in custody . . . the interviews, him guiding us to the remains of his victims' bodies . . . it all adds to the whole credibility of the notebooks.'

Kennedy paused as a new realization finally hit him. He looked at Hunter. 'And that's why he asked for you.'

Hunter breathed out and nodded.

'Because *you* add even more credibility to Lucien's character,' Kennedy said. 'You went to college together. You shared a dorm. You were the best of friends. You know how intelligent he is and he knew that you could vouch for that.' He walked over to the other side of his desk. 'I bet that he's counting on you remembering the conversation you had about the "killing encyclopedia" idea. He knew you would remember Susan Richards. You were always a major part of his plan, Robert.'

'So now that his credibility is more than established,' Taylor cut in, 'why not just ask him for the notebooks? If you're right, and the idea from the beginning was for the Bureau to get those books, he should be forthcoming with the information.'

'No, he won't be,' Hunter said. 'Not yet.'

'And why is that?'

'Because he's not done yet.'

Sixty-Two

Hunter managed only three and a half erratic hours of sleep. He was up by 5:00 a.m. By 6:30, he'd already been for a five-mile run, and at 7:30, he and Taylor were back down in sublevel five.

Like the previous day, Lucien was sitting at the edge of his bed, right leg crossed over his left one, hands clasped together and resting on his lap, calmly waiting for them.

Hunter, Taylor and Kennedy had decided the night before that pushing Lucien to talk about the notebooks now, if they indeed existed, wasn't the best strategy. His victims' remains were still the priority.

'I was wondering if you'd still be here or not, Robert,' Lucien said as his interrogators took their seats. 'I thought that maybe you'd want to see Susan's remains for yourself. I thought that you might be halfway to Nevada to see her parents by now.' He studied Hunter's expression but got nothing. 'You did find her, didn't you?' The question sounded unconcerned.

'We found her,' Taylor confirmed.

'Ah, but of course,' Lucien said as he'd just remembered something. 'Tests and more tests. You know that it's her, don't you, Robert?'

No reaction.

'But the FBI won't move a muscle until they have lab confirmation. It's protocol. Contacting her parents without being one hundred percent sure that you have Susan's remains is careless, and potentially very damaging for both sides. That's very understandable.'

'Are there any other victims buried in the vicinity of the house in La Honda, Lucien?' Hunter asked.

Lucien smiled. 'I did think about it. It's a great location. Hidden from everything. No neighbors. No one to sneak up on you.' He shook his head. 'But no. Susan was the only one in La Honda. This is a huge country, Robert. Similar places aren't that hard to find. Anyway, after Susan it took me a long time to get my shit together.' He cracked the knuckles on his hands against each other. 'We've all heard and read about the "cooling-off" period between serial murders, but let me tell you . . . it can be one hell of a dark time.'

Hunter wasn't very interested in hearing Lucien's personal accounts of how he felt, and though he knew Lucien would want to stretch every interview as much as he could, he still pushed for the information he wanted.

'So give us the name and the location of another victim, Lucien.'

Lucien carried on as if he'd never heard the question.

'On the days, weeks, months, after Susan, as the "killing drug" effect wore off –' he had drawn quotations marks in the air with his fingers – 'I was as sure as I could be that I'd never do it again. But as time went by, all the urges started to creep up on me again. And they came back stronger, more demanding. I missed the transcendent high. I missed the feeling of power that I had that night with Susan. And I knew that my body as well as my brain were dying to experience it again.'

'How long was it?' Taylor asked. 'The cooling-off period? How long between Susan Richards and your second victim?'

'Seven hundred and nine days.'

Lucien didn't even have to think about the answer. The number was etched in his brain. Every detail about everything he'd done was etched in his brain.

'I was already at Yale,' he proceeded. 'Her name was Karen Simpson.'

Hunter frowned.

Lucien looked at him and nodded. 'That's right, Robert, Karen was real, with all the tattoos, the lip and nose piercings, the left ear stretched to a full centimeter, the Bettie Page-style fringe . . . I met her at Yale, just like I told you, but I did lie about something. Karen was never a drug addict. That was just something I made up because it fit the story I wanted to tell you a couple of days ago. That's something I learned along the way. If you're going to lie, then use as many true facts as you can – real people, names, descriptions, locations, time frames or whatever. They're easier to remember, and if you need to retell your story at a later date, you reduce your chances of being caught out.'

Hunter knew the theory.

'Like I told you before, Karen was a very sweet woman. She was also doing a PhD in psychology. We used to study together. In fact . . .' Lucien gave them a goofy smile, one that said, 'I know something that you don't.' 'Both of you have already made her acquaintance.' He gave Hunter and Taylor a challenging look.

'The other framed tattoos down in that basement,' Hunter said.

'That's right, Robert,' Lucien agreed. 'The cranes.'

One of the framed human skin pieces found in Lucien's basement had a colored tattoo of a pair of cranes. The design had been taken from a painting called *Cranes on a Snowy Pine*, by the artist Katsushika Hokusai.

'She had it tattooed on her upper right arm,' Lucien said. 'Now, despite Karen being only my second victim, I decided to get adventurous.'

Sixty-Three

There was something in the way Lucien phrased his last words that seemed to freeze the air for an instant, as if evil had been waiting around the corner all this time, and was just about to make its presence felt.

'As I've said,' Lucien continued, 'the urges started coming back to me a few months after I left Stanford, but they didn't become unbearable until much later. At first, I thought I could deal with them. I thought that they'd be easy to curb, but just like every repeat offender eventually finds out, I was wrong.'

Lucien used both of his hands to rub the back of his neck while closing his eyes and tilting his head back. After several silent seconds, he breathed out.

'There was a difference this time. Like I said before, I had never looked at Susan as a potential victim until the night it all happened. This time, I knew Karen would be the one. I'd known it from the day I met her.'

'What guided you toward that decision?' Taylor asked. 'What made you choose Karen?'

Lucien pulled an impressed face. 'Very good question, Agent Taylor. Looks like you're learning.'

The tattoos, Hunter thought. Even if physically, Karen didn't resemble Susan at all, the tattoos would've reminded

Lucien of her. And as he'd already admitted, he was chasing the same high. A new victim also carrying large tattoos meant that Lucien would've been able to partially skin her just as he'd done with Susan. By repeating the same methods, the same MO, most perpetrators believe they can achieve the same feelings and highs as they have in previous murders.

Lucien looked as if this was the first time he had actually thought about the reasons behind choosing Karen.

'I guess the first thing that guided me toward Karen were her tattoos.'

Hunter didn't even blink.

'You've got to remember that large, colored tattoos weren't as popular twenty-three years ago as they are now,' Lucien said. 'Especially on women. They reminded me of Susan.' His words were dry as bone. They seemed to suck all the moisture out of the air. 'I began having dreams about them. I began fantasizing about skinning those drawings off Karen's body just like I'd done to Susan. And that was when I realized that another theory was proving true.'

Lucien nodded at Hunter as if they'd had some sort of secret bet all those years ago about which theories would prove true and which ones wouldn't.

'Subconsciously, my brain kept on going back to the same MO as I had used with Susan, and we all know the reason why, don't we? Though it had been nowhere near perfect, I knew I'd feel more comfortable going back to an MO I had used before and knew it worked. Familiarity, Agent Taylor. That's why repeat offenders rarely change their MO.' He pointed to her notebook. 'You can write that down if you want.'

Lucien got up, poured himself a glass of water from the washbasin, and returned to the edge of his bed.

'But I decided that I wasn't looking for comfortable. I wasn't looking to do something I'd already done. That wasn't part of what I had planned in my head. So I started to think about what I'd do differently. Even before I met Karen, I knew I would do it again. There was no doubt in my mind anymore. The urges had become too great for me to resist them. I knew that it was just a matter of time, and finding the right victim. So the search for a new hidden place began.'

'Where is she?' Hunter asked.

'Oh, she's still in Connecticut,' Lucien confirmed. 'Actually, not that far from New Haven and Yale University.' An otherworldly feeling appeared to radiate out of Lucien, like a fatal sort of calm that could creep out just about anyone.

'Where exactly?' Hunter pushed.

More for effect than anything else, Lucien hesitated, moving his head from side to side as if half in doubt.

'I'll tell you, but let me ask you this first.'

Taylor was attentively observing Lucien. She would never forget the evil smile he threw their way.

'Do you know what a LIN charge is?'

Sixty-Four

Lucien had met Karen Simpson right at the beginning of his second year at Yale University. Karen had just transferred from some place in England, and was still settling in. Lucien had never forgotten the first time he saw . . . no, heard her. That was what caught his attention at first, her voice . . . her British accent.

It was right at the end of a rather boring lecture in Investigative Psychology and Offending Behavior, when Karen put her hand up to ask a question. Lucien had already gathered his books together and was ready to leave when the sound of her voice made him stop. There was something in the calm and unconcerned way in which she pronounced every word. There was a charming cadence to her sentences that was almost hypnotizing to the ear. The icing on the cake was the way everything was dressed up in the most charismatic British accent.

Lucien's eyes found Karen sitting at the other end of the lecture hall, almost hidden away among the other students. She couldn't have been any taller than five-foot-two, Lucien guessed. He took a step to the side to get a better look at her. Her makeup looked quite different – heavier, more Gothic than most. She was wearing a dark T-shirt with 'The Cure' written on it and a photograph of someone with messy dark hair, heavy black eye makeup, and badly applied red lipstick.

But what really grabbed his attention was the large colored tattoo on her right upper arm. As he caught sight of it, it made him hold his breath for a moment or two. All of a sudden his memory was slapped with images of Susan and what had happened that night just over two years ago. Images of him carefully slicing the skin off her arm. The memories brought with them a tremendous head rush, something he hadn't felt since that night, and for an instant Lucien felt light-headed and almost lost his balance.

What is that? he thought as he recomposed himself, squinting his eyes at the tattoo. It looked like a couple of large birds, but from where he was standing he couldn't be sure. What he was sure of was that Karen Simpson would never graduate from Yale. Her fate would be much, much different.

It didn't take Lucien long at all to befriend Karen. In fact, it happened later that same day. From a distance, he'd followed her around campus for the next couple of hours, until a perfect opportunity presented itself during mid-afternoon. Karen had just stepped out of the Psychiatric Hospital building, just south of the old campus, when she paused, seemingly looking for something inside her ruck-sack. She rummaged through it for about two minutes before giving up. After letting go of a deep, exasperated breath, she allowed her eyes to circle around her, looking a little lost.

'Everything OK?' Lucien asked, recognizing the opportunity and tentatively approaching her. The expression on his face was pleasant, innocent.

Karen smiled shyly. 'Yes, everything's fine. I just seem to have lost my campus map, which is not the best thing to do on your first week in a campus this big.'

Yale University is spread over 837 acres of ground, with over 11,000 students.

'That's very true,' Lucien agreed with a sympathetic chuckle. 'But you might be in luck. Give me a sec,' he said, lifting a finger in a "wait" gesture before reaching into his own rucksack. 'Here we go. I knew it would be here somewhere. Have this one.' He handed Karen a new campus map.

'Oh!' Her eyes lit up with surprise. 'Are you sure?'

'Yes, of course. I know my way around quite well. I just never really cleaned out my bag, so that map's been there for a while.' He gave her a "What can you do?" kind of shrug. 'Anyway, where do you need to go just now?'

'I'm trying to find Grove Street Cemetery.'

Karen's British pronunciation of *cemetery* brought a new smile to Lucien's lips.

'Wow, that's quite a walk from here.' He pointed south. 'Why do you want to go to the cemetery, if you don't mind me asking?'

'Oh, no, I don't really need the cemetery. That's just my point of reference. I need to go to the Dunham Lab building, but I remember that it's just across the road from the cemetery.'

Lucien nodded. 'Yes, that's right, but hey, I'm heading that way myself. I can walk you there if you like.'

'Are you sure?'

'Yes, of course. I'm going to the Becton Center, which is right opposite the Dunham Lab building.'

'Oh, that's a piece of good luck,' Karen said, hooking her rucksack over her right shoulder. 'Well, if it really is no bother, that would be great. Thank you very much.'

Then, with a thoughtful expression on his face, Lucien looked at Karen a little sideways. 'Wait a second.' He pointed a finger at her. 'You were in the Investigative Psychology and Offending Behavior lecture this morning, weren't you?' His performance could've won him a place in drama school.

Surprised flourished on Karen's face. 'I was indeed. You were there?'

'Yeah, sitting right at the back. I'm doing a psychology PhD.'

Even more surprise now.

'So am I. I just transferred from University College in London.'

'Wow, London? I always wanted to go to London.' Lucien offered his hand. 'I'm Lucien, by the way.'

And so they became friends.

Lucien already knew he would kill again. He'd started fantasizing about how he would do it around eight months ago, and the more he thought about it, the harder it got to control his impulses. Meeting Karen Simpson filled him with an immense feeling of relief, as if he'd just found a long-lost piece of a puzzle that had been eating at his brain for months.

Lucien didn't want to overdo it, though. He knew that people would see them together, so he didn't want to appear like he was Karen's best friend, or even a romantic interest. Those were the first people whose doors the authorities would come knocking once she disappeared. No, Lucien was careful to appear like just another student in Karen's circle of friends. Even an acquaintance, rather than a friend.

His planning took another six months. Four of them were spent searching for a hidden place where he'd be able to take Karen and take his time, undisturbed. He finally found an abandoned shack hidden deep in the forestland by Lake Saltonstall, not that dissimilar to the one he'd found back in La Honda. One thing Lucien was very certain of was that he would skin Karen alive. Skinning was what had given him the biggest high that night with Susan. And that meant he would have to keep Karen in captivity for at least a few hours.

But Lucien also wanted to experiment. He didn't want to use his hands on Karen's neck like he'd done with Susan. He wanted something new, something different. The idea came to him one morning as a friend of his, who was reading Molecular, Cellular and Development Biology at Yale, told him about an experiment gone badly wrong inside Pierce Laboratory. As his friend described what had happened, Lucien felt his blood prick inside his veins. He now knew how he wanted Karen to die.

Sixty-Five

Yale University closed for summer in mid-May. Lucien had been eagerly waiting and planning for it for some time, and he played his cards absolutely right.

Around April Lucien had asked Karen if she intended going back to England for the summer holidays.

'Are you joking?' she had replied. 'Summers in England are like a mild spring around here. I've been looking forward to my first summer in the US for quite a while now.'

'Are you staying around here?'

'No, I don't think so. I'm thinking about taking a trip down to New York first. I've always wanted to see New York, you know, Broadway and all. Maybe even get a new tattoo. There are some great studios over there. After that, I was thinking I could perhaps travel down to Florida and the coast. Spend a few days at the beach? They don't call it the sunny state for nothing.' Karen smiled.

'Are you planning on doing all that by yourself?' That was Lucien's key question.

Karen shrugged. 'I guess.' She looked at him inquisitively. 'But I could do with a travel mate, what do you say, Lucien? It could be fun . . . New York, then the beach?'

Lucien saw the opportunity but he screwed up his face and gave her a quick excuse, saying that he already had a few things organized – a few summer jobs. He knew that if he'd said 'yes', Karen would probably tell someone else that they'd be traveling together – a friend, a professor, her parents, whoever. Then, if she never came back from their summer trip but he did, his name would be right at the top of the police's enquiry list. On the other hand, if Karen disappeared when she was supposed to have taken a trip on her own, questions wouldn't start being asked until much later. Many would just assume that she had given up Yale after one year and gone back to England. It probably wouldn't be until her parents started worrying from the lack of communication that a few alarm bells would start ringing.

They met again just five days before summer break, and Karen told Lucien that she was planning on leaving for her New York and Florida vacation in four days' time. That gave him three to get everything prepared. But Lucien had been meticulously organizing everything for two months. He had almost everything he needed in place. The only things missing were a few chemical canisters, and he knew exactly where to get them.

Lucien dropped by Karen's efficiency apartment the day before she was due to leave for New York. His plan was simple. He would invite her to take a drive with him to Lake Saltonstall that morning for a picnic, saying that they'd be back before nightfall. If Karen said that she couldn't for any reason, then Lucien would invite her for a quick goodbye drink later that evening, which he was sure she would've said yes to. Anyway, the final purpose was the same – to be alone with Karen either at a remote picnic site or inside his car before she was due to leave.

Karen said yes to the picnic.

They set off at around 11:00 a.m. He drove at a steady pace, and the ride to the isolated location he'd chosen by the lake took just under twenty-five minutes. But this time Lucien didn't subdue his victim inside his car. There was no surprise attack. No needle to the neck. Lucien did actually prepare a picnic, with sandwiches, salads, fruit, donuts, chocolates, beer and champagne. They ate, drank and laughed like a couple of best friends. It was only when Lucien poured the last of the champagne into Karen's glass that he added enough sedative to throw her into a deep, dreamless sleep for at least an hour.

It took less than five minutes for the drug to work.

When Karen reopened her eyes, there was no more picnic, no more outdoors. She came to very slowly, and the first thing she realized was that her head ached with such ferocity, it felt like an animal was inside her skull, clawing at her brain.

In the poor light and through the pain, it took her eyes four whole minutes to finally regain focus. As they did, she struggled to understand her surroundings. She was sitting inside a dark, stuffy and soiled room. The walls seemed to be made of plain wood, like a large tool shack in someone's back garden. But something inside her told her that she wasn't in anyone's back garden. She was somewhere else. Somewhere no one would find her . . . a place where no one would hear her if she screamed. And as that realization dawned on her, that was exactly what she tried doing – screaming. And that was when she became aware that her lips weren't really moving. Her jaw wasn't moving either. Panic took hold of her body and she tried to look around her. Her neck wasn't moving.

Oh, Jesus!

She tried to move her fingers.

Nothing.

Her hands.

Nothing.

Her feet and toes.

Nothing.

Her legs and arms.

Nothing.

All she could move were her eyes.

They stirred down to her body, and she saw that she was sitting down on some cheap metal chair, unrestrained. Her arms were loose and falling down the sides of the chair.

For a second, she thought she was dreaming, that she would very soon wake up back in her bed, that she would laugh and wonder why her brain had produced such tormenting images, but then there was movement in the shadows to her right, and the fear she felt growing inside her told her that this was no dream.

Her eyes darted in that direction.

'Welcome back, sleepyhead,' Lucien said, stepping out of the darkness.

It took Karen just a few seconds to notice that everything about him seemed different, starting with what he was wearing – a long, lab-like, plastic, see-through coverall. His sneakers were also covered with blue-plastic shoe covers.

Lucien smiled at her.

Karen tried to speak but her tongue felt heavy and swollen. Only undecipherable noise came from her throat.

'Unfortunately, you won't be able to say much,' Lucien explained. 'You see, Karen, I've injected you with a succinylcholine-based drug.'

Fear exploded inside Karen's eyes.

Succinylcholine is a neuromuscular-blocking agent. It blocks transmission at the neuromuscular joint, causing paralyses of whichever skeletal muscle was affected. In Karen's case, her entire body. The nervous system, though, stays intact. She would still be able to feel everything.

Lucien checked his watch. 'You'll be in this state for a while longer.' He stepped closer. 'You know, I'm not a big fan of tattoos. I'm not sure if I've told you that before, but I will admit that that design you have on your upper right arm is very nice. Japanese, isn't it?' As he said that, he moved his right hand from behind his back, and the metallic blade glistened in the dim light.

There was no room for any more fear in Karen's eyes. They just teared up as more unrecognizable sounds escaped her throat.

Lucien stepped closer still.

'The main reason why I paralyzed you,' he said. 'Was because I wouldn't want you to wiggle about and mess this up. This is very delicate work.' He looked at the blade – a laser-sharp surgical scalpel. 'This will hurt a little bit.'

Tears just rolled down Karen's cheeks.

'But the good news for you is that ... I've done this before.'

Sixty-Six

Karen implored her body to move. She tried to gather together all the strength she had left inside her, all the willpower she could muster, but it simply wasn't enough. Her body just wouldn't respond, no matter how hard she willed it to. She tried screaming, talking, pleading, but her tongue still felt like a huge hairy moth inside her mouth.

Slowly and skillfully, Lucien used the scalpel to rupture the skin at the top of Karen's shoulder blade. The first blob of blood came out, and he used a piece of gauze to clear it up. He proceeded to gradually slice and very carefully pull the skin off her arm.

Karen's head had been paralyzed in a sitting-up sleeping position, slumped forward and slightly to the right. Her chin was low and almost touching her chest. Lucien had placed her in that position deliberately. He knew that once the drug had taken effect, Karen wouldn't be able to move her neck, only her eyes. He wanted her to be able to see.

And so she did.

As Lucien moved closer, her eyes shot right and she saw the scalpel pierce her skin and the blood come out of her arm, but she was so scared that the pain effect was delayed. It took several seconds for a sharp and deep penetrating pain to finally hit her, releasing an animal-like, guttural growl that came from deep inside her.

The skinning, together with Karen's contagious fear, filled Lucien with a mind-numbing satisfaction he couldn't explain. Much better than any drug he could think of.

The entire process didn't take him very long, and at the end of it Lucien was floating on air, high on the chemicals his brain had released into his bloodstream. He would've completed the skinning in half of the time, but Karen could only manage a few minutes before she passed out. Lucien wanted her awake, he wanted her panic, and so he interrupted the skinning process to bring her back to consciousness before starting again. That took time.

When he was finally done, he waited for Karen to come to again and lifted the bloody, tattooed piece of skin to show her.

Her internal organs weren't paralyzed, and as her eyes caught sight of what used to be part of her upper right arm, her stomach shot half of its contents back up her esophagus and she vomited all over herself.

'Don't worry, Karen,' Lucien said as he began to clean her up.

Karen shuddered inside at his touch.

'That's the only tattoo I want from you. I will not be taking any of your other ones.'

Karen had five tattoos in total.

'But I do have a surprise for you.' Lucien got up and disappeared into the shadows for a moment.

Karen heard a muffled scratching metallic sound, as if Lucien had begun dragging a beer keg across the floor. When he reappeared, she finally saw what he was dragging, and it was no beer keg. Lucien had with him a couple of metallic tanks, very similar in appearance to the large oxygen tanks one would find in hospitals. But somehow Karen knew that the contents of those tanks wouldn't be oxygen.

At the top, a hose was attached to the nozzle of each tank. Lucien placed the tanks about five feet in front of Karen's chair before returning to the shadows. Seconds later, he resurfaced, bringing with him a telescopic boom microphone stand that had been specially adapted. The alteration was that the stand had two boom arms instead of one.

He placed the stand in between Karen and the tanks before adjusting the two boom arms – one up, one down. The up one was leveled at Karen's chest, the down one at her waist.

Karen's eyes were following every movement with anticipation and an enormous sense of dread. She could almost feel her organs trembling inside her.

Lucien proceeded to hook a tank hose to each of the boom arms, so both hoses were now pointing directly at Karen.

'I have a question for you, Karen.'

There was nothing Karen could do but just stare at him.

'Have you ever heard of a LIN charge?'

He twisted both tanks so that their labels were facing Karen. As she read them and understood what their contents were, her heart froze.

Sixty-Seven

Taylor had frowned at Lucien's question, but Hunter knew exactly what he was talking about.

LN_2, LIN and LN are all known abbreviations used for liquid nitrogen. A LIN charge is a supercooled liquid nitrogen blast. It became known as a LIN charge because the military had created liquid nitrogen grenades and explosive charges that could be magnetically attached to structures like doors, walkways, bridges and so on. Their main purpose was to hyper-freeze anything – alloys, metal, plastic, wood – making them extremely vulnerable and easy to breach. The real problem comes when a LIN charge hits human skin.

Liquid nitrogen grenades differ from all other known types of grenade in one simple way. Their charge doesn't need to break or penetrate the skin of the target in order to kill them.

The premise behind their effectiveness is based on the special chemical properties of the most abundant mineral on earth – water.

Water is the only naturally occurring substance on the planet that expands when cooled. If a human body is struck by a blast of supercooled liquid nitrogen, it will become very cold, very fast. When that happens, blood cells will freeze instantly in what is known as a 'shock freeze'. The real messy part comes because blood cells are made of approximately 70 percent water, and the water in the blood cells will begin to expand very, very rapidly. The result of all those water molecules in one's bloodstream expanding so quickly is total body hemorrhage. The subject will bleed from just about everywhere – eyes, ears, mouth, nose, nails, sexual organs *and* through the skin.

Because of the supercooled charge, the molecules' expansion doesn't stop, and in consequence every single blood cell in the human body eventually explodes. It's an excruciating death, and a totally horrifying sight.

For Taylor's sake, Lucien briefly explained the entire process.

'I'll tell you this,' Lucien said to Hunter and Taylor. 'What happened to her body once I blasted it with liquid nitrogen was hell-scary, even for me. It was like everything inside her exploded, and all that blood came pouring out through . . .' He sighed deeply and scratched his beard, sweeping his eyes over his barren cell. 'Everywhere, really. I spent four days just cleaning and disinfecting that shack so wild animals wouldn't take over once I was gone.' Lucien paused, remembering. 'My friend back at Yale told me that they were performing this experiment on a live frog in one of the labs. It involved liquid nitrogen. When he told me what had happened, I just tried to imagine how a human body would react. But even my fertile imagination didn't reach as far as reality.'

If Hunter or Taylor had any doubts that they were sitting before pure evil, those doubts had just vanished in the last few minutes. Neither of them wanted to hear any more details.

'The location, Lucien?' Hunter asked. His voice was steady and reasonable. 'Did you bury her around Lake Saltonstall?'

Lucien ran a finger around the grooves surrounding one of the cinder blocks on the wall to his left. 'That I did. And I have a surprise for you. I revisited that site four more times after Karen, if you know what I mean.' He pursed his lips in a 'What can I do?' way and followed it with a careless shrug. 'It was a good site, well hidden.'

'Are you saying we'll find five bodies at the site, instead of only one?' Taylor asked.

Lucien held the suspense up for a moment longer before nodding. 'Uh-huh. Would you like their names?'

Taylor glared at him.

Lucien laughed. 'But of course you would.' He closed his eyes and breathed in as if his memory needed an extra burst of oxygen. When he reopened them again, they looked dead, emotionless. He began.

'Emily Evans, thirty-three years old, from New York City. Owen Miller, twenty-six years old, from Cleveland, Ohio. Rafaela Gomez, thirty-nine years old, from Lancaster in Pennsylvania. And Leslie Jenkins, twenty-two years old, from Toronto, Canada. She was an international student back at Yale.'

Lucien paused and drew in another deep breath.

'Would you like me to tell you how they died as well?' His lips smirked, but his eyes didn't.

Hunter had no intentions of sitting in that basement and listening to Lucien boost about how he had tortured and killed every one of his victims.

'The location, Lucien, nothing more,' Hunter said.

'Really?' Lucien pulled a disappointed face. 'But it was just starting to get fun. Karen was only my second victim. I got better with each new one, believe me.' He winked at Taylor suggestively. 'Much better.'

'You're a fucking psycho,' Taylor couldn't contain herself anymore. She felt disgusted just looking at him.

Hunter matter-of-factly turned his head to look at her, silently pleading with Taylor not to engage.

'You think so?' Lucien seized the moment.

Taylor disregarded Hunter's look. 'I know so.'

Lucien looked like he was considering that statement for a moment. 'You know, Agent Taylor, you really do have a problem with naivety. If you think I'm unique in the urges I have, then you're unmistakably in the wrong profession.' He threw a thumb over his shoulder. 'Every single day thousands, millions of people out there have murderous thoughts. Some start having them very, very young. Every day there are people out there who in their own way consider killing their spouses, their partners, their neighbors, their bosses, their bank managers, the asshole bullies who torment their lives . . . the list goes on and on.'

Taylor glanced at Lucien as if his argument didn't have a leg to stand on.

'What you're talking about are spur of the moment, heated *thoughts*,' she returned calmly, emphasizing the word 'thoughts'. 'They are understandable, angry psychological reactions to a particular action. It doesn't mean that any of it will ever materialize.'

'The location, Lucien,' Hunter intervened. For the life of him he couldn't understand why Taylor was still feeding the fire. 'Where are Karen's remains?'

Lucien ignored him. Right then, he was more interested in pushing Taylor a little further.

'Naive, naive, naive, Agent Taylor,' he said, shaking his head. 'With every human thought, spur of the moment or not, there's always a risk that the thought might one day – fed by anger, hurt, disillusion, jealousy . . . there are a thousand factors that could help it grow – become much more than just a thought. It's called the *law of probability*. I'm sure you've heard of it. Your databases are overflowing with such examples. And it happens because anyone, and I mean *anyone*, independent of upbringing, gender, class, race, beliefs, status or anything else, could, under the right circumstances, become a killer.'

Let it go, Courtney, Hunter pleaded in his head.

Taylor didn't. 'You *are* delusional,' she replied without thinking.

Her response only amused Lucien more.

'I don't think that I'm the one who's delusional here, Agent Taylor. You see? It's very easy for anyone to say that he or she will never cross a certain line, when that line is never presented to them.'

Lucien allowed his words to float in the air, giving Taylor a moment to digest them before moving on.

'If one day they come face to face with such a line, they'll sing a very different tune. Trust me on this, Agent Taylor. It was one of my experiments – presenting that line to someone who swore she could never take a life.' Lucien looked at his nails as if considering if they needed trimming or not. 'And, boy, did she cross it.'

Taylor choked on her own breath.

Hunter stared at him in disbelief.

'Are you saying that you forced someone to commit murder as an experiment? To prove a point?' Taylor asked.

Hunter had no doubt that Lucien was very capable of such an act. He was very capable of much more. But Hunter had heard enough, and despite Taylor being the lead agent in this investigation, he lifted a stop hand at her and took over.

'The location, Lucien. Where in New Haven are those bodies?'

Lucien scratched his beard again while studying Hunter.

'Of course I'll tell you, Robert. I promised I would, didn't I? But I've been telling you things for far too long now, and it's my turn to ask a question again. That was the deal.'

Hunter could feel that coming. 'Tell us where the bodies are first, then, while the FBI verifies the site, you can ask your question.'

Lucien agreed with an eye movement. 'I can see your logic, but I'm sure that the FBI is already verifying the four names I've just given you.' He looked up at the CCTV camera on the corner of the ceiling inside his cell and smiled at it. 'Which means that I've already given you something to keep you busy. So now it's my turn.'

Lucien gathered himself before staring deep into Hunter's eyes.

'Tell me about Jessica, Robert.'

Sixty-Eight

Back in the holding cells' control room, once Director Kennedy heard the four names Lucien had given Hunter and Taylor, he immediately got on the phone to one of his research teams.

'I need proof that these people are real,' he said to the lead agent. 'Social security numbers, driving licenses, whatever.' He dictated the first three names with the respective ages and home towns, just as Lucien had mentioned. 'The fourth person – Leslie Jenkins – is from Toronto in Canada. She was an international student at Yale, probably in the early 90s. Check with Yale, and if need be check with the Canadian Embassy in Washington. I also need to know if these people have been reported missing. Get back to me ASAP.' He quickly put the phone down.

Kennedy remembered once having a conversation with a military weapons expert who had joined the FBI. They had discussed LIN grenades and charges. The weapons expert had showed him actual footage of what happens to a human body when it's exposed to a blast of supercooled liquid nitrogen. Kennedy had probably seen more dead bodies and attended more violent crime scenes than most people in the entire FBI, but he'd never seen anything quite like that footage.

Kennedy was ready to contact the FBI field office in New Haven, Connecticut, and ask them to dispatch a team to whatever set of directions Lucien was about to give them, when Lucien changed the game and asked Hunter about Jessica.

'Who's Jessica?' Doctor Lambert asked, looking at Kennedy.

Kennedy gave him a delicate headshake. 'I have no idea.'

Sixty-Nine

While Lucien's question resonated against the walls, Hunter felt the air being sucked out of his lungs as if somebody had just hit him in the stomach with a baseball bat. He looked at Lucien with narrow eyes, half doubting his ears.

Taylor couldn't help but let her gaze wander over toward Hunter.

'I'm sorry?' Hunter said. No amount of poker face could mask his surprise.

'Jessica Petersen,' Lucien repeated, clearly enjoying Hunter's reaction. The name traveled through the air slowly, like smoke. 'Tell me about Jessica Petersen, Robert. Who was she?'

Hunter couldn't tear his eyes away from Lucien, his brain trying hard to understand what was happening.

Police or medical records, he concluded. *That's the only possible way. Somehow Lucien gained access to either police or medical records, or both.* Hunter then remembered the feeling he had when Lucien kept on asking him about his mother. Hunter felt as if Lucien already knew all the answers, and he would have, if he'd gotten his hands on police or medical records. The medical examiner's report would've stated that Hunter's mother had died of a painkillers' overdose, and put the time of death sometime in the middle of the night. Finding out that Hunter's father worked nights, and therefore wasn't at home, wouldn't have been very difficult. The only other person in that household at that time was a seven-year-old Robert Hunter. Lucien would've had no problem putting together most of what had really happened that night. He just needed Hunter to fill in the gaps.

'Who was she?' Lucien asked again, coolly.

Hunter blinked the blur of confusion away. 'Someone I knew years ago,' he finally replied in the same tone.

'C'mon, Robert,' Lucien shot back. 'I know you can do better than that. And you know you can't lie to me.'

Their stares battled for a moment.

'She's someone I used to date when I was young,' Hunter said.

'How young?'

'Very. I met her just after I finished my PhD.'

Lucien sat back on his bed and stretched his legs in front of him, getting as comfortable as he could. 'How long did you date her for?'

'Two years.'

'Were you in love?' Lucien asked, tilting his head slightly to one side.

Hunter hesitated. 'Lucien, what does this have to do with—'

'Just answer the question, Robert.' Lucien cut him short. 'I can ask whatever I like, relevant or not, that was the deal, and right now I would like you to tell me more about Jessica Petersen. Were you in love with her?'

Taylor shifted on her chair.

Hunter's nod was subtle. 'Yes, I was in love with Jessica.'

'Did you make plans to marry her?'

Silence.

Lucien's eyebrows arched, indicating that he was waiting for an answer.

'Yes,' Hunter said. 'We were engaged.'

For the briefest of moments Taylor heard Hunter's voice croak.

'Oh, that's interesting,' Lucien commented. 'So what went wrong? I know that you aren't married or divorced. So, what happened? How come you never married the woman you were in love with? Did she leave you for someone else?'

Hunter gambled. 'Yes, she found someone else. Someone better.'

Lucien shook his head and noisily sucked his teeth with every head movement. 'Are you sure you want to test me again, Robert? Are you sure you want to lie to me? Because that's what you're doing right now.' Lucien's look and voice became hard as steel. 'And I *really* don't like that.'

Taylor kept a steady face, but her eyes looked lost.

'You know what?' Hunter said, lifting both of his hands up. 'I'm not talking about this.'

'I think you'd better,' Lucien countered.

'I don't think so,' Hunter replied in the same conservative tone a psychologist would use to address a patient. 'I was brought here because I thought I'd be helping an old friend. Someone I thought I knew. When they showed me your picture back in LA just a few days ago, I was sure that there had been some sort of bad mistake. I agreed to fly over here because I thought I could help the FBI clear all this up and prove you're not the man they thought you were. I was wrong. I can't help because there's nothing to clear up. You are who you are, and you did what you did. Unfortunately, no one can change that. But you said so yourself – there's no rush to any of this because there's no one we can save – and when I leave, the FBI will carry on interrogating you about the location of all your victims' remains.'

Hunter peeked at Taylor. A frown had creased her forehead after she heard the word 'leave'.

'They'll just use different methods,' Hunter continued. 'Less conventional ones. I'm sure you know what's coming. It might take a few days longer, but trust me, Lucien, in the end you will talk.'

Hunter got up, ready to leave.

Lucien looked as calm as he'd ever looked.

'I would really suggest that you sit back down, old friend, because you've misquoted me.'

Hunter paused.

'I didn't say that there was no rush to any of this. I said that there was no rush in finding Susan's remains, because you couldn't save *her* anyway.'

Something in the way Lucien phrased his words made Hunter's heartbeat stumble, pick itself up, and then stumble again.

'And I've never said that you couldn't save anyone. Because I think there's still time.' A tense pause as Lucien looked at his wrist, consulting his invisible watch once again. 'I haven't killed all the victims I've kidnapped, Robert.' Lucien accompanied those words with a look so cold and devoid of feelings, it could've belonged to a cadaver. 'One is still alive.'

Part Three

A Race Against Time

Seventy

Hidden location.
Three days earlier.

She coughed and spluttered awake, or at least she thought she was awake. She couldn't really tell anymore. Her reality was as terrifying as her worst nightmares. Confusion surrounded her twenty-four hours a day, as her brain seemed to be in a constant state of haziness – half numb, half awake.

Due to the lack of sunlight, she had lost track of time a while ago. She knew she'd been locked in this stinking hell-hole for a long time now. To her it felt like years, but it could've been just months, or even weeks. Time just trickled by, and no one was counting.

She could still remember the night she met him in that bar on the east side of town. He was older than her, but charming, attractive, well educated, very intelligent, funny, and really knew how to compliment a woman. He made her feel special. He made her feel like she could light up the sky. At the end of the night, he put her in a cab and didn't offer, or even suggest joining her. He was very polite and gentleman like. He did ask her for her phone number, though.

She had to admit that she was quite excited when he called just a few days later and asked her if she would like to go out for dinner with him. With a huge smile on her face she accepted.

He picked her up that evening, around 7:00 p.m., but they never made it to a restaurant. As soon as she entered his car and buckled up, she felt something sting the side of her neck. He'd acted so fast she didn't even see his hand move. The next thing she could recall was waking up in this cold and damp room.

The room was exactly twelve paces by twelve paces. She'd counted and recounted it many times. The walls were crude and made of brick and mortar, the floor of rough cement. The door, which sat at the center of one of the walls, was made of metal with a rectangular, lockable viewing slot about five feet from the floor. Like a prison door. There was a thin and dirty mattress pushed up against the back wall. There was a blanket that smelled of wet dog. No pillow. On one corner there was a plastic bucket she was told to use as a toilet. There were no windows, and the weak, yellowish bulb locked inside a metal-mesh box at the center of the ceiling was on 24/7.

Since she'd been taken into captivity, she'd only seen her kidnapper a handful of times, when he would enter her cell to deliver food and water, a new roll of rough toilet paper, and to swop her toilet bucket for a clean one.

So far, he hadn't touched or hurt her. He never said much either. She would scream, beg, plead, try to talk, but he barely ever replied to her. On one occasion, his simple physical response scared her so much she wet herself. Out of pure fear, her subconscious mind kept on urging her to ask him what he wanted with her, what he would do to her. So one day, she gave in and asked him. He didn't reply with words. He simply looked at her, and in his eyes she saw something she'd never seen before – unadulterated evil.

He would bring her food and water, sometimes daily, but not always. Though she had completely lost the concept of time, she could still tell that some of the intervals between rations were way too long. Certainly, way over a day or two.

Once, just after the third or fourth food delivery, she had waited for the door to open and tried surprise-attacking him with all the strength she had in her, clawing at his face with her chipped nails. But it seemed like he'd been waiting for it to happen all along, and before she was able to put even a small scratch on him, he punched her stomach so hard, she immediately doubled over and puked. She spent the rest of that day lying on the floor in the fetus position, contorted in pain, her abdomen sore and bruised.

Sometimes the rations were larger than others – more bottles of water, more packets of crackers and cookies, more candy bars, more loaves of bread, sometimes even fruit. Then he'd be gone for a long time. The larger the ration he brought her, the longer it would be before he came back, and the last ration she got was the largest of them all.

She didn't know exactly how long ago that was, but she knew it was longer than ever before. Very quickly she learned to rationalize everything almost to perfection. By the time she was running out of food and water, he'd be back bringing new supplies, but not this time.

She had run out of food some time ago, maybe three or four days. To her it seemed longer. She ran out of water maybe a day or two after that. She felt weak and dehydrated. Her lips were dried and cracked. Because of how hungry she was, the cold and dampness of the room affected her more than usual now. She spent most of her time curled up into a ball against one of the corners of the room, wrapped up in that stinking blanket. But even so, she couldn't stop shivering.

For some time, her throat had been feeling like it was on constant fire, but today more than ever. She desperately needed a drink of water. Her eyelids felt heavy and it required an effort of will to force them open. Her head ached in a way that every little movement she made felt as if it would be her last, before her brain exploded inside her skull.

She brought a hand to her clammy forehead, and it felt as if she was touching hot metal. She was burning up.

With amazing effort she lifted her head and looked at the door. She thought she heard something. Steps, maybe. Someone coming.

As crazy as it seemed, a smile came to her lips. The human brain is a very complex organ, and a fragile and shattered mind sometimes clutches at straws. Right there and then she didn't think of him as the man who would probably rape her repeatedly before killing her. She thought of him as the man-savior who was coming to bring her food and water, who was coming to take away her overflowing toilet bucket that filled the room with stench and sickness.

She held on to the wall and slowly propped herself up on her feet. With the hesitant steps of a battle-weary soldier, she gradually made her way to the door and placed her ear against it.

'Hello . . .' she called in a voice so weak that it seemed to belong to a scared child.

No reply.

'Hello . . . are you out there? . . . Please?'

. . .

'Please can I have some water?' Her voice was now strangled with tears. She was shivering so badly her teeth were shattering against each other.

'Please . . .?' She began crying. 'Please help me . . .? Just a few drops of water, please?'

She heard nothing but absolute silence.

She stayed on the floor by the door with her ear pressed hard against it for a long time – a couple of hours, probably. There was no noise. There never was. Her tired brain was so desperate it was starting to trick her. Her fever was so high, she was starting to hallucinate.

It took some time for her sobs to subside. She wiped the tears from her eyes and her dirty cheeks, and with no strength left in her to get back up on her feet again, she crawled back to her corner and her blanket on the other side of the room.

She was losing her mind. She could feel she was losing her mind.

As she curled herself back into a ball again, she started whispering to herself. 'Don't give up. Stay strong. You'll get through this. Stay strong . . .' She paused, frowning as her confused eyes circled the room. 'Stay strong . . .' she repeated and paused again, forcing her brain to remember, but it was gone. She couldn't believe it was gone.

'I'm . . .'

Nothing.

'My name is . . .'

Blank.

She desperately wanted to tell herself to stay strong, but she couldn't remember her own name.

She began crying again.

Seventy-One

'Madeleine,' Lucien said. He was still sitting on his bed with his legs stretched comfortably in front of him. 'Her name is Madeleine Reed. But she likes to be called Maddy.'

A prickling began to run deep inside Hunter's body, as if soda bubbles were racing through his bloodstream in an expanding sense of urgency.

Taylor felt as if someone had just slapped her across the face.

'What?' she asked, leaning forward on her chair.

'Madeleine Reed, or if you wish, Maddy Reed,' Lucien repeated with a shrug. 'She's twenty-three years old. I picked her up on April 9, in Pittsburgh, Pennsylvania, but she was born in Blue Springs City, Missouri.' He jerked his head toward the end of the corridor outside his cell. 'You can go check it out if you like. Her family must be going crazy by now.'

Hunter and Taylor both knew that Adrian Kennedy was listening in on the interview. He would have the name and everything else checked in a matter of minutes.

'April 9?' Taylor said, her eyes wide with surprise. 'That's four months ago.'

'It is indeed,' Lucien agreed. 'But don't worry, Agent Taylor, I've got a little system that works. It's been proven over the years.' He smiled. 'I leave her rations of food and water before I leave, and Maddy is very clever. She figured out very quickly that she had to go easy on it, or else it would all run out before I got back with more. And I'll tell you, she became quite an expert at it.' He opened his hands and studied the veins crisscrossing the backs of them. 'But I was supposed to be back four, maybe five days ago.'

He allowed the seriousness of his words to punch everyone square in the face before he continued.

'If Maddy ran out of food and water a few days ago, she'd be very weak by now, no doubt about that, but she's probably still alive. Now, how long she'll stay that way? I can't tell you.'

'Where is she?' Hunter asked.

'Tell me about Jessica Petersen,' Lucien came back. 'Tell me about the woman you loved.'

Hunter sucked in a deep breath.

'Tell us where she is, Lucien, so we can save her, and I promise you that I'll tell you whatever you want to know.'

Lucien rubbed the patch of skin between his eyebrows. 'Umm.' He pretended he was thinking about it. 'No. No deal. Like I've said, now it's your turn to answer my questions. I've given you enough.'

'I will answer them, Lucien,' Hunter said. 'I give you my word I will. But if she has run out of food and water four days ago, we need to get to her now.' The urgency in Hunter's voice filled the air with electricity.

Lucien just looked at him, unperturbed.

'What's the point in letting her die this way, Lucien?' Hunter pleaded. 'Whatever satisfaction you got from killing your victims, Madeleine's death will not give it to you.'

'Probably not,' Lucien agreed.

'So please let her live.'

Lucien looked unfazed.

'It's over, Lucien. Look around you. You've been caught. By chance, but you've been caught. There's no point in taking anyone else's life.' Hunter paused. 'Please, there must still be something human inside you. Have mercy this once. Let us bring Madeleine in.'

Lucien got back on his feet. 'Nice speech, Robert,' he said, pursing his lips. 'Short, to the point, and with just the right amount of emotion. For a second there, I thought your eyes would tear up.' Sarcasm was like a second skin for Lucien. 'But I *am* having mercy. My kind of mercy. And this is how it works. First I want to hear about Jessica; then, and only then, I'll tell you the location of Karen Simpson and the other four victims' remains in New Haven, and I'll tell you where Madeleine Reed is. After that you and Agent Taylor can go be heroes.'

Lucien saw Taylor check her watch.

'Yes, you are losing time,' he said, nodding. 'Every second suddenly became really precious, hasn't it? You don't need me to tell you that dehydration can have irreversible neuro-logical consequences. If you don't get a move on, even if you find her alive, by the time you get to her she might be nothing more than a vegetable.'

Lucien pointed to Hunter's chair.

'So sit your ass back down, Robert, and start talking.'

Seventy-Two

Hunter checked his watch, exchanged a quick, worried look with Taylor, and returned to his seat.

'What do you want to know?' he said, looking Lucien in the eye.

Lucien's smirk was triumphant. 'I want to know what happened. How come you never married the woman you were engaged to? How come you and Jessica aren't together?'

'Because she passed away.'

Taylor turned her head and caught Hunter's gaze. Something glittered in his eyes, and she thought she detected great sadness in them.

Lucien saw it too. 'How?' he asked. 'How did she die?'

Hunter knew he couldn't lie. 'She was murdered,' he replied.

Taylor couldn't hide the surprise in her eyes.

'Murdered?' Lucien frowned. 'OK, now this is getting interesting already. Please do carry on, Robert.'

'There's nothing more to it. We were engaged and she was murdered before I had the chance to marry her. That's all there is.'

'That's never all there is, Robert. That's only superficial, and that's not the purpose of this exercise. Tell me how it happened. Were you there? Did you see it happen? Tell me how you felt. That's what I really want to know. The feelings deep inside you. The thoughts in your head.'

Hunter hesitated for a split second.

'You can take as long as you want,' Lucien challenged. 'It doesn't bother me. But remember that the clock is ticking for poor Madeleine.'

'No, I wasn't there,' Hunter said. 'If I were, it wouldn't have happened.'

'That's a bold statement, Robert. So where were you?' Lucien sat back down at the edge of his bed. 'Feel free to start at the beginning.'

Hunter had never talked about what had happened to anyone. Some things he found it better to keep locked inside, in a place he barely visited himself.

'At that time I hadn't made detective for the LAPD,' he began. 'I was just a police officer with the central bureau. My partner and I were out doing rounds in the Rampart area that day.'

'I'm listening,' Lucien said once Hunter paused for breath.

'Though Jess and I were engaged, we didn't live together,' Hunter explained. 'We were making arrangements to, once I became a detective, which was only a few weeks away, but at that time, we still lived in separate houses. I was supposed to see her that night. We were having dinner together. She'd made reservations in a restaurant somewhere in West Hollywood. But that day, toward the end of the afternoon, my partner and I were dispatched to check on a domestic-violence disturbance in Westlake.

'We got to the address in less than ten minutes, but it all sounded quiet. Too quiet. The husband must've seen our black and white unit approaching through the window. We got out, walked up to the door and knocked. Actually my partner, Kevin, knocked. I walked out to the side of the house to check the window.'

'So what happened then?' Lucien urged Hunter.

'The husband shot Kevin with a sawn-off twelve-gauge shotgun through the letterbox flap on the door. He was hiding behind it, waiting for us.' Hunter looked down at his hands. 'The gun was loaded with heavy double-slug termi-nator ammo. From that distance, the round practically tore Kevin's body in half.'

'Wait,' Lucien said. 'So just like that, this guy shot a cop through the door?'

Hunter nodded. 'He was high on crack-cocaine. He'd been high on it for several days. That was also the main reason for the domestic violence. His brain was soup. He'd locked his wife and his little daughter in the house, and had been abusing and beating them. His little girl was six.'

Even Lucien paused for thought. 'So what did you do after he'd torn your partner in half with a shotgun?'

'I returned fire. I pulled Kevin away from the door and I returned fire.'

'And . . .?'

'I aimed low,' Hunter said. 'Lower half of the body. I wasn't looking for a kill shot, just to maim. Both of my shots got through, but with reduced velocity from breach-ing the door. The first hit the husband on his right thigh, the second on his groin.'

Lucien coughed a laugh. 'You shot his dick off?'

'It was unintentional.'

This time it was a full, throaty laugh. 'Well, if the scum-bag was abusing his six-year-old little girl, then I guess he deserved it.'

Taylor found it rich that someone like Lucien would call anyone a scumbag.

'He survived?' Lucien asked.

'Yes. I called for backup, but the amount of blood he was losing, together with being shot in the groin, scared him sober. Before backup and the ambulance arrived, he opened the door and gave himself up.'

'But your partner didn't make it,' Lucien concluded.

'No. He was dead before he hit the ground.'

'Too bad,' Lucien said, with no emotion in his voice. 'So I guess that you never made it for dinner with Jess that night.' He paused and studied Hunter. 'Do you mind if I call her Jess?'

'Yes, I do.'

Lucien nodded. 'OK, I apologize and I'll rephrase. So I guess that you never made it for dinner with Jessica that night.'

'No, I didn't.'

Seventy-Three

Los Angeles, California.
Twenty years earlier.

Hunter had helped place Kevin's body in the coroners' van before having to recount the details of what had happened to the detectives now assigned to the case. After that, he drove to the Rampart General Hospital to check on the progress of the man he'd shot.

A doctor came out of the operation room to update him. The man, who went by the name of Marcus Colbert, would live, but he would probably walk with a limp for the rest of his life, and he would never again have active sexual relations with anyone.

Hunter's head was an absolute mess, but he still had to go back to his precinct and fill in several reports before he could go home.

Protocol dictated that after a shootout with fatal victims, any LAPD officer involved must have at least a couple of sessions with an LAPD shrink before, pending a psychological evaluation, being allowed to return to full duties. His captain told him that his first session with the appointed psychologist would be in two days' time.

Hunter sat in an empty room, staring at the pen in his hand and the empty reports in front of him for a long time. The events that had taken place earlier that day kept on playing and replaying in his mind like an old movie stuck on an endless loop. He couldn't believe Kevin was gone – cowardly shot dead by a paranoid crackhead on a drug binge. They'd been partners since Hunter had joined the LAPD, a year and a half earlier. Kevin was a good man.

By the time Hunter was finally done with the reports, it was coming up to ten in the evening. Understandably, he'd forgotten all about his dinner plans with Jessica. He gave her a call to apologize and explain why he hadn't turned up or called earlier, but the phone rang a few times before going straight to the answering machine.

Jessica was a very pretty and intelligent woman, and she fully understood the complications that came with dating a law enforcement officer – the long hours, the last-minute cancellations, the worries for Hunter's well-being, everything. She also knew that once Hunter made detective, those complications would step up a level or two, but she was in love, and to her that was all that mattered.

Hunter left a short message apologizing, but he didn't go into any details; he would tell her everything when he saw her. But Jessica was also very sensitive, and though he'd tried to conceal it, he was sure that she would pick up the sadness in his voice, the seriousness of it all.

Hunter found it strange that Jessica hadn't answered the phone. He didn't believe she'd gone out, not at that time on a Tuesday evening. Maybe tonight, she was just a little more upset than the previous times he'd had to cancel on her right on the last minute. Despite his head being all over the place, he still managed to think straight enough to stop by a 24-hour grocery shop and pick her up some flowers.

He got to Jessica's place just before 11:00 p.m. and, as he parked on the street outside and looked back at her house, he was overwhelmed by a dread sensation so intense it nauseated him. He'd never felt anything like it before. But then again, he'd never lost a partner before.

Hunter stepped out of the car and approached the house, but with every step, the dread sensation inside of him multiplied itself exponentially.

Sixth sense, premonition, gut feeling, whatever name anyone would like to call it, by the time he got to the door, Hunter's was screaming at him. Something wasn't right.

He had a copy of the keys, but he didn't need them. The front door was unlocked. Jessica never left the front door unlocked.

Hunter pushed the door open, stepped into Jessica's dark living room, and was immediately hit by a faint, metallic, copper-like smell that practically paralyzed his heart and sent a roller coaster of shivers up and down his spine.

Blood does not have any smell while flowing through one's body. It's only when it comes into contact with air that it acquires a very distinctive, non-chemical, metallic smell, very similar to copper. Hunter had been surrounded by that same smell that afternoon.

'Oh, God, no.' The terrified words dribbled from his lips.

The flowers hit the floor.

His trembling hand reached for the light switch.

As brightness bathed the room, Hunter's world was sent into darkness. A darkness so deep he wasn't sure if he would ever find his way out of it again.

Jessica lay face down in a pool of her own blood by the kitchen door. The living room around him was a mess

– broken lamps, tossed furniture, open drawers – distinct signs of a struggle.

'Jess . . . Jess . . .' Hunter ran to her, calling out in a voice that didn't even seem to belong to him.

He kneeled by her side, his trousers soaking in her blood.

'Oh, God.' His voice broke.

He reached for her and turned her over.

Jessica had been stabbed several times. There were lacerations on both of her arms, hands, chest, abdomen and neck.

Hunter looked at her beautiful face and his vision clouded with tears. Her lips had already faded to a pale color. The skin on her face and hands had acquired a peculiar shade of purple. Rigor mortis hadn't set in yet, but it was well on its way, which told Hunter that she'd been murdered less than four hours earlier – around the time he was supposed to have picked her up for dinner. That knowledge sent the darkness inside of him plunging into new depths. His soul seemed to abandon him, leaving behind just an empty body, drowning in sorrow.

Gently, Hunter pulled her hair away from her face, kissed her forehead, brought her to his chest and hugged her tight. He could still smell her delicate perfume. He could still feel the softness of her hair.

'I'm so sorry, Jess.' A suffocating kind of anguish drowned his words. 'I'm so terribly sorry.'

He held her in his arms until the tears stopped coming.

If he could've exchanged places with her, if he could've breathed his life into her body, he would've done it. He would've given his life for hers without a second thought.

He finally let go of her, and as he turned his head he saw something he had completely missed. Written in blood on one of the living-room walls were the words, cop whore.

Seventy-Four

As Hunter finally told Lucien about that night, a dark, endless pit, like an old wound that had never really healed, reopened in Hunter's stomach, dragging his heart down, and bringing back an emptiness inside of him he'd fought for twenty years to leave behind.

Everyone was silent for a long moment.

'So you lost both of your partners in the same night,' Lucien said. If Hunter didn't know better, he could've sworn there was a pinch of sorrow in Lucien's voice.

Hunter blinked once, pushing the memory as far away from his mind as he could. 'Madeleine, Lucien, where is she?'

'Wait a second, old friend, not so fast.'

'What do you mean, not so fast?' Hunter replied. His eyebrows curved into an angry look. 'You've heard all there is to hear about what happened to Jessica. That was what you wanted, wasn't it?'

'No, that was just part of it.' Lucien lifted both of his hands in a truce gesture. 'But since you told me what happened that night, I'll give you something in return. It's only fair. Are you listening?'

It took Lucien just two minutes to give them specific directions of how to get to the site by Lake Saltonstall in

New Haven, where they'd find Karen Simpson's remains, together with the four other victims he'd mentioned earlier.

Hunter and Taylor listened to everything very attentively and without interrupting, but they were sure that Adrian Kennedy would be taking notes from the holding cells' control room, and within minutes he'd have an FBI team from the New Haven field office dispatched to the site.

'Now,' Lucien said when he was done, 'if you want me to give you Madeleine, let's go back to Jessica and what happened after she was murdered. Was the perpetrator ever caught?'

'Perpetrators,' Hunter corrected him. 'Forensics found two sets of prints in the house, neither of which matched anything in the police archives.'

Lucien's expression showed surprise. 'Was it a sexual attack?'

'No,' Hunter replied, and his eyes glistened with relief, 'she wasn't sexually assaulted. It was a robbery. They took the few items of jewelry she had, including the engagement ring on her finger, her purse, and all the cash she had in the house.'

'A robbery?' Lucien found that strange.

So did Taylor.

'So why kill her?' Lucien asked.

Hunter paused. Looked away. Looked back at Lucien. 'Because of me.'

Lucien waited but Hunter didn't offer any more. 'What do you mean, because of you? This was a revenge attack? Someone wanting to get back at you?'

'No,' Hunter said. 'Jessica had several photographs of the two of us together scattered around the house. In many of them I was in uniform. Those picture frames had all been smashed. Some had the word "pig" written in blood on them. Some had the words "fuck the police".'

As things became clearer, Lucien's head moved sideways slowly. 'So, once they found out that she was engaged to an LAPD officer, they decided to kill her just for fun.'

Hunter said nothing. He didn't even blink.

'I'm not trying to teach an old dog new tricks,' Lucien said. 'But have you looked at gang members? Gang members have a never-ending hatred for the police hardwired into their brains, especially in a city like Los Angeles. The only other people who hate police officers as much are ex-cons, but if the fingerprints weren't on file, then those are clearly ruled out.'

Hunter knew that full well; he and the detectives assigned to the case had hammered every single gang contact they had for information. They got nothing, not even a whisper.

'We're wasting time here,' Hunter said, irritation starting to come through in his voice. 'There's nothing more to say about Jessica or that night. She was murdered. The people who did it have never been caught. Tell us where Madeleine is, Lucien. Let us bring her in.'

Lucien still wasn't ready. 'So you blamed yourself for her death.' Lucien didn't ask. 'Actually, you did it twice, didn't you? First for being a cop, because you knew that was the reason why they killed her. And second because you didn't make it to her house for dinner as you were supposed to.'

Hunter stayed quiet.

'The human mind is a funny thing, isn't it?' Lucien spoke in a practiced, therapist's voice – deep, calm and reasonable. 'Even though you know full well that neither of the two reasons you've been blaming yourself for years are actually your fault, even though you understand the psychology behind the "why" you've been blaming yourself, you still can't avert the guilt.'

Lucien chuckled and got back on his feet. 'Just because one understands psychology, Robert, doesn't mean one is immune to psychological traumas and pressures. Just because one is a doctor, doesn't mean one doesn't get sick.'

Was that what Lucien was doing? Hunter asked himself in thought. *Using Jessica's murder as an example to defend his own sordid actions? Just because Lucien knew that kill-ing people was wrong, just because as a psychologist he probably understood his urges and where they were coming from, it didn't mean that he could control them.*

'And that's the reason why, since then, you've always been a loner, isn't it, Robert?' Lucien said. 'Because you blame yourself for what happened. She was killed because she was close to you. I bet you promised yourself you'd never let that happen again.'

Hunter wasn't in the mood to be psychoanalyzed. He needed to end this. And he needed to do it now. Any answer would do. 'Yes, that's the reason. Now tell us where Madeleine is.'

'In a moment. You haven't satisfied the psychologist in me yet, Robert. What I really want to know about is what happened inside your head after Jessica was murdered. The earthquake of feelings that I know you went through. You tell me that, and I'll give you Madeleine.'

After twenty years, Hunter had learned how to live with those feelings.

'What is there to know?' he asked evenly.

'I want to know about the anger inside you, Robert. The rage. I want to know if you were angry enough to kill. Did you go after them?' Lucien asked. 'The perpetrators? Jessica's killers?'

'An investigation was launched,' Hunter said.

'That's not what I asked,' Lucien shot back with a shake of the head. 'I want to know if *you* launched your own crusade to find her killers, Robert.'

Hunter was about to reply when Lucien interrupted him.

'Don't lie to me now, Robert. Madeleine's life depends on it.'

Hunter could feel Taylor's eyes on him.

'Yes. I have never stopped searching for them.'

Hunter's answer seemed to excite Lucien.

'So here's the million-dollar question, Robert,' he said. 'If you found them, would you take them in, or would you impose your own justice on them . . . your own revenge.'

In silence Hunter scratched the back of his hand.

'You would kill them yourself, wouldn't you?' Lucien's smile was confident. 'I can see it in your eyes, Robert. I saw it while you were reliving that night. I bet Agent Taylor saw it too. The anger. The rage. The hurt. Fuck being a detective. Fuck the law that you swore to uphold. This would take priority over everything. Over your own life. If you came face to face with the people who took Jessica from you, you'd murder them without an ounce of hesitation. I know you would. I know you've thought about it hundreds, maybe thousands of times.'

Hunter breathed in through his nose, and out through his mouth.

'Hell, you might even torture them a while just to see them suffering for what they did. That would be fun, wouldn't it?'

Lucien saw a muscle flex on Hunter's jaw.

'As I've said before,' he continued, 'under the right circumstances, anyone can become a killer. Even those who are supposed "to protect and to serve".' His dead stare could've melted ice. 'Remember, Robert, a murder is a murder. The reasons behind it have no relevance, be it justified revenge or a sadistic urge.' He brought his face to less than an inch from the Plexiglas. 'So one day, you still might become the same as me.'

Lucien was indeed using Jessica's murder to, in a sick way, give reason to the things he'd done,' Hunter thought. *First appealing to psychological reason, now the emotional ones.* Hunter was sure that Lucien had read the police reports. Knowing Hunter as well as he had all those years ago, he would've figured out that Hunter had never stopped searching for Jessica's killers. He had pushed for Hunter to tell the story purposefully, so that he could degrade it and use it as an example and rationale for his own twisted acts.

Despite Hunter's anger, he still had only one priority in his mind. He'd figured that in his head, Lucien had achieved what he wanted. There was nothing else to say.

'Tell us where Madeleine is, Lucien.'

Lucien chuckled. 'OK. But I can't just tell you the location, Robert. I have to take you there.'

Seventy-Five

It took Taylor a moment to register what Lucien had said. She scowled at him.

'Come again?'

Lucien stepped away from the Plexiglas. His expression showed no concern at all.

'I can't just give you instructions to where she is, Agent Taylor. That won't work. I have to take you there myself.'

Hunter didn't seem surprised. In fact, he was expecting it. It was only logical. Because Madeleine's life depended on them getting to her fast, it was too risky to rely on simple verbal or written instructions. What if when they got to the vicinity of where she was supposed to have been held captive, the instructions suddenly became unclear because the surroundings had changed? What if they took a wrong turn? What if there was a mistake in the instructions, deliberate or not? They would've lost valuable time trying to get Lucien to re-explain everything over a phone line, or video link.

No, Lucien had to go with them. He had to personally guide them there.

Taylor's eyes sought Hunter. He gave her a subtle nod.

Lucien smiled. 'There's one more thing,' he said, winking at her. 'There will be only the three of us on this trip. No other FBI agents. No one following us either, by land or air. You, Robert, and I will go, not a person more, not a person less. That's the deal. No negotiation. You break the deal, or I suspect that we're being followed in any way, I guide you nowhere. Madeleine dies alone, forgotten and forsaken, and I'll make sure the press finds out why. I can live with that. Can you?'

Taylor knew she was in a no win situation. Nothing had changed since they'd discovered that Lucien was the only one who could guide them to his victims' remains. He still held all the cards, even more so now that there was supposedly a live victim. He could call the shots any way he saw fit, and at the moment, there was nothing either Hunter or Taylor could do about it.

'As long as you understand that you'll be hand-and ankle-cuffed, and we'll be armed. You try anything, and I swear we'll gun you down.'

'I would've expected nothing less,' Lucien replied.

'We'll be ready to leave in fifteen minutes.' She stood up. 'Where are we going?'

'I'll tell you when we're on our way,' Lucien replied.

'I need to know if we need a plane or a car.'

Lucien nodded his agreement. 'A plane first. Then a car.'

'I need to know how much fuel we'll need.'

'Enough to get us to Illinois.'

As Hunter and Taylor took their first steps back toward the door at the end of the corridor, Lucien halted them.

'I guess that day is closer than you think, Robert,' he said.

Hunter and Taylor both paused and turned around to face Lucien again.

'What day is that?' Hunter asked.

'The day that you might become the same as me.' If Lucien's voice had sounded cold and emotionless before, this time it sounded like it could've come from some ancient devil ... completely heartless. 'Because for the past two days, my friend, you've been sitting before the man you've been seeking for twenty years.'

Hunter felt his stomach curl into a ball.

'I was the one who took Jessica from you.'

Seventy-Six

Hunter didn't move, didn't breathe, didn't blink. It was like his whole body went into lockdown.

'What was that?' Taylor was the one who asked the question.

Lucien's gaze was cemented on Hunter, but other than the initial frown of confusion at his statement, he got nothing else from the LAPD detective.

'You think I'm saying this just to get under your skin, don't you, Robert?'

Despite the awkward feeling starting to gain momentum deep inside of him, Hunter still looked calm.

'Which you obviously are,' Taylor cut in. There was no disguising the irritation in her voice. 'You ran out of tricks and now you're just stalling. You know what? I wouldn't be surprised if there is no Madeleine Reed held captive anywhere. I wouldn't be surprised if you'd just made her up because you ran out of acts for this little performance of yours. I think your chamber is empty. You're panicking, and now you're firing blanks because you know the game is really up.'

Lucien faced Taylor, a smirk stretching his lips. 'Is that really your argument, Agent Taylor? I'm firing blanks because I know the game is up? Is that the best you can come up with?' He coughed a laugh before his stare turned to ice once more. 'Wow, I could eat a bowl of alphabet soup and shit a better argument than that.' Lucien jerked his chin at the CCTV camera just outside his cell. 'Why don't you go ask your people who have been listening in on us? Go ask them if Madeleine Reed is real or not. I'm sure they've been busy running a few checks.'

'Even if there is someone named Madeleine Reed from Pittsburgh, Pennsylvania,' Taylor shot back, still keeping her composure, 'who has been reported as missing sometime after April 9, it doesn't mean you've got her, or that you even know where she is. A list of names can be easily obtained over the Internet from every missing-persons bureau in the country. You are well prepared. You proved that. I'm sure that even someone as arrogant as you must have entertained the possibility that one day you might be caught. It's reasonable to think that you'd have a few tricks already prepared for that eventuality. But even if you were the one who had kidnapped Madeleine, you can give us no proof that she's still alive. You could've killed her months ago, and you know that there's no way we can know for sure. So now you just picked her name out of the many that you've tortured and murdered, and are using her to give you a last chance outside.'

Taylor took a breath, looked at Hunter, and then back at Lucien.

'I wasn't joking when I said that we'll gun you down if you try anything,' Taylor continued. 'If you think this trip will give you a chance at escaping and we're not going to take decisive action because we think you might have information that'll lead us to a live victim, you've got another think coming.'

'Now that's a much better argument than the firing blanks one, Agent Taylor,' Lucien said, clapping his hands three times. 'But as you've just pointed out, there's no way you can know for sure. So when you find out that there really is a Madeleine Reed, who was reported missing in Pittsburgh, Pennsylvania, after April 9, can you really afford to call my bluff?' He gave her a couple of seconds to think about it before adding, 'Because if you do and I'm not bluffing, the amount of shit that will rain on you and on the FBI will last a lifetime.'

Hunter was barely listening. Lucien's words were still bouncing around in his head – *'because for the past two days, my friend, you've been sitting before the man you've been seeking for twenty years. I was the one who took Jessica from you.'*

Every atom in his body wanted to believe that Lucien was just bluffing, but Hunter had seen something in Lucien's eyes – a disquieting defiance that he knew usually only came with certainty.

'I can see your eyes wild, Robert,' Lucien said, taking his attention away from Taylor. 'You're trying to decide if I'm telling the truth or not. Maybe I can help you with that.' He ran his tongue over his top lip. 'Yellow-fronted house, number 5067 on the corner of Lemon Grove Avenue and North Oxford, in East Hollywood.'

Hunter felt his throat constrict. That had been Jessica's address. But if Lucien had read the police reports, that information would've been very easy to obtain.

Lucien read his mind.

'I know, I know,' he conceded. 'That proves nothing. An address is easy to acquire. But how about this. Out of the photographs you mentioned Jessica had scattered around the house, the largest of them all was in a silver frame on a small table by the dark brown leather sofa in the living room. The picture was of the two of you at some sort of LAPD dinner party or award ceremony. You were in uniform and proudly displaying an award. She was wearing a purple dress with a matching purse. Her hair was loose, but thrown to one side, over her left shoulder.'

Still with his gaze firmly set on Hunter, Lucien paused, giving his old friend's brain a chance to try to match his words to the images locked away in Hunter's memory.

And then he delivered a final blow.

'But you know the real difference between that and all the other photographs that were vandalized in the house, don't you, Robert? That was the only one on which the word "PIG" was written vertically, instead of horizontally.'

Seventy-Seven

Hunter felt his heart stall, his blood freeze in his veins, and the pit in his stomach turn into a black hole that threatened to swallow his soul into oblivion. He wanted to speak, but his voice seemed to have gotten stuck in his throat.

His eyes were focused on Lucien, but not his mind. All of his thoughts had traveled back to the night that part of him had died with Jessica. He didn't need to search long. Every detail of what he'd seen that night had been locked away somewhere in his brain. Accessing those memories was painful, but simple. He could practically see the photograph Lucien was talking about, right in front of him – the smashed glass, the silver frame, and the word 'PIG' written in large blood letters – vertically. As Lucien had said, that had been the only photograph on which a word had been written that way.

Trying his best to think logically, Hunter somehow managed to restrain his anger before it boiled out of his body.

If Lucien had somehow managed to get his hands on the crime-scene police reports from Jessica's murder, then there was also a possibility that he'd managed to obtain copies of the crime-scene evidence report and inventory, which Hunter knew were very detailed.

Hunter breathed out.

Lucien picked up on his doubt.

'Still not convinced, huh? Isn't the brain's defense mechanism intriguing, Robert? To try to avoid the intense psychological pain that it can see coming, it will, sometimes, even subconsciously, try everything to find an alternative answer. It will even disregard facts and try to hang on to things it knows not to be true. But I can't blame you, Robert. If I were in your shoes, I wouldn't want to believe it either. But the reality is – it's true.'

Taylor could feel on her skin how volatile the air had become down in that basement corridor.

'You're bluffing again,' she tried one more time, her voice angry and a few decibels louder than before. 'Robert said that there were two perpetrators. Forensics found two sets of fingerprints at the scene. Are you going to tell us that you had a partner this once? *And . . .*' she stressed before Lucien could respond, 'we now have your fingerprints on file. One of the first things the FBI's computer system does is to check the fingerprint of any apprehended individuals for a match against the records in IAFIS, which are linked to any unsolved crimes. If your fingerprints had matched any of the ones found inside Jessica's home, or at the crime scene of any other unsolved crime, we would've had red alerts screaming at us from all four corners days ago.'

IAFIS is the Integrated Automated Fingerprints Identification System. After collecting a DNA sample, the FBI computer system also does the same check against the National DNA database.

Lucien waited patiently for Taylor to finish.

'As I have brought to your attention before, Agent Taylor, you can be quite naive sometimes. Do you think that staging a crime scene is hard? Do you think that making a murder look like a by-product of a robbery is difficult? Do you think that acquiring and planting someone else's fingerprints inside Jessica's house would've posed a problem to someone like me?' He laughed. 'I can give you the names of the two men those fingerprints belonged to. Not that you'll be able to verify it anyway, but I can also give you the location where you'll find their remains. I wanted it to look like a robbery by gang members. I wanted the police to look for two suspects, instead of one. Why do you think the FBI had no clue I existed, Agent Taylor? Why do you think that after so many murders, your Behavioral Science Unit was never able to link any of them? Why do you think you haven't been searching for a murderer who's been killing people for twenty-five years?'

Defeat and anger began to draw lines across Taylor's face.

'It's called deception, Agent Taylor. Making the police believe one thing, while the truth is something very different. It's an art, and I'm very good at it.'

Lucien reverted his attention back to Hunter.

'Maybe this will clear all the doubts from your mind once and for all, Robert. You said that all the jewelry Jessica had in the house was taken, but did you tell the detectives exactly what was taken?'

Hunter felt an awkward sensation crawling like a rash across his skin.

'Of course not,' Lucien said. 'I doubt you knew every piece of jewelry she owned. But I can tell you exactly what was taken. She kept everything inside this cute little flowery box on the dresser in her room. Next to another picture of the two of you. A picture that wasn't touched, wasn't vandalized. The two of you at the beach.' He paused, and in Hunter's face saw the punch hit its target. But he wasn't done yet. 'I took the whole box. But from her body, other than the engagement ring you've already said was taken, I also took her two single diamond earrings, and her dainty necklace. The pendant on it was a white gold humming bird. Its eye was a tiny ruby.'

No amount of self-discipline would've been able to keep Hunter's anger locked inside this time. He exploded forward and slammed both of his fists against the Plexiglas several times.

Tears welled up in Hunter's eyes. The deep pain in them was as clear as words on a page. Without even realizing, and through gritted teeth, a single word escaped his lips.

'Why?'

Seventy-Eight

Hunter's outburst was so sudden and so violent that it made Taylor jump on the spot. Lucien, on the other hand, barely blinked. He was expecting it.

When Hunter's fists finally stopped pounding the Plexiglas, the skin on his hands had turned red raw and was already starting to bruise. His whole body was trembling with rage, sadness and confusion. Lucien was simply enjoying the show, but he didn't fail to hear Hunter's question.

'You want to know why?' Lucien said.

Hunter just glared at him. He couldn't stop shaking. At that particular moment, he was in a place very far away from his sane starting point.

Lucien gathered himself, lifting up as if what he wanted to say needed an injection of strength into the nape of his neck.

'The real reason is because I couldn't help it,' Lucien explained. 'I'd really missed you, Robert. I missed the only true friend I ever had. So eight months before the incident with Jessica, I decided to look you up in Los Angeles. I didn't get in contact with you first because I wanted to surprise you. I wanted to see if you'd recognize me if I suddenly knocked on your door.'

Hunter allowed his hands to drop to the side of his body.

'I found out where you lived,' Lucien continued. 'That wasn't very hard. So I just hung around your apartment block one evening, waiting for you to come home. I thought that maybe after the huge surprise, or at least what I thought would be a huge surprise for you, we could go and grab a beer somewhere, talk about old times . . . catch up.' Lucien shrugged. 'Maybe deep inside I had a masochistic desire to see if you would pick anything up – any psychopathic traits, I mean. Maybe I wanted to check if you could see behind my everyday mask. Or maybe it wasn't that at all. Maybe I was so confident that I just wanted to put myself through a test, to prove to myself that I was that good. And what better test than to spend a few days in the company of the best criminal behavior psychologist I knew. Someone who was also a police officer, and about to become a detective. If you weren't able to read the signs, Robert, then who would?'

Hunter's stomach was in turmoil, and he had to concentrate hard not to be sick.

'But that night you didn't come home alone,' Lucien proceeded. 'I watched you park your car, get out and, like a gentleman, go around to the other side and open the passenger's door for someone. Out stepped this beautiful woman. And I have to hand it to you, Robert, she was stunning.'

Hunter held his breath to stop his chest from heaving with emotion.

'I couldn't really tell you what it was exactly,' Lucien said. 'But one thing that my experiences had already taught me, was that despite all the desires, despite all the violent thoughts and impulses one gets, despite the unstoppable drive to take someone's life, there still needs to be some sort of trigger to finally push one over the edge.'

Immediately, Hunter and Taylor's thoughts went back to the passage they'd read in Lucien's notebook, which Kennedy had showed them the day before.

'With Jessica it was the way she looked at you when you took her hand to help her out of the car, Robert,' Lucien moved on. 'The way she kissed you right there in the parking lot. There was so much love between the two of you that I could feel it on my skin all the way from where I was standing.'

Hunter's fingers closed into a fist once again.

'I tried, Robert. I tried to resist it. That's why I never approached you that time. I didn't want to do it. I didn't want to take Jessica from you. I left Los Angeles the next morning, and I did all I could to forget about her. If ever I tried to resist an urge, that was it. But what neither of you will ever understand is that once that trigger goes off inside your head, you're doomed. The obsession drives you crazy. You can delay it, but you can't contain it. It comes back night, after day, after night, hammering your brain, until you just can't take it anymore. Until the visions take over your life. And that point came eight months later.'

Hunter took a step back from the Plexiglas.

'So I planned everything to look like a robbery,' Lucien said. 'I killed two men just to get their fingerprints. I knew they would never be found, so no matter how hard and long the police searched for them, the prints would never be matched to anyone. I returned to Los Angeles. I saw the two of you together again, and then I followed her back to her place.'

Even Taylor was now starting to feel numb.

'There was no torture,' Lucien added. 'No sexual gratification. I did it as fast as I could.'

'No torture?' Taylor interjected. 'Robert said that there were stab wounds all over her body.'

'Post-mortem,' Lucien replied, his eyes seeking Hunter. 'If the autopsy team was competent enough, they should've found out that her first wound, the one to her throat, was the fatal one. All the others were inflicted post-mortem. That was part of the "robbery-deception" plan.'

That fact had always intrigued Hunter once he'd read the autopsy report. He had put it down to a burst of anger from the perpetrators because Jessica was engaged to a police officer.

'I staged the scene with the broken picture frames, the vandalized photographs, the disturbed house and the stolen jewelry and money. And that was it. That's how it happened. That's *why* it happened.'

Hunter's eyes remained unblinking on Lucien's face as he stepped up against the Plexiglas once again, the fingers on both of his hands still clenched into fists.

'You were right before, Lucien.' His voice was so calm, it scared Taylor. 'Screw being a detective. Screw what I've sworn to uphold. You *are* a dead man.'

He turned and walked out of that corridor and basement.

Seventy-Nine

Ninety seconds later, Hunter and Taylor were standing inside Director Adrian Kennedy's office. Doctor Lambert was also there.

'I understand that this whole scenario has changed for you, Robert,' Kennedy said, as Hunter stood looking out the window. 'No one could've anticipated that sort of revelation, and I am deeply sorry. I'm not going to lie to you and say that I completely understand how you feel, because I don't. No one does. But I have a pretty good idea.' Kennedy's voice sounded fatigued.

He walked over to his desk and picked up a printout that was by his computer monitor before retrieving his reading glasses from his breast pocket.

'But there's one thing that hasn't changed,' he said before reading from the printout. 'Madeleine Reed, twenty-three years old, born in Blue Springs City, Missouri, but at the time was living in Pittsburgh, Pennsylvania. She was last seen by her housemate on April 9, just before she left her apartment to go out for dinner with someone she'd met a few days earlier in a bar. Madeleine never came back that night, which her housemate found strange, because Maddy – that's what everyone called her – didn't make a habit of spending the whole night with anyone on her first date.'

Hunter kept his focus on the world outside Kennedy's window.

'Two days later, she still hadn't turned up,' Kennedy added. 'That was when the housemate, someone called Selena Nunez, went down to the police station and reported her as missing. Despite all efforts from the missing-persons' investigators, they've got absolutely nothing. No one knows what this mysterious man who took her out for dinner on the evening of April 9 looks like. The barman at the bar Madeleine was the night before remembers her. He also remembers seeing her talking with someone who looked to be a little older than her, but he didn't pay enough attention to the man's face to be able to give the police an accurate description.' Kennedy adjusted his reading glasses on his nose. 'Madeleine worked for CancerCare. Her specific job was to provide support and friendship to children with terminal cancer, Robert. She's a good person.'

Kennedy offered the printout to Hunter.

Hunter didn't move.

'Look at her, Robert.'

A few seconds went by before Hunter finally dragged his eyes away from the window and onto the sheet of paper Kennedy had in his hand. Attached to it was a second print-out – a 6x4 portrait photograph of Madeleine Reed. She was a very attractive woman, with light and seemingly smooth skin, eyes that had a slightly oriental appearance and were green in color, and hair that dropped in a vibrant black sheen past her shoulders. The smile she had on when the photograph was taken looked pure and innocent. She looked happy.

'The fact that Lucien might know where Madeleine Reed is being kept hasn't changed, Robert,' Kennedy said again.

'You can't walk away from this now. You can't turn your back on her.'

Hunter studied the photograph for a while longer before returning the sheet to the director in silence.

Kennedy took the opportunity to press on. 'I know you don't work for me, Robert, so I can't order you to do anything, but I do know you. I know your moral values. I know what you stand for and what you've dedicated your life to. And if you allow your emotions to dictate your actions now, no matter how hurt and angry you feel inside, you won't be able to live with yourself later. You won't be able to face yourself in the mirror. You know that full well.'

A headache was pinching and pricking behind Hunter's eyes.

'I've been searching for Jessica's killers for twenty years, Adrian.' Hunter's voice was low and full of hurt. 'Not a day has gone by since that I don't regret not being there for her that night. Not a day has gone by since that I haven't promised her and myself that I would find them, and when I did, I would make them pay, no matter the consequences to myself.'

'I understand that,' Kennedy said.

'Do you?' Hunter questioned. 'Do you, really?'

'Yes, I do.'

'She was pregnant,' Hunter said.

The air was knocked out of Kennedy's lungs. He looked back at Hunter with confusion on his face.

'Jessica was pregnant,' Hunter repeated it. 'We had found out that morning, through one of those off-the-shelf pregnancy tests, but we both knew it was true. That was the reason for her booking the restaurant that night. We were supposed to be celebrating. We were both ...' Hunter paused to catch his breath: '... so happy.'

Taylor felt a paralyzing chill run through her. She wanted to say something, but she didn't know what, or how.

'Lucien didn't only take the woman that I was supposed to marry from me, Adrian,' Hunter said. 'He took away the family I was supposed to have.'

Kennedy looked down at the floor in solemn silence. His way of paying his respects and recognizing Hunter's pain.

'I'm sorry, Robert,' Kennedy finally said. 'I never knew that.'

'No one did,' Hunter replied. 'Not even her family. We wanted to wait until Jess had seen the doctor so we had official confirmation.' Hunter's gaze returned to the window. 'I asked the coroner to omit it from the autopsy report. That was not the way I wanted her parents to find out, and I saw no point in adding to their pain.'

'I can only imagine your pain, your anger, and how devastating that must've been for you, Robert,' Kennedy said after a long and dark silence. 'And I am so sorry.'

'And nevertheless you still want to put me inside an enclosed space with the person who I've been searching for for twenty years and swore revenge on, without the security of the Plexiglas wall between us.'

'He's been caught, Robert,' Kennedy said back, in a measured voice. 'Lucien is sitting in an underground, escape-proof prison cell five levels below the FBI's Behavioral Science Unit. He *is* going to pay for everything he's done. He's going to pay for what he did to Jessica and to you.' He pointed to the printout. 'But this girl may die if you don't get in that plane with Lucien. I know you don't want to let that happen.'

'You can send someone else.'

'No we can't, Robert,' Taylor, who was standing by Kennedy's desk, said, turning to face him. 'You heard what Lucien said downstairs. You and me and him. Not a person less, not a person more. We break that deal, and if Madeleine isn't already dead, she will die – alone – probably until the last second still holding on to some hope that someone will find her. We owe this to her, Robert.'

Hunter said nothing.

'Courtney is right, Robert,' Kennedy said. 'If Madeleine isn't already dead, we're losing precious time here. We've got to act now. Please don't let your anger and sorrow take away Madeleine's chances of being saved. Her only chance of being saved.'

Hunter looked at Madeleine's photograph attached to the printout once again.

'She's not dead,' he said, not an ounce of doubt in his voice.

'What?' Kennedy asked.

'You said, "If Madeleine isn't already dead".' Hunter shook his head. 'Madeleine Reed isn't dead. She's still alive.'

Eighty

The unwavering conviction in Hunter's voice was reassuring and confusing in equal measure.

Taylor's question came not from words, but from a slight shake of the head complemented by narrowing eyes.

'She's alive,' Hunter told them again with a firm nod.

'How can you be so sure?' Doctor Lambert asked. 'Don't get me wrong, Detective Hunter. I do agree with Director Kennedy. I believe you must act now, but you must also be prepared for the fact that you could already be too late to save this poor girl's life, or even for the fact that Lucien could be sending you on a wild goose chase. He's a deceiver by nature, with years of experience. As Agent Taylor said during your last interview, Lucien might be looking at this as his last chance outside, which gives him a better chance at trying something than if he's sitting in a cell five levels underground.'

'That could be,' Hunter replied. 'But Madeleine is still alive.'

'So I'll repeat Doctor Lambert's question,' Kennedy took over. 'How can you be so sure, Robert?'

'Because Madeleine Reed is Lucien's trump card,' Hunter said. 'He's been holding on to it from day one. When did you first bring him here to the BSU?'

'Seven days ago,' Kennedy answered. 'You know that.'

'And yet he hasn't mentioned her until now,' Hunter reminded them. 'As Doctor Lambert said, Lucien's got a lot of experience. He's been playing this game for a very long time. Even though he was caught by chance, every move he makes is calculated to the last detail. And an experienced player knows one major rule about trump cards.'

'Never play them too soon,' Taylor said. 'You hold on to them until the best possible moment.'

Hunter nodded. 'Or until it's imperative that you do. You've all mentioned how impressive Lucien's internal clock and calculations are, right? He knows exactly how much food and water he's left Madeleine. He's already said that she'd learned how to ration everything almost to perfection. He's calculated the threshold. He's known it from day one, and I'm sure he's got a very accurate idea of where the point of no return is. And yet he saw no reason in playing his trump card until now. And that reason is – he wants to make this a race against time, because that puts us under tremendous pressure. A hell of a lot more pressure than just finding victims' remains.'

Everyone breathed in Hunter's words for a second.

'And that's also why he waited until now to reveal that he was your fiancée's killer,' Doctor Lambert said, 'because that not only puts you under extreme pressure, but it also affects your state of mind. It destabilizes you. It makes you emotional, and therefore more vulnerable, more prone to mistakes. Lucien knew that fully well.'

Goose bumps ran up and down Taylor's skin.

'But that also makes Robert more volatile,' she said. 'If Lucien weren't behind that Plexiglas wall, he'd probably be dead now.' Her gaze moved to Hunter, who returned her stare with 100 percent conviction.

'And maybe that's exactly what he wants,' Doctor Lambert said. 'Not to try to escape while he's outside with you both, but suicide by cop.'

Kennedy and Taylor frowned at him, but that was exactly what Hunter had been thinking about while staring out the window.

'Why would he be looking for suicide by cop?' Taylor asked.

'Because whatever happens, Lucien wants to be remembered,' Hunter said. 'He wants the notoriety.' He drew air quotations with his fingers. 'The "prestige" that comes with being a famous serial killer. He wants his legacy to be studied in criminology and criminal behavior classes. That's one of the reasons he's been writing this encyclopedia of his, if that really is what he's been doing.'

'I understand that,' Taylor said, 'but that will probably happen no matter what. He doesn't have to be killed to achieve it.'

'True,' Hunter agreed, 'but he also understands that his reputation would get an exponential boost if he doesn't end his days behind bars, or executed by the state. I'm sure that in his mind that would not be a suitable conclusion to his lifelong project. On the other hand, if he's shot dead by the FBI while they're trying to rescue his last victim . . .' Hunter shrugged and let the significance of what he'd said intoxicate the air.

'He becomes a legend,' Doctor Lambert agreed.

'So, if you think Madeleine Reed is still alive,' Kennedy said, addressing Hunter, 'and assuming that Lucien's got his calculations right, how long would you say we have, Robert?'

Hunter pulled a dubious face. 'My best guess is that from the time he told us about Madeleine, we would've had around twenty hours to find her. After that, I wouldn't hold out too much hope.'

Kennedy checked his watch. 'So we've got to act fast,' he said. 'We can't waste any more time here, Robert.'

Madeleine's photograph was still on the desk. It looked like she was staring straight at Hunter.

'Is the plane ready?' he said.

'It will be by the time you get to the runway,' Kennedy replied, 'but the two of you need to get ready first.'

'Be prepared,' Doctor Lambert said as everyone began moving, 'because I think you're right, Detective Hunter. Lucien will try to push both of you to the limit, and he knows that as things stand right now, he won't even need to push that hard. I think that once he gets out there again, he will do whatever it takes not to end up back here. Even if it costs his life.'

Hunter zipped up his jacket. 'And I'm fine with that.' He looked at Taylor. 'As long as I'm the one who takes the shot.'

Eighty-One

Before heading down to the SUV that was already waiting for them by one of the security exits at the back of the building, Hunter and Taylor were both asked to hand in their shirts so that two state-of-the-art, wireless surveillance microphones could be fitted onto them. The microphones were disguised as regular buttons, but so that a single button didn't differ from the other ones, every button on both shirts had to be replaced. The one just above their belly button was the microphone. It connected via a small cable to a very powerful but inconspicuous satellite transmitter that resembled a stick of gum, strapped to the small of their backs. The microphone also worked as a GPS locator. Director Adrian Kennedy and his team would know their exact location at all times. But as soon as he got his shirt back, Hunter opposed the idea.

'The fake buttons aren't the same exact color as the original ones,' he told Adrian Kennedy.

'They're close enough,' Kennedy replied.

'Maybe to most people,' Hunter said. 'But not for Lucien.'

'Are you telling me that you think he's noticed the color of the buttons on yours and Agent Taylor's shirts?'

'Trust me. Lucien has noticed everything, Adrian. He's like a sponge.'

'Well, this is the best we can do given our timeframe,' Kennedy said back. 'I need ears with you at all times, so we're going to have to roll with this.'

This could be a costly mistake, Hunter thought.

Everything was already in place by the time Lucien was escorted out of the security exit by two US Marines, ten minutes later. He was wearing the same orange prisoner jumpsuit he'd been wearing throughout the interviews. His hands and ankles were shackled by metal chains that looped around his waist, restricting his movements – his arms would not come up past his chest, and his step would never go beyond one foot, making it impossible for him to run.

'Something is missing from this equation,' Lucien said to Taylor, as she opened the back door of the SUV to allow him to climb in.

'Detective Hunter will meet us in the plane,' Taylor said, knowing exactly what Lucien was referring to.

Lucien laughed. 'But of course. He needs time to find himself and maybe check his emotions before this whole thing turns into a total fiasco, isn't that so, Agent Taylor?'

Taylor didn't reply. If she were to allow her emotions to take over, she would probably punch him in the face right there and then, and shoot both of his kneecaps off. Instead, she simply held the door open while both Marines helped him onto the backseat, locked his chains to the metal loop on the car's floor, and handed the keys to Taylor.

'I love your sunglasses, Agent Taylor,' Lucien said, as Taylor took the passenger's seat. 'They're very . . . FBI. Do you think I could get a pair, just for the sake of this trip?'

Taylor said nothing.

'I guess that will be a "no" then.'

Lucien looked at his cuffed hands for a short instant; when he spoke again his voice was controlled and measured – no excitement, no anger, just a robotic flat tone. 'How do you think this is going to end up, Agent Taylor?'

The driver, an African American Marine who looked like he could probably bench-press that entire SUV got the car in motion.

Taylor kept her eyes on the road.

'C'mon, Agent Taylor,' Lucien insisted. 'It's a fair question. I'm very interested in knowing what your expectations are. You've done great so far. You've managed to obtain information that has led the FBI to retrieve the lost remains of three victims.' His eyebrows popped up and down once. 'Assuming that your team is competent enough to follow instructions, you should also find the remains of the five victims I left in New Haven. And you have also managed to acquire information that might lead you to a live victim, which, if you succeed in saving her, will make you into a hero, Agent Taylor. That's not bad going at all for just two days of interviews. So I think my question is quite fair. How do you think this whole thing is going to end up? Do you think you and Robert will become heroes, or will this turn into your worst nightmare?'

Taylor saw the driver's questioning eyes flick toward her for a fraction of a second.

What she really wanted to do was to turn around and tell Lucien that they were going to find Madeleine Reed and finally put an end to her torture. Then they would bring him back to the BSU so that he could tell them where to find the remains of all his other victims. After that, he would either rot in prison or be executed by the state. Either way, it made no difference to her because she would never have to look at his face again. But she kept her composure and didn't say a word. She didn't even look at him.

Lucien wasn't deterred.

'Do you think he will do it?' he asked in the same robotic tone. 'Do you think Robert will avenge Jessica's death? Do you think he'll forget everything he's upheld for most of his life and let his anger take over?'

No reply.

'Do you think he'll shoot me or will he use his hands – beat me up until I stop breathing?'

Taylor didn't look, but she could tell that Lucien had that sickening smile on his face again.

They exited the FBI Academy compound heading north toward Turner Field landing strip.

'How would you do it, Agent Taylor? If I had violently taken the person who you were so desperately in love with away from you, and left you with nothing but doubts and a lot of blood, how would you take your revenge on me?'

Taylor felt her blood warming inside her veins, but still, she swallowed every word that threatened to come out of her mouth.

Lucien swopped tactics.

'How about you, Muscle-Munch?' he addressed the driver. 'If I'd broken into your home and savagely murdered your wife, and you'd been searching for me for twenty years, what sort of revenge would you take when you finally came face to face with me? You look like you could crush my whole skull with one squeeze of those banana-like fingers you have. I bet you and your wife have great fun with those.'

The driver frowned angrily and his eye sought Lucien through the rear-view mirror.

'Don't even think about answering the prisoner, Private,' Taylor said, looking at him. 'You will completely disregard whatever he says, no matter how offensive. You understand?'

'Yes, ma'am.' The reply came in a deep bass voice.

Lucien laughed out loud.

'Let me tell you what I think, Agent Taylor. I think he will do it. I think Robert will break, and he will finally get his revenge. And I think that the only way you will be able to stop him, is if you shoot him. The big question is – will you?'

Eighty-Two

Hunter and two US Marines were waiting by the small, custom-made, five-seater Lear Jet when the black SUV with Taylor and Lucien pulled up next to the plane.

In the sky, heavy clouds were starting to gather, making it feel like the whole day was changing moods – bright was being substituted by dark, blue by gray.

Taylor stepped out of the car and handed one of the Marines the keys to Lucien's restraints. They took charge of unlocking him from the backseat and taking him onboard. As they walked past Hunter and took the few steps that led up into the plane, Lucien turned and looked into Hunter's eyes. He saw nothing but hurt and anger, and he had to fight an internal battle not to smile.

Only when Lucien's chains had been securely locked to the special metal loops built onto the floor of the plane by one of its seats, did Hunter and Taylor board the aircraft.

Lucien's seat was at the rear of the cabin, enclosed by a metal cage equipped with a military-grade, assault-proof electronic lock that could only be activated through a button by the pilot's cockpit.

Taylor placed her jacket on the seat just ahead and to the right of Lucien's cage, but didn't sit down. Hunter took the

seat across the aisle from her. The pilot was patiently waiting in his cockpit.

'So, where in Illinois are we going?' Taylor asked Lucien.

'We're not,' he replied matter-of-factly.

Taylor hesitated a beat. 'What do you mean? You said we
were going to Illinois.'

'No, I didn't. I said we needed enough fuel to cover the
distance from here to Illinois. If we have enough fuel to get
to Illinois, that means that we also have enough fuel to get
to New Hampshire. That's where we're going.'

Lucien's seat was stationary, but all the others in the
plane cabin could swerve a full 360 degrees. Hunter didn't
swing his seat around to look at Lucien, he kept it facing
forward, but he wasn't surprised that Lucien was still playing games.

'New Hampshire,' Taylor said.

'That's correct, Agent Taylor, "Live free or die".'

'OK, so where in New Hampshire are we going?'

'You can tell the pilot to just head for New Hampshire.
I'll give him more details when we enter their airspace.'

Taylor passed the instructions to the pilot and returned to
her seat. Like Hunter, she preferred not to face the prisoner.

A minute later, the plane had taxied to the end of the
runway, and the pilot announced that they were clear for
takeoff. The jet engines came to life, and within twenty
seconds they were airborne. As the plane veered right, the
few rays of sunlight that managed to break through the
dark clouds reflected sharply off the aircraft's fuselage.

Hunter fixed his eyes out the window as the ground
below him slipped away. To him, the plane's bottled air felt
denser than ever, as if it had somehow been polluted by
Lucien's presence.

Taylor sat still, eyes forward, clearly trying to organize the multitude of thoughts exploding inside her head. She had a bottle of still water with her, from which she took a tiny sip every minute or two. It wasn't because she was thirsty, it was just a nervous reflex, something her body practically forced her to do almost unconsciously in order to try to calm herself down.

Hunter was also struggling with his thoughts, but this time he had twenty years of anger and frustration that were dying to break free to deal with.

They'd been flying for over half an hour when they heard Lucien's voice again.

'Do you believe that someone can be born "evil", Agent Taylor?' he asked.

Taylor sipped her water again while her gaze moved across the aisle to Hunter. It looked like he hadn't even heard the question. His full attention seemed to be in the world outside his window, not inside.

In Taylor's silence, Lucien moved on.

'You do know that there are a great number of criminologists, criminal psychologists and psychiatrists who believe that a person can be born "evil", don't you? Some sort of evil gene.'

Nothing from Taylor.

'If they believe in an evil gene, that means they also believe that being evil, or overwhelmingly violent, can be a genetic condition. Do you think that's true, Agent Taylor? Do you think a newborn can actually inherit being evil, being a killer, just like one can inherit hemophilia or color blindness?'

Another silent sip of her water.

'C'mon, humor me, Agent Taylor,' Lucien said. 'In your

opinion, can being evil and a senseless killer like me be a product of genetic inheritance?'

The thought making headlines in Taylor's head right then was, *Why didn't they equipped this plane with a sound-proof, Plexiglas cage instead of a metal bar one?*

'Twenty-seven,' Lucien said, resting his head against the chair's backrest.

Reflexively, Taylor's eyes peeked at Hunter again. He was still looking out the window, but she was sure he'd heard Lucien. Had he just completely changed subjects and was now giving them coordinates? She spun her chair around.

'Twenty-seven?'

'Twenty-seven,' Lucien confirmed with a single nod.

'Twenty-seven what?'

'States,' Lucien said.

A thin mask of confusion covered Taylor's face.

'I've visited sperm banks in twenty-seven different states,' Lucien explained. 'All under a different name, and with a life résumé that would impress the Queen of England. It's all part of a very long, ongoing experiment.'

Taylor felt the acidic taste of bile rise up in her throat.

'So, if you believe that being a killer can be a product of genetic inheritance, Agent Taylor,' Lucien said, 'then, in a few years' time, we might all have some surprises.'

Just being in the same enclosed space and breathing the same air as Lucien was making Taylor feel queasy.

'You're not only sick,' she said with a disgusted look on her face, 'you're completely deranged.'

The cabin speakers crackled once before the pilot's voice came through.

'We're approaching the border between Massachusetts and New Hampshire. Do I have any new instructions?'

Lucien's face seemed to come alive.

'Let the adventure begin.'

Eighty-Three

Hidden location.
Two days earlier.

Madeleine Reed's eyes blinked slowly and dopily several times before she was finally able to open them. Focus did not come instantly. In fact, it took almost two minutes for shapes to start making sense to her broken and exhausted mind.

She was still curled up against one of the corners in her captivity cell, with the dirty and smelly blanket wrapped around her fragile body like a cocoon. But no matter how tight she wrapped that disgusting rag around her, or how small she made herself against that wall corner, she couldn't keep the cold away. The fever might've gone away, or gotten worse. She couldn't tell anymore. Every atom in her body ached with such intensity that she was constantly on the verge of passing out.

The only sound inside her cell was the afflicting buzzing of flies flying around the overflowing bucket of excrement in the opposite corner from where she was.

Madeleine coughed a couple of times, and her dry throat together with her face and head immediately felt as if they were on fire and about to explode. The nauseating pain made her eyelids flutter like butterfly wings for a moment, and she rested her head against the wall, hoping she wouldn't drift off into unconsciousness once again.

She didn't.

As she gathered herself together one more time, she looked at her unrecognizable bony hands and fingers. Her nails were all broken and their beds crusted with dried blood. Her knuckles were red and swollen like an old lady's who suffered from acute rheumatism. She had never been that thin. She had never felt so weak, so hungry, so thirsty.

Madeleine realized that there were parts of her blanket that were still wet. Probably from when her body was soaking wet due to her high fever. She was so desperate that in a moment of madness she brought the blanket to her mouth and eagerly sucked on it, trying to get some of the moisture from the fabric onto her cracked lips and dry mouth. But what she got was a mouthful of dirt and such an obnoxious taste it immediately made her gag.

When she stopped coughing, Madeleine looked around her cell, but dehydration and malnutrition had already started to affect her physiologically and neurologically. Her eyes didn't have the strength to focus on anything that was further than about a meter away.

Empty plastic water bottles were scattered around the floor. Not even a drop was left in any of them, but that didn't stop Madeleine from reaching for one and trying again. She brought the bottle to her mouth and threw her head back, crunching and squeezing the bottle with both of her hands.

She got nothing.

Exhausted by the effort, she let the bottle fall to the floor again.

Her eyelids fluttered one more time. She felt desperately tired and overwhelmed by sadness, but she didn't want to fall back asleep. She knew that the extreme tiredness was her body shutting down. It just didn't have enough energy to stay awake. It didn't have enough energy to keep all of her organs working properly. It was like a huge factory shutting down certain departments because it didn't have enough resources to keep them operational.

Madeleine remembered watching a TV documentary about that once. How a dehydrated and malnourished body would slowly eat itself away. First its fat storages, then the proteins and nutrients from the muscles until it was all gone and its energy all depleted. After that, the body would start shutting down. Main organs like the liver and kidneys would stop functioning properly. The brain, which is made up of approximately 75 to 80 percent water, would really feel the damaging effects of dehydration. Its response would vary from person to person, and it would be completely arbitrary, ranging from very vivid hallucinations to a total meltdown. At that point, the damage caused to the cerebral mass would be irreversible.

With no more nutrients, the body runs out of energy, becoming overexhausted. But nothing on earth is as complex and as intelligent as the human body and the human brain. Even under such intense duress, its defense mechanism will work to the best of its ability. To try to save the little energy it has left, and to avoid the person dying in agonizing pain, the exhausted body will force itself to fall asleep. Once that happens, the body will slowly and quietly shut itself down completely and mercifully. The person's eyes will never open again.

Madeleine knew she was dying. She knew that if she fell back asleep, she would probably never wake up again. But she also didn't know what else to do. She felt so tired that even moving a finger felt like running a marathon.

'I don't want to die,' she whispered to herself in a weak and out-of-breath voice. 'I don't want to die like this. I don't want to die in this place. Somebody, please help me.'

Then a crazy idea came to her. She'd heard stories of people who drank their own urine. As disgusting as that might sound to her, she also knew that to some people that was a sexual turn-on. But her fatigued brain was fighting to keep her alive. Anything else, disgusting or not, would come a very distant second.

Without giving it another thought, Madeleine reached for one of the empty water bottles again. With tremendous effort she got back on her feet, unbuttoned and unzipped her dirty and now ripped trousers, and pulled them down to her ankles. Her panties followed. Holding the bottle in the right position, she closed her eyes and concentrated as best as she could, squeezing her leg and stomach muscles tight.

She got nothing.

Her body was so dehydrated she had nothing to give. But she wasn't about to give up. She tried it again, and again, and again. For how long, she had no idea. But finally, after what seemed like an eternity, a few tiny drops splashed against the bottom of the bottle. Madeleine became so happy she started laughing hysterically. That was until she looked in the bottle.

The few drops of urine she had managed to squeeze out of her were of a dark amber color, and she knew that that was a very bad sign.

The darker the color of human urine, the more dehydrated the body is.

If a person drinks a lot of liquids, like water, a healthy liver and kidneys will filter it very fast, taking in what the body needs and discarding the rest. The discarded liquids will fill the bladder. When the bladder is full, the person feels the need to go to the bathroom. Urinating is the body's main way of getting rid of what the body doesn't need, including toxins, but not always. If a person hydrates him/herself constantly, then the bladder will still get full due to all the excess liquid, but in that case, what the body is getting rid of is mainly the extra water or liquids the person has consumed. The toxin content of the urine will be minimum. The less toxins, the lighter the color of one's urine. The opposite is also true.

Judging by the color, Madeleine knew that the few drops she had in that bottle were probably 99 percent toxin. If she drank it, it would be like drinking poison. It wouldn't help her stay alive. It would speed up her death.

She stared at it for a long moment, the bottle shaking in her hand. She wanted to cry. In fact she did, but in her advanced stage of dehydration, her lacrimal glands could produce no tears.

Finally, strength left her and she collapsed to the ground. The bottle rolled away across to the other side of her cell.

'I don't want to die.' The words barely escaped her trembling lips, but she couldn't battle anymore. Her whole vision blurred as her eyes began closing. She had no more strength to keep herself awake.

She had no more hope.

She had no more faith.

She allowed her eyes to close, and began accepting what to her was now inevitable.

Eighty-Four

Since Lucien's hands would not come up past his chest due to his restraints, he bent forward so he could scratch his nose.

Taylor had swerved her chair around to face him, while Hunter still kept his facing forward.

'OK,' Taylor said. 'So we've entered New Hampshire's airspace. Where do we go from here?'

Lucien took his time. 'Damn, these are uncomfortable. You wouldn't be so kind as to scratch my nose for me, would you, Agent Taylor?'

She scowled at him in silence.

'Yeah, I didn't think so.' Lucien finally sat back up. 'Tell the pilot to fly due north. Let me know when he is over White Mountain National Forest.'

The White Mountain National Forest is a federally managed forest that totals an area of 750,852 acres. About 94 percent of it is located in the state of New Hampshire. It's so vast, no private aircraft flying over it could miss it.

Taylor passed the instructions to the pilot and returned to her seat.

They flew for another twenty-seven minutes before the pilot's voice came through the speakers again.

'We're just about to reach the south border of the White Mountain National Forest. Shall I keep on flying north or is there a new piece of this puzzle?'

Taylor faced Lucien one more time and waited.

Lucien was staring at the back of his hands.

'Now it gets good,' he said, without lifting his eyes. 'Tell the pilot we're going to Berlin.'

Taylor stared at him in disbelief. 'Say that again.'

'Tell the pilot we're going to Berlin,' Lucien repeated, casually. His gaze lingered on his hands for a while longer before moving to her.

Taylor didn't move, but her expression went from surprised to angry in record time.

'Relax, Agent Taylor,' Lucien said, 'I'm not referring to Berlin, Germany. That would've been too far-fetched even for me. But if you check the map of New Hampshire, you'll find that just north of the White Mountain National Forest, there's a small town called Berlin. Its municipal airport, interestingly enough, is located eight miles north, by another small town called Milan.' He laughed. 'How European, isn't it?'

Taylor's expression relaxed a little.

'Tell the pilot we need to land at Berlin's municipal airport.'

Taylor used the plane's intercom to pass on the new instructions to the pilot.

Hunter had been thinking about this for a little while, and he could hardly believe how well prepared Lucien was. *How long has he been planning this for?* he asked himself.

The state of New Hampshire was one of the few that did not have a specific FBI field office. Its jurisdiction fell under the Boston field office in Massachusetts – way too far for

Director Kennedy to have a backup team dispatched. Even though Lucien had given them detailed instructions that no one was to follow them, by land or air, Hunter knew Adrian Kennedy wouldn't simply comply with the requests of a serial murderer. Kennedy would no doubt be extremely careful because he knew the life of a kidnapped victim was at stake, but he would also want to have a plan B in place. With no FBI field office in New Hampshire, that meant if Adrian Kennedy wanted a second, local team tagging Hunter and Taylor, he would have to contact the county sheriff's department, or the local police department. Neither would be trained in high-profile surveillance, and that was a risk too far. Lucien had factored all this into his sick equation.

'I've just contacted the municipal airport in Berlin.' The pilot's voice came through the cabin speakers one more time. 'We're clear for landing, and we'll be starting our descent in five minutes.'

No one could see how much Lucien was smiling inside.

Eighty-Five

After being airborne for just under two hours, the Lear Jet touched down at the small landing strip in Berlin's municipal airport in New Hampshire. It quickly taxied to a spot at the end of the runway, away from the other small planes, and waited. The pilot had already alerted the airport's traffic control center that the plane was an official FBI aircraft on federal business, and not to be approached.

'So what now?' Hunter asked Lucien even before the plane came to a complete stop. This was the first time Hunter had addressed him since Quantico.

'Now we get a car,' Lucien replied, and pulled a dubious face. 'But this isn't LAX, Robert, there are no car-rental companies in the airport's foyer. Actually, there isn't even a foyer.' He jerked his head toward the window. 'You'll see. You'll be lucky if you find a vending machine somewhere around here.'

Taylor threw a questioning look at Hunter.

'You can call a rental company if you like,' Lucien proceeded. 'I'm sure you can get a number for one either in the town of Berlin or Milan, but it will take them about twenty to twenty-five minutes to get everything arranged and a car out here. If you don't want to wait, I suggest you improvise.'

'Improvise?' Taylor said.

Lucien shrugged. 'Commandeer a car or something. Like in the movies. You're the ones with FBI badges. I'm sure the folks around here would be very impressed by them.'

Taylor considered what to do.

'Remember that every second counts for poor Madeleine,' Lucien added. 'So feel free to take as long as you like.'

'You stay here with him,' Hunter said, already moving toward the plane's door. 'I'll go.'

Taylor agreed with a nod. Right now she really didn't want to leave Hunter alone with Lucien.

'Let's go,' Hunter said as he stepped back into the plane.

'We've got a car already?' Taylor asked, jumping to her feet. Hunter had been gone for less than three minutes.

He nodded. 'I sort of borrowed it from the guy who runs air traffic control here.'

'Fair enough,' she said. She didn't need any more explanation. Taylor then unholstered her weapon and pointed it at Lucien. 'OK, we're going to do this nice and slowly. When Robert presses the release button to the door to your cage, the floor chain loops will also disengage. You will then stand up, *slowly*, step out of the cell, and stop. Do you understand?'

Lucien nodded, unimpressed.

Taylor gave Hunter a head signal. He hit the button by the door to the pilot's cockpit before also unholstering his weapon and placing Lucien dead in his aim.

An electronic buzzing sound echoed loudly throughout the passenger cabin. Lucien's cage door clicked open and retracted. The metal chains that kept his ankles and hands shackled together were also released from their floor and chair restraints.

'Up slowly,' Taylor said.

Lucien complied.

'Now step forward and outside the cage.'

Lucien complied.

'Walk toward us and the exit, nice and slowly.'

Lucien complied.

Taylor moved over and positioned herself behind Lucien. Hunter stayed ahead of him. He came down the steps first. Lucien and Taylor followed shortly after.

A red Jeep Grand Cherokee was parked just a few meters from the plane. Hunter walked over and opened the back door.

'Nice car,' Lucien commented.

'Get in,' Hunter replied.

Lucien paused and looked around him. There was no one about. Berlin's municipal airport was nothing more than a landing strip of asphalt built next to a forest. There was no airport foyer, or lounge, or anything. Two mid-sized hangers, large enough to fit maybe a couple of private planes each, were located east of the runway. Just south of them were a few smaller administrative buildings. That was all there was, nothing else.

Lucien looked up at the sky. Night was fast approaching, and with it a cold breeze was settling in. His eyes stayed in the sky for a long while, searching, listening.

He saw and heard nothing.

'Get in,' Hunter commanded again.

With Geisha steps Lucien moved toward the car. Hunter held the door open. Like an educated lady, Lucien sat down first before bringing his legs in. With his hands and feet shackled to his waist, it was easier that way.

Hunter closed the door and signaled Taylor to go over to

the other side. She did. Only once Taylor had taken her place in the backseat did Hunter get into the driver's seat.

Taylor's gun was still aimed at Lucien.

'I want your back against the seat,' she said. 'And your arm on the door's armrest at all times.' She pulled down the back seat's center armrest, creating a flimsy division between Lucien and herself. 'You make any sudden movements, and I swear I'll blow your kneecaps. Is that simple enough for you?'

'Perfectly simple,' Lucien replied.

Hunter started the car.

'So where to from here?' he asked.

Lucien smiled.

'Absolutely nowhere.'

Eighty-Six

Hunter had been right. Director Kennedy would always have a plan B for any situation.

Exactly ten minutes after the Lear Jet with Hunter, Taylor and Lucien took off, a second jet left Turner Field landing strip in Quantico. This one was carrying five of Kennedy's top agents, all of them expert marksmen skilled in covert operations. With them they had a satellite-tracking device that specifically tracked the GPS signal coming from Hunter and Taylor's microphone buttons. They also had ears in the plane, as the surveillance microphones transmitted back not only to Director Kennedy at the FBI Academy, but also to the second jet and its agents.

Inside the FBI Operations Control Room back in Quantico, Adrian Kennedy and Doctor Lambert were following both planes' progress on the radar screen. They had also been listening to every word that had been uttered between Hunter, Taylor and Lucien. As soon as their jet landed at Berlin's municipal airport, Kennedy reached for the phone in his pocket.

'Director,' Agent Nicholas Brody, the team leader in the second jet, answered his cellphone before the second ring.

'Bird One just landed,' Kennedy said.

'Yes, we saw,' Brody replied. They were also following the first plane's progress on their radar application.

'Tell your pilot to start flying in circles right now,' Kennedy said. 'Do not, and I repeat, do not fly over airspace which is visible from the ground from Berlin's municipal airport. I'll call you back when you're clear for landing.'

'Roger that, sir.'

Agent Brody disconnected from the call, passed the new instructions to the pilot, returned to his seat, and waited.

Eighty-Seven

Hunter met Lucien's cold eyes in the rearview mirror. The smile on Lucien's lips was a mixture of arrogance and defiance.

'What was that?' Taylor asked, her patience more than wearing thin.

Lucien kept his gaze on the rearview mirror, his eyes battling with Hunter's.

'We're going absolutely nowhere,' he said again, his tone controlled and even.

Hunter calmly turned the engine off.

'What do you mean, Lucien?'

'I mean exactly what I said back in my cell,' Lucien said. 'The deal was – just the three of us, no one following. You break the deal, I take you nowhere. I thought I had made that perfectly clear.'

Hunter took his hands off the steering wheel and turned his palms up.

'Do you see anyone other than the three of us? Anyone following us at all?'

'Not yet,' Lucien replied confidently, before his eyes moved up and to the right, 'but they're up there, probably waiting, flying around in circles. You know it and I know it.'

Taylor's inquisitive eyes also found Hunter's in the rear-view mirror. He kept his gaze on Lucien.

'No, we don't know that,' Hunter said. 'And neither do you. You're assuming it. So you want us to sit here while Madeleine runs out of time because of an assumption?'

'My assumptions are always very accurate because they're based on facts, Robert,' Lucien said.

'Facts?' Taylor this time. 'What facts?'

Lucien's stare finally left the rear-view mirror and moved to Taylor. On its way, Lucien noticed that her grip on her gun had slacked just a touch.

'Let's see, Agent Taylor, we can get a move on as soon as you and Robert take off your shirts and throw them out the window. How about that?'

'Excuse me?' Taylor said. The offended look she managed to pull could've won her an Oscar.

'Your shirts,' Lucien repeated. 'Take them off and throw them out the window.'

Silence from Hunter and Taylor.

'You disappoint me, Robert,' Lucien said. 'Did you think I wouldn't notice the buttons on both of your shirts?'

A muscle flexed on Taylor's jaw.

Lucien addressed her. 'It was a good try, but the colors don't quite match the ones you had earlier.' He lifted his right index finger and pointed at Taylor's shirt. 'Those are about two shades darker. I'm guessing that what we have here is a microphone, a GPS satellite transmitter, and perhaps a camera?'

There was no reply.

'Disappointing. I'd imagined that the FBI would be more careful than that.' Lucien shrugged. 'But then again, I didn't give you guys that much notice, did I?'

Hunter's earlier thought came back to him: *this could be a costly mistake.*

'So,' Lucien carried on, 'we have a few options here. You can both take off your shirts and throw them out the window . . .' He gave Taylor a provoking wink. 'And that would no doubt add to my pleasure here in the backseat. Or you can rip the buttons off, one by one, and throw them out the window.' Lucien was still staring at Taylor. 'I bet you have a beautiful belly button, Agent Taylor.'

'Fuck you,' Taylor couldn't contain herself.

Lucien laughed. 'Alternatively, you can keep your shirts on with the buttons intact and just rip off the satellite transmitter, which I'm sure is taped to your bodies somewhere.'

Without even noticing it, Taylor looked like an angry kid who had just been caught on a lie.

'Please,' Lucien added, 'waste as much time as you like thinking about it.' He placed his head against the leather headrest and closed his eyes. 'Let me know when you've made your minds up.'

Hunter unbuckled his seatbelt, leaned forward a little and ripped the satellite transmitter from his lower back.

With her weapon still aimed at Lucien, Taylor did the same.

Back in the Operations Room in Quantico, Director Adrian Kennedy heard a scraping sound. A moment after that, Hunter's microphone went into complete silence. A couple of seconds later, so did Taylor's. The two dots that represented both of them on the radar screen they were looking at faded to nothing.

The agent sitting at the radar station quickly typed several commands into his computer before finally looking up at

Kennedy, who was standing by his side. 'We've lost them, sir. I'm sorry. There's nothing we can do from here.'

'Sonofabitch,' Kennedy whispered between clenched teeth.

Inside Bird Two, circling around the sky near Berlin's municipal airport, Agent Brody ran his hand through his close-cropped hair and uttered the exact same comment.

Eighty-Eight

'That's much better,' Lucien said, once Hunter and Taylor had both dropped their satellite transmitters out their windows. 'Now, let's be on the safe side, shall we? Take off your belts and drop them outside the window as well.'

'That was the only transmitter we had on,' Taylor said.

'Noted,' Lucien said with a polite nod. 'But forgive me for not trusting you at this particular moment, Agent Taylor. Now, if you please, the belts.'

Hunter and Taylor complied, dropping them outside the window.

'Now empty your pockets. Change, credit cards, wallets, pens . . . all of it. And your watches too.'

'How about this,' Taylor said, showing Lucien the keychain that belonged to him. The one they had used to get access to the house in Murphy in North Carolina.

'Oh, you'd better hang on to that, Agent Taylor. We'll need it to get into this place.'

Hunter and Taylor dropped their watches and whatever they had in their pockets out the window.

'Don't worry,' Lucien said. 'I'm sure the pilot will collect everything once we drive off. Nothing will be lost. Now, since we're on a roll here, let's do the same with your shoes too. Take them off and leave them outside.'

'The shoes?' Taylor asked.

'I've seen transmitters hidden inside heels, Agent Taylor. And since you've already abused my trust once, I'm not leaving anything to chance. But if you want to waste more time, you'll get no opposition from me.'

Seconds later, Hunter's boots and Taylor's shoes hit the asphalt by the side of the car.

Lucien leaned forward slowly and looked down at Taylor's feet.

'You have very pretty toes, Agent Taylor.' He nodded his agreement. 'Red, the color for passion. Interesting. Did you know that it's estimated that maybe as many as thirty to forty percent of men have some sort of foot fetish? I'm sure that there're people out there who'd kill just to be able to touch those pretty toes.'

Cringing at his words, Taylor instinctively moved her feet back, as if trying to hide them away.

Lucien laughed animatedly.

'And last but not least,' he continued. 'Let's get rid of the cellphones, shall we? We all know that they have trackable GPS systems.'

As much as this was making them mad, Hunter and Taylor couldn't argue. Lucien was still holding all the cards in this game. They did as they were told, and the phones were dropped outside their windows.

Satisfied, Lucien smiled at Hunter via the rearview mirror.

'I think we're good now,' he said. 'You can start the car again, Robert.'

Hunter did, and the satellite navigation system came to life on the 8.4-inch touchscreen on the dashboard.

'You won't need that,' Lucien said. 'There's no road name, or number or anything. Just a dirt path.'

'And how do we get there?'

'I'll guide you,' Lucien said. 'First thing we got to do is get the hell out of this shithole of an airport.'

Eighty-Nine

Director Adrian Kennedy stared at the radar screen inside the Operations Room at the FBI Academy in Quantico for a long time, trying to figure out what to do next.

'We can try to track the GPS signal in their cellphones,' the agent at the radar station offered.

Kennedy shrugged. 'We can give that a spin, but this guy is too smart. He figured out the buttons just because they were a couple of shades darker than the original ones for chrissakes. Who notices the color of buttons on someone else's shirt?'

'Someone who knows what to expect,' Doctor Lambert said. 'Lucien never expected the FBI to simply bend over and accept his demands. He knew we would try something, and he was ready for it.'

'And that's exactly what I mean,' Kennedy said. 'If he was ready for the buttons, I don't think there's a chance he would allow Robert and Agent Taylor to proceed carrying their cellphones with them. Even a ten-year-old kid knows that a cellphone GPS system is trackable.' He looked at the agent at the radar station. 'But by all means, give it a spin.'

The agent called an internal FBI application on his computer. 'What's the agent's name?' he asked.

'Courtney Taylor,' Kennedy replied. 'She's with the Behavioral Science Unit.'

A few more keyboard clicks.

'Found her,' the agent said.

The application he had called up on his screen listed the trackable GPS ID for every cellphone issued to an FBI agent.

'Give me a few seconds.' The agent began typing ferociously. A moment later, the word 'locating' appeared on his screen, followed by three blinking dots. Just a few seconds after that, the screen announced: 'GPS ID found'.

A new dot appeared on the radar system.

'The phone is live,' the agent said. 'The GPS is still transmitting, which means it hasn't been destroyed, and the battery is still in it. The location is exactly the same as we had before. They're still on the runway at Berlin's municipal airport.'

'Either that,' Kennedy said, 'or they were told to leave their phones behind.' He looked at Doctor Lambert, who nodded.

'That's what I would do.'

The cellphone in Kennedy's pocket rang. It was Agent Brody inside Bird Two.

'Director,' Brody said once Kennedy answered the call. 'Our pilot has just been in contact with the pilot in Bird One. He said that the car with the target is gone, but they left behind a pile of stuff on the runway – cellphones, wallets, belts, even shoes. The target is taking no chances.'

Kennedy had his answer.

'What do you suggest we do?' Brody asked. 'With no ears on the ground anymore, and no accurate target location, landing can be too risky, and even if we get away with it without the target noticing it, we don't have a dot to follow once we're on the ground.'

'I understand,' Kennedy said. 'And the answer is: I'm not sure yet. Let me call you back once I figure something out.' He disconnected. His tired brain was working hard to come up with an idea. And then a thought came to him. 'The car,' he said, looking at Doctor Lambert and then at the radar station agent. 'Robert got the car from the guy who runs air traffic control at the airport. His name is Josh. We heard that whole conversation through Robert's button mic, remember? Josh said he just got the car, a Jeep Grand Cherokee, a couple of months ago.'

'And a lot of new cars,' the agent said, picking up on Kennedy's line of thought, 'already come equipped with an anti-theft satellite tracking system. It's definitely worth a try.'

Kennedy nodded. 'Let's get Josh on the phone right now.'

Ninety

As soon as he drove through the airport gates, Hunter found himself on East Side River Road.

'Make a left,' Lucien said, 'then take your first right. We've got to cross the small bridge into the city of Milan. Unfortunately, it doesn't quite compare to the one in Italy. No Duomo Cathedral to see here. Actually, nothing at all to see here.'

Hunter followed Lucien's instructions. They crossed the bridge and passed an elementary school on their right before coming to a T-junction at the top of the road.

'Hang a right, and just follow the road on,' Lucien commanded.

Hunter did, and within a few hundred yards he drove past a few houses, some small, some a little larger, but nothing too exuberant.

'Welcome to the city of Milan, New Hampshire,' Lucien said, jerking his chin toward the window. 'There's nothing here but rednecks, fields, solitude and isolated places. It's a great place to disappear, go under the radar. No one will disturb you here. No one cares. And that's one of the greatest things about America – it's riddled with similar towns. Every state you go, you'll find tens of Milans and Berlins and Murphys and Shitkickersville. Just God-forsaken places where many of the streets don't even have a name, where people don't notice you.'

Taylor felt the weight of Lucien's keychain in her pocket and thought back to the seventeen keys it held. Each one of them could belong to a different anonymous place scattered around the land. Just like the house in Murphy.

Lucien read her like a book.

'You're wondering how I come upon these places, aren't you, Agent Taylor?'

'No, I'm not,' Taylor replied just to contradict Lucien. 'I don't really care.'

Hunter checked her in his rearview mirror.

Taylor's reply didn't deter Lucien.

'They are actually quite easy to come by,' he explained. 'You can buy them for next to nothing, because they are neglected, abandoned, half-destroyed places that no one wants or cares about anymore. If there is an owner, he or she usually just wants to get rid of the burden, so any offer is an offer, no matter how small. No refurbishment needed either. On the contrary, the more fucked-up, dirty, rotten and putrid the place is, the better. And you know why that is, don't you, Robert?'

Hunter kept his eyes on the road, but he knew exactly why: *The fear factor*. You throw an abducted victim into a soiled, rancid and dark place, infested with rats or cock-roaches, and the place alone will scare the life out of them.

Lucien didn't need an answer. He knew Hunter knew. Lucien moved his head from side to side, and then forward and backward to try to release some of the tension in his neck.

'This particular house,' he continued, 'was sheer luck, but a great find. It belonged to someone I met while at Yale. His great-grandfather built it some one hundred years ago. The house was passed down from generation to generation, being refurbished twice before it finally ended up as my friend's property, but he hated everything about this place – the location, the looks, the layout and, according to him, its legacy and its history. In his mind, the house was cursed, a jinx. His mother died in an accident in the backyard. A few years later, his father hanged himself in the kitchen. His grandfather also died there. He said that he never wanted to see this place again. If he did, he'd burn it to the ground. I offered to buy it from him, but he wouldn't have it. He just gave me the keys, signed away the deeds and said, "Take it. It's yours."'

Once they passed the initial cluster of houses, the scenery began to change. To their right, following the banks of the river, were nicely cropped fields that stretched as far as the eye could see. To their left, nothing but densely populated forests.

After about two miles, Hunter started noticing several little dirt paths that sprang out from the main road, leading deeper into the forest fields on their left. From the road, he couldn't see how deep they went, or where they'd lead.

Lucien was still watching Hunter through the rearview mirror.

'You're wondering which one of these will take you to where Madeleine is, aren't you, Robert?'

Hunter locked eyes with him for a quick moment.

Lucien gave Hunter a tight smile. 'Well, we'll be there soon enough. And for your sake, I really hope we're not too late.'

Ninety-One

He's going to keep on pushing.

Taylor's finger tightened around the trigger on her weapon once again, as anger began to boil her blood.

Lucien noticed it, and calmly leaned his head against the window.

'Easy on that trigger, Agent Taylor. I don't think you can, or want, to shoot me just yet.' He winked at her again. 'Plus, I'm sure that that would really piss Robert off. He wants that privilege for himself.'

Without any warning, Hunter's memory threw several images of Jessica lying in a pool of blood in her living room at him. His grip stiffened around the steering wheel until both of his fists had gone white.

The road swerved slightly to the left, then to the right, then to the left again. There were no crossroads and no tight bends, just dirt paths every so often leading away from the main road and into the unknown. The forest-land to their left seemed to get denser the further they went. There were no lampposts, and darkness began to clothe them like an ill-fitting suit, tight and uncomfortable. Hunter switched the inside lights on. There was no way he would allow Lucien to hide his movements in darkness.

'How much further?' Taylor asked.

Lucien turned and looked out his window before carrying his gaze across to the one on the other side.

'Not long.'

The road swerved left again in a half-moon shape, following the contour of the river on their right. The nicely cropped fields were all but gone. Now they had only dense forestland on both sides of the road.

'Keep your eyes peeled for a sharp left turn that's coming up, Robert,' Lucien said. 'Not a dirt path.'

Hunter slowed down and drove for another one hundred and fifty yards.

'Yep,' Lucien said, and nodded, 'that's the one. Right ahead.'

Hunter bent left.

The road, now flanked by more forestland, seemed to stretch forever into undiluted darkness. Since they'd left the airport, they hadn't crossed a single vehicle in their path. No one in their rear-view mirror either. The further they went, the more it felt like they were driving away from civilization and into some sort of twilight world. One thing was for sure: Lucien knew how to pick a secluded hiding place.

They drove for another mile before the road turned into a bumpy dirt path. Hunter shifted down and wondered if he should engage the four-wheel-drive just in case.

'We're lucky,' Lucien said, 'it looks like there's been no rain lately. These roads can easily turn into a nightmare of water pools and deep mud when rain comes.'

Hunter slowed down a little more, moving from one side of the road to the other, choosing the best path, trying to avoid making the car jerk too much.

'There's a right turn coming up,' Lucien announced, tilting his head to one side to get a better look at the windscreen. 'We've got to take it, Robert.'

'This one?' Hunter asked, pointing to a turn about twenty-five yards ahead of them.

'That's it.'

Hunter took it.

They were now clearly driving through the middle of nowhereland. The last sign of human life they'd seen had been miles back. If a bomb exploded right where they were, no one would hear it. No one would care. No one would come.

The road got bumpier still. The next mile seemed to take them an eternity to cover.

'One more left turn coming up,' Lucien said, 'and we'll be almost there, but keep your eyes open, Robert, it's a tiny path, and it's quite hidden away.'

Hunter saw it after another fifty yards, but he almost missed it. It really was a minute path. If they weren't specifically looking for it, no one would ever notice it.

Hunter veered left. The trail was barely wide enough for the Jeep to fit through, and everyone heard the shrubs and bushes scrape the side of the vehicle.

'Ooh,' Lucien commented, 'I don't think the air traffic controller back at the airport will be happy about this, but then again, since his car was commandeered by the FBI, I'm sure it will be federally insured.'

This time, Hunter had nowhere to go to swerve away from the bigger bumps and holes. Good thing that they were in a brand-new car and the suspension was strong and steady.

They had to sit tight inside the shakemobile for another half a mile, until the road came to an abrupt end. Hunter put the car in neutral and looked around him. Taylor did the same. There was nothing but forest surrounding them.

'Did we take a wrong turn somewhere?' Taylor asked.

'No,' Lucien replied. 'This is it.'

Taylor looked out the window again. The Jeep headlights reflected on the shrubs and trees.

'This is it? Where?' she asked.

Lucien nodded toward the front of their vehicle. 'We have to walk the rest of the way. You can't get there by car.'

Ninety-Two

Hunter was the first to leave the Jeep. Once he was out, he unholstered his weapon and opened the back door for Lucien. Taylor followed shortly after.

'Now what?' she asked, looking around her.

'Through there,' Lucien said, indicating a few loose tree branches that'd been piled up against each other just ahead and to the right of where the Jeep was parked.

'We're going to go deep into this forest with no light and no shoes?' Taylor asked Hunter, looking down at their bare feet.

'Not much I can do about the shoes,' he replied, before reaching back inside the car for the glove compartment. He came back with a Maglite Pro Led 2. 'But we do have light.'

'That's handy,' Taylor said.

'I knew night was approaching,' Hunter said. 'And I wasn't counting on Lucien's hiding place being very straight-forward. So I also asked the air traffic controller for a flashlight.'

'Robert Hunter,' Lucien said, nodding and pursing his lips as if he was about to whistle. 'Always thinking a step ahead. Too bad you didn't foresee the shoe problem.'

'Let's go,' Hunter commanded.

They assumed the same formation as when they were leaving the plane. Hunter took point, Lucien came second, and Taylor stayed four to five steps behind Lucien, her weapon always trained on his back, just a couple of inches below his neckline.

Hunter quickly removed the branches Lucien had indicated, and it revealed a well-worn trackers' trail.

'Just follow it,' Lucien said. 'The place isn't very far from here.'

Despite already being in a hurry, Hunter's gut feeling filled him with an extra sense of urgency, as if something he couldn't quite pinpoint was off, but he didn't have much time to dwell on it.

'Let's move,' he said.

The flashlight had an ultra-bright and wide beam, which made things a little easier.

They took to the trail and, surprisingly, Lucien didn't try to slow them down with the excuse of his shackled legs. He didn't have to. Pebbles and little rocks and sharp-edged dried sticks forced Hunter and Taylor to move a lot slower than they would've liked.

They had covered only about thirty yards when the track swerved hard right, then left, and then it really felt as if they had crossed some sort of twilight gate. All of a sudden the bushes, trees and scrub gave way to a plain field – a clearing in the middle of nowhere.

'And here we are,' Lucien said with a proud smile.

Hunter and Taylor paused, their eyes looking around in disbelief.

'What the hell is this?'

Ninety-Three

Hunter shone his flashlight on the structure standing before them.

It was a stiff and squared, ivy-covered brick house, with white Romanesque columns that must once have been imposing outside the front entryway. Now, only two of the original four were still standing, and those had cracks running from top to bottom.

The house had been built one hundred years earlier, and then reconfigured again twice after that, so whatever remained of its first incarnation as someone's grand hillside home was now merely memory. Add to that the disfiguration caused by the elements and a total disregard and lack of care for a property, and you'd end up with the carcass of a house they had in front of them – a battered shell of a home of long ago.

Three out of the four outside walls still remained, but they all had several holes and major fissures in them, as if the house belonged in a warzone somewhere in the Middle East. The south wall, on the right side of the house, had almost entirely crumpled onto a pile of rubble. Most of the internal walls had also collapsed, giving the place nearly no room separation, and filling it with what looked like destruction debris. The roof had caved in almost everywhere, with the exception of the old living room at the front of the house, the corridor beyond it, and the kitchen on the left, where it was still partially in place. Weed and wild vegetation had grown through the floorboards and among the debris just about everywhere. The windows were all broken, and some of the window frames had been ripped from the walls as if by some sort of internal explosion.

'Welcome to one of my favorite hiding places,' Lucien said.

Taylor blinked the surprise away. 'Madeleine?' she yelled out, taking a step to her right.

No reply.

'Madeleine?' she yelled again, this time even louder. 'This is the FBI. Can you hear me?'

She got nothing back.

'Even if she's still alive, she won't be able hear you,' Lucien said.

Taylor looked at him with fuming eyes. 'This is bullshit. There's nobody here.'

'Are you sure about that?' Lucien questioned.

'Look at this shithole. This is not a hiding place. How can you hide or keep anyone locked in a place without doors or walls? Where anyone can simply walk in, or out?'

'Because no one knows this place exists,' Hunter said, trying to analyze the area surrounding the house. 'And no one will ever come looking for it out here.'

'Right again,' Lucien said, looking at Taylor. 'Hence the term *hidden* place.'

'This is bullshit.' Taylor couldn't hide the anger in her voice. 'You're telling us that you left Madeleine somewhere in this ghost shell of a house – no windows, no doors, no walls, and she never walked out?'

Lucien's gaze went to Taylor and right then his eyes looked like dark vials filled with venom.

'Not somewhere inside it, Agent Taylor.' He paused and ran his tongue over his bottom lip like a lizard. 'Buried underneath it.'

Ninety-Four

Lucien's words sent fear crawling like a rash across Taylor's skin. Her now confused gaze immediately returned to what was left of the house, before moving to the soil surrounding it.

'Well, not exactly buried,' Lucien clarified. 'Let me show you.' He lifted both cuffed hands and pointed toward the north side of the disfigured structure. 'Through there.'

In a hurry, Hunter and the flashlight took point again. Lucien and Taylor followed.

'My friend's grandfather,' Lucien said, as they started walking, 'and by friend, I mean the person I got this place from, was a hardcore, old-school patriot. I was told that he had his best years in this house during the USA versus USSR era. You know, "death to all communists" kind of thing. And he really subscribed to that ideology. And there was plenty of talk about a very possible atomic war.'

As soon as they reached the side of the house, Hunter and Taylor understood what Lucien was talking about.

On the ground, halfway along the north wall, they could see a very large, external, thick metal, basement-entry double door. The doors were locked together by a Sargent and Greenleaf military-grade padlock, very similar to the one they'd found in the house in Murphy.

'My friend's grandfather,' Lucien continued, 'in his paranoia and deep belief that an atomic war was inevitable and imminent, refurbished the whole place, extending and adding a substantial bomb shelter to the original basement.' He nodded at the padlocked doors. 'The house might look like an earthquake site, but the shelter has more than lived up to its expectations.' He indicated the padlock. 'The key for that is on the keychain.'

Taylor immediately reached for it.

'Which one,' she asked urgently, holding up the bunch of keys.

Lucien leaned forward and squinted at them for a second. 'The sixth one starting from your left.'

Taylor selected the key and reached for the padlock.

Hunter and Lucien waited, and as they did, Hunter's awkward sensation that something wasn't quite right came back to him. He looked around him for an instant.

'What's at the back of the house?' he asked.

Lucien studied him for a moment, and then let his gaze move toward the far end of the house.

'A very badly treated backyard,' he replied. 'There's a large pond as well, which now looks more like a deep pool of mud. Would you like me to give you a tour? I have all the time in the world.'

Click. The padlock came undone. Taylor unhooked it from the doors and threw it away before grabbing one of the handles and pulling it toward her. The door barely moved.

'Heavy, aren't they?' Lucien commented with a smirk. 'As I've said, this isn't a regular cellar, Agent Taylor. It's a fallout shelter.'

'I'll do it,' Hunter said.

Taylor stepped back while Hunter first pulled the right door open, then the left one.

They were immediately hit by a breath of warm, stale air. The doors revealed a concrete staircase that took them down a lot deeper than one would've imagined. There were at least thirty to forty steps.

'Deep, isn't it?' Lucien said. 'It's a well-built shelter.'

Hunter went down first, and they all moved down in a hurry.

At the bottom, they were greeted by another heavy metal door with a very sturdy lock.

'The seventh key,' Lucien announced, 'the one to the right of the one you used on the padlock.'

Taylor moved forward and unlocked the door before pushing it open.

The air inside the dark room beyond it was leaden with dust, and felt even staler, but there was something else in the air, something that both Hunter and Taylor could easily recognize because they'd been around it too many times.

The smell of death.

Ninety-Five

Sometimes sour, sometimes putrid, sometimes sickly sweet, sometimes bitter, sometimes nauseating, and most of the time a combination of everything. No one can tell you what death really smells like. Most would say that there's no specific smell to it, but anyone who's been around it as many times as Hunter and Taylor had been would recognize in just a fraction of a second, because as soon as you smell it, it chokes your heart and saddens your soul in a way that nothing else does.

As they sensed death, Hunter and Taylor were filled with a disquieting fear, and the same thought exploded inside both of their heads.

We've wasted too much time. We're too late.

Hunter shone the beam of his flashlight into the room and moved it around the place almost frantically.

It was empty.

There was no one there.

Lucien took a healthy deep breath, like a hungry man taking in the aroma of freshly cooked food.

'Wow, I've missed this smell.'

'Madeleine?' Taylor called into the room, her gaze chasing after the beam of the flashlight. 'Madeleine?'

'It would've been very stupid of me if I had left Madeleine

locked inside the very first room one comes to in the shelter, wouldn't it?' A cryptic smile graced Lucien's lips.

'Where is she?' Taylor asked.

'There's a light switch on the wall to the right of the door,' Lucien told them.

Hunter reached for it.

A feeble yellowish bulb at the center of the ceiling flickered a couple of times, as if in doubt whether it would come on or not. It finally did, and it brought with it an electronic hiss that echoed annoyingly around the room.

They found themselves in a semi-bare room, twenty feet square. Two of the thick, solid concrete walls were adorned by a few handmade bookshelves, all of them loaded with books that were covered by a thick layer of dust. The wall to the left of where they stood had a single steel door set right in the center of it. The door had a dappled gunmetal look to its surface, as though it were meant to draw the eye. Against the wall directly in front of them was a console desk that must've been at least fifty or sixty years old, where a multitude of buttons, switches, levers and old-fashioned dial gauges could be found. A switched-off computer monitor hung on the wall just above the console desk. This was definitely the shelter's main control room.

The floor was simple polished concrete. A plethora of metal and PVC pipes of different diameters crisscrossed the ceiling in all directions, disappearing through the walls. A couple of medium-sized square cardboard and wooden boxes were piled up one on top of the other in one corner of the room. They looked to be supplies.

Hunter's eyes began searching the room.

How many victims has Lucien tortured and killed locked away in this hellhole, he thought.

'Madeleine is through that door,' Lucien said. 'I suggest you hurry.'

'Which key?' Taylor asked, holding the keychain up to Lucien once again.

'Second to last key on your right.'

Taylor holstered her weapon and moved purposefully toward the gunmetal door. Lucien and Hunter followed and the formation inverted: Hunter took the rear, three steps behind Lucien.

Taylor slotted the key into the door lock and twisted it left. With two loud clicks, the lock chamber rotated 360 degrees once, then twice.

Taylor's heart picked up speed inside her chest as she turned the handle and began pushing the door open.

Police instincts, hyper-sensitivity, training and experience, psychic ability, whatever it is that one has in these situations, Hunter and Taylor both sensed it at the same moment – a new life, a new presence, as if unlocking the door had given the cue for their cop's intuition to kick in.

Once again, an identical thought crossed both of their minds: *Maybe we're not too late. There's still hope.*

But that hope vanished fast, because that new life, that presence they'd sensed, wasn't past the door ahead of them. It was behind them.

Ninety-Six

Click.

They felt the new presence, but before Hunter or Taylor had a chance turn around, they heard the sound of a bullet being chambered into a 9mm semi-automatic handgun.

'If any of you two fuckheads move, I'll blow your fuck-ing heads off. Is that clear?' The voice that came from the opposite end of the room was sharp, firm and young. 'Now get your goddamn hands up above your heads.'

Hunter tried to identify the specific direction where the voice was coming from. He was positive that the bullet chambering sound, together with the first few spoken words, had come from the general direction where the piled-up boxes were – probably the perpetrator's hiding place, but there was barely enough space behind them for a midget to hide. His next sentence, though, had come from a different direction all together, which meant he was moving, but the reverberation inside the room coupled with the incessant light-bulb hiss made pinpointing the perpetrator's exact location an almost impossible task.

Hunter was pretty sure that he could spin around and squeeze out a shot before the perpetrator realized what was happening, but that would only work if he knew exactly where to place the shot. Guessing wouldn't cut it – if he missed, he'd be a dead man. He decided not to risk it.

'Did you all fucking hear me or what?' the young voice said again, but this time with a much more disturbed edge to it. 'Hands above your heads.'

Hunter and Taylor finally lifted their hands.

Lucien turned and smiled triumphantly at Hunter as he moved past him.

'I did good, didn't I?' the young voice asked. 'I followed the instructions just like you taught me.'

'You did great.' Hunter and Taylor heard Lucien reassure whoever else had joined them in that room. 'OK,' Lucien said, now addressing them, 'this is when I have to ask you both to put your guns on the floor, and without turning around, kick them back toward me, one at a time. Robert, you go first. Nice and easy. And let me add that my friend here has a very itchy trigger finger. And he never misses.'

A few hesitant seconds.

'The fuck you waiting for, big guy?' the young voice said. 'Let's go. Put your gun on the floor and kick it back before I put a hole in the back of your head.'

Hunter cursed himself, because the little voice inside his head had been telling him that things didn't feel quite right since they'd got to the derelict house. But in his hurry to try to save Madeleine Reed, he'd disregarded his instincts and proceeded inside the fallout shelter without properly check-ing the control room.

'Do it, Robert,' Lucien said. 'He really will blow your brains all over these walls.'

'Fucking right, I will. You think this is a game, big guy?'

The voice had moved closer. Hunter was almost certain that he was just a little to his right. But Hunter was now holding his weapon high above his head, while the kid behind him had his directly aimed at Hunter's skull. The advantage had swung the other way. Hunter had no way out.

'OK,' he said.

'Nice and slowly,' Lucien commanded. 'Squat down, place your gun on the floor, then get back to a standing position again before kicking it back toward me.'

Hunter did as he was told.

'Your turn, Agent Taylor,' Lucien said.

Taylor didn't move.

'Bitch, did you hear what he said?' the young voice asked with overwhelming anger.

Lucien lifted his hands, signaling his accomplice to give him a minute.

'I'm well aware of many of the FBI's protocol field rules, Agent Taylor,' he said, keeping his voice steady and unthreatening. 'I'm also aware that some of those rules are not supposed to have any exceptions whatsoever. High on that list is the rule that mandates that an FBI agent shall never surrender his or her weapon to a suspect or perpetrator during a hostage situation.'

Taylor clenched her teeth in frustration.

'Make no mistake here, Agent Taylor, this isn't your typical hostage situation. This is a life or death situation . . . for you and Robert, that is. If you don't slide your weapon over to me, you *will* die. It's not a threat. It's a certainty. You need to make a judgment call, and you need to do it sharpish.'

'Fuck this explaining bullshit, Lucien,' the young voice blurted out. 'Let's just kill these two fucks and get it over with.'

The new ring to the kid's voice told Hunter that he was right on the edge; going over it wouldn't take much.

'Your call, Agent Taylor,' Lucien said. 'You've got five seconds, four . . .'

Hunter's gaze was fixed on Taylor's tense body. 'Don't be a fool, Courtney,' he said under his breath.

'Three, two . . .'

Hunter got ready to move.

'OK,' Taylor said.

Hunter breathed out.

Taylor proceeded to slowly place her weapon on the ground before using her foot to slide it across the floor toward Lucien.

Hunter and Taylor heard the sound of metal chains scrapping the floor for an instant.

Lucien had picked up Taylor's gun.

'Nah ah,' the young voice said as Taylor began to turn. 'No one told you to turn around, bitch. Keep your eyes on the Goddamn door in front of you, or I'll blow your fucking head off.'

Taylor paused.

'He really means it, Agent Taylor,' Lucien said.

'Does this bitch think I'm kidding?'

Even without looking, Hunter and Taylor could sense that the newcomer's aim had moved to the back of her head. All he needed was a reason.

Taylor didn't give him one. She finally complied, and her eyes returned to the door.

'Now I'm going to have to ask you both to kneel down, and put your hands behind your heads,' Lucien said, while at the same time, unseen to Hunter and Taylor, signaling his accomplice. 'Do it now.'

Once more, Hunter and Taylor had no way out. They had to do as they were told.

'So what now?' Taylor asked. 'You're just going to shoot us in the back?'

'Not my style, Agent Taylor,' Lucien replied.

Clunk.

They heard the sharp sound of metal cutting through metal. A few seconds later they heard it again, this time followed by that of a chain running through a loop before falling to the ground.

'I was just being cautious while I got rid of these chains. Oh, now this is much better.'

The next sound Hunter and Taylor heard was a loud thud, as a heavy metal object was thrown across the room to the other side and collided with the wall.

'Now please, stand up and turn around,' Lucien commanded.

They did.

Standing next to Lucien, holding a Heckler & Koch USP9 semi-automatic handgun, was a wiry and small man, a little like a professional horse-racing jockey in build, who looked to be only about twenty-five years old. He wore a crooked smile that seemed to bend in the same direction that he hunched his shoulder, giving him a skewed and somewhat menacing look. His head was completely shaven, and his blue eyes glowed with an intensity that was unsettling. He had a large, badly healed scar that ran from the left side of his chin, all the way to the back of his right ear, crossing his right cheek. Even from a distance, Hunter could tell that the scar had been made either by a blunt knife, or a thick piece of glass. Across the room he also saw the heavy-duty, 48" bolt cutter that Lucien had used to free himself.

'Remember when I told you that it wouldn't be hard for

me to find an apprentice if I wanted to?' Lucien said with a lopsided grin. 'Well, I did want to, and just as I'd said, it wasn't hard at all. So let me introduce you to Ghost.' He gestured toward the shaved-headed man to his right. 'I call him Ghost because he moves like one, so light and silent you won't ever hear him coming. And due to his size and amazing flexibility, he's able to hide in places you can't even imagine.' Lucien allowed his gaze to move to the cardboard boxes. 'I know it's hard to believe, but he was actually inside one of those.'

One of Ghost's front teeth was chipped. Every few seconds he nervously ran his tongue across its jagged edge, giving him a very edgy look, as if he was about to lose control.

'I like her,' Ghost said, his gaze falling over Taylor as if she were naked. 'And she's got pretty toes. I *reeeeally* like that. Let's just kill the big guy and take her with us. We can have some fun with her.'

Taylor didn't shy away from Ghost's eyes, the anger in her stare colliding with the desire in his.

'Did you arrange everything the way we'd planned?'

Ghost nodded. His attention was still on Taylor.

'I don't want you to think that I've been lying to you all this time,' he said, 'because I haven't. Why don't you open that door, Agent Taylor?' He indicated the gunmetal door. 'And see what lies behind it.'

Taylor held Lucien's stare for a while longer before turning around and pushing the door open. On the ceiling of the corridor beyond it, two very weak fluorescent tube lights flicked and hissed as if they were about to blow. Their light seemed to travel down the hallway in slow motion, and as it reached the end of it Taylor's heart almost stopped beating.

Ninety-Seven

Hunter had also turned to see what lay beyond the door.

The corridor was long and narrow. The walls were made of solid concrete, just like the shelter's control room. There were several doors on both sides of the hallway and one directly at the end of it. All of them in the same dappled gunmetal color as the one Taylor had just opened. They were all shut, with the exception of the one at the far end.

The light that propagated from the fluorescent tubes wasn't strong enough to properly reach the last room, so all they got was a sort of hazy silhouette, but even so, Hunter and Taylor had no problem identifying the shape of a naked woman's body. She was sitting on a chair. Her head was slumped forward awkwardly. Her hands looked to be tied behind her back, and she didn't seem to be moving.

Taylor felt a nauseating shiver start right at the pit of her stomach.

'Ghost,' Lucien said, 'the lights.' He nodded at the control desk.

Still with his attention locked on Hunter and Taylor, Ghost took a couple of steps to his right and flicked a switch on the old-fashioned control console.

Inside the room at the far end of the corridor, another weak light bulb struggled to come to life for a few seconds before finally engaging. It bathed the room in a pale yellow-ish glow, and right then every muscle in Hunter's body tensed.

Madeleine Reed wasn't dead. On the contrary, she was pretty much alive, but compared to the picture they'd seen of her inside Director Kennedy's office just hours before, she wasn't even a shadow of the woman she used to be. Her weight had drastically plummeted. Her smooth skin looked like it had aged forty years in just a few months, and it now clung to her bones as if she were a terminal cancer patient. The dark circles under her eyes were so intense they looked like surgical bruises. The eyes themselves seemed to have sunk into her skull just a little, but enough to give her a cadaver's appearance. Her lips were dry and chipped, and her body looked weak and extremely fragile.

As the light inside the room came on, Madeleine blinked desperately several times, her sad and confused eyes struggling with the brightness after who knows how many hours of darkness. Focus took a while, but when it finally came, her drained brain had to battle to understand the images in front of her. She slowly lifted her head, and the look on her face went from puzzled, to hopeful, and then to pleading, before at last settling on desperate. Her lips moved, but if any words did come out, their sound wasn't strong enough to reach anyone at the other end of the hallway.

With the room now under its own light, Hunter and Taylor could finally see the entire picture.

Madeleine was indeed naked, her hands were surely tied to each other behind the chair's backrest. Her feet were tied to the chair's legs.

As her eyes at last registered people at the other end of the corridor, she started shaking. Her breathing came in little gasps, as if there weren't enough oxygen in the room.

'Madeleine,' Hunter said, reading the first signs of acute panic on her. He knew she'd been conditioned. She'd been tortured and scared for so long that her immediate psychological response to seeing anyone down in that hellhole was to flood her body with terrifying fear. Right now, to her, everyone was a threat, because everyone she'd ever met down there had tortured her.

'Listen to me, honey.' Hunter's voice was as calm and as warm as he could make it sound. 'My name is Robert Hunter, and I'm with the FBI. We're here to help you. Stay calm and we'll get you out of here, OK?'

Hunter felt so useless saying those words. He wanted to go to Madeleine, free her hands and feet, get her out of that fallout shelter, and reassure her that she was safe, that the nightmare was now over, that no one would hurt her anymore. But he couldn't do any of that. All he could do was throw empty words traveling down that corridor, and hope that was enough to keep Madeleine from losing control.

Madeleine's lips moved again; again, the sound of her words weren't strong enough to reach anyone's ears in the control room. But Hunter had no problem reading her lips.

'Please help me ...'

Hunter quickly peeked at Ghost. He was standing by the control console, his weapon firmly in his grip, his stare burning a hole in the back of Taylor's head. Lucien was standing just a step to his left, but his attention seemed to be everywhere – nothing would escape him. If Hunter tried anything, he'd be dead.

Lucien nodded at Ghost, who flicked a different switch on the control console. The door to the room Madeleine was in slammed shut, no doubt sending even more fear snowballing into every molecule in her body.

Reflexively, Taylor turned to face Lucien and Ghost. 'No. Please, no.'

The suddenness of her movement caught Ghost by surprise, almost tipping him over the edge, his arm tensing even further and his finger half-squeezing the trigger on his gun.

'You better stay where you are, bitch.'

'Please,' Taylor said, her hands up in a surrender gesture. 'Shutting the door on her will make her panic even more.'

Lucien nodded in a carefree way. 'Yes, I know.'

Anger radiated from Taylor. 'You sonofabitch.'

'Let her go, Lucien,' Hunter said. 'Let Madeleine go. You don't need her anymore. You don't need to take her life. She means nothing to you. Take me and let her go. Let Courtney take Madeleine out of here, and take me.'

'You dumb fuck,' Ghost said. His gun was still aimed at Taylor. 'Reality check, big guy – we already have you, and the whore inside the room, and the pretty FBI bitch with the pretty toes here.' He blew Taylor a kiss while rubbing his groin. 'Soon you'll be all mine, bitch. And I'll make you scream. You can bet on that.'

Taylor's self-control completely escaped her.

'Fuck you, you tiny pencil-dick ugly fuck.'

Maybe it was Taylor's words, or maybe Ghost had just had enough of this game, but the overload switch in his head flicked.

'No,' he said, with so much anger it almost drooled out of his mouth. 'Fuck you, you stupid whore.' He squeezed the trigger on his gun.

Ninety-Eight

FBI Academy – Quantico, Virginia.
Forty-five minutes earlier.

It didn't take the FBI long to get in contact with Joshua Foster, the air traffic controller at Berlin's municipal airport. The call was immediately transferred to Director Kennedy in the Operations Room.

'Mr Foster,' Kennedy said, switching the call to speakerphone. 'My name is Adrian Kennedy. I'm the director of the National Center for the Analysis of Violent Crime and the Behavioral Analysis Unit of the FBI. I believe that you were in contact with one of our agents. His name is Robert Hunter. You handed him the keys to your Jeep.'

'Ummm, that's correct.' Understandably, there was a nervous edge to Joshua Foster's voice.

'OK, Mr Foster, please listen carefully,' Kennedy said. 'This is very important. I understand your car was brand new.'

'Yeah, well, I got it about two months ago.'

'That's great. Now did the car come equipped with a location transponder, a GPS locator, in case of theft?'

'Actually, yes, it did.'

Kennedy's face lit up.

'But I don't have the transponder tracking code with me,' Foster said, anticipating Kennedy's next question. 'It's back at my house.'

'We don't need it.' The agent at the radar station took over. 'All we need is the car's license plate and I can find the transponder tracking code from here.'

'Oh, OK.' Foster gave them his Jeep's license plate number.

'Thank you very much, Mr Foster,' Kennedy said. 'You've been a great help.'

'Could I ask . . . ?' Foster tried saying, but Kennedy had already disconnected the call.

'How long will it take you to find this tracking code,' he asked.

'Not long at all,' the agent replied, already typing something into his computer.

As Kennedy waited, his cellphone rang inside his jacket pocket again. It was Special Agent Moyer, the agent in charge of the expedition sent to Lake Saltonstall in New Haven. They were looking for Karen Simpson's remains, together with those of four other victims.

'Director,' the agent said, his voice firm but a little subdued, as if to show respect. 'Sir, the information is one hundred percent legit. So far, we've dug out the remains of exactly five bodies.' There was an awkward pause. 'Would you like us to carry on digging? The area here is pretty vast, and if this was the perpetrator's preferred burial ground, who knows how many more we might find.'

'No, that won't be necessary,' Kennedy replied. 'You won't find any more bodies.' He had no doubt Lucien had told the truth. 'Just prep the ones you found for transportation. We'll need them here in Quantico ASAP.'

'Understood, sir.'

'Good work, Agent Moyer,' Kennedy said before hanging up.

'Got the transponder tracking code,' the agent at the radar station announced, as he entered a few more commands into his computer.

Everyone's eyes were glued to his screen.

'Tracking now.'

The seconds felt like minutes. Finally, the map on the agent's screen repositioned itself to show the location of a bright, pulsating dot.

'We've got the Jeep's location,' the agent said excitedly. A short pause. 'And it doesn't look like they're moving anymore.'

'Yes, I see that,' Kennedy said, frowning at the screen. 'But where the hell are they exactly?'

'Right in the middle of absolutely nowhere, by the looks of it,' Doctor Lambert commented.

According to the map, the Jeep was parked at the end of a nameless dirt path deep inside a dense forestland several miles from Berlin's municipal airport.

'We need a satellite image of the area instead of a map,' Kennedy said.

'Give me a second,' the agent replied and immediately started typing again.

Two seconds later, the map on his screen was swapped for a satellite image of the area.

Everyone frowned at the screen for a moment.

'What is this?' Kennedy asked, pointing at what looked like a construction site not that far away from where the Jeep was parked.

The agent zoomed in on it and readjusted the resolution. 'It looks like an old abandoned house, or building of some sort,' he answered. 'Or at least what's left of it.'

'That's it,' Kennedy said, 'that's where they are. That's where Lucien was keeping his victim.' He reached for his cellphone and called agent Brody inside Bird Two. They needed to land and get to that house – NOW.

Ninety-Nine

Hunter saw it before it actually happened.

He saw something explode inside Ghost's cold eyes, as if he'd been injected with an overdose of pure anger and evil, and right then he knew Ghost had passed the point of no return. But even though he saw it, this time Hunter wasn't able to move fast enough. He wasn't able to get between Taylor and Ghost. Ghost's trigger-squeezing reaction took only a split second.

As the hammer hit the firing pin in Ghost's gun, it was like it'd activated a real-life slow-motion switch for Hunter. He practically saw the bullet leave the gun barrel, travel through the air and whizz past the right side of his face, missing it by just a fraction. In a reflex reaction, he began turning toward Taylor, but he didn't have to. From that distance, even a novice wouldn't have missed, and he could see in Ghost's eyes that he was no first timer. A millisecond after the shot, he felt the warmth of splattered blood and brain matter hit the back of his neck and side of his face, as Taylor's head exploded with the impact of the fragmenting bullet.

The air inside the room was immediately filled with the smell of cordite.

Hunter still managed to turn fast enough to see Taylor's body be propelled backward and slam against the dappled gunmetal door, before falling to the ground. The wall behind her was immediately colored in crimson red with speckles of flesh, gray matter and blonde hair. The bullet had hit her almost perfectly right between the eyes. Due to Ghost's diminutive height and his position in relation to Taylor, the bullet traveled in a slight upward and left-to-right angle. The damage was mind-boggling. Most of the right upper part of her head and cranium was missing, blown off by the devastating effect of the Civil Defense bullet – a special type of round designed to mushroom (like turning inside-out) and fragment on impact, sending tiny pieces in all directions.

Taylor never had a chance.

Hunter quickly turned back to face Ghost, whose aim had now moved to Hunter's face.

'Make a move, tough guy, c'mon, make a move, and I'll blow your brains all over her rotting corpse.'

Hunter felt every fiber in his body go rigid with anger, and he had to use all his willpower not to lunge at Ghost. Instead he just stood there, his breathing labored, his hands shaking, but not from fear.

'Yeah, that's what I thought,' Ghost said. 'Not so tough after all, are you?'

'WHAT THE FUCK WAS THAT?' Lucien shouted. He looked even more surprised than Hunter was. 'Why the fuck did you shoot her, Ghost?'

Ghost kept his weapon trailed on Hunter. 'Because the bitch was getting on my nerves,' he replied in a serious but unconcerned voice. 'You know I hate when anyone talks about me that way.'

Lucien took a step back, running a hand across his forehead.

'The foulmouthed bitch got what she deserved.' Ghost shrugged, as if all he'd done was throw a dart at a dartboard. 'What does it matter anyway? They were both going to die, weren't they? They've seen our faces, Lucien. You and I know that they would never walk out of here alive. And all this chit-chat bullshit was pissing me off, so I just sped things up for her.' He nodded at Hunter. 'And you know what? I'm just gonna do the same for him.'

Ghost's face burned with sadistic desire, and Hunter saw the same determination of moments ago flood Ghost's eyes.

There was no time for a reaction.

Another squeeze of the trigger.

Just like before, the bullet found its target with amazing accuracy.

One Hundred

Sky above the city of Milan, New Hampshire.
Forty minutes earlier.

Inside Bird Two, Agent Brody and his team were starting to lose hope.

Their plane had been circling the outer perimeter of Berlin's municipal airport for several minutes now. The pilot had already told Brody that he'd need a plan of action soon. The plane had enough fuel for another thirty to thirty-five minutes of flight time, but if they weren't landing in Berlin, they would need to land somewhere else and refuel before flying back to Quantico. That meant turning the plane around and flying to a different airport.

The nearest airport to Berlin was Gorham municipal airport – about five to ten minutes due south depending on the wind. As a precaution measure, the pilot always allowed an extra ten minutes of flight time in case of landing traffic or some other unforeseen circumstance. That left them with a maximum of another ten, maybe fifteen minutes' circling time. After that, the pilot was turning the plane around and heading toward Gorham.

Brody had his cellphone on the table in front of him. He was staring at its dark screen as if hypnotized. When he finally checked his watch, another seven minutes had passed. Three more minutes and this operation was over. He had to call Kennedy.

As he reached for his phone, it rang.

One Hundred and One

This wasn't the first time Hunter had stared down the barrel of a gun. It wasn't the first time he'd been in a life or death situation either, but Ghost was too far away for Hunter to be able to get to him in time, and he was too close for Hunter to be able to dive away from the bullet.

This time there was no way out.

In that split second before Ghost squeezed the trigger, all Hunter could think of was how sorry he was for not being able to protect Taylor, and for not fulfilling the promise he'd made Jessica all those years ago while he held his fiancée's mutilated body in his arms.

Despite what he was facing, Hunter didn't close his eyes. He didn't even blink. He would not give Ghost the satisfaction. His gaze stayed on Ghost's face. And that was how he was able to see his head explode.

It was a perfect shot. The bullet hit Ghost on his left temple. Its hollow-point cavity was immediately filled with fluids and tissue, forcing it to mushroom as it began traveling past the cranium wall and across Ghost's brain, savagely ripping apart everything in its path.

The mushroom effect of a hollow-point reduces the bullet's velocity considerably, and in most cases there will be no exit wound. The bullet will generally lodge itself within its target. But again, at such close range, the power of a .45-caliber round was more than enough to propel the bullet all the way across Ghost's shaved head.

When it occurs, the exit wound of a .45 mushroomed Civil Defense bullet is impressive. In Ghost's case, it was the size of a grapefruit. Half of the right side of his face, from his ear to the top of his head, exploded out as if an alien being had hatched out of a large egg. Bone, blood, brain matter and skin splattered against the wall and the control console to his right, covering everything in a sticky, gooey red mess.

The terribly loud sound of the fired shot made Hunter jerk, but he still kept his eyes open. He saw the anger, the determination and the evil dissipate from Ghost's eyes, before his whole body was basically lifted from the ground by the force of the shot's impact. It slammed against the control console and flopped to the ground like an empty flour sack. A pool of blood quickly began to form around his head.

His gun also hit the console, but it slid away to the other side of the room, ending somewhere behind the cardboard boxes.

Hunter's heart was racing like a Drag car. Adrenaline had flooded every vein in his body, making him shake. His gaze finally moved to Lucien. He could still see a thin plume of smoke traveling in the air from Lucien's shot, but again, before Hunter could react, Lucien had already aimed Taylor's gun at him.

'Stay right where you are, Robert. I really don't want to, but if need be, I'll put a bullet right through your heart. And you know I mean it.'

Hunter stared at him, unable to hide his surprise for what he'd just done.

'I've never liked him anyway,' Lucien explained in his usual matter-of-fact manner. 'He was just a dumb, sadistic kid with no purpose, who was traumatized when young, and because of that he loved torturing and killing people just for the fun of it.'

Coming from Lucien, Hunter found the comment very rich.

'And he just outlived his usefulness,' Lucien moved on, not even a pinch of remorse or pity in his tone. 'Like all the previous ones. They all do eventually, so I just find myself a new little helper.'

Hunter's focus was on Lucien's gun.

'Believe me if you like, but I had no intention of killing Agent Taylor, unless I absolutely had to, but unfortunately she touched on a very delicate subject when it came to Ghost. You see, he came from a very dysfunctional family. Both of his parents abused him physically and psychologically in ways that are hard for even me to imagine. They forced him to walk around the house naked all the time, and they made constant fun of him, especially of his manhood, calling him a series of derogative names. Would you like to guess one of them?'

Hunter breathed in. 'Pencil-dick.'

Lucien nodded once. 'That's the one. Unfortunately, the same name Agent Taylor threw at him.'

For a deeply traumatized and disturbed person, a single word, a sound, a color, an image, a smell . . . a multitude of simple things can easily reopen a terribly painful wound. Usually the person's reaction is highly unpredictable, but in the case of a violent person, violence is almost always present within the reaction. In the case of a psychopath like Ghost, that violent reaction is usually fatal.

'When Ghost was seventeen years old,' Lucien added, 'he finally had enough. He tied his father to a bed, castrated him, and left him to bleed to death. After that, he used a baseball bat to beat his mother's head into a paste. He was too damaged. I knew I'd be getting rid of him soon anyway.'

Despite the bloody chaos of the control room, Hunter forced himself to think as clearly as he possibly could. His main concern came back to him, and he turned his head to look down the corridor behind him. His eyes caught a glimpse of Taylor's body on the floor, and his heart sank yet again. He looked back at Lucien.

'Let Madeleine go, Lucien,' he said one more time. 'Please. If you really want another victim, take me instead. She means nothing to you.'

'True, and that's exactly why I should kill her, Robert,' Lucien said. 'Because she means nothing to me. Now you were my best friend. We have some history. Why would I want to kill you instead of her?'

'Because you already took half of my life when you took Jessica from me,' Hunter replied. 'And I know you don't like to leave things half done.'

As much as Hunter tried to hide it, Lucien recognized real emotion in his voice.

'So this is your chance, Lucien,' Hunter continued. 'Let her go and finish what you started with me, because if you don't, I *will* kill you.'

Despite the seriousness of his words, Hunter spoke as if he were talking to someone inside a library, his voice quiet and steady.

'OK,' Lucien said, taking a step closer to the blood-covered control console, his weapon still targeting Hunter's heart, 'let's see if you are a man of your word, Robert.' He flicked a switch and the door at the end of the corridor swung open again.

Hunter turned and faced the hallway.

Madeleine immediately looked up. She looked even more petrified than before.

Hunter knew that she'd heard both shots, and they'd no doubt scared her imagination into fantasizing the worst as to what was happening outside and, worse, what would now happen to her.

She looked to be almost hyperventilating; right then, nothing in the world could make her stop shaking.

Lucien jerked his gun toward the hallway. 'Let's go join her, shall we? I have one last surprise for you.'

One Hundred and Two

Hunter had to step over Taylor's body to reach the hallway. Lucien followed, but at a safe distance. There was no way Hunter could mount an attack before Lucien fired at least two shots at him.

As Hunter started down the corridor, Madeleine's eyes met his and he could see only one thing in them – pure terror.

'Please help me.'

This time Hunter could finally hear her. Her weak and quivering voice was drowning in fear.

'Madeleine, please just stay calm,' Hunter said in his most confident voice. 'Everything will be just fine.'

Madeleine's gaze moved past Hunter and found Lucien, and it was as if the monster that had been haunting her worst nightmares since she was a little girl had just materialized in front of her. Fear grew inside her like a hurricane, and she began screaming and wiggling her fragile body in the chair.

'Madeleine,' Hunter said again. 'Look at me.'

She didn't.

'Look at me, Madeleine,' he repeated, firmer this time.

Her stare moved to Hunter.

'That's right. Good girl. Keep your eyes on me and try to stay calm. I'll get you out of here.' He hated himself for lying, but in the situation he found himself in, there wasn't much else he could do.

Madeleine still looked terribly scared, but something in Hunter's tone seemed to work. She looked directly at him and stopped screaming.

'Get in, turn left, walk five paces and kneel down, Robert,' Lucien said as they got to the door.

Hunter did as he was told.

The room was completely bare, except for the chair with Madeleine and a small module with two drawers at the opposite end from where Hunter had kneeled down. There was a faint aroma of urine and vomit, fighting the harsher odor of disinfectant right inside the door, as if someone had been violently ill, and the clean-up had been sloppy.

Lucien entered the room after him, turned right and approached the module. He opened the top drawer and reached for something inside.

Madeleine's eyes wavered toward him.

'Look at me, Madeleine,' Hunter called again. 'Don't worry about him. Keep your eyes on me. C'mon, this way.'

She looked back at Hunter.

'You are very good with hostages, Robert,' Lucien said, moving to the left side of Madeleine's chair.

Hunter finally saw what Lucien had retrieved from the drawer – a stainless-steel blade, about five inches long.

'You know,' Lucien said, 'I really hate guns.' With a quick hand movement he released the ammo clip from Taylor's .45 Springfield Professional. It fell to the floor, and he kicked it behind him, across the room from where Hunter was. In another very quick double-hand movement, he pulled back the slide, ejecting the bullet in the chamber.

Hunter kept his attention on him. He finally began to see a chance.

Lucien then moved the gun away from him and used his finger to depress the recoil spring plug. In no time at all he had completely stripped the gun, dropping all the separate parts onto the ground.

Hunter breathed out, his muscles tensed-ready as he wondered if he could get to Lucien fast enough.

'Don't even think about it, Robert,' Lucien said, taking a step forward and positioning himself partially behind Madeleine's chair. The blade, now in his left hand, moved to her neck, while with his right one he pulled her head back by the hair. He could see that Hunter was dying to lunge at him. 'You move a muscle, and I'll slice her neck open.'

Madeleine felt the cold blade dig at her skin and her heart almost stopped. She was so petrified that this time she wasn't even able to scream.

Hunter held steady.

'I know you despise me, old buddy,' Lucien said, smiling slightly, almost apologetically. 'And I don't blame you. Without knowing the real purpose behind everything I've done, anyone would. To everyone I'm just a psychopathic sadistic killer who's been torturing and killing people for twenty-five years, right? But to you I'm much more than that. I'm the person you've been hunting for twenty years. The person who so savagely mutilated the only woman you've ever loved. The woman you were going to marry. The woman that would give you a family.'

Hunter felt the anger and rage inside him start to gather strength again.

'But I'm much more than that,' Lucien said. 'In time you'll understand. I'm leaving you and the FBI a gift.' He jerked his head in the corridor's direction. 'You'll have no problems finding it. But that will come later, because right now I'm going to give you a chance to fulfill the promise you made to yourself and to Jessica all those years ago, Robert. And this is going to be the only chance you'll ever get, because if you don't kill me now, you'll *never* see me again. Not in this lifetime.'

Hunter's heart shifted gears inside his chest.

'The problem is,' Lucien continued, 'the moral dilemma that is about to storm through your head and throw your conscience into a tormenting mental battle, old buddy.' Lucien's gaze flicked to Madeleine for a moment before returning to Hunter. 'Let me clarify what I mean by asking you one single question.' He paused, his stare almost drilling holes into Hunter's eyes. 'And that question is: If you come after me now, how are you going to contain her bleeding and get her to a hospital before she bleeds to death?'

In a super-fast movement, Lucien moved the knife from Madeleine's neck down to her body, and stabbed her on the upper left-hand side of her abdomen, just under the ribcage. The blade penetrated all the way to its handle.

Hunter's eyes widened in shock.

'No!' he shouted as he sprang forward, but Lucien was ready for it, and before Hunter could get to his feet, Lucien used the sole of his boot to kick him square on the chest. The powerful blow sent a winded Hunter tumbling backward. Lucien extracted the knife from Madeleine, opening the wound and causing it to start bleeding profusely.

'Keep your promise to Jessica, or save Madeleine, Robert,' Lucien said as he moved toward the door. 'You can't do both. Make your choice, old friend.' He disappeared down the corridor.

One Hundred and Three

It took Hunter a couple of seconds to be able to breathe again, and when he did, his lungs and his chest burned as if he'd sucked in hot coal. Reflexively his hand moved to his chest, and his eyes to the door. His socks scrambled across the floor, trying to maintain some sort of grip as he fought to get back on his feet.

Once he finally did, his primal instinct kicked in and he dashed toward the door. There was no way he was letting Lucien get away from him. He knew Lucien meant what he'd said – if Hunter didn't kill him now, he'd likely never get another chance again. Lucien had surely planned his escape to the last detail. It had taken then FBI twenty-five years to apprehend him the first time – who knew if they ever would again?.

Hunter had taken only three steps in the direction of the corridor when his eyes caught a glimpse of Madeleine. Blood was pouring out of her open wound in volumes. Her head had slumped forward again. Her eyelids were half-shut. Life was fast draining out of her.

Hunter had a pretty good understanding of anatomy. The wound was to Madeleine's upper-left side of the abdomen, just under the ribcage. The blade Lucien had used was about five inches long, and he had driven the entire blade into her flesh. Judging by the amount of blood she was losing, Lucien had punctured a vascular organ.

Left upper side, Hunter thought. *The blade has punctured her spleen.*

He'd also noticed that Lucien had twisted the blade as he removed it from her body, enlarging the rupture to the organ and the entire wound-channel. If Hunter didn't contain the bleeding now, in three to five minutes Madeleine would be dead from loss of blood. Even if he managed to contain the external bleeding, there was nothing he could do about the internal hemorrhaging. He still had to get her to a hospital and an operation room fast.

Hunter blinked once. His priorities were colliding just as Lucien had predicted.

Lucien was getting away.

You'll never see me again. Not in this lifetime.

Hunter blinked again. The mental battle Lucien had talked about was now in full flow inside his head.

Keep your promise to Jessica, or save Madeleine, you can't do both. Make your choice, old friend.

Hunter blinked one more time, and then rushed toward Madeleine.

He immediately kneeled down next to her, ripped his shirt from his body, jumbled it into a ball and, using his left hand, placed it over the wound, applying just enough pressure. The shirt immediately became soaked in her blood.

'Look at me, Madeleine,' he said, while he stretched his right arm out, reaching for the blade that Lucien had dropped. 'Look at me,' he said again.

She didn't.

Streeeetch. Got it.

'Madeleine, look at me.'

She tried, but her eyelids began to flutter.

'No, no, no. Stay with me, honey. Don't close your eyes. I know you're tired, but I need you to stay with me, OK? I'm going to get you out of here.'

Hunter took a quick look behind the chair. Her hands were tied together by a plastic cable tie, just like her feet to the chair's legs. Still applying enough pressure over the wound with his left hand, he tilted his body to the right and used the blade to slice through the cable tie behind the chair.

Madeleine's hands fell loosely by her side, as if she were a ragdoll.

Hunter quickly sliced through the two cable ties at her feet.

'Madeleine . . .' He dropped the blade and reached for her face. Touching her chin, he gently shook her head from side to side. 'Stay with me, honey. Stay with me.'

Madeleine's drowsy eyes found his face.

'That's it. Keep your eyes on mine.' He reached for her left hand and placed it on the shirt over her wound. 'I need you to hold onto this and press it against your body as hard as you can, do you understand, honey?'

He reached for her right hand and placed it over her left one, now making her hold the shirt against the wound with both hands.

Madeleine didn't respond.

'Hold onto it and press it against you as hard as you can, OK?'

She tried, but she was way too weak to be able to apply enough pressure to properly contain the bleeding. Hunter had to do it himself, but he also needed to carry her out of that fallout shelter, into the Jeep outside, to which he still had the keys in his pocket, and on to a hospital. Unless he became an octopus in the next second or so, pulling that off would be a very hard task to accomplish.

Hunter placed his left hand over both of Madeleine's, helping her apply pressure to the wound.

Think, Robert, think, he told himself, looking around the room. There was absolutely nothing he could use.

He thought about running back to the shelter's control room and searching the place for some sort of tape or rope, something he could tie around her body to hold his shirt in place, but that would take too much time, and time was something he didn't have.

Think, Robert, think. He was still looking around the room.

That was when his thought process went from A to Z in a split second – Ghost. Ghost had a small frame, with a very narrow waist, but Madeleine had lost so much weight that he was sure Ghost's belt could loop around her torso.

'Maddy, hold on to this shirt as tight as you can. I'll be right back.'

Madeleine looked at him with dopey eyes.

'Hold on tight, honey,' he repeated. 'I'll be right back.'

Hunter let go of her hands. Immediately, more blood flowed out of her wound. Madeleine simply didn't have enough strength to keep applying the necessary pressure. Hunter had to move fast.

He got to his feet and dashed down the corridor like an Olympic sprinter. He reached the control room and Ghost's body in three seconds.

Ghost was wearing a cheap black leather belt with a conventional square frame and prong buckle. Hunter undid it and pulled it off his waist with a single strong pull. In no time at all, he was flying back down the corridor. By the time he reached Madeleine again, he'd lost only nine seconds.

Madeleine's hands had almost let go of his shirt.

'I'm here, Maddy, I'm here,' he said, grabbing the shirt with his left hand and reapplying enough pressure to partially contain the bleeding.

Using his right hand, Hunter lifted Madeleine's back from the chair's backrest, and wrapped Ghost's belt around her torso and over his blood-soaked shirt.

'This is going to feel a little tight, OK?' he said, and gave the belt a strong tug.

Madeleine coughed several times. No blood in her mouth. That was a good sign.

Perfect fit. The buckle slotted into the first hole.

'OK, honey, I'm going to pick you up, and we're getting the hell out of this place, OK? I'm going to get you to a hospital. Stay with me. I know you're tired but don't fall asleep, OK? Keep your eyes open. Ready? Here we go.'

Hunter picked her up from the chair with both arms and got to his feet. The belt tourniquet held in place. Madeleine coughed again. Still no blood.

Hunter dashed out of the room and down the corridor as fast as he could.

One Hundred and Four

Outside darkness was almost absolute, but after coming out of what could easily be considered Satan's basement, breathing the fresh night air felt like a god's touch.

'Madeleine, stay with me. Don't close your eyes,' Hunter said as he paused almost at the top of the long staircase. He couldn't really see if Madeleine had her eyes open or not, but he knew that he had to keep talking to her. He couldn't allow her to doze off.

He still had the Maglite in his pocket, so he adjusted his position on the steps – left leg two steps higher than the right one – and awkwardly reached for the flashlight with his left hand. Grabbed it. Switched on.

Madeleine was struggling with her eyelids.

'You're doing fine, honey. Stay awake?'

Hunter's sense of direction was as sharp as they came. He remembered that they had approached the basement entrance from his left, so he turned and started moving that way fast.

Debris, rocks and sticks began digging at the soles of his feet, but he gritted his teeth and blocked out the pain as best he could.

'You're doing great, Madeleine. We'll be in the car in just a moment, OK?'

Madeleine didn't reply. Her head dropped to Hunter's shoulder.

'No, no, no ... hey, no dozing off now. Tell me your name, honey. What's your full name?'

'Huh?'

'Your name. Tell me your full name, honey?'

Hunter also wanted to test her level of consciousness.

'Maddy,' she replied.

Her whisper was getting weaker. Despite the tourniquet, her blood was now covering Hunter's arms, the whole lower half of his torso, and beginning to soak the top of his trousers. Because of the running action, some had also spurted upward, spraying his chest and face.

'That's great. That's really great. Is Maddy short for something?'

'Huh?'

'Maddy is short for something, isn't it?'

'Madeleine.'

'Wow, that's a beautiful name. But what's your last name?'

No reply.

'Maddy, wake up. Stay with me, honey. What's your last name? Tell me your last name.'

Nothing. Hunter was losing her.

He took his eyes off his path to look at her face, and that was when he felt something cut into the sole of his left foot. The pain shot up his leg like a rocket, making him stumble awkwardly, lose his balance and almost fall to the ground. The shake and stumble movement jerked Madeleine awake. Her eyes butterflied open and she at last looked at him.

Despite the pain, Hunter smiled. 'We're almost there. Keep your eyes open, OK?'

Hunter's running had turned into a desperate limp, as his left foot screamed in agony every time it touched the ground.

They finally reached the front of the house.

'FBI, stop right where you are or we'll put you down.' The shout came from Hunter's left. He turned his head in that direction, but a light was immediately shone on his face, preventing him from seeing who had called the order.

Hunter came to an abrupt halt.

In the next second, four other lights appeared out of the darkness – one more to Hunter's left, two to his right, and one directly in front of him. All the lights together provided enough brightness for Hunter to better see what he was faced with. He was surrounded by FBI agents. All of them had their weapons trained directly on him. No doubt this was Kennedy's backup team.

'Place the woman on the ground and take three steps back, nice and slowly,' the same person who had instructed him a moment ago yelled out.

'I'm *with* the FBI,' Hunter shouted back, a touch of anger overshadowing any relief in his voice. 'My name is Robert Hunter. I had to dispose of my credentials back on the runway of Berlin's municipal airport. You can check with Director Adrian Kennedy, if you like, but do it in your own time, because this woman needs *immediate* medical assistance.'

Agent Brody, the one who had called out the commands, took a step closer and squinted his eyes at Hunter. It took his memory an extra couple of seconds to match Hunter's blood-streaked face to the photograph Director Kennedy had emailed him.

'Stand down. He's with us,' Brody instructed his team, urgently moving toward Hunter. 'There are supposed to be two of you,' he said as he got to Hunter. 'Agent Taylor?'

Hunter gave Brody a subtle headshake that told him everything he needed to know.

Two other agents joined them. The remaining two kept their distance, their flashlights and weapons checking the perimeter.

'And the prisoner?' Brody asked, as they started moving toward where the Jeep was parked again.

'On the run,' Hunter answered. 'Where's your car?'

'Parked behind the Jeep you took from the air traffic controller.'

'When did you get here?' Hunter asked.

'About a minute ago. We were just moving toward the house when we saw you come out.'

'And you didn't cross paths with Lucien?'

They reached the cars. Brody's team had a GMC SUV.

'No.'

One of the agents opened the back door. The other helped Hunter place Madeleine on the backseat. He gently brushed the hair from her forehead.

'Madeleine, stay awake, OK. We're almost there.'

Madeleine blinked tiredly.

Hunter looked at the agent holding the car keys.

'You need to get her to a hospital now.'

The agent was already jumping into the driver's seat.

'I'll get her there.'

Hunter turned to the second agent. 'Get in the back with her. *Do not* let her fall asleep. Tell the medical team that she received a stab wound to the left upper side of her abdomen, approximately five inches deep. The blade reached the spleen, and was twisted counterclockwise on its way out.'

The agent nodded and jumped into the car.

Madeleine's lips moved.

'What was that, honey?' Hunter asked, leaning down. His right ear came within an inch of her lips.

'Please don't leave me.' Her voice was now barely audible. Shock was settling in.

'I won't. I promise. These men are going to take you to a hospital now so they can treat you, OK? I'll be right behind them. I won't leave you. First, I'm just going to get the bastard that did this to you.'

Hunter closed the door and looked at the driver. 'Go, now.'

One Hundred and Five

As the car drove away, Hunter faced Agent Brody.

'You came in this way and you didn't cross paths with Lucien?' he asked again.

'No,' Brody confirmed.

Hunter's gaze moved to the forest surrounding them.

'There's another way to get to this house,' Brody said.

Hunter looked at him.

'You can see it if you look at a satellite picture, or a map.' Brody explained. 'It goes around the long way. It takes you up to the back of the house.'

Hunter had suspected that there was another way to get to the house when he saw Ghost, because he had to have driven here. No way would he have walked.

'Let's go,' Hunter said.

They quickly moved back in the direction of the house. The other two agents saw them, and promptly joined them. They moved past the stairs that led down to Satan's basement and carried on toward the rear of the property.

The house's backyard was as dilapidated as the building itself. Lucien had told the truth. There was a small pond, or something that once had been a pond. Now it was just an ugly pool of mud. There was also an ample concrete pathway, most of it cracked and full of holes. Parked on the right-hand side of the dirt path that led away from the house was a beat-up fifteen-year-old Ford Bronco. They all drew their weapons and approached the car slowly and carefully. It was empty. No doubt that was Ghost's vehicle.

This time it was Brody's turn to study the forestland surrounding the house.

'Do you think he's on foot?' he asked. 'Tracking away through the forest?'

Hunter walked over to the dirt path, kneeled down, and used his flashlight to check the ground.

'No,' he replied after a few seconds. 'He's got a motor-bike.' He pointed to the tire tracks he found.

'What kind of head start has he got on us?' Brody asked.

'Five to six minutes, maximum.'

Brody reached for his cellphone. 'He can't be that far then. I'll call Director Kennedy. He'll be able to organize roadblocks all around this perimeter.'

Hunter closed his eyes and cursed himself again for not seeing this coming. He said nothing to Agent Brody, but he knew roadblocks wouldn't work. Not in this forsaken place, and not with the minimum amount of time they had.

A perimeter airtight roadblock requires manpower, and a hell of a lot of vehicles, something Hunter was sure the city of Berlin or Milan in New Hampshire didn't have. He'd be surprised if both of their police departments together mounted up to more than eight men and four cars. Kennedy would have to request the help of the police departments in adjacent cities. The closest FBI field office was a whole state away. By the time Kennedy managed to gather together the manpower he needed to shut the roads and pathways to try to contain the area, Lucien would certainly have already crossed state lines.

Hunter knew that none of this had been coincidence. All of it had been planned. Lucien had left absolutely nothing to chance.

One Hundred and Six

Four hours later.

The entire fallout shelter was now swarming with FBI personnel. Courtney Taylor's body together with Ghost's had both been placed in zip-up body bags and taken to the airport, where they were to be flown back to the chief medical examiner in Quantico.

Brody's team agents had made it to the Androscoggin Valley Hospital in Berlin in record time. Madeleine Reed was still being operated on, but the doctors had told both agents that due to the precarious condition her body was in – very malnourished and partially dehydrated – her chances of survival weren't the best. But as long as there was a chance, there was hope.

Hunter and Director Adrian Kennedy were in the shelter's control room. Hunter had run Kennedy through everything that had happened since they'd lost their satellite communication back at the airport.

Kennedy had listened to everything with a somber expression on his face, and without interrupting. When Hunter told him how Agent Taylor was executed at point-blank range, and the reason for her execution, Kennedy squeezed his eyes tight and let his chin drop to his chest. Hunter actually saw him quiver with rage.

'How did this happen, Robert?' Kennedy finally asked when Hunter was done. 'How come this Ghost character was here waiting for you? He couldn't just have been here the whole time, could he?'

'Probably not,' Hunter replied.

'So how come he was here waiting for you? How come he knew exactly when you were coming?'

'He didn't.'

Kennedy pulled an annoyed face. 'What do you mean, Robert?'

Hunter had been thinking about this for some time.

'The FBI has certain secret procedures that will only come into action if a code word is spoken, or a code number is keyed in, or something along those lines, right?'

Kennedy nodded and paused for a second. 'You're saying that Lucien had a dormant procedure in place? A pre-planned strategy in case he was captured?'

Hunter agreed with a head gesture. 'I'm sure he did. There's a reason why Lucien has managed to torture and kill so many people for so many years without anyone suspecting a damn thing, Adrian, even people close to him. And that reason is: he's too well prepared. He's methodical, meticulous, disciplined and he's very well organized. What happened in here was planned a long time ago.'

While he pondered over Hunter's words, Kennedy let his eyes circle the room once again. They paused on the pool of blood by the door that led into the corridor – Agent Taylor's blood. Sadness and anger collided inside his eyes.

'I'm sure that Lucien had told the truth about having left Madeleine with enough food and water to last her just a few days,' Hunter carried on. 'But a simple code word or signal would've gotten this whole plan in motion. If he weren't already here, Ghost would've made the trip from wherever he was to keep her from dying. He obviously got here with plenty of time because he managed to feed and rehydrate her enough. He knew that within days of the code signal, Lucien would've made whomever had him under custody bring him here.'

Kennedy stayed quiet, his mind grinding through the information.

'Ghost wasn't his first ever "apprentice",' Hunter added. 'Lucien said so.'

Kennedy looked at Hunter, intrigued.

'Lucien said that Ghost had outlived his usefulness, *like all the previous ones*. He said that they all did eventually, so he just finds himself a new little helper.'

A thoughtful pause from Kennedy.

'I'm sure that the only reason Lucien found apprentices was so that plans like this could work if he ever needed it. He probably found them, taught them the procedures, kept them for a while, then got rid of them and found a new one, and the process would start again.'

'Because in the long run they'd become a liability,' Kennedy said. 'A risk he didn't need.'

Hunter nodded.

Kennedy still looked uncertain. 'But to get the procedure in motion, Lucien would've had to have gotten the code word or signal out to this Ghost character. So how did he do that?'

'Phone call?'

Kennedy shook his head. 'Lucien did not have access to a phone. He wasn't granted any phone calls. He was incommunicado at all times.'

'Since he was taken in by the FBI, you mean,' Hunter said back. 'But he was arrested by the sheriff's department in Wheatland, Wyoming. Any calls then?'

A pause, then Kennedy shut his eyes for a second as if in pain.

'Sonofabitch,' he whispered. He now remembered reading in the arrest report that the arrested subject was granted a single phone call. The call went unanswered. A code telephone number – a dead line that was never supposed to ring, unless . . . That was the code signal.

'How did this Ghost guy get in here,' Kennedy asked. 'You said that the door to this hellhole was padlocked from the outside.'

'Last room on the right down the corridor,' Hunter answered. 'There's a door inside that leads to another passageway, which leads to an exit at the back of the house. Ghost got in through there. The first room on the left,' Hunter said, pointing to the corridor, 'is an observation room with two computer monitors. Lucien had eight motion-sensor equipped CCTV cameras hidden outside. As soon as anything moved within range of the cameras, a red-light alarm would go off inside the whole shelter.' Hunter indicated a red bulb on the wall behind Kennedy. 'One of the cameras is set on a tree at the end of the dirt path that leads to the front of the house.'

'Where you parked the Jeep,' Kennedy said.

'That's right. That would've given Ghost more than enough time to pull Madeleine out of her cell – the last room on the left – tie her to the chair, and come hide inside that box.'

Kennedy turned and looked at the cardboard boxes pushed up against a dark corner.

'He hid in there?'

Hunter nodded. 'He had a small frame, and according to Lucien it sounded like he also had the flexibility of a contortionist.' An awkward pause. 'This was all rehearsed, Adrian. We walked into a trap, and I'm sorry I didn't see it coming.'

'A very well-prepared trap,' Kennedy said. 'Lucien put you and Agent Taylor under incredible time pressure to save a hostage's life. He put you under even more mental pressure by revealing he was your fiancée's murderer just minutes before forcing you to bring him here. The door was padlocked from the outside, and we all believed that Lucien always worked alone. There was no reason for you or Agent Taylor to suspect that there'd be someone in here waiting for you.'

'I still should've checked the room properly,' Hunter said. 'I'm so terribly sorry for what happened to Courtney.'

No one said anything for about a minute.

'He's not going to stop killing,' Kennedy finally said. 'We both know that. And when he kills again, we'll pick up the trail and we'll hunt him down.'

'No, we won't,' Hunter said.

Kennedy glared at him.

'He killed for twenty-five years without anyone ever knowing, Adrian. No links. Lucien doesn't follow a pattern. He doesn't repeat the same MO. He experiments. He kills indiscriminately – old, young, male, female, blonde, brunette, American, foreigner. Nothing matters to him, except the experience. He could kill someone later today, he could have done it already for all we know. We could find the body, search the crime scene, and we still wouldn't be able to say with any certainty if the killer had been Lucien or not.'

'So you believe what he told you?' Kennedy asked. 'That we'll never see him again?'

Hunter nodded. 'Unless we outsmart him.'

'And how do you suppose we do that?'

'Maybe we can find something in those books.'

Kennedy's gaze moved to the dust-covered books on the shelves.

'Those are the notebooks you were looking for,' Hunter explained. 'Lucien told me that he was leaving us a gift. Well, that's it. There are fifty-three books in total. All of them are somewhere between 250 and 300 pages long.'

Kennedy approached one of the shelves, randomly picked up one of the notebooks, and flipped it open. The pages were all handwritten. There was no date stamp, no mention of time whatsoever. Groups of written pages were separated by a single blank one, as if to isolate them into numberless and nameless chapters.

'I don't know exactly what we'll find in them until we go through all of them thoroughly,' Hunter said. 'But I did have an idea.'

'I'm listening.'

'I skimmed through a couple of them before you got here. Judging by what I saw, these books will not only contain Lucien's emotions, frame of mind, how he felt during the build-up and aftermath of a murder, his different MO's and so on, but also everything he did, everyone he met, and *everywhere* he's been since he started this murderous encyclopedia, including hide-out places like this one. Places no one knows about.'

Kennedy caught on fast. 'And right now Lucien needs a place to go. A hiding place. And the house in Murphy and this fallout shelter are probably not the only two hiding, or captive, or torture places he has under his wing.'

'Precisely.'

Kennedy thought about it for a beat. 'Our problem is that if you're right, Lucien might be halfway there already, and I'm sure he won't hide in the same place for too long. He'll get organized quickly, and then he'll probably vanish.'

Hunter said nothing.

Kennedy looked back at the shelves. Fifty-three books, each about 300 pages long. Hunter could see the doubt in his eyes.

'How quickly can you organize a team of the best speed readers you can find, Adrian?' he asked. 'People who can skim through pages fast, looking for something specific. In this case, a location.'

Kennedy checked his watch. 'If I get on to it now, by the time I get these books back to Quantico, I'll have a team there waiting for me.'

'So if we're fast enough, we'll have our list by the morning,' Hunter said.

'Then we'll hit every place on that list at the same time,' Kennedy agreed.

'I know it's a long shot,' Hunter said, 'but with Lucien, we need to take every shot we get, because we won't get many.' He walked over to the bookshelves and collected eight random books.

'What are you doing?' Kennedy asked.

'I'm the fastest speed-reader you'll find.'

Kennedy knew that to be true.

'I'll go through these, and you can get your people to go through the rest. You'll have my list in a few hours.' Hunter started moving toward the exit.

'Where are you going?

'To the hospital. I promised Madeleine that I would be there.'

Kennedy knew that going after a list of places wasn't the only reason Hunter wanted to go through those notebooks. If he could, he would've taken them all.

'Robert,' Kennedy called out.

Hunter paused.

'Finding Jessica's passage in one of those books will not soothe the pain. You know that. On the contrary, it will feed the anger and the hurt.'

Hunter studied Kennedy for a brief moment. 'As I've said, Adrian, you'll have my list in a few hours.' He took the stairs out of Satan's basement.

One Hundred and Seven

The doctors had just finished operating on Madeleine Reed when Hunter got to the hospital. They told him that she had lost a lot of blood. A minute or two longer getting her to the theater and there would've been nothing they could've done for her. But whoever had contained the external bleeding with the belt tourniquet had done a good enough job. If not for that, she would've died from loss of blood five minutes before the agents got her to the emergency unit.

The doctors also told Hunter that the operation had gone as well as they could expect. They had managed to contain the internal bleeding and suture the spleen wound shut before the organ failed, but Madeleine's strength was already at its minimum before they operated. Now, all they could do was wait and hope that Madeleine's weak body would somehow find the strength to wake up and breathe on her own. That her will to stay alive would be strong enough. The next few hours were absolutely critical. At the moment, machines were keeping her alive.

Hunter sat in an armchair pushed up against the corner, just a few feet away from Madeleine's hospital bed. She lay flat and still under a thin coverlet. Different-sized tubes came out of her mouth, nose and arms, and connected to two different machines, one on each side of the bed. Even with the coverlet, Hunter could tell that her abdomen was heavily bandaged. The heart monitor on the right side of the bed beeped steadily, drawing a hypnotic peak line on its dark monitor screen. While that line peaked, there was still hope.

Before taking a seat, Hunter had stared at Madeleine's face for a long time. She looked peaceful, and for the first time in God knows how long, not scared.

Her parents had been notified just about half an hour earlier, and they were on their way from Missouri.

'I know you're strong enough, Maddy,' Hunter had whispered to her. 'And I know that you can beat this. This time Lucien won't win. Don't let him win. I know you'll walk out of here.'

Hunter had been flying through Lucien's notebooks all night. It was 4:18 a.m. and he'd already skimmed through six out of the eight notebooks he had with him. So far, his list contained three different locations Lucien had used as a torture chamber. Each one in a different state.

He hadn't come across any mention of Jessica and what had happened that fateful night twenty years ago in Los Angeles. Truthfully, he didn't really know if he was relieved or angered. He wasn't sure how he would feel if he did come across the pages that described that night's events.

Hunter sped through the pages for another twenty minutes when something made him stop. It wasn't something on the page he was on, but something his eyes had gone over a couple of pages back, but his tired brain took a few extra seconds to process it. He quickly flipped back to the page and read the passage again.

Where had he heard that before?

Hunter wracked his brain for a few minutes searching for it.

And then it finally came to him.

One Hundred and Eight

Hunter quickly exited Madeleine's room and found a bathroom down a long and empty hallway. Once inside, he reached for his cellphone and dialed Kennedy's number. He knew Kennedy would still be awake.

Kennedy answered his phone with the second ring. 'You've speed-read through all eight notebooks already?'

'Almost there,' Hunter replied. 'One more to go. How's your team doing?'

'They've each been through four of the notebooks,' Kennedy explained. 'But I've got nine of them on the go, five notebooks each. At this rate, we should have a list by dawn.'

'That would be great,' Hunter said. 'But you'll have to ask them all to go back to the beginning and start again. They need to look for something else other than the locations. Create another list.'

Hunter could practically hear Kennedy frown.

'What? What do you mean, Robert? What else? What other list?'

Hunter quickly told him.

'Why?'

Hunter explained the reason why, and now he could almost hear Kennedy thinking.

A long pause.

'I'll be damned,' Kennedy said in an outbreath. 'Do you think . . .?'

'It's another shot,' Hunter replied. 'And we agreed to take every shot we could.'

'Absolutely . . .' Another thoughtful pause. 'If you're right, Robert, we *might* get a result. The problem is that that result could come tomorrow, next week, next month, or any time in the next twenty or thirty years. There's no way of knowing.'

'To get my hands on Lucien, I'm prepared to wait.'

'OK,' Kennedy agreed. 'But the team is just about to finish with the locations list, and you know that we can't lose time on that, so let's get that list first and then I'll tell them to start again.'

'OK. You'll have my list of locations within the next hour.' Hunter disconnected and went back to Madeleine's room.

He finished skimming through the last notebook he had with him in thirty-one minutes – no new locations. His location list contained three entries. He texted Kennedy his list, went back to the first notebook, and started it all over again.

When Kennedy called Hunter at 11:22 a.m., Hunter's eyes were strawberry red from tiredness and reading fatigue.

'I thought you'd like to know,' he said. 'We have fifteen locations in total, spread across fifteen states. FBI and SWAT teams are getting ready as we speak. We should be ready to coordinate a mass crackdown in about an hour to an hour and a half.'

'It sounds good,' Hunter said.

'How are you doing with the second list?'

'Almost there. Give me another half an hour. How's your team doing?'

'Exhausted and overworked. Living on strong black coffee. People here are calling them "the pink-eye squad".'

'Yeah, I guess I can relate.'

'They should also be finished in the next hour. How's Madeleine doing?'

'Still unresponsive.'

'I'm sorry to hear that.'

'She'll come out of it,' Hunter said. 'She's a strong woman.'

Kennedy had to admire the confidence in Hunter's voice.

'Once you get the new list, you know what to do, right, Adrian?'

'Yes, of course.'

They disconnected.

Back inside Madeleine's hospital room, it took Hunter just another twenty-four minutes to complete his new list. This time he had four entries. He texted the new list to Kennedy and received a reply back in five seconds: '*Will initiate procedures as soon as I have all the entries. Locations crackdown will be in T–53 minutes. Will keep you posted.*'

One Hundred and Nine

Hunter received the next text message from Kennedy in exactly fifty-three minutes.

'*Locations crackdown is a go. Will keep you posted. Second list now completed – every procedure initiated.*'

There was nothing Hunter could do now but sit and wait. He massaged the back of his neck for an instant. Exhaustion had slowly worn its way into his brain, joints and muscles. Every time he moved, he could feel the tendons pulling tight across his whole body, as if they were about to snap. He closed his eyes only for a moment, and the next thing he felt was his cellphone vibrating in his chest pocket.

Hunter had dozed off for eighty-four minutes. To him, it felt like two seconds. He quickly left the room and answered Kennedy's call.

'We've drawn a blank, Robert,' Kennedy said. 'Lucien was in none of the locations.' Kennedy's voice sounded defeated, as if all hope had gone out of him. 'And it doesn't seem like he'd been in any of them for weeks. Judging by the photographs I've received back from the crackdown teams, some of those places were a torture haven, a slaughterhouse. You wouldn't believe the torture paraphernalia found in them.'

Hunter was sure he would believe it.

'It will take our forensics teams weeks, maybe months, to sift through everything in those fifteen locations, and it still might give us no clue to Lucien's whereabouts. I'd say that those notebooks are our best bet of finding anything . . . if there is anything to be found. But they have to be read thoroughly and scrutinized to the minutest detail, and that will also take a long time.' Without realizing, Kennedy let out a beaten sigh. He had no doubt that by the time they finished analyzing everything Lucien had left behind, the killer would be long gone, vanished forever. As Lucien had said, they'd never see him again.

One Hundred and Ten

Hunter came to a sudden stop as he returned to Madeleine's bedroom. All the hairs on the back of his neck stood on end. Madeleine was still lying flat and still, but her eyes were open, or semi-open, her eyelids struggling with their own weight.

Hunter rushed to her bedside.

'Madeleine?'

She blinked hazily.

Hunter gently touched her hand. 'Madeleine, remember me?'

She blinked again and her eyes finally found his face. She didn't say a word, but her lips stretched into a thin, but very truthful smile.

Hunter smiled back. 'I knew you'd beat this,' he whispered. 'I'm going to go get a doctor. I'll be right back.'

She gave his hand the faintest of squeezes.

Hunter rushed out of the room, and in less than a minute was back with a short and plump doctor who walked as if carrying his body weight was an everyday penance. As the doctor approached Madeleine's bed, Hunter felt his cellphone vibrate in his chest pocket again. He excused himself and quickly left the room.

'Robert,' Kennedy said as Hunter answered it, 'the second list, the idea you came up with?'

'Yes, what about it?'

'You're not going to believe this.'

One Hundred and Eleven

Seven hours later.
John F. Kennedy International Airport, New York.

'Would you like a drink while we wait for the rest of the passengers to board, Mr Tailor-Cotton?' the young stewardess asked with a bright smile. Her blonde hair was pulled back and styled into a perfect bun, and her carefully applied makeup accentuated her facial features perfectly. 'Perhaps champagne, or maybe a cocktail?' she offered.

Champagne and cocktails were some of the many perks of flying first class.

The passenger's eyes broke away from the window and found her pretty face. The nametag on her blouse read KATE. He smiled back.

'Champagne would be perfect.' His voice was soft, with a gentle Canadian accent. His dark green eyes had an intense, but knowledgeable look in them.

The smile never left the stewardess's lips. She found Mr Tailor-Cotton mysteriously charming, and she liked that.

'Great choice,' she said in reply. 'I'll be right back with a glass.'

'Excuse me, Kate?' he called, as she was turning away. 'How long before we take off?'

'We have a full flight tonight,' she replied. 'And we just started boarding all the other classes. If no one is late, we should start taxiing toward the runway in no more than twenty to thirty minutes.'

'Oh, that's great. Thank you.'

'But if there's anything I can do to make this short wait more comfortable for you, just let me know.' Her smile gained a flirtatious sparkle.

Mr Tailor-Cotton nodded, with a flirtatious smile of his own. 'I'll keep that in mind.'

His gaze followed her as she started down the aisle. When she disappeared past the dividing curtain, his attention returned to the window. He'd never been to Brazil before, but he'd heard great things about it, and he was really looking forward to spending time there. It would be a nice change.

'I've heard that the beaches in Brazil are simply breathtaking,' the passenger sitting directly behind Mr Tailor-Cotton said, leaning forward. 'I've never been there before, but I've heard that they're like paradise on earth.'

For a split second Mr Tailor-Cotton's heart almost froze, then he smiled at his own reflection staring back at him from the airplane window. He would recognize that voice anywhere.

The passenger behind him stood up, moved forward, and casually leaned against the armrest of the single seat across the aisle from Mr Tailor-Cotton.

'Hello, Robert,' Mr Tailor-Cotton said, turning his head to look at Hunter.

'Hello, Lucien,' Hunter replied calmly.

'You look awful,' Lucien commented.

'I know,' Hunter admitted. 'You, on the other hand, have done a great job on the look. Different hair color, contact lenses, the beard is gone, even the scar is gone. All that in the space of just a few hours.'

Lucien looked like he was accepting a compliment.

'You can do wonders with makeup and a little prosthetics if you know what you're doing.'

'And you have mastered that Canadian accent to perfection,' Hunter admitted. 'Nova Scotia, right?'

Lucien smiled. 'You still have a great ear, Robert. That's right. Halifax. But I do have a collection of accents I've mastered. Would you like to hear some of them?'

That last sentence was delivered with a perfect Midwestern accent – Minnesota to be precise.

'Not just right now,' Hunter replied.

Lucien looked at his nails, unconcerned. 'How's Madeleine?'

'She's alive. She'll make a full recovery.'

Lucien looked back at Hunter. 'You mean physically, right? Because mentally, she's probably fucked-up for life.'

Hunter's stare became even harder. He knew Lucien was right again. The trauma Madeleine had experienced would stay with her for the rest of her life. The true extent of its consequences wouldn't be known for many years. Neither would the lasting psychological effects.

There was a long, silent break.

'How did you find me?' Lucien finally asked.

'Your notebooks,' Hunter explained. 'Your lifelong project. Your "gift" to us, as you put it. Or, better yet, your encyclopedia.'

Lucien looked at Hunter, curiously.

'Yes,' Hunter said, 'I still remember the day you mentioned the idea to me back in Stanford.'

Lucien smiled. 'You thought it was a crazy idea.'

Hunter nodded. 'I still do.'

'Well, the crazy idea became a reality, Robert. And the information inside those books will forever change the way the FBI, the NCAVC, the BAU, and every law-enforcement agency in this country, maybe in the world, look at violent and sadistic repeat offenders. It will make you understand things that up to know no one ever did, and otherwise the world never would. Intimate things and thoughts that have never been explained. Things that will exponentially better your chances of capturing those offenders. That's my gift to you, and to this fucked-up world. My work and those books will be studied and referenced for generations to come.' He shrugged. 'So what if I took a few lives in the name of research? Knowledge comes at a price, Robert. Some much higher than others.'

Hunter nodded as his eyebrows arched. 'All that knowledge about psychology and criminal behavior, and you failed to see your own psychosis. You're not a researcher, Lucien, much less a scientist. You're just another run-of-the-mill killer, who, to justify your actions and feed the sociopath inside you, deluded yourself into believing that what you were doing was for a noble cause. It's pathetic, really, because it's not even original. It's been done so many times before.'

'Nothing I've done has been done before, Robert,' Lucien shot back.

Hunter shrugged carelessly. 'I'm not your therapist, Lucien. I'm not here to help you and this isn't a session, so you can carry on deluding yourself as much as you like.

No one cares, but the good thing was that in your books, you were kind enough to note absolutely everything concerning your experiments – locations, methods used, victims' names, and much more. I spent the night going through some of them.'

'You read through fifty-three books in one night?'

'No, but I managed to skim through eight of them. And that's where I got lucky, and you didn't.'

Lucien's expression showed interest.

'While skimming through one of them, I came across the name of one of your victims that I knew I'd heard somewhere before – Liam Shaw.'

Lucien's eyes went cold.

'It took me a little while to place it,' Hunter said, 'but I did eventually remember. That was the name you were using when you were first arrested in Wyoming.'

Lucien stayed quiet.

'You were also kind enough to very thoroughly describe all your victims,' Hunter continued. 'And that was when I realized that Liam Shaw shared several physical characteristics with you – same height, same body type, same skin complexion, same facial shape, including the shapes of his eyes, nose and mouth. You were also of similar age.'

Still silence from Lucien.

'Then I remembered something else you'd said in one of our interviews. You told Courtney that the reason you were caught wasn't merited to the FBI. They weren't investigating any of your murders, or any of the *aliases* you used.'

Lucien shifted on his chair.

'Well, that got me thinking, so I went back and checked for all other *male* victims you described in the books. There weren't that many, but all of them shared those same physical characteristics with you.'

Lucien scratched his chin.

Hunter tucked his hands inside his trouser pockets. 'And that was why you picked them. Not because you wanted them to be part of your encyclopedia of torture and death, but because you were creating a list of identities you could steal at the drop of a dime.'

Lucien's gaze moved back to the window and the darkness outside.

'Some of your male victims were prostitutes,' Hunter moved on. 'Some were people who were down and out on their luck, but all of them had one major thing in common – they were all lone souls. People who were misunderstood and probably cast aside by their family and friends somewhere else. People who had left their lives behind to start something new in a new city. People with no attachments to anyone. The ones who'd never get reported as missing. The forgettables. The ones no one would miss.'

'They've always made the best victims.' Lucien still sounded unconcerned.

'Because of their natural physical resemblance to you, taking their place was never a hard thing to do – a little makeup, some hair dye, maybe some contact lenses, a new accent, and, "Goodbye Lucien Folter, hello new identity." In this case, Anthony Tailor-Cotton, from Halifax in Canada.'

Lucien finally caught up with Hunter. 'So you and the FBI spent the night flying through those books, looking for every male victim's name you could find.'

Hunter nodded. 'A nationwide APB was put out for every name in the list we came up with. But I'll admit that our hopes were very, very low. The best we were hoping for was that maybe, if we were very lucky, a few years from now one of those names would show up in a credit card transaction somewhere. Just a sniff of a clue to where you could be. Now, you can imagine our surprise when within a couple of hours we got word that Anthony Tailor-Cotton, holder of a Canadian passport, just like one of the victims described in one of your notebooks, had purchased a ticket for a flight to Brazil tonight.'

'I guess I should've taken an earlier flight,' Lucien commented.

Hunter could easily see Lucien's logic. Initially he had two options. One was to stay in the USA and lay low for a while . . . a long while, and while doing so, he would probably have to live under the shroud of a disguise. His name would've made the list of the top ten most wanted by the FBI, and his picture would've been circulated to every police department and sheriff's office in the country. Lucien Folter wasn't the unknown ghost of a killer he used to be anymore.

Option number two was to disappear quickly, preferably somewhere outside the USA. Hunter knew that Lucien didn't underestimate the FBI. He knew that his encyclopedia would be scrutinized to the tiniest detail, because that was exactly what he wanted. He was counting on the Bureau linking the name of one of his victims to the same name he was using when he was arrested, and then making the physical connection between all of his male victims and himself. So, if Lucien disappeared quickly and to somewhere outside the USA, then when all those connections were made it wouldn't matter, because the FBI wouldn't be able to get their hands on him anyway. He just never imagined that the Bureau would've managed to connect everything in a matter of hours.

'Maybe you should've,' Hunter said. 'Like I said, this

time I got lucky and you didn't, because the name "Liam Shaw" so happened to be in one of the eight books I had with me. If I hadn't come across that name, it would've probably taken the FBI a few months to connect the dots, by which time you would've been long gone.'

Hunter's eyes finally left Lucien's face and moved down the aisle toward the dividing curtain at the front. All of a sudden the curtain was pulled aside and Director Adrian Kennedy, together with four FBI agents, began making their way toward Hunter. At the opposite end of the aisle, four armed NYPD SWAT officers had appeared, and were also making their way toward them.

For the first time, Lucien showed real surprise.

'You're going to hand me over to the FBI?'

Hunter said nothing.

'That's very disappointing, Robert. I thought you were a man of your word. I thought that you had promised not only yourself, but also the memory of your *murdered* fiancée, that you'd find who'd so violently taken Jessica from your life, and kill him. That's what you've been searching for for twenty years, isn't it? To avenge Jessica's death. Well, here I am, old friend. All you have to do is put a bullet through my head and your twenty-year-long search is over. You can be proud of yourself.' Lucien quickly checked the aisles. 'So c'mon, Robert. Here I am, a sitting duck. I promise you I won't react. It'll be an easy shot.'

Hunter shifted on his feet.

Kennedy and everyone else were getting closer.

'I thought you'd said that more than anything else, Jessica deserved justice. Are you telling me that you're going to betray that promise, Robert? You're going to betray the memory of the only person you ever loved? The woman who you wanted for your wife? The woman who was carrying your baby?'

Hunter froze.

Lucien saw the hurt in his face. He pushed.

'Yes, I knew she was pregnant. She told me when she begged me not to kill her, but I did it anyway. And did you know that yours was the last name that came out of her lips before I cut her throat open? Before I murdered her and your child?'

Hunter saw red as his blood began to boil. The thoughts inside his head made no sense anymore. His actions were no longer guided by sense and logic, but by pure rage. His hand was shaking with devastating anger when he reached for his gun holster.

Kennedy saw the look on Hunter's eyes, but he was still several steps away from him.

'ROBERT, DON'T DO IT!' he shouted down the aisle.

Too late.

One Hundred and Twelve

Hunter had acted so fast that his hand had moved onto his gun holster and then back in Lucien's direction in just a split second.

Lucien flinched and Hunter saw his body go rigid, but not from fear – from expectation – from satisfaction in his accomplishment. That satisfaction was short-lived.

Hunter dropped a pair of handcuffs on Lucien's lap.

Lucien looked up at him, confused. Hunter was holding no gun.

'You're right,' Hunter said. 'Jessica deserves justice. Her parents deserve justice. My unborn child deserves justice. And I deserve justice for what you've done. Nothing would please me more than to put a bullet in your head right here, right now. But we're not the only ones who deserve justice for what you've done, Lucien. The parents, the families, and the friends of every single victim you tortured and killed over so many years deserve justice too. They deserve to know what really happened to the people who most of them still believe and hope are just missing. They deserve to know where the remains of their loved ones are. They deserve to be able to give them a proper burial according to their beliefs. And most of all, they deserve to know that the monster who killed those loved ones will never kill again.'

Hunter looked at Kennedy, who was now just a couple of feet away, and then back at Lucien.

'For that reason, yes, I'll betray my promise to myself and to Jessica. And this time, there will be no more interviews, no more talks, Lucien. You have no more bargaining power, because we have your books, and everything we need to know is in those pages, including the location to the remains of every one of your victims. This really is where it ends for you.'

Hunter nodded at the SWAT agents to his left. 'You can take him now.'

One Hundred and Thirteen

Despite his insomnia and the carnival of thoughts dancing around in his head, Hunter was so exhausted that he finally managed to sleep for a total of four hours.

After Lucien's arrest, he had flown back to Quantico. As Kennedy had put it before, he was still officially 'on loan' to the FBI and, as such, he needed to fill in his last report. That was done late last night.

Hunter had woken up before dawn. Kennedy had arranged for an FBI jet to fly him back to Los Angeles early in the morning, and Hunter couldn't wait to get out of that place. Everything still felt too surreal in his mind. Only a few days ago, he was supposed to be boarding a plane to Hawaii, his first vacation in so long, he couldn't even remember the last time he had one. Instead, he was whisked away to the FBI Behavioral Analysis Unit in Quantico, and into something that could only be described as a hellish nightmare. So much was revealed in so little time, his head seemed like it would never stop spinning.

Hunter was all ready to go. His few belongings were already packed into his rucksack, and he had nothing else to do but wait for the driver to come pick him up. He walked over to the window on the east wall and placed his cup of coffee on the ledge. Outside, still under the cover of the night, several FBI recruits had already started their grueling exercise and running routines.

Hunter looked up at the star-filled sky as he reached for his wallet. From it he retrieved a twenty-year-old photograph. The colors had partially faded, but other than that, the picture was still in pretty good condition.

Hunter had taken that photo himself, a day after he and Jessica had got engaged. She was standing on Santa Monica pier, smiling at the camera, her eyes glistening with an overwhelming happiness. Staring at the photograph, Hunter's heart was filled with a barrage of old and brand new emotions. He felt a knot coming to his throat, but then he remembered the words Director Kennedy had told him in the early hours of the morning.

'Before you go, Robert, I want to make sure you understand something. I'm not going to pretend I know, because I can't even begin to imagine what's going on inside your mind right now. But I can tell you this, no matter what; you *must* stand proud, because thanks to you, we estimate that we'll be able to bring closure and final peace of mind to at least eighty families around the USA. Lucien's twenty-five-year murderous spree is finally over. You ended it. Don't ever forget that.'

Hunter knew he never would.

Acknowledgements

It's a well-known fact that writing is regarded as a solitary occupation, but I have found out that though authored by a single individual, a novel is never the achievement of one alone.

My most sincere thanks go to all the incredible people at Simon & Schuster UK and to my editor, Jo Dickinson, whose great input and valuable suggestions made the story and the characters in this thriller come alive. Also, to my copy editor, Ian Allen, for his incredible work and attention to detail all throughout the manuscript.

Words can't express how thankful I am to the most passionate and extraordinary agent any author could ever hope for – Darley Anderson.

To the fantastic team of extremely hard-working people at The Darley Anderson Literary Agency, I owe my eternal gratitude.

Thank you also to all the readers and everyone out there who has so fantastically supported me and my novels from the start. Without your support, I wouldn't be writing.